HAUNTED

Junctions Murder Mystery Series

Book Two:

HAUNTED

L. E. Fleury

First paperback edition December 2023.

Editing by Joyce M. Gilmour.

Cover design by Heylea, LLC.

Cover photo enhancements by
Kelly Rainbow Butterfly.

Special thanks to BETA reader,
Louise Ginsberg.

Published by Heylea, LLC.
cabininthewoods2021@gmail.com

ISBN: 979-8-9890236-1-5 (paperback)

I dedicate this book

…to the Father: Thank you for giving us eternal life.

…to the Son: Thank you for your Blood Covering that gets us
back Home.

…to the Holy Spirit: Thank you for enriching our earthly
sojourn.

"I will say of the Lord, He is my refuge and my fortress: my God; in him will I trust. Surely he shall deliver thee from the snare of the fowler, and from the noisome pestilence. He shall cover thee with his feathers, and under his wings shalt thou trust: his truth shall be thy shield and buckler. Thou shalt not be afraid for the terror by night; nor for the arrow that flieth by day; Nor for the pestilence that walketh in darkness; nor for the destruction that wasteth at noonday."

Psalm 91: 2-6 (KJV)

PART I

Smoke and Mirrors

CHAPTER ONE

Skunks

Dawn emerged as an ethereal glow, silhouetting the towering silo and roofline of the barn on the old Wilson Dairy Farm. The structure, along with the horse barn which was located just a couple hundred feet north across the barnyard, was still cloaked in the last dark, wet sweep of a rainy night. Only one electric bulb, screwed into a porcelain fixture, glowed weakly from the north end of the dairy barn, dimly illuminating various rough clapboard surfaces, chipped rock foundations, damaged corners, and lumpy pathways across the yard of this family-run business. Within the old clapboard farmhouse standing close to the road that marked the west boundary of the property, Jessie and Laura Wilson and their teenaged son, Jack, still slumbered.

Almost directly across from the Wilson house, snuggled into the inside of a tight curve in the Old Colchester Road, the Thompsons' farmhouse was also still dark. Again, a lone light bulb cast its soft rays across the back yard from its perch high above a narrow door on the north side of the small barn. The outline of a compost pile, heaped high in the corner of last summer's garden, leaned hard toward the barn, testing the strength of the barbed-wire fence. Between the house and garden, weeds struggled up amongst rocks which bulged stubbornly from the soil. Beyond the range of the soft electric light, deep shadows covered the property of this small family farm. It was the predawn of Saturday, October 10, 1953, in the township of Essex, Vermont.

Things were unusually quiet.

The Old Colchester Road originated at the north end of the village of Essex Junction, just past where the train crossing met Grove Street, right next to the now-defunct creamery. Grove Street turned slightly north, stopping at the Indian Brook Bridge, and becoming Old Colchester Road, from that point northward. This hard-packed dirt road ran past a few houses on the left, then a couple of cornfields on the right, until it made a sharp turn to the west between the Wilson and Thompson homes. From there, it passed the north end of the Thompson driveway (marked by a large maple tree), past their barbed-wire enclosed garden on the left, and on the right, the Wilsons' cornfield, now chopped down into neat rows of cornstalk stubble. A few hundred feet ahead, it passed an x-shaped sign which warned of a single railroad track. From there, the road dropped down a very short, deep slope, to intersect with Vermont Route 2A, also known as the "new" Colchester Road.

There was no traffic disturbing the stillness of this early hour.

Across Route 2A, the continuation of the dirt road dropped sharply down to another crossing over Indian Brook, rising again at the other side of a small bridge up into a neighborhood of a half-dozen houses, snuggled close to the woodlands of upper Case Road. These homes, though built near that tree line, were still visible through the vaporous veil of diminishing darkness, all the way back from the intersection of the two Colchester Roads.

Suddenly, right back there at that very junction, something moved. Where the scent of pungent, damp soil hung heavily over the weed-filled undergrowth, there was a rustling through the tall grass. The movement proceeded slowly through the ditch between the raised bed of the railroad tracks and the asphalt edge of Route 2A. In the shadow of the steep slope's side drop-off, a nocturnal creature waddled around past a metal obstacle. Then, as suddenly as it had started, the shuffling stopped. There was a precipitous silence.

Shortly, the vibrations the creature had felt in the ground could be heard: the faint sound of footsteps grinding steadily, heavily, into the hard-packed dirt of Case Road. As the treading became increasingly louder, a shadowy figure emerged from the deep gulley of the brook crossing below. Rising higher with each dug-in step, the hooded head appeared first, then the torso, leaning forward, arms swinging, and finally, the legs, bent in concentrated effort from the steep climb. It paused at the edge of the highway, panting, and seemed to check for traffic before making a dash across the road into a special spot in the tall grass, just under the edge of the old slope. Quickly, the shadowy runner bent to lift an object of considerable weight and size, almost throwing it onto the edge of the highway. As the object hit the asphalt, the runner turned to see what was now moving in the grass, but it was too late. A shout pierced the darkness, and the phantom body rose, suspended momentarily in midair, before it swooped away down the highway, hell-bent toward Essex Junction.

The near-sighted skunk proceeded cautiously through the grass, waddling up over the railroad tracks, carefully making its way over to the compost pile in the Thompsons' garden. The overwhelming stench of its spray attack now filled the air, wafting across the back yard toward the house where Cecil Thompson had just dragged himself out of bed. As he dressed, the skunk odor became obvious. He carefully pulled back the dark green pull-down window shade, noting the maple tree, now visible in the first real light of dawn, was still a vibrant red and gold showpiece. The rainy night had not hastened the inevitable fading and crumbling of the foliage just yet. Satisfied, he softly closed the window, careful not to wake his wife, Winnie, and stepped quietly out into the dining room.

Directly in front of him was the dining room table, where he left his rimless eyeglasses in the exact same spot every night. He reached down and lifted them gently over his nose and ears. They were smudged, so he removed them, drew a large, red patterned handkerchief out of his overalls pocket, breathed upon the lenses, and slowly proceeded to rub the glass surfaces clean.

As he worked, he glanced around the dining room, which was tastefully wallpapered in a blue silver-white floral pattern, right from Sears and Roebuck, like all the other wallpaper in this home. Once more, he appreciated the home he had inherited from his folks some years ago. To his right was the sitting area, furnished with two new Sears and Roebuck recliners (one gold, one dark blue), placed on either side of a doily-topped table, upon which sat a radio, a lamp, and an ashtray. Behind the recliners, a cushioned window seat, covered with magazines and newspapers, lay invitingly in front of the bay window which looked out across the driveway, past the garden and the railroad track, to the now dawn-lit trees of upper Case Road. His head tilted back as he yawned at the five plaster of paris bluebirds — two adults and three babies — frozen in flight over the central stretch of the ceiling arch separating the sitting area from the dining room where he stood. The birds were Winnie's, of course, not anything he would have chosen on his own. "Like they're good luck, or something," he murmured, just before he licked his dry lips. But that was a small issue, not to be pursued.

Brushing that thought aside, Cecil slipped his eyeglasses back in place, satisfied his vision was now unencumbered. Latching his thumbs under the straps of his hickory-striped bib overalls, he breathed deeply and pulled the front pockets up over his forty-nine-year-old paunch. As he did, something caught his eye to the left, down the hallway which led to the parlor, the front door, and the stairway that climbed to the little apartment on the second floor. The dusty-blue painted walls were set off by white woodwork, including the white panes of the double French doors on the left, which opened into the seldom-used parlor. The Christmas tree was set up in there every year, and it was used occasionally as a guest room because of a generously sized chaise lounge against the east wall, but the room was rarely occupied and almost never heated. However, on this particular morning, one of the French doors was slightly open.

That was disturbing.

Cecil sock-footed across the old, polished hardwood floor, which continued on down the hallway. He stopped in front of the unlatched French door on his left, carefully pulling it open, and peering into the quaint room.

Dawn's rosy light now shown through nylon curtain panels of the front window which framed a view of the Wilson farm across the road. A soft glow bathed the quiet interior of the parlor, turning the gold brocade drapes and tan satin-striped walls into shades of dusty rose. Carefully, Cecil visually checked each item in the room.

To his left, a photo-decorated piano, its cover closed over the ivory keys, held court on the inner wall, while a small sofa squeezed between two petite stuffed side chairs in front of the other curtained window on the north wall.

His gaze moved right to the chaise lounge, stretched out just under the front window. It was covered in a brocade fabric with a deep red chain pattern crisscrossing luxuriously across the contours of its surface. In the center of its seat, the lap robe crocheted by his deceased mother-in-law, Marie, lay in a lacey heap.

Uncle had paid another visit to the parlor.

***

Uncle was Winnie's nearest and dearest family member. He was the youngest brother of her mother, Marie. When they lost both parents in a fishing accident on Lake Champlain, Marie took her four-year-old sibling to raise as her own, right along with her infant daughter, Winnie. It was an easy transition, literally just a move next-door for Uncle, and so the two children grew up in a poor, but innocent environment up there in Swanton, Vermont.

The two youngsters resembled each other, both having small, dark eyes on each side of a straight nose, and both being short of stature. Although they were like sister and brother, she still called him "Uncle"; he called her "Pooh," short for "Winnie the Pooh."

It was a close relationship until Maria died in late 1927. That event marked some big changes for these two young Abenaki children. Winnie, who had just turned fourteen, was suddenly the apple of her father's eye. Chief Raven's Wing hovered over her, a stern but loving taskmaster, determined she would prosper in every possible way. But the Abenaki chief was unusually hard on Uncle, whose native name was Shining Waters, urging the boy to buckle down during his last year of high school.

That spring, Uncle graduated from high school and headed for the big city of Burlington, in search of his fortune. A series of jobs came and went. By 1929, however, it was evident there was no fortune to be made, what with the crash on Wall Street and the advent of the Great Depression. The job hunting became a futile pursuit. Further, somewhere in the spring of 1930, he learned that Pooh had been taken to Canada. He was devastated, not having been there to support her as he had in their childhood. But what was done, was done. It was a discouraging time for the young man. As a last resort, he joined the United States Army in 1931. Years later, World War II sent him home on furlough with a souvenir: a white streak of hair from his left temple to the back of his head, where a bullet had creased his skull. He laughed and called himself, *Seganku*, the Abenaki word for "skunk."

Before he returned to the front lines, the infantryman watched Pooh become Mrs. Cecil Thompson, at the Cathedral of Immaculate Conception in Burlington. He managed to go north and take a walk along Swanton's Missisquoi River before leaving. This time when he left his home town, he was gone right on through the beginning of the Korean War in 1950. He retired with twenty years of active service, in the spring of 1951. Winnie was overjoyed to have him back in her life, and after some months of convincing her husband, who was running this little family farm on Old Colchester Road, Uncle was brought on board as a hired hand. The war-weary veteran moved into the little attic apartment at the top of the white stairway just behind where Cecil stood at this moment, quietly closing the French door. He moved right, coming to the foot of the stairs, checking to see that the door at the top was closed. It was.

"Sad little drunk," Cecil thought.

***

Uncle had established a Friday night pattern, not long after Cecil hired him. The job entailed a "free board and room" deal, in exchange for helping around the place, with a twenty dollar bill every Friday at noon. Since the retired soldier was receiving a government check every month, it all worked out quite well. Sometime around three in the afternoon, his official day off started. At first, it wasn't every single Friday, but eventually it did become routine. Regardless of the season, the weather, or anything else, Uncle pocketed his twenty, walked down the one mile of Old Colchester Road to Essex Junction, bought a bottle of cheap wine at Yandow's

Market, and a small order of fries from Al's French Fries, right next-door. He ate the fries while sitting in the old wooden train depot across the street, sneaking a sip from the bottle whenever he thought he could get away with it, and then toddled home with his libation in a bag, usually arriving at the brick farmhouse before dusk, "… drunk as a skunk," as Cecil would say. Sometimes Uncle would arrive in worse condition than usual, dipping deeply into a pit of despair and regrets. It was at these times he would slip into the parlor, wrap himself in his beloved sister's lap robe, and dissolve in a pool of grief. It wasn't that he was loud and upsetting to the household; in fact, the other two were often unaware he was even in there. But when they were, the depth of his grief was evident. Nothing — no kind word, no sympathetic hug could console him. It would just take whatever time it took, and then he would wipe his face, fold the robe neatly across the back of the lounge, and quietly closing the French door behind him, slip away up the stairs to his disheveled bed.

But he would always be ready to resume his work schedule by three o'clock on Saturday afternoon.

***

Cecil turned his attention back to where he was at the foot of the stairs, looking directly south at the large front door to the house. The door, with its etched window, opened out onto the screened-in porch that stretched along the rest of the front of the house. He stepped forward to test the inside door's secured doorknob, then peered out at the porch door, located at the street side of the porch. The hook-and-eye lock was latched. Cecil saw nothing unusual on the porch; just the two aqua metal chairs, each with a small metal table for its own ashtray, sitting side by side at the far end of the metal porch swing with the faded flower cushions.

Apparently, no one had been out *there* last night.

Satisfied that things were pretty much in order, Cecil slipped along the hardwood floor back into the dining room. Winnie would be getting up soon. He shuffled carefully to his left past the telephone stand, heading toward the mostly white kitchen at the south end of the house. Quickly, he plugged in the coffee pot prepared the night before. By the time he came out from the bathroom just left off the hallway to the west-facing back door, the electric pot was sighing and heaving its way to a delicious brew. Like the recliners and the wallpaper, the pot, of course, was from the Sears and Roebuck store over there in Burlington where Winnie was into her eighteenth year of employment. So was the refrigerator, the electric stove, and the can opener which sat on the linoleum shelf near the sink. The white porcelain sink sank into the blue, striated pattern of that shelf along the south wall of the room. Above it was a window, where beyond a view of the southern entrance to the driveway, a few hundred feet of the Old Colchester Road, lined with maples and birches and still another Wilson cornfield, provided a pleasant, familiar scene.

"Time for a cup of java," he murmured, as he reached into the white cupboard and pulled out a white Corning Ware cup. He poured the hot coffee and picked up the translucent vessel, blowing softly upon it for a minute, then touching it lightly to his pursed lips. One sip. Then one more. He belched lightly, then slowly, sweetly drained the cup.

"Time to get to work. Those cows won't milk themselves."

He passed the bathroom and proceeded down the long narrow hall that led to the back door. This was the mudroom where boots and barn clothes were kept. There, Cecil sat down heavily upon the bench against the right wall. As he pulled on his barn boots, he glanced across the small room to the back stairway which also led up to Uncle's apartment.

"Damn! He's done it again," he spoke aloud. The stairway light was on. *"Probably all night."* Cecil took two big steps to the bottom of the stairs and reached for a long string which was looped through eye hooks all the way up the blue and white striped wallpaper of the stairway's far wall. He pulled it firmly, and the bare light bulb at the top of the stairs blinked out with a soft "chi-chink."

"It's like having a teenager in the house," the man whispered to himself.

He pulled a red and black plaid jacket off the hook by the back door, slipping it on without buttoning it. Then, as he did every morning, he picked up the gray "engineer" cap from the second hook, holding it by the brim, and placed it gently over the silvery hair, so as not to disturb the carefully combed hairstyle: parted in the middle and slicked straight back on the sides.

The last part of his getting-to-work ritual was to unlock the back door. The round, metal knob sported a decorative metal plate behind it, with a keyhole just under the knob. With one hand, he held onto the doorknob, and with the other, he reached for the key which was always left in the keyhole. Turned to the left, the door was locked; to the right, the door was unlocked. Cecil tried to turn the key to the right. Nothing happened. He tried again, and then a third time... but it would not budge.

It was already turned to the "unlocked" position.

That was it. The blue eyes turned dark with frustration. He turned on his heel and pounded up the creaky stairs, barn boots and all. At the top, he lowered his head to miss the ceiling which sloped to his right, raising his fist to bang on the door... but it, too, was ajar. Pushing the door open, he called, "Uncle! Get your lazy, stinking butt out of that bed!" and strode past the tiny bathroom on his left, into the small kitchen. "Uncle! Get up! I want to talk to you, mister!" Across the kitchen, the bedroom door was wide open. Cecil moved toward it and poked his head into an organized mess of a room. On the left, an unmade bed lay empty. At the head of it, wrinkled pillows were propped up against the west wall, while a rumpled blanket draped over the foot of bed, almost touching Cecil's feet. On the north side of the bed, snugged up under the sloping wall, a bookcase held all the precious possessions of a bachelor: magazines, a baseball cap, a screwdriver and a couple of mismatched screws, a soiled, empty saucer with a spoon on it — all neatly pushed back on each shelf. On the floor below, odds and ends of shoes stood in a loose line like inebriated soldiers. The open closet to his right held shirts and pants, each in their own pushed-together bunches. Boots, slipper socks, more magazines, and a few old newspapers lay in organized chaos on the closet's floor.

Cecil could see the man was not in the room. He turned around and shouted toward the front stairs, where a small living room held its own against the ever-imposing slope of the ceiling. Stepping over to peer into that area, Mr. Cecil Thompson began to be more curious than frustrated. Obviously, Uncle was not here.

Turning once more, Cecil made a quick survey of the kitchen, and noticed the coffee pot turned upside down in the sink. It still had the strainer full of coffee grounds in it. That was quite odd, because the three of them always saved the grounds for the compost pile. It appeared Uncle did not take the time to pour them into the empty coffee can under the sink. Cecil knew the little gardener did that faithfully.

Nearby, right in front of the only window in the kitchen, a white card table held Uncle's favorite coffee cup: a heavy, clear glass vessel inherited from his dear sister. It was only half-full of coffee. Illuminated from the morning light behind it, the coppery brew cast a soft amber brush stroke across the soiled table top.

The usual two folding chairs were there, also. One was drawn up to the left side of the table, the other pulled away and turned toward the window, as if Uncle had been watching the rainstorm… or maybe something else.

But as he descended the groaning back stairway Cecil reminded himself that it was still the man's day off. No matter, the barn was where that little runt had to be, so that was where he would get an earful from his heretofore benevolent boss. Enough was enough.

As he stepped out onto the small back porch, the cool morning air held just enough skunk odor to be irritating. The darned thing was most likely still around, probably snout-deep in compost. He shrugged it off, having other things on his mind. Normally, he would have paused to take a pack of Camels out of his plaid jacket's pocket, finger-pop one cigarette loose, pull it out of the package with his lips, and light up. But this morning, he stopped just long enough to check out his back yard, just in case… whatever.

The slim line of wet grass between the porch and the driveway provided more evidence of the rainstorms that seemed to have lasted on and off through the night. Cautiously, he viewed what he could of the muddy driveway, although the south access to the road, which could be seen from his kitchen window, was now hidden by the back corner of the old house. He settled for focusing on the rest of the drive, which stretched in a tight curve around the back of the house, ending at the north access, right beside the big red maple. In effect, the driveway mirrored the sharp curve of the road between him and his neighbors. There was something comfortably orderly about that. Things were kept in place. Spaces were clearly delineated.

He also liked being able to see the neat lineup of vehicles on the east, or "near" side of the barn. Usually, in front of the large sliding barn door was their 1947 Dodge sedan, which Winnie drove to work five days a week. To its left, would be his old 1939 Ford pickup, and just to the left of that, his John Deere tractor. All of them would normally be facing toward the barn, like ducks in a row. But last night, Winnie had pulled the Dodge into the barn to keep it out of the rain, because she had just had it cleaned up at a Cathedral High School carwash in Burlington. The large barn door was still open, and Cecil could see the back of the car, and the bottom edge of the hayloft just above to its left, full of the fragrant harvest from this last summer. In fact, everything seemed to be in place — the yard, the vehicles, the harvest — until he spotted the opened narrow barn door at the north end of the building. This entrance to the milking parlor was always, always kept closed at night.

So, of course, that's where Uncle had to be. Cecil clomped across the driveway toward the open door, barn boots slapping against his calves, muttering to himself, ready to "...fire that no-good polecat." Even before he had yanked the door wide open, he yelled, "Uncle! What do you think you're doing, huh?"

Automatically, he twisted the butterfly light switch on the wall to his left, illuminating the whitewashed walls of the milking room. In the sterile white light, he viewed the five stalls facing the long whitewashed wall to the left: a wall which divided the barn almost in half, north to south. His three cows — two Holsteins and a Guernsey — waited patiently to be milked. There was no grain parceled out for feeding, and the iron-handled faucet for the pipeline that brought fresh water into the individual water bowls at each stall was definitely still turned off. The man had not been in the milking room. Further, there was no movement in the elongated hayloft opening high above the furthermost two of the five stanchions.

He stepped down the two cement stairs, and slap-walked across the cement floor, to peer through one of the little all-in-a-row windows on the west side of the barn. He blinked, straining to see through the cloudiness from temperature changes on the lenses of his glasses. After a moment, there was no doubt. Uncle was not out there, either. If that scoundrel was somewhere out here in the barn, it certainly wasn't because he was starting the Saturday morning milking chores.

Since he hadn't stopped to have that cigarette on the back porch, Cecil decided there was time enough to take a look around in the front half of the barn. Milking had to be done pretty much on schedule, or "the girls," as he called them, got uncomfortable and made a lot of noise. But today, there were still a few more minutes, and so he trudged across the smelly barn floor, back up the two cement steps where, instead of going back outside, he shuffled to the right through the open doorway which led into the hay storage area of the barn.

Here, the building showed its age. To his left, a dusty workshop shelf, running almost the entire length of that north wall, lay half-hidden in the shadows. Thin shafts of light could be seen through the cracks between the boards of the uninsulated wall, faintly illuminating old chains and other odd-looking objects draped haphazardly from the rafters above. Aged floorboards sagged under the weight of the Dodge parked alongside the workshop shelf. Cecil stepped carefully across the rotting floor, his right hand extended, until he caught the long pull-string for the light. He pulled, and the metal-shaded light up high over the car swung gently back and forth, making shadows move under its undulating glow. Cecil stood still right there in front of the hood of the car, looking around slowly and carefully.

The workshop was quiet. Upwards, on the other side of the Dodge, the hayloft lay silent, bits of hay draping awkwardly off the edges, as though ready to slip earthward at any second. Just to his right on the north-south dividing wall, his shovels, pitchforks, and a worn broom were hooked over a neat row of ten-penny nails, ready for service at a moment's notice.

"Wait a minute..."

He turned fully around and took a second look at that collection of long-handled tools. Slowly, he stepped forward to touch an empty space on the wall, just under an unoccupied nail. A sharp breath registered his surprise.

"No…"

He looked again, patting the empty space, dread filling his heart. *"Oh no… no…"* His father's antique three-pronged pitchfork was missing.

He could visualize this treasured farm instrument very well: a shorter, slimmer, smoothly worn wooden handle attached securely to a long, slender metal fork which extended gracefully into the thin lines of the three very pointed, very sharp tines. Unlike the wider pitchforks hanging down the row, it was lighter and easier to handle while pitching, flipping, or winnowing. This one had a shorter handle and was probably used by the worker who caught the hay as it hit the top of the wagon, to spread and balance the load for safe transportation. As far as he knew, he reminded himself anxiously, this particular pitchfork was no longer manufactured.

Below that line of tools, the floor was bare except for snatches of hay and loose pebbles tracked in from outside. He squinted, visually checking out the storage area under the loft at the south end of the barn. From where he stood, nothing seemed out of order; about six feet from the car, a permanent wooden ladder, centered on the east-to-west edge of the loft, led straight up. Just behind it in the low-ceilinged storage area beneath, containers of feed corn and other shadowy shapes sat darkly in place. But surely, that pitchfork was somewhere around. He focused on this new, pressing search, not thinking about Uncle now, more concerned about this valued piece of memorabilia from his childhood.

"Okay, better take a closer look at the storage area under the loft." He had hardly made it across the twelve feet toward the storage area behind the loft's ladder, before he saw something against the background of morning light now flooding through the opening of the large barn doorway to his left. The slim line of a shadow… no, a silhouette… leaning slightly

away from the side of the Dodge, brought him to a sudden stop.

"There it is, stuck in a pile of hay! I recognize the handle, and the curve of the fork. Yes!!"

Relieved, he did a quick turn, and headed for this recovered treasure, eager to hang it back up on its nail hook. His head jerked as the toe of his boot slammed against something solid, causing him to nearly plummet forward into the mound of hay. An instinctive reaction stopped the fall, and as he looked down past his flailing arms, he saw a white tennis shoe lying on its side. Not sure of what he was seeing, he stood still for a couple of seconds, then pushed it gingerly with his foot. It did not budge. Suddenly he saw the thick ribbing of a white bobby sock top, unrolled upward on the pale calf of a leg, and then, to the right, another shoe, sock top and leg and then the royal blue, bright gold and royal blue panels of a skirt. He drew back, took in the whole picture, and his jaw dropped. What he had thought was a mound of hay was, instead, a young girl's body, lying face down in a pool of blood, his father's pitchfork savagely driven deeply into her lower back, all the way into the floorboards beneath.

His throat filled. "Ahww-www, gee-awd..." He turned his face away, trying to get control of the nausea. "Ahww-www, hay-ell..."

He took a big breath and swallowed hard, then instinctively stepped forward to rescue his valuable pitchfork. His rubber boot slipped across a wet floorboard. Automatically, he grabbed the nearest rung of the ladder to regain his balance. As he straightened up, the smeared trail of blood caused by his slipping step brought him back to reality: forget the pitchfork. Right in front of him was a dead young girl — violently, viciously killed.

"Oh, my dear God... no. No."

All he wanted to do was to get out of there. He did not try to go out the milk house door where he could rinse the manure smell off his barn boots with a convenient hose. Instead, he circled behind the loft ladder and stumbled out past the rear of the car into the light, giving the sliding door just a little wider push as he passed it. Without further pause, he took off across the driveway, and up the stairs to the back door, not stopping at the bench in the mudroom to remove the soiled footwear. He saw his wife down the length of the hall, in the kitchen, sitting at the mottled white Formica and chrome dinette set. As usual, the radio in the living room was going full blast. Jan Peerce was singing one of Winnie's "bluebird" songs, **The Bluebird of Happiness**. His operatic voice filled the room, urging the world to find hope in the encouraging twitter of a bluebird. It would not soften the shock about to hit Winnie-the-Pooh.

The little lady was in her faded pink bathrobe, drinking coffee. Suddenly she saw him. She turned to visually follow the electric cord up to the blue plastic circle of the wall clock above the table, then looked back at him.

"You done out there already? It's only five after six."

Cecil stopped abruptly at the doorway into the kitchen. The pale blue plaid wallpaper seemed to fade in and out on the wall above the bright white wainscoting behind where Winnie was sitting. The man opened his mouth, but the words did not come. He licked his dry lips, and took some short breaths, as Winnie rose quickly from her chair to turn off the radio. Moving closer to peer into her husband's pale face, their eyes met, and she saw the shock. "What?" she asked, placing her small hands over his heart, her fingers smoothing gently across the roughness of the overall bib, to calm him.

"What?"

He exhaled slowly, the jaw slackening, a frown line deepening between the knitted brows. Then he took another deep breath, and spoke softly. "There's a dead body in the barn, Win. A young girl. My father's pitchfork is in her back."

Her hands dropped quickly to press tightly over her mouth. She stared at him for a few seconds, processing what her husband had just told her. Then her hands slid downward, one over the other, moving as if to protect the hollow of her throat. "What happened?"

"I don't know." He shook his head. "I can't imagine such a thing happening in my own barn, for Pete's sake, and with my own pitchfork."

"What are you going to do?"

He swallowed and shook his head, again. "Have to call Chief Rob, I guess. Have to report it, that's for sure." He looked at her, scanning his petite wife from the top of her salt-and-pepper hair, down past the faded robe to her slippered feet. "Guess you'd better get dressed."

"Guess I'd better," she said, scooting toward the bedroom. At the dining room table, she stopped and turned around. "You going to be alright to make that call?"

Cecil stuck his trembling hands into the side pockets of his overalls and lied, "I'm fine."

CHAPTER TWO

Cops

Surprisingly, he made the call without incident, even remembering the telephone number. Lily, the secretary/dispatcher, answered the phone.

"Essex Junction Police Department."

He cleared his throat before he spoke. "Hello, Lily. This is Cecil Thompson, up on Old Colchester Road."

"'Morning, Cecil. What are you doing on the phone so early? Aren't you supposed to be milking by now?"

"Uh... I... uh, really need to speak to the chief. Is he anywhere around?"

The tone of Cecil's voice caught Lily's attention, switching her manner into official mode. "Chief Rob is over at Muncy's Diner. I can have him call you back, if you like."

"That would be good. As soon as possible, Lily."

"Your call sounds urgent, Cecil. May I inform the chief as to the nature of the problem?"

He paused.

"Cecil?"

He just didn't want to say it.

"Please feel free to share your information, especially if it will expedite whatever action Chief Rob needs to take."

He cleared his throat again. "Uh... there's a dead body in my barn."

He heard her catch her breath. "Yes, sir. I will notify Chief Rob immediately. He should call you back in just a couple of minutes, okay?"

"Okay."

"Oh, and Cecil, whatever you do, don't touch anything."

She hung up before he could answer.

Winnie hurried out from the bedroom, dressed in a cotton dress. A row of buttons descended down the front, almost to the hem of the pale green plaid. A baggy white sweater topped it off, keeping the morning chill from her arms. She stopped in front of the sitting room, right under the arch. "Did you get him?" she asked, as she twisted to the left and then to the right, looking down across the curve of her forty-three-year-old calves, checking for crooked seams at the back of her nylons.

"He's going to call me back."

"Good," she replied quietly. "We should probably wake Uncle up."

The shrill of the telephone broke into the conversation. Still standing over it, Cecil picked it up immediately.

"This is Chief Rob. Is that you, Cecil?"

"Ay-yuh, it's me."

"Lily tells me there's a body in your barn." It was more of a question than a statement.

"Ay-yuh — a young girl, I think. Next to the car. It's a helluva mess, Chief."

"Well, it's not really in my jurisdiction — you actually reside in Essex Township, not here in the village of Essex Junction — so I have to notify the sheriff, right away. But," he reassured Cecil, "I will be right up there, okay?"

"Appreciate it."

"But, Cecil, be sure you don't touch anything. Don't move anything, okay?"

"I... I did give the front barn door a push."

There was a moment of silence. "I'll be right up. You stay in the house until I get there."

Winnie moved slowly toward the kitchen. "What did he say?" Her little brown eyes never left her husband's face as he repeated the conversation back to her. At the end, she was a little surprised. "I always thought of us as being part of the village. We do so much down there in the junction." She walked purposefully across the room and headed down the back door hall. "I'm going to get Uncle up."

"He's not there."

She stopped and turned to look at the clock again. "Of course he is. It's his day off. He's sleeping in like always."

"He's not up there," he insisted, but she was already on her way, padding softly up the creaking stairs.

Cecil pulled the chrome-legged dinette chair a little farther out from the table and sat down heavily on its mottled white plastic cushion.

"What the heck just happened, here? A dead body in my barn, and a missing hired hand." He leaned forward on his elbows and picked up Winnie's half-empty cup. *"Sure don't like the sound of that… dead body, and a missing Uncle."* He brought the cup slowly up to his mouth and took a sip of the lukewarm coffee. *"But that's nonsense. That little runt… although he was in combat in the Army…"* He shuffled his feet, and took another sip. *"No, that just isn't who he is. Uncle wouldn't do something like that."* He felt a tinge of guilt. *"Maybe I've been too hard on him. Or maybe I should have been more aware, more alert."* But then, he shook his head. *"Naw, I am who I am, too focused on whatever is in front of me, just get it done, and I just plain do not like surprises."* He snorted softly. *"Guess I'm just as much of a stinker as he is."*

She was standing at the foot of the stairs, and when she spoke, her voice was trembling. "He's not up there. We need to look around. He has to be someplace around here." She was already pulling on her boots.

"Chief told us to stay in the house, and that's what we're going to do."

She jumped up and grabbed her blue nylon windbreaker. "Uncle is missing. There's a dead girl in the barn, probably murdered," she replied. "I need to know what's going on. I'm going out there."

Before she could say more, he was bounding toward her, a look in his eye that made her stand still. He reached for her, wrapping his arms around her trembling little frame. She returned the embrace, burying her face into his soft belly. The front panels of the red plaid jacket concealed her head, and she muffled a couple of little sobs into the overalls. After a moment, she took a long, shaky breath, and exhaling, gently pushed him away. "I'm sorry, Ceese, but you just smell so bad with those boots on. You're stinking up the whole house, you."

He tried to chuckle in agreement. "You're talking like a Frenchman, again." He grabbed her hand. "Let's just go back and sit down at the table for a couple of minutes."

As they began to sit down, she suggested, "Maybe you could just take them off until he gets here."

"Not a good idea." Then, turning around, he said, "But I could step into the bathroom and wash them off in the bathtub."

She winced, but gave a nod of approval. Before he went all the way in, he leaned his head back out. "Promise me you won't move."

She clucked her tongue and waved him to get on with it.

***

Just as Cecil finally stepped back out of the bathroom, the sound of a car pulling into the driveway drew them both to the kitchen window. It was Chief Rob's patrol car. They watched as he stopped the vehicle, shifted, and backed it out onto the road, then pulled onto the right shoulder to park it.

"He must not have had the siren on," Winnie said. "Sometimes they just use the flashing lights."

Out on the back porch a few seconds later, the two of them stood at the top of the steps, ready to descend as soon as the chief came into sight. However, he appeared from behind the corner of the house, his right hand raised in a "stay put" signal, and, catching their attention, brought that same hand close to his own face, tapping his index finger against his lips, commanding silence. He glanced toward the barn, drew a gun from his left-sided holster, and proceeded toward the open doorway. Once there, he kept the door between him and the inside of the barn, as he checked the edge of it, looking up, then down to the wooden threshold. A moment later, he turned slowly and stared hard at the body lying between the loft and the car, and then, looking up into the hay hanging off the loft's edge, moved quickly across to the back of the ladder. There he paused, more closely examining the situation.

Sirens could be heard in the distance. The Thompsons turned to see which way they were coming from, but could not tell. When they looked back, the chief was up the ladder, his head just above the loft's floor, slowly turning left and right, as though searching for something. Suddenly, he looked back over his shoulder, aware that the sheriff was on the way.

He had holstered his gun and was climbing back down when the sheriff's car bumped up over the railroad track. It came to a sliding stop at the side of the road, just before the north end of the driveway. Before the sheriff and his deputy could even get their doors open, a second vehicle bounced over the track and plowed into a sudden stop on the other side of the drive, right in front of the red maple.

Maxwell Duncan had lived in Vermont all of his life, mostly in the Colchester area. He had been elected Chittenden County Sheriff in 1948, and ruled with an iron hand. Today, there was a murder in the township of Essex, and he was here to take care of it. The three-man police department from the village sure wasn't going to handle this; it was in his jurisdiction.

A deputy sheriff with a camera moved ahead of him along the driveway toward the barn area, taking pictures of the muddy tire tracks and footprints. Two other deputies walked slowly along beside him, one with a tablet and pencil, the other with a roll of tape to mark the crime scene. When they reached the back porch steps, he turned and reached up to shake Cecil's hand.

"'Morning, sir. I'm Chittenden County Sheriff, Max Duncan." He moved up the steps and the Thompsons backed up to make way for this tall, robust figure of a man.

"This is no way to start the day, now, is it?" Winnie's head drooped, and Cecil shook his head to confirm the statement. "Are you folks all right? Do you need medical assistance or anything?" They declined it politely, even though their knees were numb with tension. The sheriff looked at them for a brief moment. "Okay, folks, Deputy Smith will be taking down some information from you… names, times… things like that. I, myself, will be talking to Chief Robert Allen over there. I assume you know him." He paused to note the heads bobbing in affirmation. "Meanwhile, if you don't feel good or something, you let Deputy Smith, here, know right away, and we'll get some help for you." With that, he turned back down the steps and caught up with the cameraman just in front of the barn door opening. He was pleased to see the Chief of Police was standing still, careful not to pollute the crime scene.

The sheriff had watched Robbie Allen grow up in Essex Junction, a good-looking, popular kid, the left-handed star player on the baseball team, graduating at the head of his class at police academy, coming back to be the rookie, and now — here he was — Chief of Police. Normally, it would be a really good feeling to see success like that. However, Maxwell was careful not to get too involved with this guy, because in the two short years after he was hired, Chief

Robbie had made quite a reputation for himself. Max saw that the man was one who just naturally landed in the spotlight. That was a political threat. Further, he realized this young man was as smart as a whip. He was going to have to be careful about working with Chief Robert Ethan Allen.

"'Morning, Sheriff."

"'Morning, Chief. I see you beat me to it, here."

"Yeah, I thought these folks might be in danger. And I've been careful." He motioned toward his vehicle. "Parked down there, then walked straight up here. So, the fresh tracks are mine…"

Sheriff Max waved his camera guy to cover that whole end of the drive. "All the way to the road," he said. Chief Rob shifted his weight just a little.

Turning his attention to the corpse, the sheriff asked, "What do we have going here?"

"Oh, it's definitely murder. You can see the pitchfork from here."

Max squinted his eyes and peered into the barn. "Smells like skunk in here." Then he turned to the deputy with the tape and directed him to start cordoning off the area, starting at the barn door, all the way around to the milk house door. "Then start inside, as soon as Norm is done taking pictures. We don't want any trouble with unhappy detectives." He turned and called Norm to get on with it, get back to the barn, and, "Be sure to use that flash bulb attachment inside. We need to get some sharp shots of the body and all, and then I can get in there and take a look." He turned to the chief. "You touched that body, Chief?"

"No, sir."

"Been anywhere near it?"

"Pretty near. But I didn't touch it." He shifted his weight again, as Max eyed him carefully.

"Just how near would that be, Chief?"

"I went in to check the loft."

"Maybe that's why *you* smell like skunk." The chief's lips became a thin line. "So, you walked in there, and climbed the ladder?"

"Yeah. Thought maybe there might be somebody up there."

"You thought maybe the murderer would still be hanging around?" Not waiting for an answer, he yelled to Norm: "You gonna be all day?" Norm came running up to the barn, inserting the first flash bulb as he ran, stopped at the threshold, and started to click away, moving methodically, in a wide semicircle around the body. The sheriff continued to direct operations. "Right. Get this part done, and then you can get the rest."

Chief Rob cleared his throat. "There may have been a second victim, maybe needing help, maybe only injured. I thought we should check that out, right away." He seemed to be satisfied with his own explanation. The sheriff just folded his arms and grunted. For another five minutes, the two officers stood quietly and waited for Norm to finish up. Once, Chief Rob tugged at his collar.

Finally, the picture taker looked up. "I'm done here, Max."

Chief Allen waited while the sheriff moved in for a closer look. Years of experience came into play as the older man stood and looked, then moved right, still eyeing the victim. After a few minutes of shifting positions, peering, sniffing, and going back to double-check this or that, Sheriff Max waved him to come closer. "Come in here and see if you can ID this body for me, mister."

Chief Rob stepped over to take a closer look. "Looks like an Essex Junction cheerleader's outfit." Then he bent closer toward the head, which was face down on the floor. It was covered with a navy blue watch cap, and there were golden-red curls falling loosely from the edges.

"Aw, crap." He stood up and pushed his chief's hat to the back of his head, like most of the 1950's movie cops did.

"We a-a-all should have seen this one coming," he said softly.

CHAPTER THREE

Tripped Up

About a year earlier, on Monday, October 6, 1952, Scottie Allen let the screen door slam with a bounce as he left the two-story home he shared with his mother, Grace, and his older brother, Rob. He skipped sideways down the two steps to their sidewalk which led out onto Vermont Route 15, otherwise known as Main Street in the village of Essex Junction. The alert fifteen-year-old checked for traffic before crossing the street, looking all the way to the left down past Drury Brickyard, then toward the train tracks several long blocks to the right. Bounding to the other side, he made a right in front of the little First Methodist Church and struck his unique stride — long legs thrown forward, heels digging hard into the sidewalk, the outward-pointing toes slapping firmly into place. Moments later, he began to pull out his tucked-in shirttail, letting it hang loose over his belted slacks. His mom was a stickler for tucked-in shirts, but Scottie usually found a way to circumvent that little rule. At last, the light blue dress shirt was flapping happily against his backside. He hitched the zippered notebook and two textbooks under his right arm into a more comfortable position.

It was a beautiful Vermont fall morning, with the foliage just breaking into its golden glory along Main Street. Scottie noted nature's leafy artist's palette as he moved along, with the half-interest of a teenager who has seen the art show before, until he finally crossed Church Street, the last small bylane before reaching downtown.

Trees and shrubs in front of the Congregational Church on his left were about to break into multiple rosy-golden hues, while across Main Street the old village cemetery lay peacefully under a lacey, burnt-orange canopy. Passing Al's French Fries takeout shack, Scottie's gaze slowly followed a slight curve to the left, looking for familiar cars parked in front of Yandow's Market. There was only a bicycle leaning on its kickstand. The youngster smiled, recognizing the racing bike, bright blue and very sharp looking. He knew it belonged to the local priest, Father Thomas.

"A priest who rides a racing bike for fun; who would ever have thought they'd see that in the village of Essex Junction?"

Even though the dinging-flashing railroad crossbar was quiet, he checked northward up the tracks, all the way over to the dark brown train depot, before he stepped out toward his eventual target: the intersection of Essex Junction's busy traffic circle. The sidewalk turned into worn, gray planks, crisscrossed by several train tracks. Scottie was careful not to get tripped up. Shortly, he was once again back onto the firm footing of the Main Street sidewalk.

Minutes later, he arrived at the intersection of five streets. Vermont Route 15, along which he had just walked from home, was just one spoke in the wagon wheeled intersection. A cement post about five feet high stood in the very center of the traffic circle, its yellow light flashing warnings for drivers to yield and proceed according to traffic laws. Vehicles already in the circle had the right-of-way, and traffic was to move in a counter-clockwise direction until reaching the street onto which the driver wished to exit.

From where Scottie stood, Route 15 resumed at a two o'clock position and became Pearl Street, which rose slowly to level out in a southwest direction and continue some seven miles or so, through the town of Winooski, leading all the way to Burlington, where that route ended.

Lincoln Hall was located there at the start of Pearl Street, just on the right. As far as Scottie knew, that was where the police department, fire department, and — he wasn't sure — maybe the town hall was located. All he was sure of, was that this is where Chief of Police Robbie had his office. As the younger brother, he had not been allowed to go there, for reasons he had not quite figured out… something about his mother wanting to keep him from all the "ugly" things of the world. At fifteen, he had already made a mental note to correct all of that, but things had been too busy up to this point, to get all those details in order.

The next exit, at the twelve o'clock position from where he stood, was Park Street. It ran between Robinson's Oil on the right, and the Lincoln Inn on the left, on past the historic Park Street School building, and all the way out to what he thought was an old dam, or something. Most folks taking Park Street, however, were pulling into the inn's parking lot for a delicious meal at either the coffee shop or the formal dining room, or for just a relaxing overnight stay in one of the New England style rooms of this Essex Junction icon.

Directly across the intersection from the inn and to Scottie's far right, was the Lincoln Street exit off the wagon wheel. This led out to the new Colchester Road, officially Vermont Route 2A. It went to the village's north boundaries, somewhere past the creamery and the railroad crossing at the end of Grove Street, all of which were several long blocks from where he stood. It was in this direction he would walk to the high school as soon as he "accidentally" ran into Penny this morning.

Scottie checked his Timex watch, a gift from Rob last Christmas. His brother had the watch inscribed, "To Ira from Ethan." It was a reference to their famous last name… at least, it was pretty prominent in Vermont history. And right now, he knew his popular brother was probably at Muncy's Diner, just to his left there on Main Street. Many times he would drop in to sit for a minute, to be with Rob while he was on official duty. He checked his watch again, then shook his head.

There wouldn't be time — too much stuff going on, what with the cheerleading tryout results being posted this morning. Penny would be, in her own classy way, very excited, so of course he would be there with her. He moved forward past Muncy's toward the fifth exit off the traffic circle, and nearest to his left, Maple Street. Hanging out with Robbie would have to wait.

Still, he was proud of his ten-years-older brother, the Chief of Police in Essex Junction. The siblings were close, Rob taking the place of the father who had died too soon. Scottie followed his brother's lead, learning to serve the public, and happy to be included in the semi-celebrity status that came with it. Historically, the two brothers felt, it was not something new for them, because they believed they were descendants of Ira Allen, brother of Ethan Allen, the well-known Revolutionary War hero. Both Ethan (years older than Ira) and his youngest brother were key founders of the Republic of Vermont. The ancestral trails were a little cloudy, but the more Rob and Scottie studied them, the more it all just seemed to fit. Just a couple of years before this sunny fall day, Scottie had been delighted to learn that Ethan had had the same flamboyant personality Robbie exhibited, while the younger brother, Ira, was more socially minded, a man of justice and fair play, sort of like he imagined *himself* to be.

Indeed, Scott Ira Allen was happy to be who he was. He was also happy to have his brother's good looks: tall and lanky, blondish hair, the same steel-gray eyes, and square-toothed smile.

"*Only, he doesn't have a case of 'terminal acne.'*" Scottie grimaced, and then grinned to himself. "*At least Penny doesn't seem to mind.*" He glanced down to locate the source of a light ticking sound on the sidewalk, to see the plastic-coated end of his brown shoelace click lightly against the cement.

"Oh-oh, don't need to trip on my own shoelace in front of the prettiest freshman girl at EJHS."

He bent down to tie the lace again, rubbing the toe of his brown oxford shoe with the side of his fist, then picked up his notebook and books, and stood up.

And there she was, just off to his left, rounding the corner off Maple Street, headed his way.

Her five-foot-one body gracefully skipped alongside her very best friend, trying to keep pace with the longer stride of the five-foot-eight Diana. Penny was an excellent amateur tap dancer, well up to the task of keeping up, and still make delightful conversation. Today, Scottie noted, the verbal exchange seemed animated, happy. Her soft, brown pageboy hairdo bounced with each step, while the bangs lifted and fell in the breeze, gently caressing the arch of her eyebrows. Under those brows, he knew, were the most beautiful liquid dark brown eyes, shaded by the longest eyelashes in the world. Below that, a pretty, softly rounded nose hovered over a delicious, plump mouth... a mouth which could easily spread wide over a glistening smile. He watched as they approached, enjoying the way the gray felt poodle skirt swayed with each shift of her hips as she waltzed along. She clutched a notebook — much like his own — both of her slender arms holding it securely in place across her bosom. Diana, who had just turned sixteen, often dominated the conversation. Suddenly, she stopped Penny and said something he could not hear, then both girls bent over with laughter before, still chuckling, they resumed their rhythmic walk. Only a moment after that, he locked eyes with his favorite girl in the whole universe.

The three of them commenced the final trek to school — north onto Lincoln, past the greenhouse, and finally turning left at the Roman Catholic Church to hike uphill on Prospect Street to Essex Junction High School. It was a walk orchestrated by the shuffle of one of the three moving forward or backward, to maintain the inclusiveness of good friends, a walk they had often made, a walk that always seemed to work. Today, they just ambled along, purposely avoiding the subject of cheerleading tryouts and the decisions which hung on the hall bulletin board at that very moment.

***

Meanwhile, quite another scenario was evolving, only a few blocks away. On Summit Street, which commenced at the crest of Pearl Street — State Route 15 to Burlington — and tee'd to an end at Prospect Street right in front of the high school, another freshman strode purposefully toward an important destination — that very same bulletin board on the first floor hall of the school, where the list of new cheerleaders was posted. The full skirt of her lavender gingham dress rippled softly with each determined step. Glorious golden-red curls whipped around her shoulders as her slender body bent forward like a runner about to cross the finish line. The ivory skin of her extraordinarily beautiful face was enhanced by the natural sweet pink in her cheeks, and her silver eyes glinted brightly above the little nose with the flaring nostrils.

Roxanne Foxx was on a mission.

She bounded across Prospect Street and up the walkway to the front door of the old federal-style brick school. There her adoring sidekick, Marsha, spotted her approach and pulled the door open.

"Roxie… Roxie… now don't get mad." Her pale blue eyes were filled with apprehension.

Roxie came to a sudden stop. She glared at her skinny friend. "What do you mean, 'Don't get mad'?"

Marsha pushed back her greasy, blonde hair. "Well, you made it, but…" Her voice trailed off. She wiped the corner of her mouth with the back of her hand, something that for some reason offended this beautiful goddess friend.

Somewhere in her short life, Roxie Foxx had acquired a unique little singsong sound. It appeared to be a cross between a grunt and a prolonged nasal hoot, executed in the two musical notes, E and B-flat. "Uh-huhhh!" This was her signature attention-getter, invariably announcing her arrival to a room full of people. It was also her very own way to give approval, and sometimes, to put annoying people in their proper place.

This time, Roxie hooted in disgust, then hastened toward the bulletin board. It was located on the wall directly across from the door that Marsha still held open.

"Shut the door, for Pete's sake," the beautiful one murmured as she crossed the shiny wood floor. The board was framed snugly between two classroom doors, the home ec room on the left, a junior high classroom on the right. She bent forward to peer at the list, her hands together, fingertips pointed forward. Almost immediately she sucked in a big breath, and stamped hard. Then her two feet drew together, side-by-side, and her whole body started to rock front-and-back in place... rocking, rocking, while the fingertips of both hands tapped firmly against each other, again and again and again. This continued for a full minute, until finally, she read it out loud: "First sub. First substitute."

"But you'll be the first one they call, if anybody gets sick, Roxie."

It took a moment.

The rocking slowly subsided. After several seconds, the finger-tapping stopped. The reddish-gold curls shook just once as she jerked around, a little smile on her pouty mouth. "That's right, Marsh. That's exactly right. But maybe I can do a little better than that."

She moved over to ascend a couple of steps up onto the west side staircase which wound upward from the basement below to the front hall where she stood, continuing on up to a landing between the first and second floors. There, students passed the tiny teachers' lounge each day to climb up to the second floor, where four classrooms and a large study hall completed the facility. An identically wide staircase ran to and from all of the same places, but at the opposite, east end of the building. However, instead of the teachers' lounge, the office of the high school principal, Randall Marvin, was located on that landing between the two upper floors.

But at this moment, there on the second step up of those west side stairs, this young girl stood transfixed, her body once again undulating ever-so-slightly, by the rocking of her feet against the stair step, over and over and over.

Slowly, slowly, Roxie no longer looked fourteen years old. A change came over her countenance as she stood quietly rocking, deep in thought, staring across to — but apparently not seeing — the other staircase. Her enchanting, silvery eyes glazed over, signaling thoughts adrift in some other dimension. For a little while, she did not move from the position on the stairs, seemingly transfixed by some mysterious force. Seeing what was happening, Marsha, who had seen this too many times before, groaned, picked up her books, and disappeared quietly down the hall into a classroom.

Moments passed. At length, the gorgeous redhead came back to EJHS, took a long, slow breath through her nose, and reached slowly into a side pocket of her dress to pull out a small plastic tube.

She was leisurely applying the lip balm to her pretty little mouth when the front doors again burst open. A small group of would-be cheerleaders and their buddies hurried to the bulletin board. There was a moment of hushed breathing, then murmurs and a "Yes!" here and there. Roxie heard it all happening, but her eyes were on the entrance. Sure enough, before the exclamations and sad sighs were over, Scottie, Diana, and Penny walked slowly into the hall, stopping at the sight of the group around the list. Paula, one of the girls who made the cut, ran up to Penny, declaring, "You made it,

Penny-pal! You made it! We both made it!" Penny covered her smile with her hands, as someone else hugged her. Congratulations moved through the group, for each member of the new 1952-53 cheerleading squad.

"Okay, we need to pick up our uniforms at three o'clock after school today," Paula said. "The first game is this Friday, so we need to practice at least once before that."

Scottie worked his way in for a closer look at the list, secretly noting that all of them were "good lookers." Diana, however, stood back and watched, glad for Penny, but filled with sympathy for those who did not make the cut. There were five or six of them huddled off to the side, so the tenderhearted girl stepped forward to give them encouraging hugs. Other students were now arriving for school, thinning out the intense little crowd. As he moved back around to watch the drama, Scottie felt a hand on his shoulder, and turned to see Roxie, tears streaming down her lovely face.

"Please," she said softly, "I need to talk to you."

"What?" He turned to include Diana in the conversation, but she was still doing hug therapy.

"Please, could you meet me at lunchtime today? In the publishing room for *The Commentator*. Please… I'm in danger, Scottie. I need your help."

"Uh… no. No, I won't be doing that, Roxie. Find yourself another hero."

"But I could be… seriously, seriously hurt, Scottie."

He moved away, trying to get across the hall to catch up with Penny. He was decidedly uncomfortable with this girl's too-intimate cry for help. Still, she was following him, calling his name in a loud whisper. This was not for him. He turned back to tell her that, but was silenced by the terror on her face.

"Oh my God, Scottie! Please help me!" she spoke through tight lips, eyes wide with fear.

"No!" He headed toward his first class, as fast as he could move.

At the end of that very first class, he ran into her in the rush of the hallway. She stepped from nowhere into his path, grabbed his arm and whispered an agonized "Please-please-please!" into his ear, before disappearing into the crowd. That next class was so clouded by her words that he left with very few notes and a ton of guilt. *"What danger? Seriously hurt? What was she talking about?"*

This was a girl who had become known, in her short time at EJHS, to live "on the edge," a person whom very few people trusted, one with a "loose reputation." It was certainly possible she had pushed the envelope too far, but she was a still just a fourteen-year-old, younger than most of her classmates, and no matter what reputation she had, she was still at risk. She could be beaten, or worse. Maybe she needed some good advice, or maybe just some protection, or both. Maybe he could get his big brother to help.

"Yeah, that might work. The Allen brothers, working in tandem. Yeah."

But he would have to know what the problem was, first. So, when she tearfully tugged his sleeve in the hallway shuffle after math class, he agreed to meet her in the publishing room of the school newspaper, right after his third and final class of the morning.

*****

Penny had promised to accompany Diana to the tryouts for the senior play, this year an original piece by one of the seniors. Because of the large numbers in the cast, lower-classmen were allowed to try out for a part. Diana had caught the acting bug way back in the seventh grade right there in this very same school building. Back then, there was only the study hall or a borrowed grange hall stage for drama presentations. But now, there was the brand new gym with the huge stage and even some velvet curtains which operated on hand-pulled ropes. This was going to be special. Auditions were to be held at a quarter past noon, and since there were mostly non-speaking parts, Diana figured she could probably make it. The girls excused themselves from lunch with Scottie, much to his relief. He had no desire to explain why he, himself needed to be absent from their usual lunch date. Before he knew it, he was down the stairs to the basement, walking past the boys' room toward the old cloakroom where the school paper was created. A black and white sign on the door read, *THE COMMENTATOR.*

He grasped the door handle and turned it, but it stopped short. *"Locked?"*

He looked around, confused, and then he heard the click of the lock. The door opened to a tiny crack, and then flew open. "Quick!" Roxie whispered, pulling him inside by his shirtsleeve. In one swift movement, she closed the door and whirled around, clasping her arms around his neck and burying her face into the hollow of his shoulder.

"Hey, Roxie… let go." He tried to pull her arms down, to back away from her, but the hysterical sobbing and murmurs of "Thank you, thank you, thank you…" drowned out his hoarse whisper. Desperate, he reached up and grabbed her wrists, and yanked as hard as he could. She fell back, but he continued to hold her forearms in a tight grip, for fear she would try to grab his neck again.

"Get hold of yourself!" he commanded. But her head fell forward, the gorgeous curls touching his chest, and he thought she was going to pass out. "For heaven's sake, Roxie. Get it together, will ya?"

Suddenly, she drew a hard, fast breath, and lifted her face toward his. "Scottie, I know you don't like me. I… I know you don't even like me." She sniffed and swallowed. Her shoulders shook twice with smothered sobs. "Thank you, thank you, thank you so much for meeting me even though you really don't want to. This…" Her shoulders shook again, as she took her next breath. "This is really nice of you."

He waited for her to take one more breath. After a few more seconds, he thought maybe he could loosen his grip, perhaps even let go of her arms altogether.

"I need a Kleenex." She kept her head down to hide the stuff coming out of her nose. "May I have my arms back?"

"No more surprises, kiddo. Promise?"

"Yes. I promise. I won't touch you again."

He let go slowly. As she backed away and reached for the tissue in her dress pocket, he saw the red marks his fingers had made on the delicate skin of her wrists. A huge pang of guilt shot through his gut.

"Ahw-w-w, Roxie. Aw, cripes, kiddo. Just look at that. Why did you grab me like that? Now look what's happened."

"Yeah, well," she blew her nose gently, dabbing it carefully as she spoke. "It's not the first time I've had bruises. I get bruises all the time." She folded her arms, shifting her weight onto her left foot. Slowly she started bouncing her right heel ever-so-lightly, rhythmically against the cement floor. The toes on that right foot never left the floor, and the ensuing jiggling motion that started there undulated upward, turning her whole body into a gently bobbing entity. Scottie had seen this happen before. It had always made him uncomfortable.

"What? No, no. You don't have bruises all the time. We see you every day. What are you talking about?"

She ignored him. "I know it's partly because I have delicate skin," she whispered softly. "But that doesn't mean I can be slapped and kicked around, and nobody helps me." Again, the shoulders heaved, temporarily interrupting the bounce of her slim body. "I'm starting to get really, really scared. I'm afraid of what he's going to do next."

"What do you mean? Who is 'he'?"

Roxie hesitated, seeming to assemble her words carefully. She shifted her weight to both feet, standing straight as a rod. Then, slowly she raised her hands up to chest level, thumbs and index fingers of each hand pinched together, and began tapping those two sets of pinched fingertips against each other. Scottie had seen this same odd motion before, also. It was kind of weird, but he had always passed it off as a physical twitch she could not overcome.

Roxie's voice was suddenly stronger, more under control. "I don't want you to tell anybody. I just want you to help me avoid… escape… another beating. He is *so* mean."

"*Who* is so mean?"

She was concentrating on the tapping fingertips, now just a few inches from her face. "You have to promise not to tell."

"Okay." But he changed his mind quickly. "Well, no, I can't promise not to tell something like that. It could be, you know… what if something really bad happened, and I never alerted my brother? He's the Chief of Police, for crying out loud."

Her lips became a thin line. Without taking her eyes off the tapping fingertips, she continued in that more powerful voice. "Are you going to help me, or not?"

It took him three seconds to decide. "Not," he said, turning toward the door.

She grabbed the back of his shirt. "Wait — wait!" There was a little pause before she spoke. "It's my stepfather."

Scottie shoved his hands into his pants pockets.

Now she had his attention, and suddenly, she didn't sound like a fourteen-year-old freshman at EJHS. It was a voice from seductively deep down in her throat, completely foreign to the young girl who was speaking.

"This man has a really bad gambling problem. You would never know it, but he bet his buddies down at the bus company three hundred dollars on me to make cheerleader."

Scottie pulled his hands out and crossed his arms as he stifled the laugh, but the grin could not be contained. "Oh, yeah?"

"This is not funny, Scottie." She blinked a couple of times before the tears filled her eyes. "He told me this morning that I had better come through for him, or I'd get more of…" She bent forward and stifled a sob. Then she choked it out: "He kicked me in my privates."

"What?"

"He did…" She lifted her skirt and slip to display a red bruise in the inside of her right thigh. "Look."

He raised his hands to wipe out the picture, turning his head away. "Aw, jeez, Roxie, don't show me your underwear."

"Look!" she insisted. "I want you to see this. Look at this! Can you imagine what he's going to do to me when I come home a loser?"

"Wait a minute." He turned to correct her. "Put down your skirt, for Pete's sake." She slowly obliged. "That's better. Now," he put both hands on his hips, trying to take command of the situation. "I just read that list this morning. Didn't you make substitute or something? That means you *did* make the cut. What's wrong with that?"

She froze. She did not know he had read the list. No words came out of her shiny lips. No breath passed through the flared nostrils. There was only a blank, cold, silvery stare that lasted way too long.

"Oh my gosh… she's lying."

Finally, she turned slowly away from him, flipping the ringlets along the side of her head with her left hand. "He doesn't count that as a win, and neither do any of his buddies. I have to be on the first team, or I'm going to be really, really hurt by this man." The pitiful voice was back.

"Yeah?"

She turned back around, moving closer to look deeply into his eyes. Again, he noted, this was not the look of a fourteen-year-old, but he let her continue, because he didn't know what else to do.

"I would be so grateful, if you would only help me. I think I would probably do just about anything to escape from George Foxx's hateful hands."

He couldn't believe her, but decided to play along with it. Pausing first, just long enough to appear to be thinking about the offer, he answered in the sexiest voice a fifteen-year-old could muster. "So-o-oo, what do you need for me to do... to help you, I mean?"

She leaned closer. "Well, it won't be easy, but I know you can do it. All you have to do is," she tapped her finger lightly on his chest, "talk your sweet little girlfriend into stepping down." Seeing his reluctance, she reassured him. "Scottie, all you have to do is tell her the details — in confidence, of course — and I'm sure she will do all she can to help."

"There it is."

He resisted the urge to laugh, carefully pushing her hand away. "Why don't you ask her, yourself?"

She hooted impatiently at his ignorance. "For Pete's sake, Scottie, she won't listen to me. She doesn't trust me. But she'll listen to you. She's in *love* with you. That makes all the difference in the world." The pleading tone returned, almost like she had rehearsed it for weeks. "What do you say? Will you help me?"

That was it. He smiled a wicked smile, moved slowly to within inches of her beautiful face, as though to kiss her, and let her have it: "Not a chance, you lying little witch."

With that, Scottie was out the door. Just before he reached the stairs, he heard the parting threat.

"You're not going to get away with that, mister! You wait and s—"

She may have said more, but the tall form of John, the janitor, rose up from where he was pulling supplies from the bottom shelf of his storage closet under the stairs. He ran one hand over his balding head, addressing the young man who was grinning triumphantly. "What's the matter with her?"

"Umm, she just got tripped up in a big, fat lie, John. She's mad, but she'll get over it." He reached over and grabbed a bundle of paper towels for the home ec room. "Here, let me help you with that." In a moment, the two of them were up the stairs and out of Roxanne Foxx's sight.

Scottie handed the towels to the home ec teacher. "There ya go!" he said, grinning at her class of junior high girls. She nodded her appreciation, at the same time giving him a reproaching look. Quickly, she tapped her watch. "Thanks, but classes start in two minutes, young man."

***

Monday's first afternoon class for Scottie was glee club. He loved it, mostly because it was one of the few classes he shared with Penny, but also because he just plain loved to sing. He was sure there was a talent for this in the Allen family. His mother had been a leading soprano in various church choirs throughout her growing-up years, and he remembered his late father, a member of a local chapter of the Barbershoppers, singing in the shower, his fine baritone resonating throughout the top floor of the house where he, his mother, and his brother still lived. Surely, singing was in his blood.

He arrived on time at the gym and hurried over to the raised stage on the north wall, where chairs were set up for the twenty or so members of the glee club. Climbing the stairs to the stage, he spotted Penny in the soprano section, but she was looking at her sheet music. He moved on to the baritone section and took his seat.

Shaking out the papers he had picked up from his chair, he glanced to the right, over to the girls' alto section, where

Diana was leaning forward to give him a quick wave. He nodded back. But as she slipped back in her chair, he noted a pale, tight face just beyond Diana's right, staring at him. It was Roxie. Her gaze was purposely aimed at him, and she was not happy.

Mrs. Desmond had black-brown eyes that scanned back and forth over the glee club battleground like military binoculars, looking for a target. The intensity of that glare was enough to send shivers up the spine of a United States Marine. She was as fiercely focused on discipline as she was at landing on the right note at the right beat. So when she hit that piano with a jolting series of C-chords, members of the club sat down and shut up. From that point, they did vocal exercises, cleared up fine points on this or that piece, until finally, toward the last part of the session, they were swept up in a melodious rise and fall of voices so surprisingly elegant, that it stirred them to the very core of their juvenile souls. None of them could really explain it, but they actually looked forward to the next week's target practice with "Dead-eye Desmond."

The class was over before he knew it, and he moved quickly to make contact with Penny before they both moved on to the second class of the afternoon. He was delighted that she was waiting at the bottom of the stage stairs, her luscious smile, just for him. He clasped her hand as they walked out of the gym.

"I have to pick up my cheerleader uniform before I leave today," she said.

"What time?"

"Three o'clock. But they are never on time, you know that."

He thought for a moment. "I can wait for you in study hall."

She tilted her head upward, glowing. "Okay."

***

Scottie's last Monday afternoon class was social studies, held in one of the second-story rooms. Today there was a special speaker, Father Thomas, from Holy Family Roman Catholic Church, just down the hill from the school. The thirty-five-year-old priest leaned his tall body back against the clean side of the blackboard, speaking easily to the attentive freshmen. It wasn't often a man of the cloth from *any* denomination showed up in a classroom.

His topic was *The Role of the Church in Society*, and while there wasn't a whole lot of talk about God, he did offer plenty of godly solutions to social problems. For the last five minutes of class, he was taking questions, when one student asked the bottom-liner: "Sir, what would you say is the driving force that inspires churches to do all these good things?"

Father Thomas's bright blue eyes widened just a little, and a kind smile spread over his deeply freckled face. "That's an astute question, my friend." Using his fingers as a comb, he pushed the dark auburn hair straight back from his forehead, letting his hand rest for a few seconds on the crown of his bowed head. Then he looked up. "I would say it has to be *unconditional love.*"

Seeing the question in their eyes, he explained, "Now, unconditional love is just exactly that. We are to love with all the patience and wisdom and forgiveness we possibly can… no strings attached. We leave all final judgment to God, Himself. We are to be His loving hands, which is not easy, but His love is the *source* of our strength and that's the one thing we must try to show the rest of the world."

Mrs. Collins, the teacher, sensed a great ending to a special talk, and hastened forward to thank Father Thomas, her graying head bobbing graciously. There was some polite "thank you" applause. As the students filed out of the classroom, Scottie, having learned well from big brother, paused long enough to shake the man's hand. "Good talk, Father Tom. Hope I can live up to all that stuff."

The freckles moved with the slightly wrinkled brow. "It's not an easy assignment, for sure."

Slightly puzzled by that remark, the youngster slowly made his way a few doors down to the large study hall. He turned his attention to the task at hand — maneuvering his way through the waves of students who were moving toward the downward staircases, heading home, or to other after-school activities. Amongst them were several newly chosen cheerleaders, heading for the gym to pick up their uniforms. Penny was one of them. He tried to spot her, but as usual, his short-and-sweet girlfriend had gotten lost in the crowd.

Once inside study hall, he unzipped his notebook, laying it wide open on a vacated desk. What did he need to take home today? He slipped into the seat, intending to check homework assignments. But his mind went back to the priest's closing remark: "It's not an easy assignment, for sure."

"Not an easy assignment? That can't be right. It has to be pretty easy to be nice to people, especially to needy people."

He pondered that concept for a few minutes, then changed his mind about a couple of things. *"It has to be easy to help people you like, but was probably hard to help people you had no respect for. Still, even bad people have to be helped now and then. And then how do you know who deserves to get help first... the good people or the bad people? And if God wants us to give unconditional love, how does a person protect himself from dumb mistakes, like helping a criminal to live, so he could hurt or kill somebody else, maybe in the very next day? What kind of a 'driving force' is this? We're talking life and death, here."* More minutes passed.

A shout arose from the stairwell, just outside and below the study hall door. Immediately, there was a shuffle of footsteps accompanied by more high voices, and the slam of the doors which led to the enclosed walkway between the school and the gym. Scottie looked at the clock on the wall. It was three forty-five. The cheerleaders were finished, and heading home. He checked his homework quickly, expecting Penny in just a couple of minutes.

Another shuffle of feet, this time followed by the slam of the same set of doors, signaled an activity other than that of exiting cheerleaders. Whatever it was, some people had returned to the gym. He closed and zipped the notebook. Curious, he hefted the books and notebook under his arm, ready to go downstairs to see what the shuffling was all about. Not one step was taken before Diana suddenly appeared in the doorway, breathing hard, her huge blue eyes full of concern.

"Penny," she said.

"What?"

"She... she's been hurt." She saw his face go tight, and waved him to follow her. As they were descending the stairs, she continued. "It was a stupid, stupid accident." At the landing in front of the teachers' lounge, she turned around. "Some of the cheerleaders were practicing their kicks, and they got silly and carried away." He moved ahead of her down the next flight of stairs to the first floor. "She walked past one of them, and tripped over that girl's swift kick. Penny actually left the floor with both feet, then came down on her knee really hard, Scottie." The intense young man was down the last flight, pushing the double doors open. "It looks like a bad sprain, is all. It could be worse." He was bounding across the walkway to the steps which led to the gym when she said, "It was that stupid show-off, Roxie."

"It was Roxie who tripped her?" He was poised at the top step, ready to pull open the door to the gym. Diana nodded. "You sure about that?" She nodded again. His jaw went hard. "That was no accident."

On the other side of the door, he spotted Penny across the gym, sitting at the very front edge of the stage, right leg draped downward, the injured left one stretched out along the edge. Mrs. Collins, the social studies teacher who also oversaw the cheerleading activities, was just putting an ice-filled towel on that knee. His girlfriend's face was twisted in pain.

Principal Marvin, who dealt with teenage drama every day, several times a day, saw it coming. He stood his ground, arms akimbo, until Scottie got within ten feet, and then he raised a calming hand. "Slow down, Scott. She's going to live." He twisted sideways to give the boy a man-hug. "These things happen. She'll be fine." He walked the lad over to his girlfriend, one controlling arm firmly around his shoulders. "It was just an unfortunate accident."

Scottie opened his mouth to object, but stopped short at the sight off to his right. There on the floor in a hysterical heap, lay Roxie, surrounded by other cheerleaders. Her body heaved with sobs and moans of "Oh, no, no, no..." The hovering band of teenage girls were reaching out to her, patting and stroking her head... shoulders... hands. But she seemed to be beyond comforting, awash in a deep chasm of absolute grief and guilt.

Scottie shook his head and snorted. "She should get an Academy Award," he muttered.

Mr. Marvin raised his eyebrows, causing the horn-rimmed glasses to slide down his nose. "What?" his rubbery lips inquired. "What are you talking about?"

The young man heaved a deep, exasperated sigh. "She's the first substitute, sir. Now she's probably going to get to be a regular for a while."

Immediately he slipped away from the principal's suddenly slackened arm, moving toward the beautiful gaze now locking with his. He reached up to touch her hand, but drew back, afraid to cause more pain. "What can I do? I'm so sorry..." His words drifted off into a whisper.

"My mom is on the way. She'll take me to the doctor." She took a deep breath. "Oh boy, this really, really hurts." Suddenly, the tears welled up, and she blinked hard.

"It should never have happened, Penny... I'll make it up to you."

"It's not your fault," she whispered.

He bit his lip.

***

Within the next half-hour, Penny had been transported by three-handed chair to the back seat of her mother's car, and was on her way to the doctor. The small group at the gym slowly dispersed, picking up their books and uniforms and headed down the sidewalk. Scottie stopped to tuck in his shirt, and was the last one out the door.

Roxie kept her head down as she crossed Prospect Street, starting toward home in Indian Acres, the new housing project on the other side of Pearl Street. She never noticed Scottie until his heavy footsteps caused her to look back. Immediately, she came to a stop right in front of Summit Street Grade School.

"Are you following me?"

"Just want to talk to you for a minute."

"Well, make it fast, I have things to do." She resumed her walk, as he ambled along beside her. Out of the side of her eye, she saw his jaw and mouth moving as he got ready to speak.

"I can't believe you could do such a thing."

"What? Accidentally hurt somebody?" She shook her lovely head. "It was a stupid, stupid accident."

"The heck it was! You did it on purpose, and I can't believe you think you can get away with it. I *am* going to tell Mr. Marvin what happened this morning in *The Commentator* room." He took an extra step to keep up with the sudden increase of her pace.

"No, you aren't."

"Oh yes, I am. You're not getting away with something like this, Roxie. I won't let you."

She came to a sudden stop and pushed the full load of books and uniform she was carrying straight onto the boy's chest, holding it there as she hooted. "Uh-huhhh! I'll tell you what you're going to do, Mister Blabbermouth. You are going to shut up, and I *do* mean *shut up*." Her words took on the same deep-throated voice he had heard that very morning. "If you don't, Mr. Marvin, and the whole school, and the whole village of Essex Junction are going to hear *my* version of what happened in *The Commentator* room... and it's not at all like *your* version." She pulled back the bundle, steel-cold eyes staring hard at him.

"What do you mean, 'my version'?"

"You tried to rape me, *that's* what, you stupid jerk."

He sucked in a startled breath, then laughed incredulously. "Nobody will believe that."

"Oh yeah?" She held her bundle at an angle so he could get a good view of her bruised wrists and forearms. "I have all the evidence I need. I have all the right bruises, in all the right places."

A picture flashed before the young man's eyes, of Roxie holding up her skirt.

"And that's not to mention, the eyewitnesses."

"What eyewitnesses? There was no one else in that room."

"Good old John, the janitor, for one. He saw you come grinning out of that room; he heard my pitiful cries for revenge." She noted the surprise on Scottie's face. "Who did you deliver those paper towels to, huh? And were you still grinning from the big put-down you just gave me, you moron? I'll just bet there were a whole lot of eighth grade girls and a home ec teacher who will remember that little incident."

The fifteen-year-old's mouth fell open, speechless. But Roxie was not finished.

"By the way, when I went to the gym to pick up my uniform, I made sure Mrs. Collins saw the marks on my arms. She asked me what happened, and you know what I told her? I told her I didn't want to talk about it." She smiled as she spoke the next words. "Mrs. Collins is very protective of her girls, did you know that, Mister Smart-aleck? She told me she did not like the looks of those bruises, and if I wanted to talk to her later, she would be more than willing to listen, and would see to it that I am protected in every way possible." She did a short little jiggle-dance, ending with another loud, elongated hoot, and turned to continue her journey to the end of Summit Street, at the junction of Pearl. Scottie could do nothing but follow, completely befuddled by the tangle of lies.

"Can she really do this?"

Just before Roxie crossed Pearl Street, she glared back at him. "You have twenty-four hours, buster. If you report this tripping thing as a deliberate injury, I will absolutely destroy you and your whole family's reputation in this town. It will be so down and dirty, you will never — and I mean *never* — recover." Her eyes narrowed. "I am completely capable of doing this."

Then she closed her eyes for a second, drawing a big breath as she slowly re-opened them. The eyelids drooped seductively. There was another deep breath, and suddenly, she came alive again, smiling magnanimously as she tilted her lovely head to one side. "I know you won't let me down," she said sweetly.

Scottie stood on the sidewalk at the corner of Pearl and Summit Streets, not believing what he had just heard. *"Can she really do that? Okay, maybe… but no, she would never get away with it… would she? People just are not that stupid. They know me. I need to think about this. I need to get to a quiet place and think about this."*

Automatically, he turned left toward the five corners of the Essex Junction intersection, the way back to his home. Halfway down to the junction, he had an idea: *"Robbie will know what to do. He's a cop. He's the Chief of Police of Essex Junction, for Pete's sake. He'll know how to handle this."* With each step, he grew more confident that he, and the law, had the upper hand. As he approached Lincoln Hall, he boldly decided to visit his brother at the police station. He would march into Robbie's office and tell him the whole thing. Robbie would know what to do.

A car horn honked him back to reality. It was his mother heading toward Burlington, and she was waving at him. Quickly, he put a big smile on his face and waved back. She was probably on the way to a meeting or something.

"Good thing she doesn't know what's going on."

Suddenly, he changed his mind. If there was one thing he didn't want at this moment, it was that his mother would have to suffer through the lying accusations against her younger son. His footsteps slowed down as he approached Lincoln Hall. Maybe he shouldn't tell Robbie, or anyone else, what Roxie had pulled off today. Maybe it was better to just shut up.

"Hey, kid!"

Scottie looked up to see his brother's smiling face framed in the window of his squad car. He was just pulling into the parking lot at Lincoln Hall. For a second, Scottie thought he was going to cry. He took a breath, and grimaced a phony smile.

"Hey." Because his throat was dry, he tried it again. "Hey, Robbie."

The chief saw the tense posture of his younger brother, and put the car in neutral, waiting.

"How's it going?" He watched Scottie look down, and shake his head. "*Uh-oh.*" He cleared his throat. "Got time for a milkshake?"

"Not really." Scottie shoved his hands into his pockets and looked around as though being watched.

Ten minutes later, the two brothers were alone in the Early American living room of their home. The traditional, turned maplewood arms of the moss-green sofa matched the maple arms of the two plaid easy chairs. Chief Rob's sock-covered feet rested on top of the coffee table, which was perched on the same style of Early American maple legs. His official black shoes rested just under the sofa's pressed box ruffle, which individually edged the bottoms of all three pieces of furniture. Careful to focus a neutral gaze upon the mostly shades of green braided oval rug which centered the nicely decorated room, he spoke softly.

"Okay, kid. Let's hear it."

In less than twenty minutes Scottie had given, almost action-by-action, the events of the day. At the end, Robbie leaned back into the mossy sofa cushions, rubbing his chin.

"She's got you," he said. "It's a 'he said-she said' situation." He stood up, hitching his pants back up closer to the waistline. "This young lady has our whole family by the b—" He cleared his throat: "…backside."

"Isn't there anything we can do?" Scott asked.

"Just wait until she lies herself into a corner," the police chief replied. He smiled as he bent over to look his brother in the eye.

"And she will."

CHAPTER FOUR

Shelburne Road

Raymond René Smart, also known to some by his Abenaki name, Shining Waters, was riding into Burlington with his niece, who was on her way to work at Sears and Roebuck. It was a bright autumn morning and he was full of life, jabbering away about this and that, looking forward to his weekly poker game with his group out there on Flynn Avenue, just a few blocks off Shelburne Road. It was a friendly game, played for pennies, and the only social outlet the man seemed to have, other than his Friday afternoon soirees at Essex Junction's train depot. As usual, he was doing most of the talking.

"Listen, Pooh, I can feel it in my gawdim bones. I'm going to get lucky this time, gawdimmit. I'll come home with you at five o'clock, ready and in time for the frickin' milking, with my gawdim pockets drooping with change." His heavy head of smooth, graying black hair flew backward with his laughter. "Those bah-serds won't even know what hit them, ay?"

Winnie nodded. "I know you enjoy the game, Uncle. Just don't come home broke." She already knew he would not do that, since she actually knew the men he was meeting with each week. But then, she was avoiding the real conversation.

"Aw, shoot, Pooh, you know I can't go too far with just a few hundred gawdim pennies."

She nodded again, steering the '47 Dodge through the Winooski traffic. Uncle adjusted his position in the car seat, coughed a little, and looked out the passenger window at the empty woolen factory on the right. As they started across the Winooski Bridge toward the city of Burlington, Winnie finally summoned the courage to confront him.

"Uncle," she spoke in the warmest tone she could find, "we really need to talk about this awful... this..." Her thoughts seemed to fail her for a moment.

He twitched uncomfortably in the passenger seat.

"I mean, this swearing, this cursing thing. I know we grew up with it all around us, and it seemed normal to us at the time, and I know you had twenty years of Army life, but even so, Uncle, you really did not do this as a little boy. I do not remember you talking like that. Somehow, somewhere, it came later into your life and it really is not a good thing." She glanced over at him. "In fact, God doesn't like it." She paused. "He really doesn't like it, Uncle. Okay?"

Uncle drew his legs up under the seat, defending himself against the all-too-familiar attack. "Why the gawdim hail are you hounding me about this, you?" He shot a dark look toward his niece. "What's going on here, ay?"

She gritted her teeth. "All I'm saying is that this bad, bad swearing has to *stop*." She took a breath. "It has to stop, Uncle. It's just..."

The engine lugged a bit before she shifted into second gear, assisting the car's move up the hill on Burlington's Colchester Avenue. There, the tan vehicle proceeded past some notable Vermont history, all lined up on the left. First, it rumbled past the beautiful Green Mount Cemetery where Ethan Allen was buried, then leveled out to pass the Mary Fletcher Hospital, set back on a great winter sledding hill, then alongside the front of the Fleming Museum, and finally moved past the stately brick buildings of the University of Vermont, where the statue of its founder, Ira Allen, stood atop a white marble block on the school's green. Right about there, where Colchester Avenue turned into Burlington's own version of a

Main Street, she found her tongue again. This time, however, she wisely slipped into their shared, soft spoken "Abenaki family" voice.

"Uncle, next to my husband, Ceese, you are my very most favorite person in the world, okay? I don't know what I would do if anything bad happened to you. I want you to go to Heaven." She glanced over at him. "Are you listening, you?"

His heart softened under the tonal balm of his ancestors, and the body relaxed as he responded: "Ay-yuh."

"When you use that kind of language, it is *disrespectful* to God, Uncle!" she murmured softly.

"Ay-yuh," the quiet answer came.

"This is unacceptable from the Abenaki. We are a respectful people, us." She noted his proud nod, out of the corner of her eye. "My mother, your sister, taught us this a long time ago, my uncle."

Quiet filled the car as she moved into the downtown traffic. Turning right on Church Street, she slowly approached the last few blocks of its northern length, passing by the front entrance to Sears, just before reaching the intersection at Burlington's own Pearl Street. There at the head of Church Street, the Unitarian Church stood, the steeple of this historical landmark reaching skyward like a symbol of spiritual authority. Winnie steered the car around the flashing light of the traffic circle, then proceeded to turn left onto St. Paul Street, and then one more left onto Cherry Street, into a parking place beside Sears. As she maneuvered the vehicle into a final position, Uncle flicked something away from his eye. She turned off the ignition, eyes focused on her own knees, and they sat there in silence.

Finally, he spoke. "I don't know how to do this, me."

She kept her head bowed in respect. "Just go to see Father Tom. You haven't been to confession in a long, long time. He will listen. I am sure of that, okay?"

He tilted his head back in silent protest, but the words came out anyway. "Okay, Pooh. I will try this." He blinked.

"But the Catholic Church hasn't exactly been good to our people, ay?"

She pressed her lips into a grim line. "I know, but Father Tom is different. I trust him."

***

Leaving the car, Mr. Smart hurried out onto Church Street, where Sears' front door was located. He turned south from it at that very junction, and commenced his walk down Burlington's main shopping corridor, toward the bus terminal. The aroma of fried bacon beckoned as he passed Woolworth's Five and Dime Store's lunch counter, located just inside the big front door. He scurried along, enjoying the early morning sights and sounds of Vermont's "Queen City." A little farther, the smell of shoe polish signaled from inside the open door of The Shoeshine, that a soft cloth was whacking smartly across somebody's shiny shoe. He padded easily along in his high-top tennis shoes, finally turning right at College Street to cut diagonally across City Hall Park, past the modest cement water fountain which was positioned near center on the green. Glancing briefly at the cascading water, he continued on down to the park's southwest corner. There, on the other side of the traffic flow, the Hotel Vermont and what was left of the Hotel Van Ness after last year's big fire, stood on their respective corners of Main and St. Paul Streets. Uncle, like most native Vermonters of that time, ignored both of these notable Burlington landmarks as he crossed that intersection, bearing right onto St. Paul, where Vermont Transit buses lined both sides of the street. Burlington Transit, the local branch of this Vermont-based bus company, took up most of the spaces with buses changing positions hourly, as each driver commenced and concluded his assigned routes for the day. This weekly passenger watched his step, because the Vermont Transit bus terminal was a busy place.

It was Tuesday, October 7, 1952. Uncle knew exactly where the bus for Shelburne Road was parked — second in line up from the Main Street corner, right in front of the bus terminal. He had been riding it every Tuesday for the last eighteen months, so it was pretty much a familiar atmosphere, even to the point that he had had a courteous relationship with both of the bus drivers who had been consecutively assigned that route.

The first driver had been a man named Alan, an average-looking fellow, but who possessed a head of shocking white hair, a lucky St. Christopher's Medal hanging from his change box, and a wife about whom he had very few good words. Early in that year of '52, Alan had regularly enjoyed the attention of a very young redheaded girl, just new in the Essex Junction area, who rode the bus every Tuesday after her special early morning ukulele lessons at Burlington's Edmunds High School. The eighth-grader rode into town with her mother, who worked there at the diner-styled restaurant one door north of the terminal. By the time the eight-forty bus out to Shelburne Road was boarding passengers, the girl was back down the Main Street hill from the school, ready for a free recreational ride, and to perform for the captive bus audience. Uncle and the other bus passengers routinely endured her amateur attempts to serenade them with her latest lesson. On the other hand, Alan seemed to be enchanted by each and every concert. Her special song for the day was always **That Silver-Haired Daddy of Mine**, which she sang with one eye on the bus driver. Uncle had sensed a connection between the man and the pretty teenager, but had paid little attention, both because she was obviously just a kid looking for attention, and because he really liked the white-haired man, who was so polite to this old Abenaki warrior. Alan had listened to many stories from Shining Waters, with great respect. The friendship had grown, to the point that it had gotten to be a ritual for Uncle to rub Alan's good luck St. Chris's Medal before getting off the bus to participate in the penny poker game out there on Flynn Avenue. In the end, Uncle was sad when the route was turned over to a new driver.

That second driver was hired in July of that same year, and wore the name Bill on his uniform. He took over Alan's scheduled route out to the end of Shelburne Road, and he looked to Uncle, for all the world, like a shorter version of the movie actor, James Dean. "A bit of a performer, this one," Uncle noted. On that very first Tuesday, the little silver-eyed redhead stared long and hard at this new, handsome driver, and by the very next occasion of Uncle's weekly bus ride, she was delighting "Sir William" with both a cute nickname and a charming ukulele concert. By then both her playing and singing skills had improved, so most of the passengers just sat still and listened. Over time, she became increasingly attentive and flattering in her relationship with this particular bus driver. Bill, himself, was charming and entertaining, always ready with a good war story, or a joke. The rapport between this charming bus driver and the sweet-looking youngster flourished as the summer passed. Bill, Uncle was told, had shown Roxie how to start a checking account, since she had a babysitting job — one of only a few forms of legal employment for a citizen under the age of sixteen. Although Uncle only rode the Shelburne Road bus once a week, he became aware that this winsome young lady was, indeed, a regular rider on Bill's various bus routes throughout that summer. In fact, it was Roxie, herself, who laughingly told him several funny stories about taking her small charges on bus rides with Sir William.

Meanwhile, Alan was nowhere to be seen, apparently assigned to a different, more senior bus route.

The trip today was not to be much different. Uncle climbed the steep steps up into the bus, offering his dull green bus ticket to Bill, who poked the required hole into it with his paper punch. He took his usual place in the side-seated bench just behind the driver. A couple of people entered and paid by coin, the money clanking down into the metal machine, and walked back to sit in the front-facing seats, wrestling packages into manageable spaces around themselves.

Suddenly, the sparkling redhead, ukulele in hand, bounced onto the bus. "I made cheerleader! Uh-huhhh!" she joyously announced to the good-looking bus driver.

He grinned. "Oh, and why does that not surprise me?" He continued to praise her as she flopped into her normal side-positioned seat across from Uncle. "Somebody as talented and gorgeous as *you*?"

Her whole body gyrated with glee. "I was so-oo nervous about this!" She covered her face with her hands. "You have no idea how hard this was for me." Her ukulele slipped to the floor, and before Uncle could move, Bill bolted forward off the side of his seat to pick it up for her. It was the look she gave the forty-something driver at that moment, that aroused an uneasiness in the heart of Mr. Raymond René Smart.

"My goodness," Bill exclaimed as he spotted the bruises on her arms. "What happened there?"

Roxie averted her eyes, and the tone of voice was that of a victim. "I don't want to talk about it."

Bill slid back onto the driver's seat, sitting sideways to face the door, his eyes on her. Another passenger boarded the bus, holding out a bus ticket. He punched it, and the one after it, held in the hands of a tired seamstress from the factory around the corner. A man with a lunchpail handed Bill a dollar, so the driver pushed the lever, which dispensed the change holder's columns of coins, and gave the rider the correct amount. Three young boys were right behind, stomping and yelling. And then, there at the door, stood Alan.

"Hiiii-ya, buddy!" he called out to Uncle, as he stepped up into the stairwell. "Miss ya!"

Uncle grinned. "How you been, you?"

"Trying to stay out of trouble, bud." He rolled his eyes. "Not doing that very well, but oh well." He snorted, turning toward his replacement. "Hey, Bill, you going to the company picnic?"

"Don't know yet. When is it?"

"A week from next Saturday."

"Don't know my schedule yet and I'll have to see what's up with April."

"Well, if that beautiful wife of yours needs a ride home, I'd be happy to oblige!" He turned and winked roguishly at Roxie, who quickly turned her gaze downward, where her hands covered most of the lacquered instrument on her lap. Alan's gaze followed hers, and he got the picture. Suddenly he turned, leaning forward to address Bill in a lowered voice. "Watch out for those sweet little concerts, pal," he warned. "They can gettcha inta a heap of trouble."

As he left, Alan lightly banged the panel of the folded bus door with the side of his right fist, making the girl jump. He laughed as she regained her composure. Uncle felt like laughing, too, but when he saw Roxie's flaring nostrils he thought better of it.

Bill stood to check that his bus signs read "Shelburne Rd," then sat down, pulled the black visor of his bus driver hat just a little lower, and slipped his sunglasses carefully in place. With one decisive pull on the crank, the bus door was shut with a rattle and a slam. After a slight jolt, the bus growled forward.

No one said much of anything for a while, but by the time the bus had whined laboriously eastward up the hill on Main, turning right on South Union Street past Edmunds High School, Roxie glanced up from her pout, apparently checking the atmosphere over there in the driver's seat. She rocked gently in the seat as her eyes moved across the aisle to the little guy with the skunk stripe in his hair — the one who, some time ago, had answered her question, "What's your name?" with "You may call me 'Mr. Smart.'" She had hoot-laughed at what she thought was so obviously a misnomer, but he had insisted on it, and so it was. Right now, his head was tilted back, eyes upward, and he seemed preoccupied with the long rows of ads which lined the curved edges of the bus's cream-colored ceiling.

The bus moved on down South Union. Occasionally, someone pulled the bell cord which stretched along the top of the windows in a series of eye screws, to signal an exit at the next stop. The bus scrunched to a stop to deliver them safely at their destinations, and then moved on. Side streets moved slowly by, edged with elegant houses of an earlier era. Some of the structures had spacious verandahs, some had big bay windows, and almost all of them were prime examples of the gingerbread trim so prevalent in New England architecture, accenting their eaves and windows. Once home to the more affluent, many of these structures now were chopped up into apartments, housing mostly students at UVM, or Universitas Viridis Montis, the Latin name for the University of Vermont. It was an ironic development, the destruction of these elegant interiors, done to support such a richly historic institution, but life went on anyway. The cream and green city bus groaned along under the coppery-gold branches of the elms which formed a shimmering canopy over the street. Burlington was a city of more than ten thousand American Elms, and before too long, the leaves would begin to fall all across its small town landscape, covering the lawns and uneven sidewalks with a luxurious, rustling carpet.

But Roxie wasn't looking at all of that. Instead, her attention was focused out through the large windshield to her right. When South Union finally turned a little westward, it rejoined St. Paul, and a few yards along, became Shelburne Road. It was there that the young girl seemed to relax a bit. Several blocks later, where Shelburne Road became part of U.S. Route 7, she let loose her attention-getter: "Uh-huhhh!"

The nine remaining people on the bus looked up. "Look at that! Another one, two, three, four, and if you count Gove Court, *five*-corner junction right here in the middle of

Burlington." She clutched the ukulele to her chest. "There sure are a lot of those five corners in this state." She leaned toward the bus driver. "Do they have a lot of those in Oregon, Sir William?"

The James Dean face turned just slightly toward her. Keeping the shaded eyes on the road ahead, he called out over his right shoulder. "Nope. I don't remember anything like that, princess."

She jiggled to attention. Things were back to normal.

Across the aisle, Uncle made note of that little jiggle.

The bus rolled unevenly along the route that would take it to the southern city limits, depositing more bustling bodies than it actually picked up. At the bus stop across the road from Howard Johnson's restaurant, three more people disembarked, leaving only Roxie and Uncle on board. A few hundred feet later, Bill reached forward to turn the steering wheel to the right, bringing the bus smoothly around onto Flynn Avenue. He slowly applied the brake about halfway down the street, fully expecting Uncle to step forward to his usual stop in front of St. Anthony's Catholic Church at the intersection of Pine Street. Making a bit of a bumpy stop at that corner, he looked up. "Mr. Smart, I believe this is your stop."

Uncle aroused from a deep thought. He wiped his hand across his brow. "You know what? I've got a frickin' headache. Came on all of a sudden." He wiggled his shoulders and then leaned back to lay his head toward the window behind his seat. "I think I'll skip it for today." Through his half-closed eyes he saw Roxie's furtive glance toward the bus driver.

"It's probably the fumes from this old bus," she said. "You probably need the fresh air. By the time you get to your poker game, you'll feel a lot better."

Uncle shook his head. "Nope, I don't think so. I'll just ride back to the gawdim terminal and go home." He smiled softly to hide the lie. "Always wondered where the frickin' hail this gawdim bus route went, anyway."

Bill cranked the door closed again, and the bus began to move south on Pine, past modest homes with neat little yards. Some of the trees were still green. Above the whine of the bus, a dog was barking.

"I know what'll make you feel better, Mr. Smart," Roxie said sweetly as she lifted her ukulele. "I learned a new song this last week. I'm going to play it just for you, okay?" She smiled right at him. "Just for you. See what you think of it." A chord was struck, with just a flip of her left wrist. Then once more. Clearing her throat, she lifted her head as she began to strum softly. By the fourth stroke across the strings, she started to sing in a surprisingly mature voice, unlike her usual lilting, little-girl style. She almost murmured the first few lines about discovering the perfect lover. Uncle thought maybe she was mimicking a leading actress's singing performance, but when she got a little smile on her face, he had second thoughts. By the time she got to the chorus, he was sure she wasn't just copying a movie star. He glanced over at the bus driver. A noticeable curl at the side of the man's mouth told the rest of the story. *He's frickin' enjoying this.*

Roxie warbled on with her rendition of Just My Bill. He watched her body language as she sang about being so comfy on "Bill's" knee, and he felt the angry twitch in his gut as she sang out the rest of her siren song with the final, dramatic declaration that he was "…just my Bill."

Her eyes opened. She finished the performance with a left-handed flourish across the strings, purposely not looking at Bill. Instead, she fixed her gaze on Mr. Not-so-Smart, asking with a straight face, "How did you like it?"

Mr. Smart suddenly realized he was no longer looking at an innocent young girl. She had completely disappeared. This teenager had suddenly turned into a pseudo-adult, not a real grownup, but a dangerously close replica.

He crossed his legs and then uncrossed them, staring at her phony innocence. "I like Camptown Races better."

"It's from the movie, *Showboat*," she informed the dummy across the aisle. "Sung by Ava Gardner. I found the sheet music inside the piano bench in the band room."

Uncle just stared at her.

"Who would have thought that a neat, old song like that would be inside a piano bench in the band room of Edmunds High School, right, Sir William?" She turned for his answer.

Bill was steering the front of the bus to the left onto Home Avenue.

The building complex of the Children's Home rolled by the windows behind where Roxie was sitting. A white two-storied cottage for employees stood closest to the street, while hundreds of feet behind it, a low, red barn passed by on the receding horizon. As the panorama progressed, the large main building loomed into view, red brick with white trim. Against the red background, high on the front of the building, there was a glimpse of the traditionally styled white figure of what may have been a youthful Jesus, accented by a blue background inside a white oval frame. At the bus stop on the corner of Home Avenue and Shelburne Road, the institute's half-oval driveway gracefully curved to the right, through the portico at the main entrance, just under the gaze of two of those sculptured white figures. From there, it progressed past a large complex of two three-story buildings which were connected by a low, verandah-fronted dining hall. There were steep stairs on the front of all three entrances. Originally built as a hospital for WWI veterans, it had been eventually converted into a children's home. Uncle knew the place well, having worked there the summer of 1951, just before Cecil had hired him. He watched the passing scene, not really listening to Roxie, but she continued to instruct him. When he came back to her, she was rubbing Chap Stick over her lips, still talking between swipes.

"So, what didn't you like, Mr. Smart — the song, or the way I sang it?"

The bus had stopped at the empty Children's Home bus stop at Shelburne Road, and was once again moving south. It picked up speed in front of the wide lawn of the Home, passing the shield-shaped road sign of U.S. Route 7, and heading for the city limits. As it passed Swift Street, Uncle answered her.

"I don't want to make you mad," he said with a grin.

She hooted in disgust. "I don't get mad, and you know why? My mom told me a long time ago, 'Don't get mad. Get even.'" She tapped her fingers on the ukulele. "So that's what I do. I get even."

"I just frickin' bet you do," he said softly. "So, I'll just pass on the gawdim question, if you don't frickin' mind."

He saw Bill shake his head, stifling the bristling Roxie.

Just down the road, the bus finally hit its destination. The driver turned left across the highway into a vacant spot near the parking lot at Ralph's Diner. He turned off the engine, opened the shuddering door, and stood to manually crank the large disks which changed the destination signs on the front and right side of the bus. Once that was done, he stretched his five-foot-eight body, then let his arms flop downward against his hips.

"Gonna take a brief break. The diner allows us to use the restrooms, if you're interested." He removed the change box for safekeeping, and he was out the door.

Roxie waited a respectable amount of time, absent-mindedly twisting a slender silver ring on the little finger of her left hand. Then she stood up, tucking the ukulele under her arm. "You going in, Mr. Smart?"

Uncle shook his head without speaking the no.

She seemed to think for a moment, then her left foot began to push rhythmically against the rubber mat of the bus's floor, moving her whole body.

"Are you mad at me, sir?" she murmured, tilting her head to one side.

He hesitated. The luxurious halo of golden hair was moving softly with the undulations.

He laughed softly, and lied again. "Nah... you're just a frickin' crazy kid."

The girl hooted in agreement. As she stepped into the stairwell, she turned back and chortled, "Well anyway, you *now know* where the 'frickin' hail' this bus route ends." She disappeared momentarily, coming back into sight as she took off at a steady trot across the dirt parking lot toward the diner.

Uncle watched her slow down as she approached the steps to the front door. Suddenly she turned to the left and slipped around into the shadows behind the building.

"I know a whole lot more than that," he muttered.

CHAPTER FIVE

Fishing

Father Thomas Ladue loved riding his racing bike. He headed out at five every morning on his routine sprint around the loop of north on Old Colchester Road, then south on New Colchester Road, repeating that same route once more before heading back to the rectory on Prospect Street. Because it was always an early ride, he seldom saw any of the residents along the route, except for the husband and uncle of Winnie Thompson, who were apparently getting ready to do the milking. Occasionally, he would see young Jack Wilson or his father getting on with their chores, just across the road. Other than that, this was just an exhilarating ride, with the angels clearing the way over the potholes and foliage debris so common on country roads. The ride was one of the blessings of being assigned at Holy Family Roman Catholic Church in Essex Junction.

So it was a surprise on the second round this Wednesday morning, as he slowed down and turned the sharp curve in the road between the two farms, to see Winnie's uncle, waving him down. He sat back on the seat, and carefully pulled the bike to a balancing stop just past the maple tree. The little man approached him apologetically.

"Jeez… I'm sorry to bother you, Father," Mr. Smart said. "But you *are* Winnie's priest, aren't you?"

"I am, indeed," the man answered between labored breaths. "Is she all right?"

"It's me who's in the gawdim doghouse." Father Tom winced, then wiped the sweat off his upper lip as he waited for the explanation. "She wants me to quit the frickin' swearing."

The younger man covered his spontaneous laugh by coughing hard, several times.

"I-I-I see." He slipped sideways on the bike to a more comfortable position, leaning with one foot on the ground. "I guess that... would put any one of us in the doghouse, wouldn't it?" The breathing was catching up with the body.

"Ay-yuh," Uncle replied, scratching his head. "She wants me to talk to you."

"I think that would be great, Mr. Smart." He leaned politely toward the man. "It *is* 'Mr. Smart,' right?"

Uncle bowed his head slightly as he responded with a gentlemanly "Yes." He blinked in surprised pleasure at his own good manners. But then a look of hopelessness crossed his face. "How the gawdim hail am I going to do that? I've been swearing practically my whole frickin' grownup life, me."

Father Tom smiled just a little. "People do change." Uncle looked doubtful. "Why don't you drop by and see me at the rectory?"

"You mean that place near the high school?" He shook his head. "No way in hail am I going in that gawdim place. What if somebody saw me, for gawd's sake?"

The smile broadened and the handlebars moved under his flexing hands. "I'm open to suggestions."

Mr. Smart studied the nails on his left hand a moment, then his face brightened. "How about we meet over a beer at the pool hall?"

This time the laughter escaped unchecked. "We could probably do that, Mr. Smart, but that's not very private, either." He glanced toward the house. "How about right here?"

"In their house?"

"Probably in your apartment, so we don't bother anybody."

Uncle covered his eyes with his right hand, as peals of laughter came from behind his ivory-colored teeth. His little body shook with every syllable. "You don't want to frickin' go there, Father. I live like a gawdim pig. *They* don't even go there, unless they have to… aww, jeez…" He snorted a quick breath. "That is too gawdim funny. Think of somewhere else, you."

Father's blue eyes twinkled at the genuine display of humility. Still smiling, he surveyed the structure for a couple of seconds. "Hey, how about the front porch? It looks pretty private. Would that work?"

A thoughtful look settled on Uncle's countenance. Collecting his wits, he turned and looked, even though the screened-in porch was out of sight on the other side of the house. He shrugged his shoulders and turned back to the friendly freckled face. "As long as Pooh is at work. Yessir, we can frickin' do this."

"Great! Would you mind calling the office and making an appointment, sir? They hold me accountable for my time… that's just how it is, or I'm the one who'll be in the doghouse." He leaned toward the older man. "And we both know what that's like, right?"

"Hail, yes!"

Father Thomas extended his hand. "I'm looking forward to some pretty good conversation, sir."

Uncle stood at attention, then stepped forward to shake the hand of this likeable young man.

"Likewise, I'm sure." With a stately bow of his head, the forty-seven-year-old veteran walked smartly off to the barn.

The priest shifted his lanky body fully onto the bike and headed carefully over the railroad track. As he pumped out onto the road toward the Junction, he chuckled, speaking softly: "I'm really going to enjoy this guy, Father. Thanks for the new challenge."

***

Some folks are just born to solve puzzles, and Thomas Ladue was one of them. As a young boy, he explored the soggy edges of Vermont pastures in early spring, looking for salamanders and pollywogs. A native of the Shelburne Bay area, he had had access to Lake Champlain, where he wandered the often-rocky shoreline in search of relics, especially American Indian arrowheads, pieces of broken pottery, and anything looking like a misplaced bit of history. Early in his childhood, he learned also to love fishing, spending hours with his dad in pursuit of "the big one." In high school, his inquisitive mind helped him to excel at science and math. So a lot of people were surprised when he decided to become a priest instead of a scientist. Tommy reminded his friends and family that he found God to be the biggest puzzle of all, and that was where he wanted to spend his life — right in the middle of that magnificent mystery.

But today, around noon, Father Tom was presented with yet another puzzle. He was having lunch with Don and Connie Collins at the Lincoln Inn's newly remodeled coffee shop. The tables and chairs had been replaced by shiny tan upholstered booths, and a counter along one side of the room. It was the latest thing in restaurant style, and the place was giving Muncy's some serious competition.

Down the hall, the formal dining room was crowded with a special award ceremony, hosted by Tupperware. The murmur and laughter of feminine voices, interspersed with applause, broke forth frequently to muffle the conversation of the three friends. Indeed, they had to raise their own voices in order to hear each other. But, being seated in a corner with a padded divider separating them from the next booth, they felt confident their words would go no further than their table. Over lobster sandwiches, the trio compared notes on ministry.

The pixie-faced Don did not look like a former WWII Army Air Corp bomber pilot. A man of quiet humor, he enjoyed the look on people's faces when they found out. Right now, this soft-spoken fellow drank deeply from his warm coffee.

"Been a pretty uneventful week for us. No progress with the youth group thing. Nothing in Winooski. Just the Congregational Church here in the village, still doing its occasional talent show and skate night thing. What's happening with you, Tom?"

The couple, who had been doing Christian counseling for years, paid close attention. This was serious business.

***

In her hometown of Hempstead, Long Island, New York, Connie had studied Carl Roger's Person-Centered Therapy with great interest when she was in her mid-twenties, just starting her first high school teaching job. Being a stalwart Christian, however, it wasn't long before she turned counseling sessions into Christ-centered events, rather than client-centered ones, while still keeping much of the therapist's transparency and the client's free will choice for his own future. There, she found a balance which was both challenging and ultimately fulfilling for all concerned. It was still a pretty novel idea, having high school counselors who offered anything beyond career advice, but she managed to find an opening in a private school there on the island, where she was hired as both teacher and career guidance counselor, a title which offered the perfect venue.

Don was stationed nearby at Mitchell Field. She met him while volunteering at the Chaplain's Office. He wandered in early for a men's Bible study, which he just happened to be leading. It wasn't long before he came on board with the Christian counseling thing, and they were married one year later in that very same chapel. Over the next few years, they honed their skills, all on a volunteer basis. By the time they left, they were well-known as a counseling team with an unusually high success rate.

When he retired from the Corp, the sixth-generation Vermonter wanted to get back to Burlington. They ended up finding a nice little ranch-style on Florida Avenue in Winooski. That was close enough. And Connie was hired the next summer at Essex Junction High School, happily, in much the same capacity, only now she was teaching a social studies class. She was also in charge of the girls' gym classes, and coaching the cheerleading squad.

***

Father Tom was winding down on his update. He paused, holding the paper napkin against his chin, his elbow resting on the table. Then he sat up straight to give his prayer partners one more report.

"That marriage I mentioned last year — where the mother had to leave because the husband was bringing his girlfriends into the house?" He shook his head. "Not good news." He tapped his teaspoon against the heavy restaurant cup, then put it down carefully on the thick saucer. "They're still up there on Case Road, in the old Case house." He paused, picked up the spoon again to dip it into the coffee, stirring slowly. "I am really concerned about the girl. She's a prime target for who-knows-what." He leaned closer to the couple across the table. "Without following Jesus, there is just no basis for a wholesome life for her, her brothers, or her mother, for that matter."

"We're still praying about that one," Don assured him. "and about her best friend."

"What about *that* one?" the priest inquired. He was surprised by the meaningful look exchanged by Mr. and Mrs. Collins. "Is this something I need to know?"

Again, a look passed between husband and wife. This would have to be handled discreetly. Professional ethics dictated that no personal information about clients or potential clients was to be made public in order to protect the privacy of these individuals and their families. The three friends felt this was especially important in the arena of Christian counseling. Connie chose her words carefully.

"She showed up on Monday afternoon to pick up her cheerleader uniform, with some pretty ugly bruises on her forearms. I asked about them, but she gave me the standard, 'I don't want to talk about it' answer." She turned her sweet, well-scrubbed face toward Don, who nodded for her to continue. "To top it all off, she accidently injured one of the other girls while practicing that little kick they do. She absolutely went to pieces."

"Were you able to talk with her?"

"No. By the time we got the injured girl off to the doctor, most of the kids were gone, including her."

"That was Monday?"

"Yes."

"Same day I gave that talk to your class."

"Nice job, by the way." Her large, pale gray eyes twinkled.

"And she hasn't said a word to you?" Connie nodded *no.*

"How about Principal Marvin? Did she talk to him?"

"He would have asked me to investigate. That's my job."

The three sat there in silence, trying to put something together, but nothing seemed to fit.

Suddenly, Don looked at his watch. "Whoops! Guess I'd better get going," he said. "I have some stuff to do before I go do that swing shift." He stood up, tugging the collar of his Vermont Transit shirt. "We'll figure it out, sooner or later," he said, as he straightened the dark green tie over his belly.

Connie slipped out of the booth right behind her pudgy spouse, dragging her purse across the upholstered seat. "Tip?" she cued her husband. Don dug into his pocket. As he dropped a couple of quarters on the table, he grinned an elfish grin. "You're a good man, Father Tom." Connie smiled in agreement. As the couple left, the Father tossed a verbal pat-on-the-back toward them.

"You're not half-bad, either, for a couple of Pentecostals!"

He took another long sip from the cup, wiped his mouth, and slipped out of the seat. As he passed the man hidden behind *The Burlington Free Press* in the next booth, he noticed the police hat on the table.

"Is that Chief Rob?"

He decided not to say hello, since there was no time to chat. His one o'clock appointment was probably already waiting. Instead, he moved along, leaving the chief to read his paper.

But Chief Rob had stopped reading several minutes ago. Slowly, he lowered the paper and carefully folded it. As he stood up to leave, he paused to look thoughtfully out the window. Across the five-cornered junction, the young priest was walking quickly past the Lincoln Street Greenhouse, on his way back to the church office.

***

He had hardly closed the door behind him when the church secretary spoke. "Your one o'clock cancelled twenty minutes ago." Father Tom waited, knowing by Anna's tone of voice, that there was more. "Father Joseph is all excited about this appointment request by one Mr. Raymond Smart." He grinned at how fast word got around in that little office. "He wants you to go ahead and meet with Mr. Smart *today*, if possible. He's been waiting for that guy to come around forever."

"Call Mr. Smart and see if he's available in about a half-hour, would you please?"

"Took the liberty of making a one-thirty appointment for him, on his front porch, by the way, because I was sure you would want to make Father Joe happy." She pulled a yellow pencil out from behind the crossed braids at the back of her brown hair, tapping it eraser side down on the desk. Her little smile indicated that she was quite pleased with herself. "You may say 'Thank you, Anna.'"

"Thank you, Anna."

"And one more thing, sir. Father says, 'No gym clothes and no bicycle.' You are to stay frocked-up and use the church vehicle."

He raised both hands, palms up. "I guess I'm ready to go, then."

She handed him the keys to the old Ford. "He says to stay as long as you need to." She gave him a good-natured wink. "Beautiful autumn day for sittin' on the porch."

Out of respect for Mr. Smart's privacy, Father Tom parked the old green Ford around in back between the house and the garden, just off to one side so as not to block the driveway. Uncle had apparently been watching for him, because he appeared at the back door even before the priest was out of the car. He was wearing a clean shirt, and his hair was pulled neatly back into a ponytail.

"Ceese is taking a nap," he explained as he led Father Tom quietly through the kitchen, around the corner and down the hallway. At the front door, he turned the knob gently and the door opened with a soft tug. The two men stepped out onto the wide-bordered hall runner which lay in front of the chairs and porch swing, its linoleum now worn thin by too many years of protecting the gray-painted porch floorboards.

"We can talk here," Uncle said, motioning to the two metal chairs at the far end of the porch. Father Tom noticed a couple of heavy glass tumblers on the little folding table between them. The ice water had caused condensation on the outer surfaces, and now droplets of water were running down the sides onto the metal TV tray.

"Thanks for the ice water," Father said as he took a seat. Immediately, he picked up a glass to take a long sip, smacked his lips, and shook his head appreciatively. "Umm. That's good." He looked out over the top of the screened-in porch railings, taking in the view. When the peaceful smile came over his face, Uncle slipped into the other chair. "This is a great porch," the young man continued. "A great view, privacy, nice and cool on a warm day like today." He assessed the position of the porch a moment. "Whoever put this porch on, did it right. Look at the position of the sun, Mr. Smart. It is now…" He looked at his watch. "One-thirty in the afternoon, and this whole side of the house is in shadow — nice, cool shadow. Pretty well planned, wouldn't you say?" The older man looked around and nodded wisely. "And best of all, no mosquitoes. Somebody had his thinking cap on for that one!" He chuckled. "Nobody likes mosquitoes."

Uncle snorted. "Nobody likes them gawdi—" He caught himself, and started again. "Nobody likes 'em, that's for fri—" He clamped his jaw shut.

"Now, where I grew up over there at Shelburne Bay, we didn't have all that much trouble with those little buggers. I think it was because of the wind coming in off the lake." Out of the corner of his eye, Father saw his host nod in agreement. "Of course if there was not enough of a breeze, we got company in a hurry, especially if there was a slow-running creek nearby, with lots of shade. Used to get in the way of my fishing time." He caught Mr. Smart's eye. "You ever do any fishing, sir?" Instantly, a special glimmer came into Uncle's eyes.

"*Bingo,*" the priestly counselor thought.

"I guess you probably forget, I'm a gawdim Abenaki, me." He was grinning as he picked up the other cold glass. "Brought up on the frickin' shores of the Missisquoi River up there in Swanton."

"I didn't know you were from Swanton, Mr. Smart. And a fisherman! What did you catch up there? Perch?"

Uncle took a long drink of cold water and settled back in the chair. "Sometimes. But mostly had to go to Sandbar for them." His face relaxed. "Ay-yuh. Up there in Swanton, though… knew the gawdim Missisquoi like the back of my hand." For a little while the conversation was all about fishing, but eventually it turned to growing up Abenaki.

"For a long time, my sister, Marie, didn't tell me and Pooh we were Abenaki. We never had a gawdim clue. It was like a big, frickin' secret, for cry-sake."

"Why did she do that, do you think?"

"My cousin, Michael, who goes to UVM, says it had to do with our frickin' history, or something."

"You have a cousin who goes to UVM?"

"Hail, yes. Got some kind of frickin' scholarship, I think. Anyways, he explained it once."

Uncle then proceeded to give a somewhat convoluted and sketchy history lesson on the Abenakis: "There used to be lots of us living in New England before the settlers came. A lot of different bands. Different names, too. We were all over the frickin' place. Then there were a couple of gawdim wars, and we fought on the losing sides even though we were gawdim good warriors." He bent closer, as though to confide in his appreciative audience of one. "We would go into battle, and then when it was over, we would disappear into the frickin' woods." He grinned. "Yeah! They couldn't even *find* us!" He slapped his knee. "I'm *telling* ya!" Shining Waters laughed out loud, and the priest shook his head in admiration.

"Anyways, the winners of these wars got gawdim mad at us. So we kept hiding, dammit, 'in plain sight,' as they say. What else could we do? Some of us stayed in the woods, making frickin' baskets and stuff, to stay alive. Now that bunch eventually got to be known as the "Gypsies." But *my* family ancestors became fishermen, and the whites called us 'River Rats.'"

He shook his head sadly.

"But we were never open about being Abenaki, 'cause it could've been gawdim dangerous." He took another sip of water. "Anyways, when it come time for the white man's government to recognize the Indian nations, the gawdim politicians in Vermont wouldn't even admit that we existed." He leaned forward, lowering his voice. "Michael says Ira Allen had a helluva lot to do with that."

"Ummm, that would have been quite a long time ago, right?"

"Hail yes. But it just kept happening. Did you know they poured the tarmac for Burlington Airport right over one of them frickin' Gypsy camps?"

"Wow, really?"

"No regard, no frickin' respect. But now we are just starting to get organized, us Abenaki people. Michael is on some kind of frickin' committee, him. We want our rights back, gawdimmit."

"So there is no Abenaki Nation at all?"

"Only across the border in Canada."

The conversation turned back to fishing, and before they realized it, two hours had passed. Cecil had finished his nap, and had gone out the back door to finish up another small farm task. By the time Father Tom rose to leave, it was agreed that the two men would make their next meeting at a certain cove over at Shelburne Bay. It would be early on Saturday morning, and arrangements would have to be made with Father Joseph about hearing Saturday Confession.

"I'll be needing some help on this one, Lord."

***

Father Joseph bustled out of his office as the young priest was placing the car keys in Anna's desk drawer. His little hazel eyes sought an answer, a glimmer of hope. "Well? What happened?"

Anna had long since departed for home, so the two priests didn't bother to retire to the privacy of Father Joe's office.

"I think it went very well, for a first contact, Father."

"Good. That's good. What did he have to say?"

"Mostly stuff about being Abenaki."

"Did he seem open to the Lord?"

"He has a tender heart, I think. Wants to do better with his bad language, anyway."

The old priest's bald head bobbed in approval. "Good. That's a good sign. It sounds like a good start." He headed back toward the office, but he seemed to have another thought. "Now just remember, don't be too pushy. We need to be real careful with this one. We need to reel him in very slowly."

Father Tom Ladue smiled. "Speaking of reeling in…"

CHAPTER SIX

Games

After a couple of days of icing and keeping the knee elevated, the sprain seemed to be a lot better, so on Thursday after school, Penny made it to the final varsity cheerleading practice before the first basketball game of the season. She came swinging into the gym on crutches with Scottie and Diana at her side. All but one of the girls squealed with delight, clapping and praising her efforts. Scottie and Diana joined in the applause, then slipped into the bleachers just behind where she sat, the wrapped knee stretched out on the front bench. Roxie sat way down at the end of that seat, apparently preoccupied with a shoe lace.

The business at hand included more than just practicing the cheers; it was time to elect a captain for the squad. Mrs. Collins waved the girls into position and took a seat in a folding chair in front of the group now seated along the same front row. After a short explanation of the duties of the captain, she passed out blank slips of paper and a couple of pencils. The first game was the next evening, right there in the gym, so time was of the essence. "Vote," she commanded. Within minutes, spunky little Penny was captain of the team.

"Since I am taking her place for a while, does that mean I am temporary captain?" All eyes glanced at the stunning redhead, then turned back to focus on Mrs. Collins.

"Actually, no. Like I said just a few minutes ago, the captain only schedules practice sessions, makes phone calls to bring in a sub, and selects when and what cheers to use during a game. There should be no problem. This particular injury does not prevent Penny from performing these tasks. All she has to do is be present at the game."

Roxie feigned relief. "That's fine with me. I would rather not do all that, anyway."

"Fine. Remember, ladies, there is the pep rally during assembly on Friday." Mrs. Collins directed her attention back to Penny. "Alright, Captain, put 'em through their paces." She folded her chair and carried it out into the entry hall. To her surprise, there stood the principal, arms folded across his chest. Before he could speak, he was interrupted by the noisy chanting inside the gym:

"E-S-S-E-X! E-S-S-E-X!
E-S-S-E-X! E-S-S-E-X!
Es-sex! Es-sex!
Rah-rah-ra-a-ah!"

As Connie approached him, he asked, "Are those some kind of bruises on Roxanne Foxx's arms, Mrs. Collins?"

She was glad he asked. "Yes, and that's not all of them." He pushed the heavy glasses back up onto the bridge of his nose in order to see her better. "There is a purple mark on the inside of her right thigh. I saw it today in gym class." Mr. Marvin was aware that the girls wore a blue gym suit for that class. The legs were wide, like two skirts, but secured lightly against the thigh by elastic in the hems. The short bloomers allowed for a lot of movement, slipping freely up and down the upper leg. He could see how the coach would have spotted that mark.

"Did you ask her about those?"

"She didn't want to talk about it. We certainly can't force her. I decided not to say anything to you unless it happened again. Then you would have to notify somebody."

"E-S-S-E-X! E-S-S-E-X!
E-S-S-E-X! E-S-S-E-X!
Rah-rah-ra-a-ah!"

"I probably should know about this the first time, don't you think?"

A blush rose slowly over her throat. She looked down at her shoes, then straight back up into the principal's eyes. "You're right. My mistake."

"I know you meant well," he said as he dropped his arms. "But I sure wouldn't want any sad surprises."

"Yes, sir..." Before she could come up with a real apology, he was already outside one of the double doors on the south side of the entry, heading down the sidewalk toward the teachers' parking area.

Randall Marvin loved his job as principal of Essex Junction High School. He had come up through the ranks of the Vermont education system relatively quickly, being especially gifted in social interaction and knowing where to find the next promotion. Having a Master's in Education from UVM had also served him well. It was the enjoyment of his work and an abiding ambition to excel in every area of it, which brought him to the meeting on the second floor of Lincoln Hall. The wide-open top floor had a history of proms and wedding receptions before the new high school gym had been built in 1951. It was still the location of the Boys and Girls Club dances, usually on Friday nights, where teenagers slow-danced to the likes of Perry Como and Eddie Fisher, coming from a portable record player. This afternoon, however, a circle of chairs was gradually filling up with community leaders who wished to build a special float for the two big parades in Burlington — the Thanksgiving Parade, and the Music Festival Parade. The EJHS band was already scheduled to march in both of these events, and somebody had the big idea that an Essex Junction float could follow close behind, advertising businesses and inviting tourists to local events. It was a primitive, but cleverly conceived concept of an Essex Junction Chamber of Commerce — exactly the kind of thing that sparked the creative juices of Principal Marvin.

Most of the town fathers were there, the majority being political figures. Amongst others, representatives from the fire department, law enforcement, local businesses, and school system assembled for some lively discussion. Randall Marvin slipped into a chair, as fate would have it, right beside Chief of Police Rob Allen. Robbie immediately recognized his younger brother's high school principal.

"Afternoon."

"Afternoon, Chief." The sound of more wooden chairs being dragged from the walls into the circle punctuated his comments. "Looks like a good turnout. It should be interesting. How do you feel about this idea?"

"If it works, it could be terrific. If it doesn't, we could be the laughingstock of Chittenden County."

Once again, the horn-rimmed glasses slipped down as he furrowed his brow. "I'm afraid you are one hundred percent right on that one." There was a one-fingered punch between the lenses, lifting them back into place. "Still, wouldn't it be great, if it worked? Could be a real asset, if the community could come together on something like this."

"You just spoke the magic words, sir."

"And they are…?"

"'… if the community could come together on something like this.'"

The principal's lips worked a supple pucker. "Well, I would like to try. How about you?"

"That's what I'm here for," Robbie replied as he extended his hand to the forty-something gentleman. Mr. Marvin responded, and as the two men shook hands, the police chief looked him in the eye and said, "Let's see what we can do."

"Well, he sure lobbied for the new gym. Not bad for a small-town chief of police. Let's see what he can do about this."

An hour later, Mr. Marvin had to admit that Rob Allen was probably right. Most of the interested volunteers were pushing their own interests, and nobody could agree on the overall theme for a float at these parades, let alone something utilitarian and still attractive. By that time, it was after four o'clock, and Principal Marvin had to get home to get some supper, before getting back to the office to finish up the always unfinished work of the day. Tomorrow night was the big basketball game with Vergennes, and his presence would be required for the whole evening.

Finally, someone suggested a committee of five, chosen by lots, to draw up some plans for the next meeting. A hat full of numbered paper slips passed quickly around the circle, each person drawing one. By the time that was done, a second hat with the same number of slips was handed to the oldest person attending — a woman named Gloria — and she drew the five numbers. One of the winning numbers in this ancient game of chance belonged to Randall Marvin.

As the group descended the stairs, Chief Rob called back over his shoulder to the principal, "Let me know if there's any way I can help!" Mr. Marvin smiled his appreciation.

As soon as his feet hit the parking area outside the hall, however, the principal decided to run back to the high school, grab the paperwork he needed, and then spend the rest of the evening at home. The idea of enjoying a few minutes of balmy weather out on the verandah was overwhelmingly appealing. Within minutes, he was pulling the school's front door open, ready to head up to his office.

Mrs. Collins was on her way out.

"Practice over?"

"Yes, sir. I was just grading papers for my social studies class." She hesitated. "And, Mr. Marvin, I am so sorry… about Roxie, I mean."

He stopped and looked back at her from the foot of the stairs, not noticing that the janitor was sweeping out the corners of each step with a hand brush, just a few feet up.

"Well, we've got that all straightened out now, haven't we?" he said kindly. "We'll both do better in the future, I'm sure."

Encouraged, the gym teacher took a tiny step toward him. "If somebody did beat that girl, I'm sure they will try it again. I promise to notify you immediately."

"I know you will," he replied as he headed up the stairs. Passing the busy janitor, he greeted the man with "Hey, John! You sure keep this place looking good."

John grunted something and kept digging at the corners.

Inside the office, he called his wife. "Hey, hon. I'm on my way home." Randy grabbed a few things off his desk, stepped outside, and locked the office door. As he started down the stairs, his sprightly step quickly slowed down. John was standing directly in front of the lowest step, waiting for him.

"Did you need something, John?" he asked as he made a cautious descent toward the fidgeting man.

"No, sir." He looked down at his shoes. "But I think maybe you do."

Mr. Marvin came to a stop directly beside the janitor. "What do I need, John?"

"You need to know something."

"Okay, my friend." He leaned back against the big newel post which supported the lower part of the stairway's handrail. "I'm listening."

He gently pinched his lips together between the thumb and forefinger of his left hand, just for a second, before he spoke. "I, uh, couldn't help hearing you and Mrs. Collins talking about that girl, Roxie." He touched his lips again, just for a second, as though to cover a cough, with the fist of the other hand. "She's the one with all the reddish curly hair, right?"

Mr. Marvin tilted his head. "Let's just suppose it is the same girl. What about her?"

John told what he had witnessed last Monday during the noon hour: Scottie bursting out of the basement office of *The Commentator*, explaining Roxie's fury at getting caught in a lie, and offering to help the janitor to deliver paper towels to the home ec room.

The principal listened without comment, but his rubbery mouth twitched and grimaced throughout the story. "The reason I'm telling you all this," John concluded, "is that, later on... oh, maybe somewhere around four o'clock... she comes running out the door as I'm emptying trash outside the back of the gym. Comes running out from the back entrance to the locker rooms, all crying and carrying on. I couldn't believe it." He paused, reliving the moment.

"What did she want, John?"

"She keeps showing me the marks on her arms, saying, 'You're a witness! You're a witness, John! You saw what happened!' And then she turns around and runs back into the building." He rubbed his hand over the bald spot. "At first, I had no idea what she was talking about, but then I figured it had to be that thing down in the basement." He looked the principal in the eye. "She's a real oddball, sir. You'll want to keep your eye on her, for sure."

Principal Marvin stared hard at the floor, his lips working, working, working, as he processed the information. At length, he had one question.

"Isn't that back gym door to be locked at all times? I'm wondering how she got back into the gym."

John hung his head. "I propped it open, sir. To make it quicker to get back in. That's the reason I didn't tell you all this before." He shrugged his shoulders. "I guess that was the wrong thing to do, but when I heard you two talking about somebody beating her up, well, I thought you better know. Probably better double-check anything she tells you. This girl is a real oddball."

"Alright, John. I appreciate the input." He stood up to take his leave. "I suppose it would be a good idea to keep that back door locked at all times, don't you? Just think, that girl would have had to go through a whole lot more obstacles to do whatever she was trying to do."

"Yes, sir. But I thought you should know, even if I got in trouble."

He reached out and gave the janitor a reassuring pat on the shoulder. "Try to stay out of trouble, my friend. I have enough of that stuff to sort out already."

He was still sorting stuff out the next evening.

***

The junior varsity game was over by seven-thirty, and the bleachers along the south wall were trading one set of fans for another, in preparation for the varsity game, which started at eight o'clock. Mr. Marvin stood in his usual place near the gym doors, just off the entry way. As usual, because of safety regulations, the doors were propped open. The rumble of the crowd was like music to his ears, for he had fought long and hard for the construction of Essex Junction High School's new gymnasium and special event facility. Since then, Class-B basketball teams all over the county couldn't wait to play on this new basketball court. And tonight a local radio station was broadcasting the first game of the season from the elevated north-wall stage, just up behind where the opposing teams' folding chairs were arranged side-by-side on the gym floor. In between the two opposing teams' lines, a table stood where the play-by-play calls of the game were to be announced over an impressive loudspeaker system by, no less than, a couple of EJHS's own student team managers. As he gazed around at this dream come true, he had every reason to smile.

Scottie saw that flexing smile as he entered the gym with his big brother. Both of the Allen boys stopped at the other side of the entrance, the chief to take his on-duty position, and Scottie to call across to the smiling principal. "Gonna be a great game, Mr. Marvin!"

Mr. Marvin turned to make a happy reply, but Diana and her tall boyfriend walked in, blocking his view. He noted that Jack Wilson had probably grown another three inches since he had graduated last spring.

"Oh yes, I remember. Almost a genius, that guy. Graduated just six months after his seventeenth birthday. Hear he just decided to hang in there, eventually to take over the family dairy farm. Well, whatever he does, he will do it well and he'll be honest."

He watched the young couple follow Scottie over to the second row up, just behind the space reserved for the Essex Junction cheerleaders. The three of them sat down together, chatting and watching the crowd.

At precisely seven-fifty, the five varsity cheerleaders came running past him into the gym, followed by Penny on her crutches. Wearing her uniform, she took her seat on the front row, her injured leg lowered to her left where her foot rested gently on the gym floor. The squad lined up in front of the crowd, looking sharp in their blue and gold knee-length skirts and the off-white sweaters with a blue and gold megaphone emblem across the front. Each stood with her white tennis shoes close together, hands on hips, a big smile aimed directly at the crowd. At Penny's signal, five sets of arms — all with sweater sleeves pushed up a third of the way — shot straight up into the air and the crowd warm-up began.

The first "yell" was a familiar one, so the Essex fans joined in at the top of their voices. As the squad went through its acrobatics, more folks filtered into the auditorium, moving up into the bleachers, waving to friendly faces, and settling into either the Essex group or the visitors' seating section at the east end of the bleachers. As soon as the EJHS yell finished, the Vergennes cheerleaders hit the floor in front of their own crowd, strutting and belting out a rhythmic exhortation to "Fight-fight-fight!" Not a beat passed between the end of the Vergennes yell before the EJHS team was back on the floor doing their "Boom-a-lack-a" routine. And so it went for the next five minutes.

Roxie was at peak performance. By the time the last yell was to be squeezed in before the two teams came onto the court, she was flying high. Every ounce of energy went into the next cheer. Her eyes sparkled above the roses of her cheeks, her gorgeous golden curls floated around the movement of her head as her slender form moved back and forth with the rhythmic beat of her arms. Finally, she executed a perfect backward "C" jump at the end of the yell, then bounce — bounce — bounced joyfully back to her place on the bench. There she sat gingerly on the edge of the seat, breathing hard, and shooting a triumphant look up over her right shoulder. But Jack, Diana, and Scottie were blocking her view. She leaned back to see around them, and the couple, thinking she was looking at them, waved politely to acknowledge her enthusiasm. Scottie looked away in disgust. She smirked and moved a little to her left, glancing up over her right shoulder to make sure she was in the right spot for making a special connection.

Chief Rob wondered if anybody else was noticing the marks on her body. His eyes wandered over the audience, not sure what he was looking for, but definitely watching for an unfamiliar face, or a certain body language, or maybe even someone who just didn't fit in this particular setting. For the last two years, he had been working hard to sharpen his surveillance skills, especially at large gatherings. This evening he was concentrating mostly on those particular warning signals. He just had a hunch. Sure enough, it wasn't long before he found somebody who filled all three of those qualifications.

"Hmmm..."

The man had a familiar look about him, although the chief couldn't quite place it. Perhaps a public figure, but not quite. He looked to be forty-something, and was dressed in dark green pants topped by a formal dull green uniform shirt with what could have been a nametag above his left pocket, and an insignia of some sort on the right sleeve. Both sleeves were rolled up a couple of folds, in an after-work casual fashion.

But what was most intriguing about this guy was that he had climbed up to the very top bench of the bleachers, where he sat leaning back against the wall, slouching slightly to one side, almost as though posing for a public relations photo shoot. He did not react to the activities of the crowd, nor did he take his eyes off something.

"Definitely not part of the crowd... and what the heck is he so intensely focused on?"

Robbie turned his attention in the direction of the stranger's gaze. Up and down the first few rows of the EJHS crowd's area, for sure. Another glance at the man at the top of the bleachers. The man was smiling at someone. Back to the first or second row of the bleachers.

And there it was.

Roxie Foxx was looking up over her right shoulder, intensely connecting with someone, a little smile on her face, a cute little jerk of her head, and then turning back to listen to Penny's instructions.

The chief quickly noted the shift in the slouch of the man in the bleachers. He was sure there had been a connection there. He glanced back at Roxie. She turned once again to make visual contact.

"Oh-kayyy."

A movement caught Robbie's attention, as an attractive blonde woman sat down beside the man in the uniform. She was laughing and settling down beside him like a wife or a mother, giving him a quick kiss on the cheek. He responded by a quick hug around her waist, then pointed down toward the Essex Junction cheerleaders. He said something to her, and she peered and nodded in response.

"Alright. Her parents. No problem — if I'm right."

He glanced across the double-door entrance toward Principal Marvin just in time to see Don and Connie Collins greet her boss. Mr. Marvin was about to speak to them when the EJHS varsity basketball team came rushing out of the locker room door, suited up in shiny-white uniforms with blue and gold trim. A cheer went up from the crowd, and the chants started, overwhelming all conversation.

"Es-sex! Es-sex!
Rah – rah – rah!"

But the Chief of Police needed an answer. He crossed over to the other side of the doorway to join Mr. Marvin and the Collinses. As the noise increased, he made authoritative eye contact with all three, holding up his hands, signaling them to wait.

The Vergennes team came barreling out into the gym, where their supporters shouted and stomped out encouragement for a full thirty seconds. Finally, as the two teams went into warm-up mode on their own sides of the court, the noise settled down to the erratic squeaking of tennis shoes and the pounding of the basketballs on the gym floor, accompanied by the rubble-bump of those balls hitting the backboards above the webbed baskets. The players shouted encouragement to each other, clapping their hands and slapping each other on the backside. The warriors were psyching up for the battle.

"I need some input from you folks."

"Oh, well… if we can help," Don offered.

"Take a look up at the top of the bleachers over here," the chief motioned. "Do either of you happen to know who that couple is? Is that Roxie's parents?"

The Collinses both checked out the couple, then looked at each other and Connie laughed, her beautiful teeth glistening. "No, sir. Those two are not Roxie's parents," she answered. "They're April and Bill Flannigan. Bill works with Don at the Burlington branch of Vermont Transit."

"Oh, so that's what the uniform is."

"That's who they are!" She turned to her husband. "Hey, honey, let's go sit with them."

"You go ahead, babe. I'll be right there."

Connie set out to climb up the bleachers. As she made it to the third row up, Don turned and motioned to the two men to follow him out into the hall. Passing the student council's beverage sales table, they stepped onto the sidewalk, just outside the walkway doors.

Don turned to the Chief of Police. "Why do you ask about the Flannigans?"

"I don't feel right about how that redheaded cheerleader is looking at him, and the way he is responding to those looks," the chief asserted.

"Something you should know," Don said. "Bill has been 'mentoring' that little gal, since she zeroed in on him last July. That's when he was hired."

"What do you mean 'mentoring'?"

Don Collins's pixie face twisted into a tight mass of flesh, his non-smiling mouth stretching far back over his teeth, the squinting eyelids lost in their own folds.

"What?" the principal asked.

The protective husband shook his head slowly. "Please don't say anything to Connie just yet. She and April are good friends. Besides, nobody can prove anything." Both listeners got it immediately, reacting with an inward groan.

The chief continued, "Do you know who her parents are?"

"I've only met her mother," the principal said. "And that was when she enrolled her last year."

Chief Rob turned to Don. "What about you?"

"Met the mother once, but see her stepdad every day."

"Every day?"

"Yeah. George Foxx is my boss. He's the personnel manager at Vermont Transit's Burlington bus line."

The chief's eyebrows raised. "Really?" He touched Don's shoulder. "We need to have coffee."

Don agreed. "The sooner, the better." He turned to the principal. "Will you join us?"

Randy Marvin hesitated, his eyes on the hallway roofline. Then he smacked his lips smartly. "Tell you what, you guys are the experts on this stuff — the law and the counselor. You get back to me when you have something that I, in particular, need to pay attention to." He looked them in the eye. "We want the best solution for a pretty involved situation, right?"

Both men agreed.

"Get back to me whenever, or if ever, you need me, okay?"

The three men headed back into the gym, but at the door, the chief turned to the principal. "By the same token, sir, we need to hear from you, if anything comes up."

Randy nodded in agreement.

Inside the gym, two players from the opposing teams crouched at the center point circle, ready to leap for the tipoff, at the sound of the referee's whistle.

The game was about to begin.

CHAPTER SEVEN

Circles

It was an early departure from the Thompson farm, so that the two fishermen could be in a certain cove on Shelburne Bay just after dawn. As the old Ford trundled south on Route 15 through Essex Junction, Winooski, and Burlington, the two men talked excitedly about reports from the Ladue family's latest fishing exploits in that favorite spot. By the time they passed the dimly lit complex of the Children's Home on U.S. Route 7's Shelburne Road, Uncle was convinced he would have a small-mouthed bass or a bunch of perch to take home for Pooh to fix for Saturday night's supper.

"Schools of fish come through that area all year long," the priest was saying. "It's even good fishing in the winter… you know… ice fishing. Dig a hole in some solid ice, drop a jig down through the slush, and you'd be surprised to find out there really are perch down there. They feed off baitfish trapped under the ice."

"That's frickin' right, Father! It was sort of the same right at the river's mouth up there in Swanton. I remember one time…"

The conversation continued, and before they knew it, the shuddering green machine had taken them to their destination. Taking all the gear they had accumulated and coordinated through a half-dozen phone calls over the last two days, they set out for a quarter-mile trek to a special spot, just as the dawn was breaking behind them. The walk became increasingly easier as it became illuminated by the ever-brightening sunlight. By the time they reached the overhang at the edge of the bay, that light was glinting off rippling water. The two new fishing buddies stood and looked across the wide expanse of water for a minute. Then Uncle ventured closer to the edge of the overhang and looked down. Solid rock jutted about five feet out over the water, and receded slowly at a solid angle down to where small waves gently lapped against its still-descending wall, some ten feet below. He could not see the bottom.

"It's a frickin' fishing hole, Father. And a deep one. How the hail did you guys ever find this?"

"It's actually near our land. You just walked over onto our property line about a hundred feet back."

The smaller man looked back to where they had just come from. "How come we didn't just come from your frickin' driveway, or something?"

"It's a ways back. This is a lot shorter, believe me."

Uncle re-surveyed the fishing situation. "Okay, so how do you ice fish down there? Is there a path?"

Father Tom pointed off to the left. "Right down that way." He bent down and started to get his fishing gear in order. Mr. Smart took the cue, and went to work on his own gear. Before too long, two lines were baited and in the water.

"Got that bait down on the bottom?" the Abenaki River Rat inquired.

The priest smiled. "Yessir!"

"Okay, just a little jig or two and let it sink back down, okay?"

"Yessir!" the seasoned, but humble fisherman replied.

"Then do it again, in a few seconds."

Tom Ladue bopped the end of his fishing pole just a little. "Like that?"

"Ya-a-aas… just like that," Uncle softly replied. "But be careful. Don't get the end of the pole up too high, see?" He held his own pole up high. "If you do it like this, you can't hook the fish, see? You don't have enough torque, see?" He lowered his pole and jigged it twice, letting the bait fall back onto the bottom. "That's pretty much all there is to it."

Father Tom listened, fascinated. The man was not swearing. He decided to keep the lesson going. "Should I move left and right? Or doesn't it matter?"

"Na-ah, it don't matter, son. Just keep doin' what I told you. Jig a couple of times, and wait a few seconds, then once more, and wait. Just keep doin' it, and you'll see, you."

"Yessir. Thank you."

Uncle looked up. "For what?"

"For the lesson. I needed a bit of review, and you are helping me a lot."

A sudden pull on Uncle's pole. A sharp upward lift, and reeling in, reeling in some more, and the Abenaki gentleman had the first catch of the day: a small-mouthed bass. The two men saw no need to measure this one; it was well within the legal length. It went into the creel. By the time Uncle's line was re-baited and back in the water, the priest had come back up the path from dropping the creel into the cool water. "We should have brought an ice chest."

"Next time we will," Uncle assured him.

A gentle wind was now coming in off the lake, rustling the bright yellow leaves of a stand of birches just behind them. The chill of the early morning was subsiding, bringing the warmth of childhood memories to Tom Ladue. He shuffled his feet, then slipped clumsily down on his behind, pulling his large tackle box under him for a seat.

"I came here many times with my father and my brothers... did I tell you that, Mr. Smart?" The Indian jerked his long hair to the right in a positive response. "It's kind of ironic, you reminding me how to jig like that." He dipped the end of his pole sharply. "Like my dad was still here, you know?"

A seagull flew silently overhead, circling something the two men could not see. They watched it for a moment, until it disappeared behind the birches.

"You kind of remind me of him." Uncle's head bowed a little, as though watching something in the pool below. "He loved to fish. He was a good soldier. He wanted to do the right thing. And he had a cursing problem, just like you."

Mr. Smart turned around and stared at the priest, speechless.

"Ay-yuh," Father Tom laughed softly. "He cursed like a sailor."

Raymond René Smart began to chuckle. "Yer full of it. No. For frickin' sure?"

The priest nodded. "For frickin' sure, Mr. Smart."

The River Rat's pole moved slowly up, then shifted over his shoulder as he turned to ask the question. "Did he ever stop? I mean, did he ever, ever frickin' stop?"

Father Tom smiled. "Yes, he did."

A gleam of hope sparkled in Uncle's eyes. "How did he do it, for cry-sake?"

"It took a long time, Mr. Smart. But that doesn't—"

Another tug on Uncle's line interrupted the thread of thought for the priest. He stood back and watched the older man land another good-sized bass. This was going well for his guest. "Here, let me take it down there for you."

As he came back up the path from taking the second fish to the makeshift cooler, he said, "Well, too much coffee for me this morning. I need to go. I'll be right back there in the birches."

Uncle turned to locate the stand of trees, and nodded. "Bet you boys been doing that for years, you," he chortled. "Once us guys find a place, we just seem to favor it."

Father Tom smiled at the man's insight and he had gotten through two more sentences without swearing. Stepping along the soft, yellow moss which covered the top of the rock, he called back over his shoulder. "Been watering those trees so long, they should be three feet taller than the rest, or dead as a doornail!"

Mr. Smart let out a howl of laughter and squatted down to wait for the next catch.

Out across the bay, the wind was beginning to pick up, making little puddles of choppy waves in the deep blue-gray water. Some of the small puddles sported miniature whitecaps, while others just sparkled to life within their own little irregular boundaries. Looking north up the lake, the horizon was pale blue by now, deepening into a vibrant azure as the eye moved upward. Up there, more seagulls swooped and circled in their very own life dance. Uncle watched them, marveling once more at their graceful aerobatics, until at last, he was forced to lower his head against the more steady force of the wind, which was now whipping his long hair across his eyes. He blinked, and keeping his head low, pushed the salt-and-pepper strands back behind his ears. His attention was now automatically directed below where he crouched. There, the beating and sloshing of the waves underneath the overhang took on their own watery waltz, arousing old memories of delightful freshwater scents and sounds, of sitting on haunches and waiting patiently, of places and times long forgotten, and life along another watery shore, far north of this place. The man closed his eyes and remembered.

He never heard his fishing buddy step softly over the moss carpet, never saw the wind-driven spider float past the priest's face and land upon a crouching Indian's shoulder. He did not see Father Tom smartly smack the arachnid intruder into oblivion. He only felt the sudden strike.

It was over before either one of them realized what was happening. Father Tom was doubled over, lying on the ground, the wind knocked out of him. Uncle was down on one knee where, seconds before, he had slipped as he was trying to pull the attacker's head facedown into a death blow upon his knee. His hands were still cupped together like a solid, little hammer. He blinked several times as he gulped down the sickening terror, and slowly, slowly, came back from Korea.

Then he saw the priest lying in a fetal position, where the missed combat move had accidentally pushed him off his feet. The victim's freckled face was pale, but his eyes were wide open.

"Oh Jesus… oh, Jesus… oh, dear Jesus. Not again. Not again," Uncle murmured as he bent down to help his friend. "Oh, Jesus, don't let him be hurt." He touched the auburn hair gently. "You okay, Father? Huh? You okay?"

Father Tom gasped and sucked in a quivering breath.

"That's it. Just relax. Get your breath back." He patted his young friend on the shoulder. "That wasn't your fault, you," he said in a fatherly manner. "It was the war, son. That's what it was."

When the priest was finally back on his feet, Uncle asked him to check to see if there was pain in the midriff area. There was none, so the two men quietly picked up their poles.

"We probably have another hour of pretty good fishing here," Tom Ladue said lightly.

The subject did not come up again until the two men were homeward bound, once more passing the Children's Home on Shelburne Road. It had been quiet in the car for a while, when Uncle leaned forward just a bit, to see past Father Tom in the driver's seat. He stared at the brick buildings, now clearly visible in the morning sunlight. "I got fired from there," he said softly.

"Really? I didn't know you ever worked there."

"Just after I came home from the war."

"May I ask what happened?"

"Aw, it was the same frickin' thing that happened back there at that gawdim fishing hole this morning. Another hired hand came up behind me, just like you did. Almost killed him." He leaned back and looked out his side window. "I could have killed you, too, you know."

The priest remained silent, waiting for the rest of it.

"If my foot hadn't slipped..." He wiped a shaky hand across his brow. "I'm so gawdimmed sorry, Father."

"No need for you to apologize for something you have no natural control over, Mr. Smart. Actually, I don't think your foot slipped at all." Uncle's head turned sharply to study the priest's face. Father Tom glanced at him, then looked back at the road. "Angels are very, very real, sir."

Uncle fixed his gaze straight ahead, not knowing how to deal with that remark.

"Oh, and thanks for praying for me, Mr. Smart."

"I prayed for you?"

"Yes, you certainly did. You said, 'Oh, Jesus, don't let him be hurt.' I heard you very clearly."

The long hair hid his face as he bowed his head. "Oh, yeah. I guess I did frickin' say that."

The old Ford pulled into the Thompsons' driveway just shortly after nine-thirty. Both men had nearly caught their limit, survived a fragile bonding, and were looking forward to another fishing expedition. The day trip had come full circle, and it was good.

***

Inside the Thompson house, Winnie was finishing up the housework in preparation for the Maple Leaf Sewing Circle meeting to be held there at one o'clock that very afternoon. This was a strictly women's club thing, which happened on the second Saturday of every month. It was held at the home of a different club member every time, creating a happy combination of constantly changing settings and sewing projects, which kept the interest piqued and the meetings dynamic. She was wiping down the dining room table when Uncle came in, beaming brightly.

"A-hah!" she crowed. "The face of a successful fisherman, ay?" She tucked the dustcloth into her apron pocket. "How many?"

"Enough for a frickin' good supper, for sure." He stopped and noted the preparations in progress. "Oh, hay-ell. You got that gawdim circle of women coming again?"

"It's my turn, Uncle." The look on his face brought her to a halt. "Tell you what, you go clean those things and wrap them up good and put them in the meat drawer in the refrigerator, and I'll cook us up a nice lunch, right after Mass tomorrow. Okay?" He looked happier. "But you make sure you wrap them up good and tight. I don't want my refrigerator smelling like fish, understand?"

Uncle made a quick exit out the back door. Those fish had to be cleaned and put in the refrigerator, then every bit of that fishing equipment had to be wiped down and stashed in the barn; further, there was a need for a refreshing nap — all before the end of his day off, at three o'clock. After that, there were farm chores yet to be done and then a sandwich while listening to Saturday night radio, and finally he would be off to bed. He was sure he would sleep well tonight.

It was a comforting scenario.

***

The first of the ladies to arrive were — surprisingly enough — the ones from the farthest distance. Connie Collins, from Winooski, had picked up two passengers: April Flannigan, from Susie Wilson Road, and then Shirley Bogue, at the old Case house on Case Road. The three women toted potluck dishes, and then their craft projects, into the warm kitchen of the old brick house, laughing and talking as they moved about, before settling themselves into comfortable spots in the sitting area. Connie chose to sit cross-legged on a big cushion down on the floor in front of the window seat. She leaned back against the wall of the storage area under the seat and drew out her favorite project, a small tablecloth which she was embroidering. Her best friend, April, sat just above and to the left of her, on the window seat itself. The attractive blonde woman pulled a half-knitted sweater from her crafting bag and held it up to the light.

"I'm still not sure about the color of this thing. Is that royal blue or lavender blue?"

"I would say it's more of a dark lavender blue," Connie replied.

"It matches yer peepers," the loud lady from Case Road remarked, as she plopped her plump body into the gold recliner. Both recliners and several dining chairs had been moved into a large circle for this gathering, creating a more inclusive and cozy arrangement. "Rats!" she stretched her arms high before folding her hands and bringing them down behind her messy dirty-blonde head. "I didn't sleep worth a damn last night." Her eyes closed as she heaved a sigh. "I feel like a horse that's been rode hard and put away wet."

The other two laughed. Shirley was an entertaining lady, even if she was a bit rough around the edges.

More ladies were arriving in the kitchen. This time it was Lily, the petite Essex Junction police dispatcher with the melodious voice, and her friend, Grace. These two women had three main things in common: they sang in the choir at the Congregational Church, they loved doing crafts, and they both had names that stopped people in their tracks. Lily didn't deliberately plan to marry a man named White. She was just Lily White, and that was all there was to it. She got used to the smirks, and just went about her business.

But Grace, who preferred to be called "Gracie," had all kinds of fun with her name, Gracie Allen. Upon introducing herself, she would wait for the usual question, "Where's George Burns?" Then Gracie would come up with all kinds of funny replies. "I left him for Charlie McCarthy. Charlie makes more money," was one of her favorites. The fact that Burns and Allen — not to mention Edgar Bergen and Charlie McCarthy — were big radio stars, contributed to her own success as an amateur comedienne, and she loved every minute of it.

No sooner had those two settled into a couple of dining chairs than Anna Morgan, the church secretary at Holy Family in Essex Junction, came bounding out from the back hallway. She tossed a sealed Tupperware bowl onto the kitchen table, and quickly disappeared into the bathroom.

Somebody was knocking on the front door. Winnie hurried past the ladies. "That's Laura, from across the road," she said. "It's her first time to join us." The ladies got the message, and as soon as the tall lady with a soft smile was introduced, Shirley was the first to make her feel welcome.

"My gawd, yer a beautiful long drink of water, aren't-cha?" She pointed to a chair next to her recliner. "Park it right here, honey." As Laura sat down, Shirley continued, "How do you like yer coffee, Laurie? I'll go get you some."

"Oh, now, that's my job," Winnie protested. "I'm the hostess today. Besides, I know how Laura likes her coffee, that's for sure."

The other ladies quietly rescued the newcomer from the over-zealous hospitality of the Case Road lady, taking out their various projects, inviting her opinion on matters of size, color, and whatever else they could think of. She finally confided that she was really there in hopes that someone would teach her to hand quilt.

"That would probably be me," Anna volunteered. "I've been doing that stuff for years." The rest of the group nodded in agreement. "It's just a matter of rocking that little ol' needle just right." She drew forth a small wall hanging she was currently working on. "Just watch me for a while. Once you get the rhythm, it goes pretty fast." The lesson commenced, as other nimble fingers went to work crocheting, knitting, and embroidering, all the way around the circle. Before too long, it was time to stop for a nice buffet lunch.

As she helped herself to the potato salad, Gracie remarked, "Mmm, potato salad. This is my Scottie's favorite dish, I think."

Laura, who was standing right beside her asked sweetly, "Oh, you have a little dog?"

"What?"

"You have a little Scottish Terrier?"

Amidst the soft chuckles, Gracie's amused reply straightened her out. "No-no. Scottie is my son."

"Oh, Scottie Allen," Laura suddenly got it. "Of course. He's friends with *my* son."

"Scott is a nice kid. One of my students," Connie spoke from the other side of the nicely decorated table. She put a slice of Shirley's homemade bread on her plate. "So is Shirley's daughter, Marsha." She aimed her fresh-faced smile toward Laura. "We're pretty much all connected in this group."

"Yeah. Better watch out what you're getting into, Laura," Anna piped up. The rest of them laughed, and continued to fill their plates, until, one by one they were all seated once again. It was then, over the clink of silverware against Winnie's good china plates that the conversation took a troublesome turn.

"Okay, Winnie. I'm going to brag about you a little bit," Shirley dramatically announced.

"Oh-oh." There was some apprehension in Winnie's voice.

Shirley put her fork down on her plate, and wiped something off her lip with the back of her hand. "I just want you ladies to know what a great couple of landlords her and Cecil are, and I'll tell you why. Last summer, when the well went dry up there at the house, Cecil was toting milk cans full of fresh water to us, every other day. Two full cans every other day, right? Hauled those blasted, heavy things up there on the back of his tractor for more than a month, if you can believe that." The ladies murmured and clucked their tongues in appreciation. "On top of that, in the middle of a really sweltering hot day, Winnie came up and helped me wallpaper the boys' room upstairs, which, God knows, I never could have done by myself." She looked around her present setting. "Ya know, I keep telling her she'd be rich if only she would stop buying all that wallpaper." Howling laughter filled the room. "Anyway," she turned and looked directly at her landlady. "I just want you two guys to know how much yer appreciated. And I'm not too proud to tell ya in public." She ended her tribute with a solid affirmative jerk of her head.

Winnie, who had begun to crochet much faster than usual during Shirley's praise, laid down her work on her lap, and spoke softly. "My goodness, we're just doing our job."

"Yeah, but I want ya to know, it's appreciated."

"Well, thank you for the encouragement." She paused, picking up her needlework again. "Of course, that doesn't mean I will *ever* stop buying wallpaper!"

"Hey, you're just going to stay poor. Right, Win?" Anna quipped.

"Wallpapered all the way into the poor house," Lily chuckled.

"Well, at least they're going to look good all the way there," Gracie added.

After the good-natured banter quieted down, Gracie spoke up again: "I never knew you two owned the old Case house."

"Neither did I," Anna said.

"Actually, the property was left to Ceese's folks when Mrs. Case died. They had been watching over her for years. It was a natural progression of events, I guess. She didn't have any living relatives," Laura murmured, as she watched the rhythm of Anna's fingers.

"How old is that place?" someone asked.

"The original part is about a hundred years old, I think." Winnie put her handiwork down again. "Nobody lived in it for a long time. Let's see… she died in 1938, I think, and Ceese's folks passed on not too long after that. So, it was probably empty for fifteen years. We had to make a lot of repairs before we started to rent it out. Put in a bathroom, for one thing."

"There's still a creepy outhouse built right into the woodshed out behind the place, today," Shirley interjected.

"No kidding!" came the voice from the window seat.

"Wow!" someone else exclaimed.

"I never really knew Mrs. Case, Laura. Did you ever get to know her?" Winnie asked her neighbor.

"I actually did. I grew up right up the road from her, just on the other side of the hill." She shifted her tall frame on the dining chair, thinking back. "She was rather eccentric. Had several cats. Never went much of anywhere. Like you said, Winnie, Ceese's folks pretty much took care of her." She crossed her knees and slung her clenched hands around the top of them. "But it was the cats that I remember the most because, during the summer, they were out all over the place — in the barn across the road, in the pastures. They were regular little hunters. But in the wintertime, she kept them inside. I mean, all winter. And there was this one thing that I was shocked to discover, one spring day."

The ladies leaned forward just a little. Laura responded to their interest by settling into the storytelling.

"I was walking by the place, for some reason, and I heard this sharp rapping noise. I looked up at the house, and there she was on the front porch, banging her cane on its deck, apparently trying to get my attention. Well, I was just a young girl, and didn't know any better, so when she motioned for me to approach her, I obeyed immediately." The ladies shook their heads. "Well, when I got up close to her, she said something to me, and I could see she had practically no voice at all. It was little more than a whisper. But she did ask me if I could help her retrieve a box of canning jar screw tops which had fallen down her cellar stairs.”

Another round of shaking heads, with a couple of “Oh-oh” comments.

“She led me inside the house, and immediately there was this bad smell all around me. Didn’t seem to bother her at all. She just went over to our right to this door with a little latch on it, and opened it up. I was a little scared, I guess, because it was dark down those stairs, but she seemed distressed, and so fragile, so I peeked down the stairs, and sure enough, there was a box of jar rings — probably twenty of them — lying half-spilt onto the dirt floor. She motioned to some rickety shelves on the right wall just inside the stairwell. Apparently, the rims had fallen from there.”

Somebody hummed an “aha” noise.

“Well, by this time, I could tell that the stench was coming from that very cellar. The longer I stood there, the less I wanted to go down there. So, I turned around to tell her I was too afraid to go down there, and she was standing there like this”: Laura held onto her kneecap as though it were a cane being held by a trembling left hand, and then she lifted a tremulous right hand to her throat. Her eyes reflected the utter helplessness of an aged woman.

Somebody in the circle murmured, “Oh my goodness…”

“Well, I knew I had to go down there, so I decided to do it as fast as I could. I pushed the door as wide open as it would go, and politely asked Mrs. Case to stand in front of it, to hold it against the wall. I guess I figured that if she was going to trap me, like the mean old witch in Hansel and Gretel,” — she snickered at the thought — “I was a lot younger and could move a lot faster than she could.”

Some of the ladies smiled.

“Finally, I decided to go for it. I held my breath and went dashing down the wobbly wooden steps, pushed the tops into the box and swooped the thing into my arms to run back up the stairs, two at a time. At my second leap up those stairs, something terrifying came swishing past my bare legs with a hideous, screeching howl. I screamed and threw the box ahead of me up the stairs. I think I reached the top at about the same time the box smacked into that little old lady who was holding the door open. I was so scared, I never stopped running until I reached the top of the hill."

The ladies glanced around the circle, then gave the storyteller a knowing look.

"Ay-yuh. I figured out later, it had to be one of her cats. But then, I also figured out right after that, she had been letting those cats use the dirt floor of the cellar as a litter box all winter."

"And that's what the bad smell was," Lily concluded. "That's almost too wild to believe, isn't it?"

Winnie spoke up. "I tell you what, my husband and I both can vouch for these facts. He helped his folks dig out that cellar after the old lady died. They spread the whole thing with lime. Ceese said they tried everything they could think of to get rid of the odor, but finally decided it would take a while. That's why nobody lived in it for a long time. Just too stinky."

"Hafta tell ya," Shirley said, "it still has its moments."

"Okay, we're passing the hat right now, girls," Anna giggled. "Gotta buy a big bag of lime for Ceese and Winnie."

Shirley reached into her blouse pocket. "Hey, here's the first nickel!"

Suddenly April spoke up. Ever the antique collector, she had waited patiently for an opening. "So, Winnie, did you get blessed with some neat old furniture from Mrs. Case?"

"Not too much," Winnie replied. "Got an oversized chaise lounge for our parlor, and a treadle sewing machine."

"Marsha and I are using that. It works great, and Winnie has her electric sewing machine from Sears." Shirley brushed a greasy wisp of hair back from her eyes. "That machine sure has come in handy."

"And I guess there were a few odds and ends, tucked unseen into corners and crevices." Winnie turned to Shirley. "Remind me again. What did you find?"

"Right. You know those shelves Laurie just talked about, the ones at the head of the cellar stairs? Well, we went to replace them — not this summer, was it? No, it was the summer before. The old ones were so bad, Ceese brought me some boards, all cut to size, bless his pea-pickin' heart, and the boys and me made new ones. Painted them up real nice." She shook out the crumbled fabric upon which she was trying to do some redwork.

"And, by golly, when we pulled out the bottom piece, there was some stuff stuck under it." She looked at her landlady. "I gave you the tiny silver scissors, and the long button hook with the pearly looking handle, remember?"

"Ay-yuh. That was a good thing, Shirley. Made me respect you."

"Thank you." She smoothed the fabric over her knee. "The other thing we found was a Ouija board."

That caught Connie's attention.

"It didn't have the regular heart-shaped pointer... you know... that moves easily from one letter to the other. So, as an antique piece, it wasn't really worth much." She looked once again at Winnie. "You told me to just dump it, remember?" Winnie nodded. "Well, Marsha and I got to playing with that thing. Instead of having the real pointer, we used a lightweight drinking glass, upside down. Just put the tips of our fingers on top, and asked our questions." She paused. "Anyway, that's about all we found."

Connie cleared her throat and asked as casually as she could, "So, did you finally throw it away?"

"Oh no. We still have it. Play with it now and then, especially if Marsha's friend, Roxie, comes for an overnight stay. She always asks to play with the ol' Ouija board."

"Is it fun?" Connie needed to know something more.

"Heck, yes. The three of us just make a tight little circle around the board, and take turns asking it questions."

"And do you ever get any answers?"

"Well, we laugh a lot, because we know it's just the vibrations from our fingertips. Still, it's fun. We go at it for a couple of hours, sometimes."

For this dedicated Christian counselor, the remainder of the afternoon was experienced through a deep fog. When it was time to pick up their dishes and go home, it was April who thanked their hostess and led her silent friend out to the car. Shirley and Laura volunteered to stay and help Winnie straighten up, each being able to easily walk home. Left pretty much on her own, April took Connie's keys and drove slowly up Case Road, past the old Case house, all the way to her own home at the intersection of Case and Susie Wilson Roads. Once there, she pulled into the driveway and sat quietly, waiting for Connie to speak.

"A Ouija board," the high school counselor whispered. "A Ouija board."

April waited impatiently, not knowing where this was going, not really wanting to deal with it. She noticed Bill's car was not in the driveway, and remembered he had had a swing shift today. He would not be home until after midnight. She would have time to work on that oil painting for her son back in Oregon.

But something was not right. Something was grieving her friend, Connie.

"So-oo, tell me about this Ouija board thing. Why does it upset you so much?"

Connie shook her head.

"It's demonic," she whispered.

CHAPTER EIGHT

Communications

After an encouraging conversation with April, Connie headed homeward, driving slowly to the intersection of Susie Wilson Road and Route 15. At the stop sign, she took a right and proceeded past Fort Ethan Allen, home of the 134th Fighter Interceptor Squadron of the Vermont National Guard. She glanced to her right, admiring the stately brick structures of Officers' Row, which formed a wavy semicircle around the huge parade field. There, something nudged her memory. Something about that long row of housing with the white trim and gleaming verandahs. Something out behind them.
"Oh yeah."

She remembered a conversation that took place a few years ago, right after they had moved to Vermont. She and Don were meeting with a new prayer partner for the first time, at the Lincoln Inn in the village of Essex Junction.

"Yes, I do believe demons exist," the priest had answered her question. "I believe there are angels and I believe there are demonic beings, as well." He paused and leaned forward, his forearms crossed upon the table in front of him. "The Roman Catholic Church has documented their existence throughout its long history, and those things don't just go away."

"Ever been to an exorcism?" Don had asked.

"Once." Father Tom grimaced. "That was enough."

"I agree," Connie had said, emphatically. "I was part of a deliverance ministry for a couple of years back on Long Island. It's not pretty." She studied the freckled face across the table. "What do you think attracts those things?"

"Fear… and foolishness," he responded immediately. Then he corrected himself: "Probably foolishness first, and then fear."

"Exactly." Don picked up his glass of water to wipe the rim with his napkin. "It's like they can smell fear from a mile away. That's why all this ghost hunting is so stupid." He took a sip. "It would be better if we could just ignore them."

Father nodded. "They thrive on fear, because it gives them power, and they get all kinds of attention when they exercise that power. That's the way they draw people away from the source of all *real* power — Jesus Christ." He looked over his shoulder and then back at the Collinses. "I can give you a prime example of that right from the fort down the road."

"Fort Ethan Allen?" she whispered.

He nodded affirmatively. "Some years ago, sometime in the early forties I believe, the military built the Ethan Allen Chapel, on the corner of King and Essex Roads, right there on the base, about a block behind Officers' Row. There was also a theater built next door to it, for various types of entertainment for the troops. The name of that fun place was, and still is, the Herrouet Theater."

"Those buildings are still there, then?" she asked.

"Still there." He had the full attention of this Pentecostal Christian couple, so he continued: "I am told there was a young nun — one who had loved the theater and the chapel — actually haunting the place. Seems she died in her sleep inside the theater, which suggests she was rooming there as caretaker, or whatever, and for some reason she just hung around — a ghost who manifested and communicated with a whole lot of people. Supposedly, she's still there, too." The couple was still listening intently. "Her name, they say, is Sister Sara."

"Hmm," the couple said in unison.

"Funny thing, though," he paused for a little bit of drama. "None of those people have ever heard a *feminine* voice. It was always a soft, low voice, but definitely a male voice." He grinned. "What does that tell you?"

"It's a demon," Don said.

"Probably more than one," Connie added. "Anyway, there are no such things as ghosts — they're all demons who love to snare gullible people with their tragic stories, or whatever." She turned to her husband. "You're right, it would be better if we could just ignore them entirely. Then they couldn't deceive so many people."

"Therein lies the problem," Father Tom noted. "People have this need for the supernatural — something to fill that *persistent* hollow place inside them. The only thing that can fill it is God, Himself, but they would rather not be subjugated to a *real* authority. It's more fun to play thrilling, bone-chilling games."

"Including experimenting with cults which offer up tantalizing alternatives." Don shrugged his shoulders. "We are like little children who don't want to mind our parents. We look for *other* sources of authority — anything but that strict set of rules."

"And yet, it is that very set of so-called 'strict' rules that offers us the most loving protection we could ever, ever desire. Isn't that so sad?" Father Tom leaned back, lifting his hands palms out toward the other two. "But then, I'm preaching to the choir, here."

"Preach it, brother," Don had said. "There's a whole other 'community' out there in the spiritual world that most human beings are completely unaware of. *Somebody* needs to wake up these folks who are seeking, *very sincerely*, intellectual conclusions which have no clear limits, and no reasonable consequences. Sadly, that includes gullible folks who are stalking — and talking with — phony 'ghosts.'"

"And using Ouija boards," Connie thought, before coming back to the present.

By now, the Studebaker was rounding the curve in front of Saint Michael's College, so she started to slow down for the right-hand turn onto Florida Avenue. Saturday night traffic was starting to crowd Route 15, and she was glad to turn onto her quiet street with the neat little single-level ranchers lining both sides. The homes on her right had back yards which butted up against Saint Michael's green area, providing a backside view of the college's historic buildings. Most of the folks on that side of the street had patios, or even just picnic tables out in those back yards, where they could enjoy a bit of peace and quiet. The weather was still good, and she thought it might even be possible this evening to eat out there in their own screened-in patio. Just before she turned another curve to her tan-colored house, she noticed Mindy Strong in her front yard, raking leaves. She waved, and kept going.

"That's one unhappy woman. But then, she walked right into it, stealing Alan from his wife."

As a fellow employee, Don had had ample complaints and details from the morose Mr. Strong.

"Poor Mindy. Had no idea this forty-year-old hotshot with the striking white hair had been raised as a spoiled child, with nothing but the best, then entering adulthood, self-centered to the core. And her, a twenty-nine-year-old woman, thinking that just because he drove a Cadillac and lived high off the hog, he had all that money. Turned out it was his doting mother who had all the money. Once Mindy and Al were married, the facts came to light, and there had been war ever since — yelling, slamming doors, and a lot of alcohol."

She sighed loudly.

"And now, here they are, living hand-to-mouth, in a rented house, and he's driving a bus for Burlington Transit. What a comedown, for both of them."

Connie pulled into the driveway of 19 Florida Avenue, turned off the key, and set the brake. It was good to be home.

Half an hour later, a ham was in the oven and she was headed downstairs to the refurbished basement, where the couple's counseling office was located. She wanted to pull a couple of books from the bookcase before Don got home at six o'clock. They both needed to review information about Ouija boards.

The door bell chimed.

When she opened the door, Mindy Strong was standing there, still in her work clothes, a red bandana tied over her jet black hair.

"I hate to bother you, Connie, but I just need a minute of your time. I saw you coming home. I hope I've given you time to settle down a bit. You've probably had a busy day."

"Sure. Thank you, Mindy." She opened the door and beckoned her to enter. "Would you like to come in?"

"No-no. I still have dirty boots on. I'm fine. I just need to, uh…" She seemed at a loss for words.

Seeing the distress, Connie put on her "counseling hat."

"What can I do for you, Mindy?" she asked quietly. The young woman responded to the warmth, and relaxed a bit. She licked her dry lips.

"You do counseling, right? Marriage counseling?"

"We do." She hoped the surprise didn't show on her face.

"Um, how much does it cost?"

"Well, we use a sliding scale. It depends on your income."

Her laugh was hollow. "Oh, that's good, because I don't have any. That means I go for free, right?"

"Well, you know what? We can probably work it out." The counselor smiled, and looked at the little pieces of leaves still stuck to the knees of Mindy's dungarees. "You sure know how to rake leaves."

"Yeah! Yeah, I sure do!" The hazel eyes widened with hope. "Would that be okay?" Connie winked an okay at her. She took a big breath and said, "I need an appointment as soon as I can get one."

"My, this sounds urgent."

"It is."

"How urgent?"

"I'm really getting scared." She looked down at her boots, then back to the older woman's face. "Alan has a hand gun, did you know that?"

Connie shook her head "no."

"His temper is getting worse. He slammed the back door so hard it broke the door jamb. Scared the heck out of me. A couple of weeks ago, he dented my mother's big copper lazy susan with his bare fist." She shuddered. "Last night he kicked a hole in the bathroom wall. Ten minutes later, I heard him on the phone with his mother, cursing me out. I don't know why she's not mad at him, you know, for leaving his wife… but she sure hates me, I can tell you. Anyway, I ended up locking myself in the bedroom." Suddenly she stopped. "I'm afraid to call the police. I can't prove anything." She looked over her shoulder.

"Is Alan working tonight?"

"Yeah, swing shift out on North Avenue. Then he goes to that bar down by the old woolen factory in town, here, for a couple of drinks. Usually gets home about one or two in the morning."

"Don will be home about six. How would you like to have dinner with us?" The hazel eyes went wide again. "Alan wouldn't be mad if you had dinner with a neighbor, now, would he?" The red bandana wobbled a "no."

"Could you come at six-thirty?"

By the time the three of them sat down to dinner, Connie had informed her husband of Mindy's situation. After he said grace, he invited the young woman to fill in all the details, questioning her gingerly, so as not to lead her astray from the facts. While he noted her verbal statements, he was well aware that those were not necessarily the dominating factors during this initial interview. Connie pretty much took care of the emotional assessment, mostly by observation. Between the two of them, the decision was made that Mindy was in a possibly dangerous situation, and something had to be done.

"Do you have somewhere to go, someone to stay with for a little while?" they asked.

"Not really." She thought for a moment. "My sister lives in Albany, New York, but that's a long way, and I don't have any money for a bus ticket, or anything." She stacked her silverware and glass on her dinner plate and rose to take it to the kitchen. "I was thinking it might calm things down for a while, if Alan would just agree to come and get a little counseling."

"Actually, we probably shouldn't be doing that, what with us two guys working in the same company. It certainly couldn't be official. Maybe two friends chatting at lunchtime, or something," he said.

"Well, could you at least do that? I need, or I should say, *we* need to buy a little more time to just see if we can't work all this anger out."

"You do understand that you could be in danger, don't you?" Connie's voice was solemn.

"Yes. But maybe we could calm him down, if we just all talked, you know?" She followed Connie to the kitchen from the small dining room. "If we could just try it for a couple of months." Don was close behind, as she put the dishes in the sink. Her question addressed the two of them. "Could we just do that?"

"Well, we can't force you to go to a safer place. What we will ask you to do is have a suitcase packed and have a plan to get out of that house, at a moment's notice. Will you at least do that?"

"Yeah, I can do that."

"And I'll start having some good conversations with my fellow bus driver." He smiled the imp smile again. "Matter of fact, I'll be his best buddy at the company picnic next Saturday, how about that?"

"Oh, I had forgotten about that. Sure, that would be good." Before she was out the door, she promised, "I'll get started on those leaves as soon as I can!"

Don was helping Connie to do up the dishes when she suddenly remembered about the Ouija board.

His reaction was as she expected, and as soon as the kitchen was in order, the two of them descended to the basement office, pulling out all the books and pamphlets they could find. At the end of an hour, they agreed that somehow, somewhere, they had to alert Shirley. They weren't sure she would believe them, much less put a stop to this risky spiritual game, but there was too much at stake for them to do absolutely nothing. As they knelt by their bed before retiring for the night, Don prayed fervently for guidance.

***

The phone rang at five o'clock the next morning, just as he was getting ready to leave for a Sunday day shift. Connie took the call.

"Is this you, Connie?" The female voice was familiar.

"Yes, this is Connie."

"This is Marilyn Foxx. I met you at the Christmas party. My husband is the personnel manager at the bus company there in Burlington. Do you remember me?"

Connie motioned for Don to come closer, holding the phone out from her ear so he could hear this. "Of course I remember you, Marilyn. How are you?"

"Not so hot. I'm sorry to be calling you this early but there's a problem, and my husband says you and Don do personal counseling. Is that right?"

"That's right, we do. Um… may I ask what the problem is?"

There was a brief moment of silence. "It's my daughter, Roxanne. She… she didn't come home until after midnight… again."

"Last night, Marilyn?"

"Yeah. I tell you, I don't know how to get through to that girl."

"Sounds like she's in rebellion, and that's nothing new. There are ways to handle that problem."

"I hope so. I'm afraid if she keeps this stuff up, we'll have a social worker on our doorstep." Her voice cracked. "She's my only child. I don't want to lose her."

"Well, there are two ways to handle this. You can call the school and ask for counseling for your daughter, and that would be my job. Or, you could just work with Don here at the office."

"What's the difference?"

"School counseling has the school system for a covering. They have to work with the social worker types. With Don, it would be private counseling. I would be helping Don, of course, so I'll be there if you need me."

Don signaled that he would like to talk to the lady.

"Marilyn, Don has been listening and wants to talk to you. Is that alright?"

"Yes."

"Hello, Marilyn. I just wanted to let you know that, while it wouldn't be ethical for me to counsel any of my coworkers, I sure could try to help Roxanne. That's outside of my workplace, so that should be permissible."

"Yeah, I understand. So when can we do this?"

He turned to Connie. "Check my work schedule on the calendar, would you, babe? See if we have a compatible day this week." His wife quickly ran and scrutinized the calendar on the kitchen wall. Don chose not to continue the conversation until he heard his wife's voice. It was a long thirty seconds.

"Thursday at six in the evening," she called out.

"Did you hear that, Marilyn?"

"Yes. I can do that. Where is your office?"

He gave the address, then reassured her, "We'll do everything we can to help you. Meantime, try to be positive."

He strove to calm the situation. "I assume you and the boss will be at the picnic next Saturday."

"Uh, yeah, we kind of have to." She checked her attitude. "Yeah, we'll be there, for sure."

"Well, let's all keep that enjoyable time foremost in our minds for the next few days. It will help."

"Right. Thanks."

"Steak and corn-on-cob, right?"

She laughed softly. "Right."

"Love that annual company picnic," he said, cheerfully. But as he hung up the phone, a darkness clothed his face. It was time to inform Connie of his suspicions about Bill Flannigan.

"You going to church this morning, babe?"

"Of course. Why do you ask?"

"You're going to need it."

***

At eight o'clock that same morning, Connie telephoned the Flannigan home on Susie Wilson Road. April bounded out of the bathroom in her robe, still wet from the shower.

"Hello?"

"Hey, good morning, April," Connie said.

"Hey, yourself. Are you feeling a little more cheerful this morning?"

"I'm trying. Thanks for the pep talk yesterday, after the Circle meeting. So, now I'm trying to get my head back into 'God is in charge.' In fact, Don is driving bus this morning, and I was wondering if you'd like to join me for church, and then lunch at Ralph's Diner."

"That would be a real day trip, all the way out there on Shelburne Road."

"Yeah, well, that's where our little church is. We Pentecostals have to hide in the bushes, you know."

April laughed. "As much as I would like to, Bill is just getting up, and we're going to have a nice brunch at the Lincoln Inn. It's his birthday!"

"Oh, I didn't know that. We should have sent him a funny card."

"He would have enjoyed that. Anyway, I have to bring him his coffee. He worked a swing shift and didn't get home until really late last night."

"Oh, is that right?"

"Yeah, like one in the morning."

"Oh-oh! Well, I'll let you go then. Have a fun birthday brekkie!"

April hung up the phone with a little smile on her face. The coffee had already been poured into her husband's favorite cup, so she carefully placed it on the antique table beside the ornate wrought-iron bed. He rolled over and grunted when she kissed him on the ear.

"Rise and shine, Birthday Boy!" He opened his eyes as though surprised by his surroundings. She carefully pulled the covers back just far enough to allow him to sit up with a couple of pillows behind his shoulders. "Here," she said, as she pointed to the coffee. "Have a big slurp of this. You'll wake up in a minute." Stepping over their toy poodle, Charley, she went back into the bathroom to finish toweling off.

"What do you feel like having?" she called out to him.

"What?" he mumbled.

"For breakfast! What do you feel like having?" She peeked around the doorway. He was rubbing his eyes.

"Anything you want to fix," he murmured.

"Did you forget we're going out for your birthday breakfast, honey?" He looked at her, and she could tell he was suddenly remembering. "You need to wake up, Bill. What on earth kept you out so late, anyway?"

He was reaching for his coffee as she turned back to wrap herself in a towel.

The crash was followed by a sharp yelp from the little dog, and a string of swear words.

"What happened?" She came to a halt, avoiding the shards of porcelain on the hardwood floor. Bill was trying to get out of bed without cutting his feet. Coffee was splattered everywhere. Charley was hiding under the bedside table, trembling.

She slipped into her robe and slippers and grabbed the broom from the kitchen. It took a good forty-five minutes to clean up the mess, including stripping the bedding, and washing down every spattered surface within five feet of the impact. What had started out as a happy celebration had become a major aggravation. The birthday boy was in a royal grump, and his wife was nearly in tears.

"All right," she finally said. "Let's just forget it. I can make breakfast here. There's no sense in our pretending everything is wonderful, when you are so irritated."

He sat at the round table in the corner of the little kitchen, head down in a sullen pout. "Fine with me."

April set her jaw against the brimming tears, and stepped out onto the tiny porch of the stucco house, to give him some time to cool off. Slowly, she slid into a white wicker rocker, pulling a small, red patchwork lap robe over her knees. Her chest felt like lead. Little blonde-colored Charley jumped up onto her lap and licked her face.

The phone rang again. Almost immediately, she heard Bill answer it.

"Hello?"

There was a prolonged pause, until he chuckled. "Well, thank you very much." The volume of his conversation declined to the point that she could not hear what he was saying. But whatever he was saying, it was being said with a great deal of humor.

She sat up straight, ready for him to call her to the phone. It was probably one of the boys calling from back in Oregon. She wiped the tears away, and waited, as the muffled conversation continued. After a few minutes, she put the dog gently down, arose, and opened the front door into the house. The relaxed figure of her husband suddenly sat upright as she poked her head inside the doorway.

"Uh-huh… uh-huh," he was saying into the mouthpiece. He glanced up at her and raised an 'It's okay' hand toward her. Obviously, this call did not require her participation. Still, she did not move along, but stood there within hearing distance, curious. Annoyed, he looked up as though to say, "Do you need something?"

"Who is it?"

He rolled his James Dean eyes, covered the mouthpiece with his hand, and whispered, "My fan club."

"Oh, r-right. That needy teenager he's been trying to help."

She moved back onto the porch and waited for the end of the phone call. Her heart softened. He really was a good person, even with his unpredictable moods. This was a long-term project for him, obviously a strain on him at times. She had tried to point out that maybe he should face the facts. He really was not qualified to counsel people, let alone, a troubled teenager. But any suggestion that he was in over his head was met with a huge psychological slap of one sort or another. At any rate, she felt this attempt to help this girl was taking its toll on her husband, but he would absolutely not give up on this project.

Finally, he opened the front door and smiled. "Hey, April, I'm sorry. We just got off on the wrong foot this morning. Tell you what — let's go ahead and do this. Let's have that nice birthday brunch at the inn, okay?"

"Are you sure?"

"As sure as I'm standing here in my beeveedees."

She jumped up to hug him, then scooted to the bedroom, where she had laid out her special outfit the night before. Maybe it was going to be a good day, after all. She whisked through the usual routine, from deodorant to hair spray, finishing with a dab of Chanel No. 5. The plan was back on, and as soon as she brushed her straight blonde hair into place, she would make sure Bill's birthday present was safely tucked into the back seat of the car.

It took longer for them to get ready than she had thought, but it was all right because the inn didn't open for Sunday brunch until eleven o'clock, anyway. Once she was ready, she went out to tuck her gift into the back seat of the pale yellow 1948 Packard station wagon. The handsome automobile was referred to by most folks as a "woodie," due to its wooden door panels. She only half-noticed the new piece of thick carpet lying across the expanse created by the folded-down back seat. Since the two boys were grown and off on their own, there was little need for passenger seating back there any longer. It was only logical that the area, which was now mainly used for hauling various items, should be protected from damage. She barely noted the smears on one of the back windows, mistaking them as unusual glints of sunlight from an unknown reflective surface. Typical of her optimistic personality, her attention was on the good stuff in life, and she rejoiced that this breakfast celebration could possibly be a much-needed bonding time for this marriage. There had been too many separations during the war, and too many mysterious nightmares whenever he was home. Worst of all was the lack of communication which had permeated their relationship for the last few years. Even their boys had seen it, and worried.

A shout from her husband indicated he was ready to leave. She went back into the house, anticipating a great morning, and when she saw how sharp he looked as he came into the little living room, she felt it was worth the wait.

"Wow! Look at you!" she exclaimed.

He was wearing a sea-blue shirt which accented his slightly faded golden summer tan. An unopened, off-white tennis sweater was draped over his shoulders, with the sleeves carefully looped together over the front of his chest. Tan slacks, with an impeccable crease, brought the eye down to his casual white loafers. He was a picture of anything but a bus driver.

"You look like a movie star, honey! Hollywood royalty! Clark Gable is no longer the King of Hollywood... no doubt about it!" She was encouraged that he would do all that for this special occasion.

"So, how do *I* look, Mr. Flannigan?" She whirled around in the lacy, deep blue sundress, which she hoped brought out the color of her Irish-sky eyes. At the end of the whirl, she performed a mock curtsy, rising slowly to shake her sleek blonde hair mischievously before her knight in shining armor. *"It was corny,"* she thought, *"but it seemed to fit the mood for the moment."*

He brushed a bit of lint from one of the sleeves lying across his royal bosom, before granting her a benign smile. "Let's go eat, milady."

They were amongst the first to arrive at the inn, and were immediately seated in the main dining room. Bill insisted that April be seated on the side of the table which overlooked the scrumptious buffet, so she could take her time in selecting the very best delectables, before she even got up there. His own seat faced the main entrance into the dining room. As the beverage server poured coffee for them, April presented her movie star husband with his gift. He opened it slowly, and when he saw the wallet, he seemed pleased. "Genuine leather. Wow!" She watched him open it and inspect each little space. "Perfect," he said.

They went to the buffet table together, returning with plates heaped high with goodies they would never have eaten at home. Both were careful about their appearances, especially their weight. But today was special. April chattered away as they slowly enjoyed the meal, not noticing her husband's repeated glances past her shoulder toward the dining room entrance.

"This is such a great place to eat," she said as she finally put down her fork. "Look at the décor. Early American. Lights that look like candles. Perfect for an inn named after Lincoln, right?" She looked up for an acknowledging nod from the handsome man across the table, to be surprised at the look on his face. His eyes were focused on something behind her as he spoke out in an oddly pitched tone. "Huh… will you look at who's here." As she turned to look, he answered his own question. "It's my boss and his wife, Marilyn. The Foxxes. And will you look at that… they have Roxie with them."

"Really?" she peered toward the approaching trio. "I've met George and Marilyn before, but never actually…" Her voice trailed off as the redheaded youngster let out a sweet sing-songy, "Uh-huuuh!" and came bounding over to their table. She seemed to scrunch down to make herself look smaller, at the same time, doing her very best fourteen-year-old jiggle-dance. "Are you April? I've been waiting so long to meet you." She looked at Bill. "You didn't tell me she was *this* pretty!" The little girl voice continued: "I've heard a lot of nice things about you, and now — Wow! Here you are!"

For a moment, April thought she was talking with Shirley Temple, the child actress. Vaguely bemused, she turned to greet the Foxxes. She was surprised again. Neither one of them seemed pleased at this chance meeting, and were actually averting their eyes. Uncomfortable, she murmured a greeting and watched them politely return it. Then Marilyn spoke directly to George. "I need to…" She waggled her strawberry-blonde curls toward the restroom. And then she left without a word.

Looking back at Bill, April said, "Well, we were just leaving, but it was a wonderful meal, I can tell you." Bill stood up, pausing for a moment with one hand on the back of the chair, looking across at his boss. It was a pose that, again, resembled the teenage hero, James Dean, looking for favor from his girlfriend's parents.

"Thought I would bring our croquet set for the picnic next Saturday, George. That alright with you?"

The dark-complexioned man nodded approval, but said nothing.

It was definitely time to end this encounter, but just before they did, April reached out and touched Roxie's shoulder. "Thanks so much for the 'Happy Birthday' phone call this morning. That was very sweet." Bill looked down at the floor, then took her arm and steered the two of them toward the cashier.

George and Roxie went immediately to their table. No sooner had they seated themselves than the words came tumbling out of her stepfather's mouth. "So that's where you went while your mother was in the shower. I saw you take your bike and go. You went to the nearest phone booth, didn't you, you little sneak?"

Roxie laughed. "I know where every phone booth in Essex Junction is located. Get used to it."

"The hell I will, you stinking little sneak."

"Watch your mouth, Georgie-Porgie."

"I told you not to call me that." He pushed a lock of his ebony hair up off his black eyebrows.

She smiled sweetly and wrinkled her nose at him. "Did you, now?" She leaned forward. "And just who are *you* to tell *me* what to do? May I remind you, sir, that you are my mother's third husband, and there is a reason for that?"

She held up her index finger, touching it with her other index finger. "The first one, well, he just died in the war. No problem."

She held up the second finger, touching it the same way. "The second one just couldn't stand having a bratty little girl around. He lasted three years. In that little experience I learned that my mom will always choose me... *me*, over some stupid guy."

Finally, she tapped the top of the third finger. "Now, you... you really are crazy about your beautiful Marilyn, and because of that, you have hung around through thick and thin, for four whole years, no matter what I have dished up for you. And I have not yet dumped you. Do you know why?" She smirked. "Because you have learned to behave yourself, Georgie, that's why." She could see he was getting uncomfortable. "Now listen, you just keep those free bus passes coming, and you don't fire my special friends, and everything will be just fine. You will get to keep your lovely Marilyn, alright?"

She spotted her mother coming back from the restroom. "Otherwise, I could really hurt you, mister. I've already told some of my friends at school that you're beating me." His eyes grew wide, then narrowed into dark slits of hatred.

As Marilyn sat down, the beverage server appeared from a nearby shadow. "What may I bring you for a beverage?"

George Foxx replied quickly, "Champagne breakfast cocktail."

"Coffee," Marilyn said.

"I'll have —" Roxie looked up to order, but stopped mid-sentence. The server was Diana, best friend of the captain of the varsity cheerleaders.

Diana blinked her Lucille Ball eyes and smiled a professional smile. "What would you like, miss?"

Roxanne Foxx made steady, meaningful eye contact with the waitress. "I'd like you to not sneak up on us like this ever again." She flipped the ringlets back from the left side of her face. "And if it isn't too much trouble, I would like a glass of water. With a straw in it."

"Yes, of course," the server replied, as she disappeared into the restaurant's ambient lighting.

Marilyn sighed. "That was a surprise, running into the Flannigans. I don't even like that Bill. What a phony showoff. I feel sorry for his wife. And I am sick and tired of having to hostess people like them for things like this asinine company picnic next weekend."

"Sorry, honey, it's just part of the job."

"I know, and we are lucky just to have a job."

"What's that supposed to mean? We had to move because of me?" the girl bristled.

"That's not what I said."

"Well, it wasn't my fault."

"Of course not, sweetheart. It was just a big misunderstanding." Marilyn stood up, hiding the worry in her silvery eyes. "Hey, you two, how about we get something good to eat, here?"

***

As prearranged by a follow-up phone call, Marilyn arrived at 19 Florida Avenue a half-hour before Roxie would get off the bus and walk the short distance to the same place. That would allow time for a private assessment of this situation, especially from the mother's perspective. Since the Collinses had a policy that opposite sexes should never be alone during a counseling session, Connie slipped quietly into a chair in the corner of the small office. Don prayed a short prayer, then sat back in his creaky desk chair.

"How're you doing, Marilyn?"

The floodgates opened. In about fifteen minutes, the story came forth in bursts of anger, frustration, and fear.

Roxie's birth father had been killed in an auto accident in Europe, just two months after she was born. His daughter never knew him. The grieving mother had poured her heart and soul into the beautiful child, bringing her up in the center of attention. When the little girl was five, Marilyn had remarried. Roxie could not handle someone else being the object of her mother's affection, and she turned into a little terror. She kicked and bit and screamed at this poor gentleman, until he had had enough, demanding the unmanageable child be properly disciplined, or he would be gone. Try as she might, the doting mother could not resist the wiles of her angelic-looking little girl. The marriage only lasted three years.

Marilyn finally married George when Roxie was only ten years old. The marriage got off to a rocky start, but George really loved his wife, and he bent over backward to accommodate his new gorgeous, but nasty stepdaughter. He did everything he could think of to win her over — a new bedroom set, a new bicycle, dancing lessons, her own telephone. At first, it seemed to work.

But things eventually got worse. About six months into the marriage, the young Roxie suddenly started to exhibit an interest in the opposite sex. At the same time, she realized she was not only beautiful, but, as she put it, "Super gorgeous." She could not pass a mirror without primping and smiling. Her whole demeanor seemed to change, until eventually, testing the waters, she found she could get just about anything she wanted, if she even *hinted* she was available for a hug. This was especially alarming to Marilyn, since George had a long-standing job as a bus driver down there in Albany, and this young girl had access to free bus rides all over the place. After George got bumped up to a management position, things became even worse.

"Long story short," the mother concluded, "we had to leave Albany for a different job because a couple of the drivers' wives threatened legal action against the company, and — guess why — because it allowed a certain minor girl to hang out with these older men, not only on their buses, but at the bus barn, as well." She lifted both hands as if to push the whole situation away. "It looks like she's at it again... only, she's older, and this is really scary."

"Can you tell me exactly why this is so scary?"

Her eyes closed, and she covered them with one hand. "I don't think she's just flirting, now."

"You think she may be sexually active?"

She dropped her hand away, and stared at the ceiling. "Which shouldn't surprise me. We mature sexually very early in this family."

"Hmm, what do you mean? Is this something someone told you when you were young, or have you seen it actually as a pattern in your family?"

"It's the hormones, Don. Raging hormones, especially in the girls."

His chair squeaked as he turned to the left to look at Connie. "You want to get in on this?" he asked.

She nodded. "Tell us a little about your family history. What did people do for a living, especially the women? Can you remember any of that?"

Marilyn laughed. "Oh boy, I sure can tell you what my grandmother did. She ran a brothel in Nevada, for many years."

"What about your mother? Did she work outside the home?"

"Nope. The only money she ever earned was when people would come to our house for readings."

"Tarot cards?" Connie asked.

"No-no. She wasn't educated in that stuff, but she sure could read the ol' tea leaves."

A few minutes later, Roxie was seated in the chair Marilyn had just vacated.

"Where you going, Mom?" she said as her mother started up the stairs. "Aren't you going to stay with me?" Marilyn hesitated, as though under an invisible spell. Suddenly the child's voice had a tremble in it. "Aren't you going to stay with me, Mom?" Roxanne looked at Don, then at Connie, and when she turned back to her mother, her angelic eyes were glistening. "Mom?"

Connie stepped forward to put her hand on the girl's shoulder. "She will be right upstairs, Roxie. If you need her, she can be down here in a couple of seconds." She motioned Marilyn to ascend. Then she placed her hand gently under

Roxie's chin, tilting her lovely face up toward her own, meeting her eye-to-eye. "Now listen to me, Roxie. You are perfectly safe here. Mr. Collins and I are here to help you, not to hurt you. All you have to do is just be your own wonderful self. That's all." She winked reassuringly. "Okay?"

When she turned around to take her seat in the corner, Don was sitting there. He nodded toward the desk, and she took her cue, sitting in the "authority" seat, and letting the real authority seem less imposing over there in the corner. She knew what to do next. "Don, would you please lead us in prayer before we begin?" Roxie saw the couple bow their heads, so she followed suit, except she kept her eyes wide open to peer at the two of them through her long eyelashes. When Don said, "Amen," she closed her eyes quickly and waited a couple of seconds to open them and lift her head. Uh-hu-uh, she could play this game.

"So-o-oo, Roxie, my wife tells me you have a great singing voice." The girl looked surprised. "In the glee club, right?" She nodded. "You must like music, then."

"Yeah."

"Play any instruments?"

"Yup." She saw the question in his eyes. "Ukulele," she said, with a little kick of her left foot.

"You're kidding me!" He grinned the elfin grin. "My dad played the ukulele." He wagged his head as he remembered. "He learned to play that thing when he was stationed in Hawaii."

"Roxie has been taking lessons down at Edmunds High School. Is it once a week, Roxie?"

"Yup."

"Those special classes are held early in the morning, so you have to get up before breakfast to do that, I know."

"Yup."

"Wow, that takes some real dedication, young lady," he exclaimed. "How do you fit this into your busy high school schedule?"

Roxie shrugged her shoulders. "I don't know. I just want to do it, so I do."

"Well," he said, "good for you, as long as it doesn't stress you out." He reached down to lift his left ankle to the top of his right knee. "Which is a good point. How is your health, young lady? You eating healthy?"

"Yup. My mom feeds me at the diner where she works, right next-door to the bus terminal. And I am never hungry, that's for sure."

"What's your favorite meal?"

She snorted. "Pizza."

Both adults laughed with her.

"How about sleep? You sleeping well?" He saw her twitch a little.

"I guess I do pretty good."

"Hmm," Connie seemed concerned. "At your young age, you need all the healthy rest you can get, Roxie." She focused across the desk toward those silvery eyes. "What's happening? Are you worried about something?" The child shrugged and looked away.

"A lot of the precious young people who come in to our office for help have this same problem," Don said softly. "There is no shame in it." He slid his left foot back down onto the carpeted floor. "Are you, by any chance, having dreams, Roxie?"

The girl looked at the floor. Her silence revealed volumes.

The husband and wife exchanged glances. The desk chair squeaked lightly as Connie shifted her weight.

"Hard to talk about?" she asked. The girl shrugged and scanned the floor. "Okay, we can save that for another time." She leaned forward, her elbows upon the desktop. "Is there anything you want to ask us before you leave here? Just take a minute to think about that. The first session can be the hardest, and sometimes we forget to ask our clients about that. So if you have anything you want to ask, go ahead."

"Why am I here, anyway?" She had not even taken a moment to think about it.

"Why do *you* think you are here?"

Another shrug. "Guess I must be in some kind of trouble, again."

"Again?"

The toes and heels were suddenly rocking back and forth, causing the knees to bounce gently. Roxie slowly stretched her arms upward and forward, the wrists turning the inside of her clenched fists outward toward the ceiling over Connie's head. She pursed her lips and pushed out a whooshing sound, much like the air out of a balloon. Then, suddenly dropping her arms and pressing her feet flat down on the floor, she spoke in a low grunt. "I'm getting really tired. We need to stop now." Connie resisted another visual contact with her husband. "Okay, Roxie. That's fine." Connie stood up and moved around to the front of the desk, where she slid her bottom back onto its top. "So, we need to assign you your homework." The girl looked alarmed. "Not to worry, young lady," Connie laughed. "You're going to love this." She turned and winked at her husband. "Don, this gal is capable of writing a song, wouldn't you agree?"

He grinned. "Absolutely."

She turned back to the young client. "How about writing a song for us, Roxie? Something you can play on your ukulele?"

"Really?" The young girl's eyes came back to life.

"Have you ever written a song before?"

"Actually… actually… I have. Four of them, in fact."

Connie slapped her hands together. "I knew it. I just knew you would do something like that." Roxie sat back in her chair, obviously pleased. "But the homework is that you write a song about your dreams." The fear returned to her beautiful face. "You can do this, and do it very well, I know. Roxie, you probably have the ability to write an important song, here. It could touch the hearts of a lot of other young people, just like you. Who knows? It might even make it big on the radio. That is how much confidence I have in you." Roxie was studying her fingertips. "Promise you will give it a try?"

There was a long pause as the fourteen-year-old slowly twisted the ring on her left little finger. Then she nodded her head.

"Actually, I can do this."

CHAPTER NINE

One-upmanship

The picnic was scheduled for noon, near the old two-story bandstand in Burlington's historical Battery Park, high above the glistening shoreline of Lake Champlain. The park was located on Battery Street, which ran north-south along the length of the shore, from the railroad yard just south of Maple Street all the way to the north end of the park. Several side streets ended at Battery Street, including Pearl Street, which terminated at the south entrance, and two blocks north, Sherman Street, which ended at a traffic circle — much like the one in Essex Junction — at the north entrance of the park. The grounds of this historical landmark were shaded by American elms, whose vase-shaped forms fanned out at the tops into gracefully arched golden boughs. Here and there, a shrub marked the edge of a sidewalk. There was a canon on display, memorializing the battle which had taken place in the waters of Lake Champlain in 1813, and a stone masonry water fountain for strolling guests on a warm afternoon. A parapet wall — also stone masonry — which was just low enough to sit on, delineated the western limits of the park. From there the view opened westward, past the treetops from the narrow slip of land for the railroad tracks below, out on past the breakwater, all the way across the lake to New York State's Adirondack Mountains.

The Foxxes were the first ones there since George was in charge of the barbecue. They set up in what was about the center of the park, making sure to stake out territory on the east side of the bandstand, where they would probably have shade for most of the afternoon. Roxie, in a soft pink shorts-and-halter outfit, lined the three folding canvas chairs in a row, then spread out a beach towel nearby, also in a shady area. Her intention was to look fetching, not to sun-bathe her sensitive skin. As soon as he had the charcoal going, George helped Marilyn set up four card tables on the uneven grassy area between the barbecue and the bandstand. By that time, a couple of other families had shown up and started to set out the napkins and paper plates, carefully anchoring them down with egg-sized stones from the drain around the bottom of the bandstand, itself.

"Anything else?" Roxie asked her mother. "I want to get in a little ukulele time."

Marilyn paused and moved in to speak softly to her daughter. "Thanks for your help." Her eyes darted to one side, then the other. "Just remember our little conversation." Roxie's nostrils flared. "No, I meant every word of it, Roxanne. No shenanigans. You behave like a nice young lady today, or there will be hell to pay." The girl's head was lowered, her narrowed eyes watching her fingertips tapping against each other. The mother put her face down close to the tapping fingertips. "They will take you away from me, if you don't stop it. Don't you understand that?" The girl nodded, and put her hands down. "Good. And thanks for helping, honey." She put her arm around the beautiful child. "I really mean that." She kissed her on the top of the head, and went back to hostess the dreaded picnic.

Don parked the car up close to the playground at the north end of the park. Since it was his day off, he intended to stay all afternoon at the picnic. Connie was with him, because it wasn't a school day. The couple exited the vehicle, each looking forward across the parapet at the beautiful view. She smiled at him over the top of their black Studebaker Champion. "Wow! It's always so gorgeous."

Don looked down the line of cars in the parking area which separated the parapet seating from the rest of the park, looking for Al Strong's white '49 Cadillac Coupe De Ville. "He's not here, yet," he told Connie.

"It's only five minutes past noon. He'll be here."

A Packard station wagon pulled into the next parking space. The Flannigans jumped out and waved. "Hey, you two!" April called out. The Collinses waved back. Bill was in uniform because he had a swing shift and would be leaving at two-fifteen, right from the picnic. April's way home was arranged. She was meeting Winnie Thompson for a movie at three o'clock at the Strong Theater on Main Street there in Burlington, and would ride home to Essex Junction with her. Bill would have his Packard woodie to get him back to his Susie Wilson home that night. The Collinses were in charge of getting the Flannigan's croquet set packed up after the picnic, so people could continue to play even after he left for work.

The four of them pulled ice chests, blankets, and folding chairs from their vehicles, and headed toward the aroma of the barbecue. George was already tending sizzling steaks over the hot coals.

Roxie raised her head from the towel where she had been lying on her stomach, going over lyrics in a student-sized spiral notebook. She blinked through the bright sunshine, then focused on the foursome approaching the picnic area. Almost immediately she identified the stride and shape of "Sir William." There he was. Her gut reaction was fierce ownership of the handsome fellow.

But something was amiss. Suddenly, she frowned. Beside him, laughing and talking, was an all-too-attractive April, in a luscious lavender-blue shorts outfit, her silvery-blonde hair, swaying and glinting in the sunlight. She was actually beautiful.

Suddenly it was a contest.

The young girl checked and saw that her mother was busy arranging the salads on one of the tables. Slowly and carefully she stood up and moved off toward Bill's direction. She stopped far enough away to catch his eye. He caught her look, and turned to his wife. "I need to get the croquet set, hon."

"Do you need any help?" April asked.

Roxie came running up. "Hi, Mrs. Flannigan! Nice to see you again." She stepped back as though to notice for the first time. "Oh my gosh, don't you look cute! That color is so perfect on you!" She did a little jiggle, and looked innocently at Bill. "Is there anything else you need to bring over?"

"Just the croquet set, princess."

"I can help you with that," she offered.

"Well, if you want to." He telegraphed a "she-wants-to-help" look to his understanding wife, and walked back to the car, the teenage girl doing her gyrating dance alongside him.

For the next hour, the games for the company's employees went into full force, with Bill and April very much involved. In fact, the Flannigans seemed to be the perfect team in the croquet competition, and truly, they had done this for years. They won round after round, exchanging "thumbs-up" and joking their way through one game after another. Roxie entered a couple of them, but was not able to hit the ball into place. At first she laughed at herself, but as failure-after-failure occurred, she gave up. She was clearly out-classed in croquet skills by the lady in lavender. In frustration, she moved back to lie carefully posed on her towel, watching the activities, and waiting to be noticed.

At intervals, potato salad, beans, and steaks were consumed, along with corn-on-the-cob, dripping with butter. People were actually enjoying the company picnic, including the joined-at-the-hip Flannigans. It was time for Roxie to bring out the ukulele. Before starting, she wiped the Chap Stick across her lips. Then, sitting cross-legged on the towel, she struck up a few chords, waiting for people to notice.

"Hey, Roxie," somebody yelled. "Give us a song!"

"What do you want to hear?"

"How about Has Anybody Seen My Gal?"

"I know that one." She went right into it. People started to sing along with her, and before long, she was leading a great little songfest, right in her glory. Finally, she asked the Flannigans if they had a special request. Bill looked a little tense. Feeling especially bold, she went to a first-name basis with his wife. "What's your favorite song, April?"

"Oh, my goodness. You probably don't even know it."

"Try me."

"Oh, okay then. It's called Just My Bill. Have you ever heard of it?"

Roxie stared at her. "I just happened to find that one, just the other day. Let me see if I can remember it."

"Really!?" April was delighted. "That's 'our song'; Bill and I danced to it at our wedding." She looked at her husband, whose face was turning a soft pink.

"Uh-huuh," the singer laughed under her breath. She picked up the ukulele and started to sing, watching his reaction out of the corner of her eye. She had gotten only into the first few lines about discovering the perfect love, when April turned toward her husband. After taking his hands and wrapping them around the back of her waist, she reached up and pulled his face down toward her own, making eye contact. Then, as she slipped her arms around his neck, she started to sway, moving her feet in a little dance. Singing along with Roxie, she teased him into a few reluctant steps of his own. Finally, the handsome one slid into movie star mode, in the spotlight, performing for his public. Now, the two of them were dancing, gliding around in the little bandstand, like Ginger Rogers and Fred Astaire — in snow shoes. The rest of the folks, caught up in the energy of the moment, erupted with raucous exhortations, cheering this comedy team on, as they kept up with one handclapped beat after another.

But the songfest leader was no longer amused.

As the song and the dance ended, Bill Flannigan was laughing, enjoying the applause, but then he suddenly checked his watch. He was due to start a swing shift at three o'clock at the bus terminal, and it was well past time for him to get going. Panicking, he asked the Collinses to grab his cooler and other items, so he wouldn't have to take time to pack them into the woodie. Don grinned and nodded. Then Bill thanked George and all the gang for a great time, blew a dramatic goodbye kiss to his wife, and hurried off to work. Swept up in the moment, Sir William never even noticed the fuming princess.

Standing quietly in the shadow of the bandstand, Georgie-Porgie watched. Roxie Foxx had been royally upstaged, and he knew that could lead to consequences. That girl never really lost a contest, because she always punished anybody who outdid her, one way or another, no matter how long she had to wait to do it. He had seen this obsessive retaliatory behavior many times. Taking a sip from his bottle of Coke, he wondered how long it would take for her to *get* April.

Somewhere around three-thirty, the Collinses noticed that Alan Strong had shown up, alone.

"Hey, Al!" Don exclaimed as he took a seat beside him on the parapet. "Glad to see you made it. Sorry to see that Mindy isn't with you." He paused. No explanation was offered. He could smell the alcohol. "We've got a good croquet game going on out there. Ever play?"

"Nah. Not my thing."

"Well, it's not for everybody," the experienced counselor observed. "I'm more of a crossword puzzle guy, myself." He waited for the reply that did not come, before he spoke again. "Had one of those delicious steaks yet?"

"Nah. Not hungry."

"Not hungry, buddy?" He leaned over to speak quietly. "You're kidding, right? Why wouldn't you want a nice steak and some potato salad, on a nice Saturday afternoon? You got something going on?" He brought a pack of gum out from his pocket, casually tapping out a stick of Wrigley's. He looked over at the silent face. "Had a meal yet, today?"

"What the hell do you care, Collins?"

The sun was now shining full force upon Battery Park, baking the lacey leaf work above the dying lawn. Croquet mallets stirred up dust with each hefty stroke, as shrieks of laughter echoed throughout the carefully marked playing field.

Don sat straight up and crossed his left leg over his right knee, pulling the left foot toward his abdomen, and holding it there. "Hmm," he said as he started to chew the stick of gum. "I guess I care because I can see that you are a pretty intelligent man, and yet, you seem to be sliding into… I don't know… some kind of depression." He looked sideways at the man with the pure white hair. "Am I right, or am I just nosey?"

Alan snorted and pulled out a flask. "You're just nosey," he said, and took a little sip.

Don let his left foot slip back down to the pavement. He leaned forward, both elbows on his knees.

"Okay, Al. I don't want to interfere in your life. After all, it *is* your life." He clasped his hands together in front of his knees. "The problem is, your life is intertwined with a whole lot of other lives, and I am sure you do not want to hurt any of those other people." He sat up straight again, a hand on each knee. "I just want you to know I am available, if you need to talk, or whatever. Is that alright with you, Alan?"

Alan chuckled to himself, shook his head, and walked off to make the one important contact of the day.

The songfest had been over for a while, the little crowd dispersed, and Roxie was alone, hunched cross-legged on the towel and studying the fingertips which were tapping just six inches from the end of her nose. Her body rocked back and forth, ever-so-slightly, and she did not seem to hear the picnickers' chatter all around her.

Somebody hit the ground with a thud, right beside the disgruntled princess. She turned to see Alan, twisting his body into a nonchalant posture beside her towel. "Hello there, Foxy Roxie," he murmured softly. She didn't like the look in his eye, but something told her to hold off. She lowered her own eyes, thinking. It took her a few seconds to put it together. Finally, she stretched her sleek body out upon the thick beach towel, inching seductively toward him.

"Hello there, **Silver-Haired Daddy of Mine**," she murmured back. "What are you up to this fine fall afternoon?"

"Talking to the **Girl of My Dreams**," he whispered.

She glanced in the direction of her mother, who was deep into the croquet game, and came back to the pitiful pale blue eyes of her suitor. "Uh-huuh!" She walked her fingers of one hand to the edge of the towel, stopping to tap them softly upon the selvedge edge. Then, with a perfect Shirley Temple pout, she looked up at him and asked in her little-girl voice, "*Am* I still your favorite dream-girl, Daddy?"

About four-thirty that afternoon on October 18, 1952, the picnickers were played out and ready to go home. One half-hour later, things were packed up and most of the people were gone. The Foxxes and the Collinses were the last to leave. Roxie slipped into the back of her parents' Chevy, and they were off toward Essex Junction. The Collinses finished packing up the items belonging to the Flannigans. It was a tight squeeze, but everything finally fit in. Don made sure their suitcase was handy, since he and Connie planned to head out along Shelburne Road, all the way to the Shelburne Inn, for a relaxing overnight stay, and then attending their Swift Street church in the morning. They pulled out of Battery

Park about five-fifteen, with the croquet set rattling in the back seat.

Nobody seemed to be able to get all the facts straight after that, but the up-shoot of the story was that this young girl had convinced Mr. Alan Strong, a Burlington Transit driver, to take her in his own private vehicle, to a bus stop out on Shelburne Road, where she could meet up with her "mentor," a Mr. William Flannigan. The girl claimed that Mr. Strong pulled off into a shrub-covered "lovers' lane" on Swift Street, and there in the shadows of dusk, raped her. After a struggle, the girl managed to escape, and came screaming and running to the bus stop at Ralph's Diner, where Personnel Manager Foxx was talking with Mr. Flannagan. Mr. Foxx, who happened to be the girl's stepfather, took her to the emergency room at Mary Fletcher Hospital. After an examination, it was determined that there had, indeed, been sexual contact. The transit officials notified the authorities.

Mr. Strong was arrested about nine-thirty that evening at his home on Florida Avenue, and taken downtown. After a phone call to his mother, bail was posted, and he was home by eleven-fifteen that night. He was to appear in court later in the week. Throughout the proceedings on this particular evening, however, he seemed very calm and uninvolved. But when he got home, he and his wife had a violent argument. It ended with her storming out of the house, suitcase in hand, to screech away in the sporty Cadillac.

The next morning, at about six o'clock, Alan Strong went out to the picnic table in his back yard to take one long, last drink from his nearly empty bottle of Four Roses Bourbon. He checked his pocket for a piece of paper, lifted his .22 caliber Iver Johnson, and shot himself through the head.

He died instantly.

CHAPTER TEN

Words

On the morning of October 19, there were more than double the usual worshippers in the barn that housed the Swift Street Pentecostal Church. By the time Don and Connie arrived from Shelburne, there was parking left only out on the side of the road. The unusual attendance level was because the guest speaker, a gentleman from Montreal, Canada, was going to preach about the Underground Railroad, and the Vermont Christians just a few miles south of this gathering, who were involved in that.

Don scanned the crowd, trying to spot the guest speaker. Just as he thought he had narrowed in on the guy, Pastor James called out to him: "Brother Don! Are you ready to witness the power of God today?"

"Are we talking miracles, here?" Connie asked her husband, as she laid their jackets on two bench spaces.

Don called out to the pastor, "It's going to be a healing service, right?"

Pastor moved quickly toward the Collinses. "A lollapalooza. I heard this precious brother on the radio. He has a powerful message." He pressed his hands together in front of his chest. "I've been praying that Jesus will be glorified in a mighty way here today."

"Alright!" Don slapped the fragile fifty-year-old clergyman so firmly on the back that the fellow had to step forward to keep his balance.

As the two men spoke, more people entered, taking the last vacant bench seats. However, some had brought folding chairs, so by the time the pastor and the couple finished their conversation, rows of believers stretched almost to the back of the fifty-foot-long building.

The pastor watched, as he confided to Don, "There are more out there than we have ever imagined, just looking for answers."

"I underst —"

A sudden hush filled the whitewashed hall. Both men turned to see what people were staring at.

There, in the entrance to this little Vermont church, stood a beautiful black man. Don had grown up in Burlington, and as far as he knew, there had been only one Negro family in the whole city. They were very quiet, and he never really thought much about them. So, when he laid eyes on this "colored" man, he was somewhat surprised as, it would seem, were most of the others in the building.

The man flashed a bright smile from his ebony countenance, then stepped aside to allow his attractive wife to enter. The statuesque woman was dressed in a white hat, and a royal purple floral-print dress with a wide, lacey white collar. In her white-gloved hands she carried a small purse, which matched her low-heeled purple shoes. The man adjusted his navy blue tie, brushing his large hand down the front of his dark blue pin-striped suit, and spoke forth a booming, "Good morning! I am Deacon Peter Foster." He wrapped his long arm around his smiling wife. "This is my wife, Rehema."

"Praise the Lord! Welcome, Brother Foster!" Pastor James went flying toward the deacon, his hand extended. As he shook the guest speaker's hand, he turned to the crowd. "This man will bring blessings to us today, according to God's Word. Come and greet our guest, my friends."

Don was third in line to shake the big man's hand. The moment he felt the strong grip of this special guest, something electric shot through his body. Slowly, he turned to make eye contact with the lovely lady called "Rehema," to find himself gazing into a golden shimmer. "Welcome," was all he could think to say. As they came away from the greeting, he whispered intensely to Connie, "O-o-o-oh my goodness, babe, there is *fire* in their eyes." The couple squeezed hands briefly as they sat down to wait for the service to begin.

Finally, the small crowd took their places on the chairs and benches, and the worship music began.

The altar area consisted of an old, but recently tuned, upright piano, a slanted lectern with a tumbler of ice water on its flat upper shelf, and a couple of stuffed chairs for the pastor and whomever else may need to be seated at any given occasion. Today, Deacon Foster sat in that chair of honor. Above the two chairs, a large varnished maple wood cross was somehow attached to the windowless wall. No further décor punctuated the plain white background. Pastor James made a few announcements, and offered the opening prayer. Then he stepped back to take a seat beside the deacon, smiling over at Mrs. Foster, who was seated in the first row. At the piano, a young woman in a pink dress struck the introduction to the chorus of the opening hymn, and all those who knew the words joined in, vowing that when the roll was called up yonder, they'd be "thay-er!"

The chorus was repeated several times, with increasing enthusiasm, until, as the final chord was struck, Pastor James jumped up from his chair and shouted, "Amen? Amen? Are we gonna be there, brothers and sisters?" The little crowd clapped and shouted another "Amen."

"I believe that. Because of the Blood of Jesus, we'll be there!" He took a breath, and turned to Deacon Foster. "And I know that our guest speaker today also believes that." He turned back to the congregation. "We are so privileged to have the Fosters with us today. There is much I could say about this gifted couple, but I feel that is not my assignment.

Because of the leading of the Holy Ghost, I'm going to let the deacon step forward at this time." He smiled at the handsome black man, then turned back to the congregation. "Would you please give a great, big welcome to our special guest speaker, Deacon Peter Foster!" He led the applause with every ounce of energy in his willowy body.

The deacon rose from the stuffed chair and strode purposefully toward the piano. The little lady in the pink dress hurried away as he slipped onto the piano bench. With one strong pounce on the keys, he looked up and boomed, "This is for you, Mighty God!" Two more pounces, and then a third, in a change of key. "For your glory, Mighty Lord!" His fingers executed a soft, tremulous vibration across the keys, rising slowly into a crescendo of arpeggio after arpeggio, to a sudden stop, and a two-second silence. Then he lifted his large hands to the heavens and took a deep breath.

Suddenly, a wordless melody of praise arose from the deepest part of his throat. It came forth in a thundering bass, starting as a curious, yet delightful melody of rippling tones, culminating in a long, sweet, soulful hum. The undulating melody rose and fell in a primitive rhythm, reminiscent of the songs of thousands of slaves, laboring in captivity all across the globe. The sonorous voice continued to create spontaneous melodic variations for several minutes. It was, at once, overwhelmingly painful and ecstatically beautiful.

The captivated Pentecostal congregation was left hanging at the sudden stop. Not a soul moved. The deacon did not shift in his seat at the piano. He stared at the keyboard for a moment.

"Go down, Moses." He spoke it softly.

The piano-playing resumed, and somewhere within the first few flourishes, Rehema started to hum in short, sweet phrases, as she moved gracefully up to join her husband. He looked up and nodded. With one more sharp downbeat on the keys, the couple slipped into the old Negro spiritual, **Go Down Moses**. He sang the lead, his deep, groaning melody accenting the ache of the words, while the woman's coloratura style rose and then fell, like a glistening starburst of fireworks, all around the heaviness of the plea, to "…let my people go." By the third verse, Moses's people were in flight from Egypt. For the rest of the spiritual the couple switched solos, ending as a duet at the end of this story. Then it was over.

Caught up in this mysterious new sweetness to what had been heretofore a familiar old Negro spiritual, the brothers and sisters sat enthralled. They had never heard anything like it. They sat quietly as Rehema moved away to resume her seat, assisted by the pastor as she stepped off the eight-inch-high wooden platform. He went back to his pastor's seat as the deacon strolled over to the lectern, hands behind his back, no prepared notes and, apparently, no agenda. The tall, muscular man of God raised his head, gazing high above the little gathering before him, and in a powerful, stentorian voice, he began to enlighten them.

"Ladies and gentlemen, I would wager that you think you've just heard a spiritual about Moses's and the Israelites' flight from Egypt, and, in fact, that is what appears to be the case. But there is much more to this song than meets the eye." His smile was a sly one. "If you are a history buff, or have Negro ancestry in this country, you know what I'm talking about." The sly one leaned forward on the lectern. "*You* know that the words to this old spiritual are all in *code*." He waited, enjoying the surprised expressions. "Yes, that is correct." He stood upright and moved around to the side of the pulpit. "This whole thing is actually code talk for Underground Railroad activities." A hum went up from the listeners. "Let me show you." He ticked off the interpretations on his fingers. "The term, 'Israelites,' in the song was the code word for 'slaves,' and the 'Pharaoh' actually referred to the slave-owners. Do you get the connection there?" Another hum. "So, we have, 'Slave-owner, let my slave-family go free, or else.'" A soft shuffle as folks moved appreciatively in their seats. "And when it came to 'Moses,' well, most folks believe that was the code name for Harriet Tubman, probably the bravest, most successful rescuer of slaves in the whole Underground Railroad operation." He lifted a teaching finger toward the congregation. "And 'Go down,' referred to her many trips into the South on these missions. Of course, she was also a scout, a spy, a soldier, and a nurse, working undercover with both sides of the Civil War, so she was quite a 'Moses,' wouldn't you agree?" Once again, he smiled. "A woman of great resourcefulness, and even greater compassion, for certain."

Amens could be heard throughout the hall.

"And while we are at it, we should be made aware of a few other spirituals that were also filled with secret code words that these slaves used to encourage themselves. For instance, I am taught that the two popular spirituals, **The Gospel Train**, and **Swing Low, Sweet Chariot** were secretly referring to escape via that very means. When you have a moment, take the time to read the lyrics to these two songs. I'm sure you will be surprised. **The Gospel Train** is pretty obvious; **Swing Low...** is a little more covert, referring to a 'station' on the Ohio River, where 'a band of angels' were 'coming after me' across the 'Jordan.'" He hesitated just long enough for them to catch their breath. "And on that note, let me tell you, briefly, about just one of those fleeing slaves, and how your lovely state of Vermont played a notable part in his rescue."

He went on to relate how this young black boy had made it all the way into Vermont, finding sanctuary in the vicinity of Ferrisburgh, just twenty miles south of this little church. "Yes, down what you now call United States Highway Number Seven — also named Shelburne Road. There, a Quaker family hired him, enabling the lad to save up the finances whereby he could escape the country to find a more secure freedom in the nation of Canada." He smiled softly. "It took four years to get what was then called 'a stake,' to get him started on a new life up there across the border. All during that time, these kind folks took good care of him."

"Only once did he have to hide from the slave-hunters. Those avid antislavery locals concealed him in the old, abandoned Brick Academy on the Robinson property, where he endured three days hidden inside a slatted storage crate, before the hunters — who had no legal rights in this slave-free state in the first place — finally gave up and moved on." Deacon Foster pulled a folded white handkerchief from his breast pocket and slowly dabbed across his brow. "But, in those four years, this young man was not only planning and surviving, he was also learning about the goodness of God's people, and the goodness of God, Himself. It was something he remembered, long after he finally managed to cross that northern border. Sometime in 1859, he settled in a small town just outside the city of Montreal." The deacon smiled softly. "His name was Joshua Foster, and he was my grandfather."

Once again, the congregation chorused its appreciation.

At the same time, perceiving the speaker's excellent elocution, delivered at a carefully measured rhythm, Don whispered into his wife's ear, "This man is not just a speaker, he's an orator. Wow."

"Shh-h-h," she said.

Deacon Foster continued his story, deliberately delivered at a slow and eloquent pace. "My grandfather, Joshua, was one of those slaves who had been fortunate enough — even blessed, it perhaps may be said — to have been taught the very basics of reading, writing, and arithmetic. He received this instruction at the knee of a precious little slave-nanny whose main task on the plantation, rare though it was, included assisting in the education of the slave master's children. To do this, she had been taught these fundamentals as a very young child, herself. Keen young woman that she was, she recognized the value of such knowledge, and secretly determined to pass this treasure on to a certain inquisitive young boy, who also happened to be her only child." He turned to sweep a long arm across the breadth of his audience as he spoke. "Aaah, yes, brothers and sisters, it is a fallen world in which we live. Adam and Eve did none of us any favors. Sin abounds, and innocent hearts are broken." He grasped both sides of the lectern and bowed his head. "And when it was discovered that she had secretly educated this little black boy, the woman was beaten, and her precious Joshua was sold to a new master, all the way over at the western border of the state." He paused, his head still down. When he lifted it again, the tone of voice was more hopeful.

"But God is good. Up there in the Montreal area, Joshua found employment as a clerk in a dry goods store, married and fathered three children. The last child was born in 1869, and that bouncing baby boy was my dear father, Daniel Alonzo Foster." He reached for the ice water, holding it a few inches in front of his mouth. "That baby was exceedingly handsome, of course. Much like me," he said, teasing a polite chuckle from the crowd. He gazed sideways at the amused listeners as he took a slow, gentlemanly sip, moving his eyebrows up and down mischievously, just once, above those twinkling eyes.

Over the next few minutes, the deacon related how all three children had finished high school, and how the family had eventually bought the dry goods business, turning it into more modernized merchandise. Foster's Hardware Store became a thriving business, Daniel Foster married in 1898 and had a handsome son the very next year. The twinkle returned. "… and by the time I graduated from high school, there was money for college. Praise God for His infinite mercy. I was the first one in the family to go on to a teaching career."

"Oh! He's a certified teacher," Connie whispered.

"How about that." Don glanced around and caught more than a few surprised folks whispering the same sort of thing to their neighbors. This was something different — an educated black man, right here in their little church. All eyes turned back to the speaker, who was humbly standing with hands joined behind his back, his eyes fixed momentarily on the floor in front of him. When he raised his gaze to meet that of the crowd, mere courtesy had given way to admiration.

The teacher continued: "I have taken time to tell you my grandfather's story to illustrate the goodness of God, Himself." He cocked his head to one side. "It's the goodness of God that makes each of us realize that there is something uplifting, even in the midst of terrible circumstances. It shows us the bottom line in life. We operate in a struggle between good and evil, between God and the devil, between compassionate love and unmerciful hatred."

He stood up straight and waited, looking slowly from his left to right, his hands slowly descending to his sides. Then he ambled back toward the podium, where he turned to ask the bottom line question. "Where are *you* operating, my friend — in the love of a compassionate God, or the horror of an unmerciful devil?"

Assuming this man of God had a point to make, they waited for him to answer the question for them. Instead, he asked another question. "Are you a slave, or a free soul? Are you bound in the chains of despair, or are you resting in the confidence that you are free to receive His loving promises? Think carefully, now! Do you actually believe His Word is, as the Bible says, alive and powerful enough to fulfill His compassionate answers to your needs?"

They waited, again.

"How can you doubt God's goodness today? We have all kinds of evidence of His compassion. Look at the blood sacrifice of His Son, Jesus. Look at the self-sacrifice of His faithful servants, like the martyred saints in biblical history. What about recent history, with people like Harriet Tubman? And now… today… did you not hear the soulful song that my wife, "Compassion" just helped me to sing?"

Suddenly, he raised an apologetic hand. "Oh, yes, I forgot to tell you. This dear lady, my wife, has a name that is very meaningful. It is Rehema. That is from the Swahili language, and translates into the English word, 'compassion.'" He fixed his gaze upon her, and slowly nodded. "And that is truly who she is — a person of compassion and insight." He spoke lovingly. "That is why she is such a wonderful nurse. Not only does she minister to the physical needs of a person, but she has a gift to see into a wounded heart." He bowed his head. "Indeed, that would include most of us, would it not?" He cleared his throat.

Don caught the whispered comment from his wife. "And *she's* a nurse! Oh, my."

The deacon moved on.

"I am thinking that many of you sensed this gift as we sang a few minutes ago. Did you not hear the compassion, the hope radiating from this woman's lovely soul? Did you hear the encouragement, my friends?" He smiled at the next thought. "If so, then you have been freed, brothers and sisters, and you are free — do I dare declare it? — to be healthy and wholesome, both in spirit and in body." He drew his Bible from inside the lectern. "So now, let's consider the subject of miraculous healings."

The tap on Don's shoulder was not received well.
"What?"
The next tap was more irritating than the first.
"Oh, for Pete's sake, not now..."

When he turned to see who was disturbing this teaching, his attention was instantly refocused. April's eyes telegraphed the urgency of the interruption. Don grabbed Connie's hand, and led her out of the meeting, following April out to the roadside parking area. The woman was crying by the time they stopped to talk at the edge of the road.

"Oh Lord Jesus... I am so sorry to tell you this..." She sniffed softly. "But, Alan... Alan Strong committed suicide early this morning."

The Collinses gasped together.

"Marilyn Foxx is insisting that you counsel Roxie immediately." April dabbed her nose with the back of her hand. "Roxie... she was involved."

There wasn't enough time to properly mourn for an unsaved soul, although the thought passed through both their minds. Instead, it was decided Connie would ride back to Winooski with April, who would fill her in on the details. Don jumped into the Studebaker and hightailed it for the nearest privacy of a phone booth, which happened to be the one out in front of Ralph's Diner. After getting a sketchy version of what had happened from her, Don agreed to meet Marilyn, along with Roxie, at his office at one o'clock that afternoon. It was five minutes to noon when he pulled out onto Shelburne Road and headed for Florida Avenue.

***

By the time he pulled into the driveway, the sky had turned into a deep gray canopy and humidity hung heavily in the air. It would most certainly rain before this autumn day was over. April had parked the woodie to one side in the driveway, and the back end was opened, ready to take in the picnic items they had left for the Collinses to pack up in Battery Park. Beads of sweat dotted Don's brow as he proceeded to unload. The moist heat taxed his strength and cut his breath short, but finally the job was done. April backed her vehicle out, waved, and took off for Essex. Connie grabbed the suitcase and disappeared inside the still-cool house. At that point Don realized he had forgotten to grab the croquet set from the back seat, and would have to return it to the Flannigans later. He decided to roll the rattling rack around to the back door, just inside the screened-in patio, where he would see it and be reminded to get it back to them. It was twelve forty-five, and there was just time to step into the bathroom and rinse his face in cold water, before the Foxxes would show up.

They arrived at five minutes to one. When Connie answered the door, she was surprised to see all three of them. Both Marilyn and Roxie were wearing sleeveless tops and shorts, but George was suffering the sticky heat through his heavy Burlington Transit uniform. Noting how the girl was clinging closely to her mother, Connie quickly surmised that George had had to drive the car. She was glad she had taken time to make a pitcher of lemonade, and she brought it out into the living room on a tray with three glasses. After she offered the refreshing drink to all three, she ushered Marilyn and Roxie down into the cool of the basement office.

Only George had been interested in the lemonade. He sat back and surveyed the room, sipping slowly from the frosty glass. The place was decorated in an eclectic style — a little of this, and a little of that — but it all seemed to come together in a comfortable mix of earthy browns, tans, and off-whites. George was not into décor. He yawned, wiped the sweat off his forehead, and leaned back in an overstuffed chair. Muffled conversation rose softly from the floor below. He listened, trying to hear what was being said, but to no avail. Giving up, he turned his attention to a magazine from the coffee table, *Better Homes and Gardens*. He groaned, but flipped past all those words, checking out the chicks in the photos and ads.

A few minutes later, the door bell chime startled him. He looked up through the small windows at the top of the door, spotting an official insignia of some sort, obviously on a hat. It moved slightly, as Connie came bounding up the stairs to answer the door. Chief Rob Allen removed his hat and returned her greeting.

"Hate to bother you, but I was told I could find George Foxx here?"

"Oh! Yes, he's here," she replied as she motioned him inside.

The officer held out his hand and the two men exchanged a handshake as George was rising from the chair. "Oh no, just stay where you are," Robbie said. "I'm Chief Rob Allen, from Essex Junction. I have just a couple of questions about last night. This won't take long." Seeing the worried look on George's face, he hastened to reassure him. "You're not in any trouble, sir. I mostly need to know if there is anything we can do to help you and your family. I understand you reside in Indian Acres development; is that correct?"

George nodded.

"If you don't need me here, I am needed downstairs," Connie said politely.

"Do you mind if we two guys have a few minutes in your living room?" the chief asked.

"Not at all… go right ahead. Have some lemonade, if you like." She slipped back down the stairs.

Rob Allen sat down heavily upon the sofa beside George's chair. Lifting his damp shirt slightly off his chest, he looked at the lemonade on the coffee table in front of him, then at George. "That stuff any good?"

"Cold and wet," the man answered.

"That'll work." He poured half a glass and took a long draw from it. "Not bad." Wiping his mouth with the tips of his fingers, he grinned at George. "Would be better with a shot of something southern-tasting, though, don't you think?"

A cautious smile broke out on the swarthy countenance as the man lifted his glass in a salute. The young chief leaned back and pressed the cold glass against his midriff. He breathed in slowly, then spoke sympathetically. "Well, your family is going through quite a hard time right now, sir." Noting the nod of agreement, he continued: "In the brotherhood of law officers, word gets around fast. I got the news about two hours ago. Since your family lives within my jurisdiction, I felt I should get in touch with you, see if there was anything I could help you with." The man looked confused. "Well, like maybe we could do a drive-by for a few days — make sure she's safe at home and at school. Make sure you aren't being harassed by students who get wind of this… that sort of thing." The man looked like he hadn't thought of that. "Is there anything you need, Mr. Foxx?"

"I guess I'm more concerned about what this is going to do to my job. All that bad press about this transit company could get me fired. Then it wouldn't matter about drive-bys, 'cause we would have to move again."

Rob set his glass down on the beverage tray in the center of the coffee table. "Let me reassure you, Mr. Foxx, this matter has already been handled. Like I said, word gets around fast, and I happen to know that some higher-ups in both Burlington and Winooski have already pulled some strings, and there will be no mention of this incident in the local paper or on the radio stations." The man looked relieved. Rob saw the apprehension fade and went for the clincher. "Is there anything else you need, sir? I promise you that I'll do my best to help you in any way I can."

The man relaxed and leaned forward. "I think I need to have you stop calling me 'Mr. Foxx, sir,'" he said. "My name is George."

"Thanks, George." Successful at breaking the ice, the chief leaned back again, looking around the cool room. "Man, I could just sit right here for the rest of the day. Or at least until after it rains."

"Yeah, me, too. That bus barn will be sweltering right about now."

"You working on a Sunday, George?"

"Not usually. Had to go in to get another driver to take Alan's place." His head fell slowly forward. "Poor, stupid S.O.B." He was silent for a little bit, then wiped the corner of one eye.

Chief Rob leaned forward. "How're you holding up, yourself?"

The ebony-topped head moved back and forth in disbelief. "I'm just so tired of chasing around after that brat."

"Roxie?"

George nodded. "We got home from the company picnic, and pretty soon she says she's tired and going to bed." He raised a darkened face. "Little liar." He lowered his voice. "About eight-thirty, I peeked into her room. It looked like she was in the bed, but I had this feeling. Told Marilyn to go check on her. Marilyn came back out with two pillows in her hands. She started screaming and carrying on." He shook his head again. "What the hell could I do? I went out looking for her."

"Wow. Where the heck would you even start? I mean, has she done this before?"

"Oooh, yeah. Driving us nuts, that one." He was still speaking in a lowered voice. "Anyway, I was pretty sure where I could find her."

"Really?"

"Headed right out to Shelburne Road, all the way to Ralph's Diner. Parked in the back. Stayed there until Bill Flannigan swung his bus into the parking lot. I was there at the bus door when he cranked it open. You should have seen his face." He cast a withering look at an imaginary Sir William. "I told him to get back into the driver's seat; there would be no bathroom break on this run. He started whining 'What's wrong? What's the problem?' I told him to shut up and sit there until I told him to move." George looked straight at the chief. "I thought the guy was going to throw up, right then and there.'

"Is that right?" the chief urged him on.

"What is it about these stupid, immature men?" He set his empty glass down on the table. "They're social retards. A few months of flattery from a good-looking chick and they fly high in a fantasy world of 'Mr. Wonderful.' Then, when reality finally slams them into the sidewalk, they cry like babies."

"Guys like that have a self-esteem problem."

"Big time."

"That makes them bait for predators like..." The chief didn't want to finish the sentence.

George suddenly saw it. "Yeah," he murmured. "That is exactly what she is." The head shook slowly, again.

The policeman let that solemn thought settle in for a minute. Then he opened the door to more details. "Sooo, where did you find her?"

The stepfather looked surprised. "Oh, I guess you didn't hear that part of the story." He sat up straight. "Well, the two of us just stayed right there in our places, him in the driver's seat, me standing hidden in the stairwell of the bus. Then, pretty soon, we hear this wailing and running steps, coming closer and closer. I told him to keep his mouth shut, so he kept his head down. And then we could hear her crying and wailing, 'He raped me... he raped me,' and running so hard, she was out of breath by the time she rounded the front of the bus and nearly fell into my open arms." He held his hands palms outward, as if to stop something from hitting his chest. Then he looked straight at the chief again. "And you should have seen the look on *her* face... like, 'What are you doing here?' And, get this: *she forgets to keep crying.*"

"Hmmm." The chief made a mental note.

"So, I told Bill to continue on his route because I could handle this. Then I took her by the hand, all sympathy, and drove her over to the ER for an exam." He grinned. "She couldn't do a damned thing about it, either. I just happened to be there, and did the 'good daddy' thing." He folded his arms in deep satisfaction. "I don't know what she told the authorities, but she never got to play the damsel-in-distress for Sir William. You know, trying to get back his full attention, after she got ignored at the picnic." He looked at the cop. "Ever seen his wife? She's a real looker, that one." He laughed. "I could see, the kid thought she really needed to do something desperate to make sure she stayed in first place with this guy."

The door at the bottom of the basement stairs opened, and there were footsteps ascending slowly. George leaned over and whispered, "This conversation never took place. She *punishes* people, that one."

Marilyn led Roxie by the hand out into the living room. Those two were followed by Connie and Don. Roxie spotted the chief and put on her "victim" face as she slipped under the protective arm of her mother. The two gentlemen stood as the women entered the room. George looked at his beautiful wife. "You girls okay?" Marilyn nodded, waved the two men to be seated, then turned to Connie.

"Would it be all right if I took a couple of sips of that cold lemonade?"

"Oh my goodness! Of course. Here, let me get a couple more glasses," she said as she went back to the kitchen.

"Mom, I need to use the restroom," the girl whispered. Marilyn pointed the way, and Roxie walked slowly past the chief who was once again seated on the sofa. She looked back suspiciously at him as she left the room, as though prompted by a primitive instinct, and sure enough, caught him in what she thought was a leering once-over. She smirked, then went down the hallway where, on the left, a bathroom connected two bedrooms. She noticed that the other end of the hall opened up back into the kitchen, and the way to the back door.

The adults settled down to partake of the lemonade, now rejuvenated by ice cubes. Don introduced Chief Allen to Marilyn. George piped up with an encouragement for the distraught mother. "The chief will be looking out for Roxie for a few days, hon. Also, anything we may need."

Marilyn wasn't sure how she felt about that, but thanked the chief politely.

"We hope things went well for you in this counseling session today," the chief said. "And, as bad as things seem to be right now, I can tell you that I have seen worse than this, and it has turned out surprisingly well for all concerned parties." Then he related a similar case which had occurred some years earlier, over in Colchester. The story took several minutes to tell, but was a profoundly encouraging one, leaving Marilyn hopeful. The Collinses were both glad the officer had taken the time to help this worried mother. Then it was time to leave.

That's when they noticed Roxie had not returned from the restroom. Marilyn jumped to her feet and rushed to find the bathroom empty. "She's not here!" she yelled, heading for the other end of the hall. Connie met her at the back door and the two of them went out to the screened-in patio. No Roxie. They began to call her. Don went out to the back lawn, while the other two men went out the front door. The cars in the driveway were checked, then the garage. Suddenly, Don called out, "I see her!" The rest of them ran to where he was standing in the green area, staring across several back yards. There, Roxie was poised like a statue, looking at the picnic table where Alan Strong had killed himself. She had crossed the barrier of tape which protected the death scene.

Marilyn ran toward her. "Roxanne! Get away from there! You're not supposed to go past the tape."

The girl pivoted around, her curls whipping wildly in the heavy wind, and looked with disgust at her mother. "So?"

The Foxxes said a hasty goodbye, and were soon headed back to Essex Junction. The other three were standing next to the police car which was parked behind the Studebaker. It was time for him to leave, also, but the chief had a couple of things to say before he left. He flipped his police hat in his hands. His eyes followed the skittering leaves across the cement driveway as he spoke.

"I don't know what that young lady told you during this counseling session today, but I do happen to know what she told the authorities. She said Alan Strong raped her." He flipped the hat again. "That's what she said." A gust of wind lifted the front tuft of blond hair from his brow. He repeated his statement: "That's what she *said*."

He glanced up to see whether they were paying attention. "She also said there was a struggle, where she had tried to protect herself." He looked right at Don Collins. "Those are her very words. She said them."

He studied the hat in his hands for a moment.

"But I believe she is lying. I believe there was sex, yes, but I believe it was consensual, and I believe it was a set-up to punish Mr. Strong for some sort of offense — Heaven only knows what, and we may never know." A gold leaf rose and fell in front of his face, causing the man to step back just a bit. Recovering, he continued. "And somewhere in the mix of this whole situation there was probably the goal to get a whole lot of attention from Bill Flannigan, whose route she *deliberately* showed up on, all defiled and victimized."

He put the hat on his head and opened the car door. "I do question her motives for showing up on Flannigan's bus route, but why do you believe it wasn't rape, Chief?" Don wanted to know.

The officer slipped into the driver's seat and closed the door before he answered through the open window. "There was no struggle."

"And how do you know that?" Connie asked.

Chief Rob Allen turned the key in the ignition, then leaned his head out the window and spoke what was so obvious. "No bruises. Not even one."

CHAPTER ELEVEN

Maneuvers

The rain began with a trickle, tapping gently on the little porch roof of the stucco house. Bill Flannigan was sitting in the wicker rocker out there, smoking a cigarette. He had not rested well the night before, and then the news of Alan's death early this morning sent him into an even deeper gloom. Charley lay on the cool cement floor, resting in the shadow of the wrought-iron table with the round leather-covered top. His soulful brown eyes watched his master's hand move to tap hot cinders into the metal ashtray. As the rain increased, the toy poodle raised his little head to sniff the moisture. Suddenly he jumped to his feet, tail wagging. Bill turned to see the woodie backing off Susie Wilson Road into the driveway. His wife steered the tailgate as close to the garage as she could, and Bill remembered, begrudgingly, that the picnic items needed to unloaded. He was in no mood for that.

April jumped out of the car, holding her large purse over her head against the increasing downpour. She skipped through the damp splatter and up the two steps onto the porch. "We can unload later," she suggested. "It won't rain forever."

Bill nodded. "Heard anything else?"

"Nope. Not really." She paused, remembering. "Oh yes, Roxie was supposed to meet with her counselor this afternoon." She was brushing the raindrops off her bare arms. "How are you doing? Did you get some sleep?"

"Oh, for Pete's sake." He took a drag on the cigarette, then spoke through the exhaling smoke. "Why don't they leave her alone? She doesn't need that right now."

"Apparently, her mother thinks she does."

"Her mother," he sneered, "doesn't have a clue."

She tilted her blonde head to one side, curious. "What do you mean, she 'doesn't have a clue'? About what?"

"About that sadistic pothead she's married to," the pseudo-James Dean growled through his teeth. "She has no idea."

She stared at him, waiting for a long roll of crackling thunder to stop. "George Foxx smokes pot?"

"Yeah, George Foxx smokes pot, and he has a filthy mind." The look in his eye was alarming. She could not decide if it was hatred or fear, or maybe a little of both, but she had seen it before.

The rain was coming down hard now, splattering off the porch railings to create little rivulets of water across the gray porch floor. Seeing the dog jump up to escape them, she reached down and brought him up into the shelter of her arms. The downpour was in full force, so noisy she had to bend closer to Bill to continue the conversation.

"Who told you all that?" she called out over the brain-jarring rattle. He ground the cigarette butt into the ashtray as he rose, then pulled open the front door, motioning her to get inside. As he closed the door behind them, he looked wearily into her deep blue eyes.

"I am so tired. I am just so tired, April." Without another word, he shuffled off to the small bedroom.

She had not seen him in this shape since he came back from South Korea, where he had been a flight mechanic at Suwon Air Base, with the 4th Fighter-Interceptor Wing. The outfit had moved there from Japan in what most people thought was more a political strategy than it was a war maneuver. Nevertheless, it was there he had become a close buddy to

Lieutenant James Daley, an F-86 Sabre pilot, and one of only a few trusted friends in his life. The pilot would take Bill out for a beer now and then, each time announcing to the bartender, "Let's have a beer over here, for the guy who keeps me safe and sound every single, damned flight!" Bill worried a lot, because supplies were slow in coming, and he had to do a lot of jury-rigging to keep those planes up and running. Then one day both the lieutenant and his swept wing fighter jet did not return from combat. It was an overwhelming loss, and one which he blamed first, on himself, and secondly, on the United States government.

And then Bill had come home from a war that was never clearly won — certainly not the heroic finish of WWI or WWII. The sad thing about it was that all this man had ever wanted to be, was a real, live war hero. Instead, he carried the triple stigma of grief, failure, and shame. He felt betrayed. And now, somehow, this incident at the bus company had triggered that whole ugly thing, again. But he was more than just tired. He was fearful on a whole, new level.

"Why is he so terrified, Charley?" She snuggled her face against the dog's silky head. He gave her a lick across her forehead and poked his cold nose under the warmth of her long hair at the side of her neck. Without disturbing him, she laid her purse on the coral-colored Formica of the kitchen shelf, and then stood quietly gazing through the rainwater rippling across the kitchen window.

It was a fierce storm, much like those which followed muggy summer afternoons around the Lake Champlain region. Only now it was the middle of October, the peak color season for the autumn pageantry of the Vermont hills. As she stroked the little dog's curly back, she worried that the savagery of this storm would pound and decimate the foliage. This most certainly would be the end of the New England fall tourist season — an ending that would come all too soon — much like the stormy end of the life of Alan Strong.

"I wonder where his wife is," she whispered.

So did a lot of other people.

During the phone call to Principal Randy Marvin at two forty-five that afternoon, the question came up.

"We don't think she knows yet, sir."

"So she probably is not aware of a relationship between this girl and her husband?"

Connie hesitated. "We don't know that, either." She cleared her throat. "I just thought I should alert you to what's happened, in case anything comes up tomorrow at school."

"We won't move on this situation unless the parents ask us," he said. "And since this student is already being counseled by your husband, I don't think the authorities will require that we get involved in that part of it. At most, I believe we will be expected to watch for problems, either from Roxanne, herself, or another student."

"I understand." She hoped that would not happen. "Is there anything else, Mr. Marvin?"

"Can't think of anything at the moment. I appreciate your call, Mrs. Collins."

***

Very early on Monday morning, however, the Cadillac showed up in the Strong's driveway. Mindy disembarked and made her way to the front door, only to encounter a security lock on the doorknob. She stood there for a moment, then strolled around the house toward the back door. She stopped short at the sight of the police tape which stretched all the way from the back door of the house, around the picnic table, and then back to the very same door. It had obviously been beaten down by the heavy rain the evening before, but there it was. Confused, she stood there for a few minutes, looking left and right, trying to make sense of it all.

Then she had a thought.

She approached the picnic table. Not too far out, it became obvious there was some kind of washed-out stain across the top of the white table. Something made her stop in her tracks.

"Oh, no…"

Still, she needed to be sure of what she was seeing, and so she moved slowly toward the soiled table. At one point she stopped, but then she moved once more, closer… and… closer, until she was within the taped-off area.

"Don't go there, Mindy!" The command shocked her to a standstill. She gasped and turned to see Don Collins in his bathrobe, standing on the green near his own back yard.

"That is still an officially protected death scene. You should not be there, and should not touch anything."

"Death scene?" she asked.

He tightened the cord around his robe. "Come on over, and Connie and I will explain."

Meanwhile, Connie was on the phone to the police department, informing them that Alan's wife had finally shown up. No sooner had Don and Connie filled Mindy in on what had happened, than there was a police officer at their front door.

"We need to get a statement from you, Mrs. Strong. There was a suicide note. We need to ask you about that."

She sat up straight in her chair. "A suicide note?" Seeing the plain manila envelope in the officer's hand, she asked, "Do you have it with you?"

The officer opened the envelope and pulled out a couple of 8 x 10 photos. "These are not the actual materials, but just so you can see."

She looked at the one picturing a scribbled note. As she read it, her face flushed with anger, but no words came forth.

"So, who is 'Lizzy'?"

"What?"

"It says, 'Hey, Lizzy!' Who is she?"

She studied the scrawled note again, and slowly answered. "Um, that would be me. It's… it's something hateful he used to do. He knew I hated that name."

"So what does he mean by, 'Too bad about the insurance'?"

She held out her hand, silently demanding to see the other photo. The man handed it over, a knowing look in his eye.

She got an "Aw, damn" look on her face.

It was a photo of a blood-splattered insurance document. She recognized the company name. Alan had somehow found it, and he had known about the half-million life insurance policy she had taken out on him… and now the police knew, as well.

"Oh well, like it even matters…"

She handed the photo back to the policeman, a smug look on her face. "It's not worth the paper it's written on. It doesn't go into effect until six months after you take it out. It still has two more months to go." She stood up to leave. "You really should read your 'evidence' a little more carefully." As she opened the Collinses' front door, the policeman reminded her that they still needed a statement from her.

"Subpoena me," she said.

The officer followed her, still talking. The Collinses watched as he dogged her back around the corner toward her car. When they could no longer hear them, Don closed the door.

"Not one tear," he said.

"Well, she did say she needed to buy some time. Now I know why." Connie went back into the bedroom to get ready for a Monday at school. "And she never did get to raking up those leaves," she commented.

***

Cecil Thompson stood on the back porch of the house, looking at the leaves scattered across the driveway all the way to the barn. The beauty of the red maple had not survived the storm the evening before. It stood at the north end of the muddy drive, forlorn and nearly bare, signaling the twilight of this New England farmer's favorite season. He drew deeply on the Camel cigarette, then blew the smoke back out through his nostrils.

Fall was a time for rewards. It was the end of a hot, sweaty time in the hayfields, and a time of reaping the modest harvest from the garden which he, Winnie, and Uncle had so faithfully tended all those months. Now the hayloft was full, and Winnie, after a long summer of picking and washing and sorting, was almost finished with the canning. A few more pumpkins and squash, and that would be pretty much it. That was a good thing, because when Winnie got stressed, she did not sleep well. Over the years, he had caught her walking in her sleep on more than one occasion.

Uncle stepped out of the milk house doorway, pausing to rinse his barn boots at the water hose looped against the wall. Milking was done. It was seven o'clock on this Monday morning. Cecil could smell the bacon Winnie was cooking back there in the kitchen. While the three of them usually took turns preparing breakfast, she had insisted on doing it today. There was a reason for that, which Cecil could not remember at the moment.

Now Uncle joined his boss on the porch. Cecil put the cigarette out in an inverted tin screw-on jar cover, which had been attached with a single nail through the center, to the flat top of the porch rail.

"Did you remember the salve for Ruby?" he asked. Uncle nodded. "Poor old girl," Cecil said.

The two men stepped inside, both removing their boots and digging their toes into well-worn slippers before washing up. They took turns at the laundry tub Cecil had plumbed into the outer wall of the bathroom, each performing his own splashing, soaping, and rinsing. They shared the towel draping over the top of the wringer washing machine Winnie kept snuggled between the sink and the stairway wall. When they all finally sat down, Winnie and Uncle crossed themselves, more out of habit than in reverence, and they began to eat.

Cecil reported on the lack of progress the oldest milk cow was having. "It's too hard to milk her now. If she gets much worse, we'll have to put her down." He spread some of Winnie's strawberry jam on a half-slice of her homemade bread. "Well, at least we'll have some hamburger for a while." It was when he paused in a moment of silence that he noticed Winnie had turned off the radio. He motioned with his head. "How come that thing's turned off?"

She tossed her head. "Too much jabbering going on. Giving me a headache."

Uncle, who was eating the whites around the golden center of a fried egg, looked up in surprise. "You got a headache, you? Since when do you get a gawdim headache, anyways?"

Cecil suddenly remembered something. He took a sip of the odd-tasting orange juice Winnie had made from a can of that new-fangled frozen concentrate. The glass was promptly put down and pushed away from his plate. He cleared his throat, trying to get back to the subject. "Maybe there's something bothering her," he suggested to the retired Army veteran. "I'm sure you can relate to that… you know, like having a bad morning." Then he leaned back in his chair, preparing for what he knew would be fascinating. He wasn't sure whether it was a cultural thing, or just something peculiar to the relationship between these two, but he had seen the interaction played out before. Still, it never grew old or boring, and he always observed it with a great appreciation of what he concluded were "Abenaki ways."

Uncle popped the whole yolk into his mouth, slowly mushing it around in there until it was thoroughly tasted and ready for swallowing. Until that was accomplished, his little brown eyes were nearly closed. But finally, he looked up at her. "You got a worry, you?" he asked respectfully.

She looked down at her half-eaten breakfast. "You have spoken rightly, my uncle," she said in the Abenaki murmur.

Uncle's attention was suddenly undivided. He put down his fork and waited.

Without raising her head, Winnie continued. "There was a phone call last night. It was after you went upstairs to bed. I didn't want to bother your night's rest." She sensed his thankful nod. "I am sorry to tell you it was about your friend, the bus driver with the white hair." She crossed herself again, letting her hand rest a second upon her lips before she spoke. "He has passed over."

The Abenaki warrior sat up straight in his chair, staring at the top of her head. His breathing was short and tight. At length he inquired sternly, "What happened to this friend who respected me?" She winced as his words bounced off the white wainscoting behind her. Then, taking a short breath, she answered him softly in the cadence of her native language.

"I'm so sorry to tell you, my uncle, that he took his own life."

Cecil saw the features go hard, and turned his gaze elsewhere. The little man needed a moment of privacy. Still, he did not move from his seat at the table, caught up in the moment, and at the same time, marveling that Uncle uttered not one single swear word during this brief exchange. For some strange reason, it was always like that when they went into "Abenaki mode."

"I will speak to the one who brought you this news," the warrior finally said.

✳

"How did he take it?" the chief inquired of Lily White.

She shrugged. "Sometimes it's hard to tell with those folks. But Winnie is his closest family, and that was probably the best way to handle it." She steered the rolling desk chair under her, back to the call board, glancing for flashing lights. "What do you think we can accomplish by talking with him?"

"Just going in through the back door, Lily. This guy probably knows a little something that could give us a clue as to what really happened. The least we could do is clear Alan Strong's name." He glanced out the window to the small parking area, then turned toward his desk.

"Winnie is dropping him off on her way to work," the perky dispatcher told him. "Should be here any minute." Secretly, she wondered why Chief Rob was so interested in clearing the name of some little-known bus driver, but she knew her boss, and she was sure he was making a very calculated move. "Sometimes this is a really fun place to work," she whispered to herself.

A light flashed on the board. She reached down and pulled a cord upward, plugging it in to connect with the caller. She listened intently, then laughed. "Okay, we'll get right on it." After a quick look out the window toward the five-cornered junction, she called out, "The Donahue's dog is out in the traffic circle again, Chief."

"Chasing cars?"

"Ay-yuh."

"Good. Maybe somebody will run over that stupid mutt." She snickered as he wearily followed up, "Call that woman and tell her she has to keep him tied up, or else."

"Yessir!"

When she turned around from making the call to Mrs. Donahue, Uncle was standing right behind her at the intake desk.

"Mr. Smart!" she sang out the signal to the chief. Rising from her chair, she pointed him toward the boss's desk. "The chief is waiting for you." She looked around for a heavy paper cup near the coffee pot on the desk. "May I bring you a cup of coffee?"

Before he could answer, the chief was there, shaking his hand. "Mr. Smart, right?" The man nodded. "Come have a seat." He looked back at Lily. "If you have a minute, it would be nice to have some nice, hot coffee, Lily."

"Shu-uu-ure thing, sir," she said, as she reached over to plug into another flashing light.

Chief Robbie Allen recognized the man immediately. Although there had never been any encounters, he knew this was the man with the "drunken Indian" reputation in the little village of Essex Junction. The man had never done anything more than buy wine and French fries every Friday afternoon, partaking of his dining indulgences in the shadows of the train depot, and then walking home in a happy haze. No rowdiness, no drunk driving, no harm done. Still, he had been pretty much judged and ostracized by the locals. As he sat there beside the desk, hands carefully folded in his lap, the label did not seem to fit.

Then the man opened his mouth.

"I want to know who in the gawdim frickin' hail upset my friend so bad, he killed hisself!" The chief saw the fire in the man's eyes. "You got any answers, you?" Uncle leaned forward as he spoke. "This is not right. It doesn't make any frickin' sense."

"Why do you say that, Mr. Smart?"

"He had a gawdim Saint Christopher's medal, for gawd's sake. Who kills hisself when he's got a Saint Chris's medal hanging on his frickin' change box?" He looked at the chief for an answer. "*Nobody*, that's who," he answered for the cop.

"So you're saying his suicide doesn't make sense because he was a person who made an effort to protect himself from bad luck?"

Uncle blinked. "Um, ya-a-as…" He twitched in the hard wooden chair. "Well, not exactly." He looked thoughtful. "I don't think he was even a frickin' Catholic." A light glimmered in his little brown eyes. "Oh yeah, I remember. That girl found it on the sidewalk and gave it to him to protect him from a gawdim bus accident, or something. Made a big frickin' deal of it, like she was protecting him, herself." He sneered. "Little snot."

Chief Rob slowly reached across his desk to pick up a pencil. "And when did this happen, do you remember?"

"Nah, it was a ways back." He crossed his legs, then uncrossed them. "I just remember her doing that."

"Do you remember her name?"

"Jeez, I should, but he called her 'Dream Girl,' or some gawdim thing like that."

The chief leaned back in his chair, deftly weaving the pencil back and forth through the fingers of his left hand. "Do you remember what she looked like?"

"Hail, ya-as. All that gawdim fluffy red hair, and skinny as a starving squaw."

"So, that's the only name you can think of?"

The retired military man went into serious recall mode. In a moment, he remembered something else. "Well, the other one calls her, 'Princess.'"

"The 'other one'?"

"The other bus driver. 'Bill,' I think, because she calls him 'Sir William.'"

The pencil stopped moving. The police chief looked around, then leaned forward to make eye contact with the little Abenaki warrior. "Mr. Smart, can I trust you?" he spoke softly. "There is some serious stuff going on, and I think you may be able to help us." He intensified his gaze. "I believe something happened with your friend, Alan Strong, but I don't think it happened the way some people are telling it."

Uncle was listening.

"I think you may have some information which could help clear your friend's name. Are you willing to help me do that?" He saw that this retired combat veteran was into this, already. "I just need for you to tell me that you will keep the information private — between me and you. Would you be willing to do that?" The man looked undecided. "It is crucial that you not give out this privileged information. Do you understand that?" It was a few seconds before Uncle nodded that he understood. "Alright then, I need you to give that agreement in writing, and I need to ask you some questions." He went on to explain the legal ramifications, ending with, "If you give permission for all that, I have some important stuff that you need to know and hopefully, you will be able to help us sort it all out."

After some paper shuffling, and a few interruptions for routine police work, the chief closed the door to his office. He sat down and picked up the pencil again. He rotated it once more through the fingers as he spoke. "I think we have a situation." The thin writing instrument flipped out of his hand, falling under the desk. After fumbling around for a moment, the chief retrieved the yellow number two, inspected it to be sure the point was still intact, then went straight to the matter at hand.

"I believe Alan Strong committed suicide because he was accused of rape by that redheaded teenager, Roxanne Foxx."

"What? Rape?!" Uncle's eyes grew wide, then blinked slowly. "I sure as hail don't believe that!"

"Neither do I. I think he was set up."

"That so?"

"Ay-yuh. And I think it was Roxie who did it. I think she did it on purpose."

Uncle seemed to agree, nodding his head. "She sure as hail could do that, her."

"Some other sources have informed me that she is a person who punishes people who upset her, or whatever." The chief paused. "Does this ring a bell with you?"

Uncle's head bowed, then lifted. "Hail, ya-a-as. She told me, herself, right in front of 'Sir William,' that her own mother taught her to... let's see... 'Don't get mad; get even.'" He sniffed contemptuously. "Gawdim little snot. And then she said something about, 'So that's what I do. I don't get mad, I just get even.'" He shook his head. "And she frickin' meant it."

"What we need to know, sir, is if there was anything that she wanted to get even with Alan Strong for. Was she ever wronged by him, even in her own mind?"

"I don't remember anything."

"You never saw her mad at him for anything?"

"I need to go take a... break. You got a gawdim bathroom in here?"

Five minutes later, Uncle had one more thing to say: "It was at the frickin' bus terminal. Alan showed up. He climbed up into the bus to talk to the driver, Bill. When he saw that girl sitting there with that ukulele thing on her lap, he turned around and made some gawdim remark to Bill about not listening to those sweet little concerts, because they could make trouble, or something. She almost blew a gawdim gasket. I wanted to laugh so gawdim bad, but she was so frickin' mad, I thought I'd better shut the hail up." He coughed. "I don't know if this matters, but that's at least *one* frickin' time she got mad at Alan."

"How long ago was this?"

"Couple of weeks."

The chief rubbed his chin. "Alright, Mr. Smart, that's very helpful." He stood up to shake the man's hand. "If you have anything else come to mind, please let me know." Uncle nodded as he moved toward the door. The chief followed him quickly, to remind him, "Remember, sir, that this is privileged information. Be careful not to let anybody else know what you and I just talked about." Uncle nodded once more and left.

Chief Robbie went back to the desk and reached down to turn off his brand new Webcor reel-to-reel tape recorder which he had carefully concealed underneath. Quickly, he closed the top and picked it up. In a few seconds it was locked up inside his personal locker. He would type up this statement, himself.

After all, this was not *really* official police business.

CHAPTER TWELVE

Control

That same Monday evening, Roxie made up her mind to get back to school, and she wasn't taking no for an answer. However, her mother strongly objected that only one day off from classes, to recover from the trauma of rape, was way too soon.

"Well, at least let me go to my music lesson tomorrow morning," the girl said, leaning against the arm of the sofa in the small living room.

Marilyn looked sharply at her daughter. "There will be no lesson tomorrow. You will wait at least another week, and then afterwards," she said firmly, "there will be no riding the bus like you have been. You will take the Essex bus right back to your own high school." Roxie's whole body stiffened. "That stuff is going to stop."

"What stuff?" came the indignant question.

"Riding the buses, Roxanne. That is going to stop. No more bus passes. All you get is enough change to take the bus back to Essex Junction High School."

The girl started to tap her fingertips together.

"Stop that. Stop that right now, young lady." Roxie's nostrils flared as she kept on tapping. Her mother continued: "I won't be changing my mind on this, so forget the plotting. It's not going to work."

Marilyn turned away, almost bumping into her husband, who had come into the room from the kitchen just soon enough to hear the last few sentences. He observed Roxie's agitation, savoring the sight with deep satisfaction, but said nothing. As he turned a knob on the little television, the redhead looked at him out of the corner of her eye. He backed away from the set to slip his rear into his recliner, his eyes glued to the white screen, which flipped into a gray fog, just before the emergence of the flickering black-and-white picture. The hollow voice of John Cameron Swayze was finishing up the nightly *Camel News Caravan*.

Roxie sidled up beside her stepfather's chair. "I will still expect those free bus passes, Georgie," she murmured.

"Nope. I heard your mother."

"If you know what's good for you, I will have those passes."

"Take a hike. Your mom says 'No.'"

"You don't want to cross me, mister."

He turned around and yelled at the top of his voice, "Your mother says NO MORE RIDING THE BUSES, so SHUT UP."

Marilyn's head appeared around the edge of the kitchen doorway, a quizzical look directed toward George. He nodded an "under control" message toward her, as Roxie slinked past her mother. The girl made a hard left through the kitchen and disappeared into her bedroom, right there at the head of the hallway. She slammed the door so hard, something fell to the floor in the bathroom right next door.

"Straighten out, Roxanne!" Marilyn called out after her. "They'll take you away from me! Get that through your head, will you?"

It was a whole new frontier, as the girl would learn very soon, for now she would have to deal not only with Georgie-Porgie, but with her desperate mother.

***

Both George and Marilyn were in deep conversation with Bill Flannigan when Uncle approached the Shelburne Road bus in front of the terminal on St. Paul Street. He had arrived to get to his weekly poker game via the usual bus route a little earlier on this Tuesday morning, because Pooh had a staff meeting before Sears and Roebuck opened up there at the north end of Church Street. As he drew nearer, he noted the anger on the woman's face, and the serious look in the man's eyes. Even though he saw that the man was also wearing a Vermont Transit uniform, he was not sure who those two people were, so he obeyed an old, familiar gut-feeling. He hid himself in plain sight.

Stopping a few feet away from his target, the man bent down to tie his tennis shoe a little tighter.

"… not going to happen anymore," the woman was saying in a hushed voice.

"What the heck am I supposed to do?" Flannigan sounded desperate. "In front of a whole busload of people? You have to be kidding me."

"She's been told," the man assured the bus driver. "Now you see to it that it stops."

Bill's voice went up a full octave. "I can't stop her, for Pete's sake. Can't you see that?" He glanced back toward his bus as though to make sure he had not been heard.

"Oh? Why not?" the woman asked.

Bill Flannigan bit his lip, then took a big breath. "Because it would embarrass everybody, that's why." He whipped around and started for the bus.

"Flannigan! This could cost you your job," the dark-haired man whispered hoarsely.

The bus driver stopped in his tracks, and without looking back, shook his head in disbelief, then stepped up into his bus to start his run out on Shelburne Road.

Uncle rose up, stomping the newly tied shoe as if to try the fit. Out of the corner of his eye he saw the man wrap an arm around the woman, to guide her inside the orange doors of the diner-style restaurant. This popular eatery was located right behind where they had been standing, just one entrance north of the bus terminal's waiting room, and was known to the locals as "The Harvest."

He heard the bus engine start up, and hurried through its open door. After getting his bus ticket punched, he took his usual side-facing seat behind the white-faced driver, as though nothing had even happened. As he glanced forward to look at Roxie, there was no one there, and his gaze continued through the window toward the sidewalk outside the bus. At that moment he saw the angry man, just before he slipped into the diner behind the woman, turn and deliberately glare at Bill.

Suddenly, the bus was moving, and the pumpkin-colored doors were out of sight.

***

"So," Scottie asked the girls as the four of them stood outside of Essex Junction High School on that same Tuesday morning, "what's the plan for Halloween?" He was the only guy in this section of the drivers' education class. They had finished their lesson early, and were enjoying a little break before the next class.

"No big plans yet. What are you thinking about?" Penny asked. She looked at Diana, but Diana was making eye contact with Paula, the official "party girl" of the freshman class, and one of the cheerleading squad. Paula smiled slyly at Diana, then addressed Penny.

"Well, I'll tell ya, Penny-pal. Diana and I had this idea." She grinned mischievously, showing an even row of white teeth. "How about we do a rip-roaring scavenger hunt...?" She tilted the short, dark hairdo slightly to the left and watched Penny's nose wrinkle just a little, then continued. "...on bicycles?" Penny's nose straightened out and her eyes blinked a couple of times. Paula kept it going. "...on a designated route, out in the country?"

"Whoa there," Scottie interjected. "It's going to be dark out there in the country."

"We'll use bike lights, or flashlights taped to the handlebars," Diana said.

There was a pause.

"Where would this be?" Penny was definitely interested.

"I already cleared it with Jack's folks. We'd start from their place and include the whole Old and New Colchester Road loop. There are just enough houses on that circuit, and we wouldn't be running over trick-or-treaters in the village."

"Who writes the list?" Scottie asked, his mind already tuned into this game.

"Jack's dad said he would."

"What's the prize for the winning team?" His eyes glinted with possibilities.

The bell shrilled the signal for the next class.

"We'll get back to you on that!" Diana and Paula called out as they headed for their classrooms.

Scottie turned back to wink at Penny. "Well, waddaya say, beautiful?" he whispered as they moved along together. "How about we skip class and go make out somewhere?"

She punched him gently on the leg with one of her crutches and headed down the opposite end of the hall. He wasn't surprised. She was a good girl, for sure.

"Hey, Scottie!" The teenager turned to see a freckled seventh-grade boy holding a crooked index finger toward his chest. "Pull my finger!" the boy gleefully directed. Scottie laughed and tousled the boy's hair. "Nah, I already know that one." Then he had a thought. "See that girl on crutches? You should try it on her. Her name is Penny." The eager youngster ran down the hallway.

"Hey, Penny!"

Scottie laughed out loud as he scrambled up the stairs to his own class. Suddenly, he spotted Mrs. Collins coming down, her eyes focused tightly on something down near the front door. Once again, the incident with Roxie flashed through his mind. He wished he could stop the teacher and tell her. He wished she could know the truth about those bruises on Roxie's arms. He wished she could know. But she was already past him, intent on a definite destination. He moved back against the wall near the teachers' lounge and watched, as the woman made her way down toward the front doors of the school. Then he saw the contact. It was none other than Roxie, herself.

"What's she doing here so early on a Tuesday morning? She has music classes in Burlington. I wish I could hear what they're talking about."

The door closed on his upstairs classroom, and he bolted for it.

"I wish you would follow through on your promises, Roxie," Mrs. Collins admonished the girl. "We had an agreement that you would not attend school for two days, for your own good." She sighed impatiently. "Why are you here?"

"I made a deal with Mom," the girl reassured her. "I don't ride the buses for a week, and I get to go back to school this morning."

Connie's mind did a quick review of last Sunday's emergency counseling session at her home, and the chief's assessment of the whole "rape" thing. It did not add up that a rape victim would be anxious to get back to school this soon. Maybe Chief Allen had something, there. The counselor drew a long breath, and then threw out a little bait. Bending closely toward the teenager, she spoke carefully.

"Listen, Roxie. Alan Strong was a very troubled man. His involvement with you was wrong. That was *his* choice." She wrapped an arm around the gorgeous redhead as the two of them moved slowly into the front hallway. "The thing *you* need to do right now, is to forgive yourself for cooperating with this involvement, for playing along with it, for your own personal reasons." She physically aligned the girl's shoulders in front of her own body as she delivered the next words. "You have some responsibility in this whole thing, and it won't be resolved until you accept that responsibility." She looked deeply into the silvery eyes. "Do you understand that?"

The reflection in Roxie's eyes was chilling.

"He raped me. What else is there to understand?" she replied, as she shook herself free from Connie's grasp. Not waiting for an answer, the girl quickly climbed the east set of stairs past the principal's office.

She was looking for Marsha, who, she was pretty sure, was in study hall this period. Crossing the length of the upstairs hallway, she was pleased to see that she was right. At the door, she spotted her friend seated in the last row of the back of the room, right near the little library which was located directly above the teachers' lounge. She caught Marsha's eye and nodded a "follow me" at her before lowering her own head and walking down the side of the room, all business. The head stayed down as she climbed the two stairs up into the library, stopping just out of sight of the study hall teacher's monitoring glance. A few seconds later, Marsha stood up, taking a book and pencil with her, and meandered up into the tiny room.

"What are you doing here?" she whispered to her beautiful friend.

Roxie pulled her out of the range of the teacher's eyesight. "I need your help. I got raped Saturday night."

At the end of the ten-minute conversation, Marsha had agreed to ask her mother if Roxie could stay overnight this very night to "Get away from it all," as Roxie explained it. The redhead then gave her friend a dime for the nearest phone booth, to make the arrangements with her mom, Shirley Bogue, who would of course clear the whole thing with Marilyn Foxx. Marsha believed these two mothers would agree with everything in order to help poor Roxanne deal with this unspeakable trauma. Actually, the scheming redhead's plan was so transparent that it bordered on the ridiculous. Neither one of those two adults should have bought into it for one moment. Nevertheless, they did, just as naively as Marsha had. It was as though a mysterious veil was dropped from another dimension, and nobody but Roxie could see through it.

By three o'clock dismissal at EJHS, everything was in place, and the two girls headed for the old Case house for the night. Roxie had managed to run home in between classes to gather a few overnight necessities, and she slung that bag over her shoulder as the two girls chatted excitedly on the two-mile walk to the Bogue home. When they arrived there, it was discovered that the boys had been picked up by their dad, and would not be back until Wednesday after school. That note, signed by Marsha's father, was lying beside the telephone in the living room, just inside the doorway from the kitchen. Roxie hooted in approval, for this meant they could spend some time on the Ouija board, uninterrupted by the raucous male behavior which had often occurred before.

Half an hour after the two girls arrived at the Case house, Shirley Bogue drove her old Chevy into the undesignated driveway of her abode. She trudged up to the back porch and entered into the kitchen, glad to be done with her waitress job at The Harvest. It was there she had befriended Roxie's mother. Once again, the day had been hard and Shirley was exhausted, so she was delighted the girls had warmed up some leftover spaghetti and meatballs, and had even added some home-canned string beans to fill out the meal. They enjoyed the humble repast there in the newest part of the house — the part with no cellar under it — which consisted of a large pantry, the kitchen, and a third bedroom.

By six o'clock, the dishes were done, and Marsha was sitting quietly in the presence of her special guest, awaiting her next request. It had been a long time since her best friend had stayed overnight.

"Let's get the homework out of the way, so we can play with the Ouija board," Roxie said as she pulled a couple of textbooks out of her overnight bag. The two girls worked away at the kitchen table for about forty-five minutes, while Shirley retreated to her bedroom at the opposite side of the living room. When the girls closed their books, they slipped into Marsha's room, right there off the kitchen, to don sweatpants and t-shirts. Eagerly, they hastened back past the kitchen table and up two stairs into the original part of the house.

Shirley was already there in the old living room, with the Ouija board on the beat-up coffee table which sat low in front of a battered sofa. She had placed three sofa cushions on the floor around the square-shaped table, and as the girls came through the doorway, scooting around the end of the sofa, she was smiling about something.

The two youngsters hit the cushions with a bounce, and exclaimed in unison, "A pointer! You got a new pointer!" Although it obviously wasn't new, it was, at the very least, authentic. Shirley had a friend at work who happened to have this old planchette, but no Ouija board. She was delighted, seeing it as a one-in-a-million "coincidence." A good story to tell sometime, although it was certainly not something she would share with the ladies in the Maple Leaf Sewing Circle. It was obvious they did not approve of the game… something spooky about it, or whatever. She wasn't worried about it. It was just a fun game, and really, it was none of their business.

Shirley took her place on the cushion where she always sat, so she could lean her plump body back against the bottom front of the sofa. She lifted both hands and fluttered her fingers, ready for action. "Let's see if that thing can lay rubber."

The shrill ring of the telephone interrupted the laughter. Marsha jumped up and answered it, then stretched the cord on the receiver as far as she could before she handed it to her mom. Shirley's polite salutation changed to a familiar chat mode by the second sentence. "Yeah, she's here, and we had a nice supper, and the homework is done." Roxie knew it was her mother, checking up on her. She looked at her watch. It was seven-fifteen. A little smile curled the left side of her mouth, and she looked very pleased. Marsha recognized the look all too well; it meant Roxie was playing some kind of control game. Obviously, she was expecting her mother to call, and there it was, and that was taken care of.

Shirley handed the phone back to Marsha, to hang it up. As she laid the receiver over the cradle, the girl grinned at Roxie. "Guess that takes care of that, for one night, huh?"

Roxie's eyes blinked in surprise, but she recovered almost instantly, waggling her head matter-of-factly. "Yup." She looked across at Shirley, pausing to see if the woman was ready. "Do you want to summon Beng, or do you want me to do it?"

"Oh my gosh," the woman seemed surprised. "I forgot that. Yeah, its name is 'Beng.' We found that out last time."

"Also found out that it is neither male nor female," Marsha added. "But here's a good question. Is it an 'it,' or is it just maybe a combination of part male and part female?"

"That could be our first question," Roxie suggested.

"Alright, Roxie, you can summon. But remember, you are always respectful, and always greet this entity into your home, as you would any other guest. Got that?"

Roxie hesitated. "This is not my home, it's yours. Maybe you should be the one to summon."

"No problem." She lifted the first two fingers on both of her hands and placed them on the planchette, nodding to the girls to follow suit. As the three sets of fingertips rested on this heart-shaped instrument, Shirley gave it a little boost, beginning to trace a wide, loose figure-eight across the board. After a few swipes, she lifted her fingers to a point where they seemed to be barely touching, the same as the girls' were. The planchette slowed down and stopped.

"Good evening, Beng. Are you with us?" Shirley asked. The pointer remained motionless. "You are welcome to join us, Beng. Please feel free to speak with us." The three of them stared intently at the planchette. "We would be delighted to speak with you, Beng." Still no motion. "Don't press too hard," she said to the girls. They lifted fingers a little higher, barely, barely touching.

"Are you here with us, Beng?"

The planchette moved slightly toward the left side of the board. The girls were hardly breathing. Shirley was ready to ask for identification. "Who are you, please?"

The pointer moved back toward the right and paused. Then it moved several inches farther to the right and upward.

"Would you please spell your name?"

Slowly, slowly, the pointer began to move over the double-arched rows of the alphabet. The first place it stopped was over the letter "B." All three were thrilled at how the magnified window in the middle of the planchette defined the exact letter, much more clearly than the inverted drinking glass. The enlarged letter was so definitely encircled, there was no mistaking it.

"B," Marsha whispered.

Slowly, the pointer moved to the next letter… "E." There was a collective gasp, and they focused even more closely on the moving object beneath their feathery touch.

"N," they spoke together.

They all smiled when the pointer window stopped over the letter "G."

"Welcome to our home, Beng." Shirley paused politely, then asked permission to commence with the first question: "We are honored to have you with us. May we ask our first question?"

The planchette wove back and forth provocatively, then slid up to stop on the top left of the board, over the word, "YES."

Marsha exchanged a look with her mother, who remembered the first question they had agreed upon. "Are you a combination of male and female, Beng?"

The pointer dropped down from the "YES" spot, stopping at the twin arches of the alphabet. There was a brief pause. Then, the planchette moved slowly to the letter "M," and then on to the next letter, "Y." It picked up a little speed, making the three fingertip contacts concentrate on keeping in place, as it went from one letter to the next, wobbling and winding back and forth, until the whole word was spelled.

It was the word, "mystery."

There was a moment of mental shifting. The entity did not answer, but, at the same time, it did answer. Regardless, Shirley was not finished.

"Is this beyond our comprehension?"

Under the trio of twin fingertips, the pointer slid once more up to the "Yes."

"No, wait," Roxie said. "We just need to ask the question differently."

For the next forty minutes, the connection continued, and although the three never did get a direct answer as to the gender of Beng, there were a number of other bits of information garnered:

Beng was from the Light side, not from the Dark side.

Beng had knowledge of ages past, present, and future.

Beng had powers beyond what they could possibly comprehend. (There was that word, again.)

Beng's presence could be made known to them through fragrances.

Finally, Shirley whispered that her arms were getting tired. Marsha gave a quick nod that she was ready to stop the session.

"No, wait," Roxie pleaded. "Before we say goodbye, could you tell us our spirit names?" The planchette moved to "Yes." Delighted, she dived right in.

"What is Marsha's spirit name?"

The pointer quickly moved over the five letters: L-O-Y-A-L.

Marsha whispered the name as though embracing it. "Loyal."

"What is her mom's name?" Roxie inquired. The planchette moved a bit, then paused, and finally it slipped along to spell out the name: "Seeker."

"Yeah, that fits. That's me, all right." Shirley chuckled.

Roxie could have cared less. She leaned in a little closer. "And what's mine?" The planchette did a wide circle eight before landing on the letter P. Then it moved to the A, and on to the S. It whirled away and circled back to the S once more before hitting the remaining letters, I-O-N.

"Pass-i-o-n?" Roxie puzzled. Then her eyes widened with glee. "Passion! My spirit name is Passion. Yeah, that's right. That's exactly who I am." She hooted, letting her fingers leave the pointer for a second.

The other two whispered frantically, "Don't detach! Don't detach! We have to say goodbye before detaching!" Roxie quickly placed her fingers back upon her spot.

"It is time to say goodbye, Beng," Shirley said politely. "Thank you for a pleasant visit," she continued as she steered the planchette over the "Goodbye" letters at the bottom of the board. Once there, she spoke a courteous, "Goodbye."

The words were hardly out of her mouth before she yelled at Roxie. "Are you out of your mind, girl? You never detach without saying 'Goodbye.' Otherwise, you could leave that supernatural thing wandering around your home. I thought you knew that."

"So I forgot once. Big deal. Nothing happened."

"You'd better hope nothing happened." Shirley picked up the board and pointer and went into her bedroom just off the living room. Roxie knew it was the signal for bedtime, so she headed for the bathroom, which was located at the other end of that same living room wall. When she came out, Marsha had replaced the sofa cushions and was standing in front of the oil stove heater which was centered on the same side of the room, between the bathroom and the bedroom. She was waiting to brush her teeth. The atmosphere was a little awkward, so Roxie just went straight through the kitchen and into the double bed, pulling the covers up to her chin. But as she lay there, she felt the resonating thrill of who she really was — "Passion." She loved the very thought.

Then she heard Marsha enter the room and go over to turn on the lamp near the window. The single-bulb lamp was old, with a tattered shade and a raveling electrical cord, but it was all there was, and, for some reason, Marsha always slept with a night light. Once she turned it on, she reached up to pull the chain on the overhead light bulb's ceramic holder, which was centered in the low ceiling. As the light went out she whispered, "Goodnight, Roxie."

"'Night."

The presence of Marsha in the bed suddenly vexed Roxie back to reality. She turned onto her side, her back to the other girl, and cleared her head. The evening was not yet really over. She had plans. Eventually, she allowed herself to doze lightly for a couple of hours, every so often keeping a check on the time. Finally, it was eleven-thirty. She slipped carefully out of bed and grabbed her tennis shoes and sweater, but as she moved in the lamplight, her shadow flickered across Marsha's face. "Loyal"'s eyes opened and she raised her head up off the pillow. Seeing the shoes and sweater in Roxie's hands, she asked, "What are you doing?"

Her beautiful friend sat down on the edge of the bed in a huff, and slipped her feet into the tennis shoes. "I'm going out."

"Where?"

Roxie finished tying her shoelaces as she spoke. "Never mind. You don't need to know." She stood up and pulled the sweater on over her head. "I'll be back in a couple of hours. Just keep your mouth shut, okay?"

Marsha sighed. "So, your mom doesn't know that 'Sir William' lives less than a mile away, does she?"

Roxie sneered. "You don't think I'd be stupid enough to actually go to that house tonight, do you?"

"Passion" slipped out the back door and started an easy jog westward, up the hill on Case Road. She would have to be careful not to be seen as she passed the little stucco house at the junction of Case and Susie Wilson Roads. But if she timed it just right, as Bill Flannigan turned the yellow woodie left off Route 15, he would see her in the glow of the headlights, right there at the Susie Wilson Road bus stop.

CHAPTER THIRTEEN

Spooks

"Thank God we didn't pick the hayride theme; it would have made us look like a bunch of hicks," Emma Donahue remarked to the other four parade float committee members as they shuffled chairs into position on the second floor of Lincoln Hall. The barely five foot tall Mrs. Donahue was the proprietress of the Lincoln Street Greenhouse, and the owner of a rambunctious mutt, referred to by the neighbors as "The Traffic Circle Terror."

Soft-spoken words of agreement rumbled across the center of the room.

Father Tom produced a card table from some dark corner, and proceeded to set it up in the center of the group. At the last meeting, the group had gone over suggestions from the community, and finally settled on what they all considered to be a "real winner." The float would be an old-fashioned locomotive, complete with a coal car. Today, Principal Randy Marvin was pleased to present some drawings of the locomotive theme float, rendered by one of his talented students. As he spread them out carefully, the others observed that there were four sheets from four side-views.

"Nice job," the man from Yandow's Market commented.

"Almost professional!" said Herb, who ran The Tip Top, a one-stop shop for everything from magazines and newspapers to candy and cigarettes.

The committee then began to get to the details.

"Last time we met," Emma reminded them, reading from her notes, "we agreed there were five key elements to a good parade float."

"Number one: colorful."

"Number two: great music."

"Number three: an accurate but favorable impression of our town."

"Number four: ad signs for each Essex Junction business funding the float."

"And finally, number five: pretty girls."

"Well," said Randy Marvin, "we have some great suggestions for color, right here in these drawings. Do you all like them?"

Everyone seemed impressed. The train was right out of a Disney cartoon, appealing, and yet believable. It could have been featured in one of Walt's movies. The vote for the colors of the float was short and unanimous.

"Great. So that means we may move on to the music." As chairman of the committee, Mr. Marvin leaned back in his folding chair, crossing his outstretched legs. "Now, there are a couple of small, reasonably priced bands to choose from, who could ride in the coal car."

"What? Would you repeat that?" Emma interrupted. The principal repeated his statement about reasonably priced bands.

"I thought we had agreed to have the EJHS cheerleaders ride in the coal car," she pouted. "After all, they fulfill the 'pretty girls' requirement." She had already told her cheerleader daughter, Paula, about the plans, so this was bad news.

The principal nodded. "That's true. We did discuss that, although we did not actually vote on that. It was just a suggestion." He pushed the horn-rimmed glasses up on his nose and grinned. "Listen, people, since that last meeting, we have had a generous support offer from the our Chittenden County dairymen, if we would have their Dairy Princess, Diana Bixby, spotlighted as 'engineer' in the locomotive window of the float. We need to vote on that this evening. It is a donation of five hundred dollars, folks, and it fulfills our 'pretty girls' requirement, and leaves the coal car open for the musicians." He looked around the table, his head cocked to one side, ostensibly open to suggestions.

Father Tom jumped right in. "We sure could use that funding, and while the cheerleaders do represent the importance of sports in our high school, EJHS already is well-represented in these parades by a really great marching band."

Mrs. Donahue drew a sharp breath, but before she could speak, Mr. Marvin took back the thread of conversation.

"Not to mention, the All-State singers and musicians who represent Essex Junction in the Music Festival each year," he said with a big smile. "It seems logical that we would accept this generous donation from the dairy industry, with which this community is so firmly linked, by having our float's locomotive feature their Dairy Princess."

Mrs. Donahue gasped. "Let's take another look at this, you guys." She pulled the drawings toward her, trying to sort out a way to keep the cheerleaders in the parade. "And we sure don't want music in the float, if it's following the marching band. Did anybody figure that out?"

"We have invited the local 4-H clubs to march immediately after the band, then the float would follow a little ways behind that group," Herb informed her.

"Oh? 'We' did that, did we? Well, I would still like to take a look, here."

The four men waited patiently as she shifted the four drawings, murmuring as she moved them around and around. Once, she clucked her tongue, twice she shook her head, but in the end, she could make no case for keeping her cheerleaders on the float. She pushed the drawings together in a heap and slumped back into her chair, arms folded defiantly. At first she stared hard at their mouths as they talked, but finally she lowered her head, and quietly lost the battle. The vote to leave the cheerleaders out of the float was four to one.

Ten minutes later, Principal Marvin and Father Tom huddled together at the Pearl Street side of the Lincoln Hall parking lot. Chief Rob spotted them from a window and joined them immediately.

"How did it go?" he asked.

The two men filled him in, briefly.

"Thank God, we got around any chance that the incident with the girl and the dead bus driver would be brought up. What a relief," the priest said, as he wiped his brow with a black handkerchief.

"The last thing Essex Junction High School needs is to have one of its cheerleaders involved in a scandal," the principal said softly. "Bad enough the poor fellow is dead." He turned face-to-face with the chief. "Thanks for your good work."

"You're welcome," Rob answered Randy. "I just happened to have a few friends in the dairy industry." He reached out to shake the principal's hand. "I meant it when I said to let me know if there was anything I could do to help."

The priest needed to emphasize the point: "It was probably a life-saver. When it comes to competition between communities, things can get really political, and downright nasty. That kind of information would be real firewood, especially if we won the prize for best float, or whatever."

"People." Randy Marvin shook his head incredulously.

"That says it all," the chief laughed as he headed back inside to turn things over for the night watch. In a few seconds, he came back to pull out the squad car, right behind the other two men, and the three automobiles left the lot, homeward bound.

Just off the Pearl Street sidewalk, quite near that side of Lincoln Hall's small parking area, someone was seated on the wrought-iron courtesy bench meant for folks who liked sitting out on the little lawn in front of Lincoln Hall to enjoy lunch hour. Its one diminutive occupant had gone unnoticed by the three men, because of the large lilac bush which stood between them, even though the little woman, herself, was able to see *them* quite clearly. After the men left, she sat quietly for a few minutes, then, as the shadowy silhouettes of nearby trees grew longer across the lawn, she leaned forward, put her shoe back on — minus the pebble — and walked slowly around the corner to Lincoln Street. Deep in thought, she walked past the Brownell Library, a couple of houses, and finally into her own driveway.

Mrs. Donahue was nearly deaf, but she was an excellent lip-reader.

Paula was doing homework at the kitchen table when her mother came in through the back door. A large black dog sauntered out from under the table to greet her. The little woman closed the door quickly.

"Hi there, Blow," she said as she patted him on the head. She looked up to smile wearily at her daughter.

"Hi, Mama. How'd the meeting go?"

The mother sighed. "I'm a little put out." Her daughter's eyes asked the question. Emma sat down across the table. "Seems there has been a little action behind the scenes, and the cheerleaders will not be appearing on the parade float, after all."

"Aww, crap! I already told them! They were all excited."

"Darn. I was hoping you hadn't said anything, yet." She glanced at the open textbook in front of the girl. "How are you doing? About done?"

Paula closed the book. "Not much sense in trying to study now. I'll have this on my mind for a while." She gave her mother an exasperated look. "How did this happen?"

Emma rose up slowly, looking out the back door window from where she stood. "Tell you what, why don't you take a break and help me check things in the greenhouse? It's getting a little chilly these nights. What is it, the twenty-third of October, already?" Emma's profession was one which required vigilance, for financial disaster could come from just a few hours of neglect. Chrysanthemums and poinsettias were in need of careful attention at this time of year, to be placed in areas of correct temperatures, some covered for protection, some for shortened daylight so they would turn color.

The dog moved closer to the door as the Donahue women prepared to go out.

"Stay, Blow!" Paula commanded, holding her palm toward his nose. He whined, and settled uneasily upon the linoleum floor, the long plume of his tail still moving. The ladies slipped quickly out the door, leaving the frustrated dog alone, again.

Blow answered to that moniker, but his real name was "Diablo." It was given to him because of his rather odd appearance. When Emma brought him home as a Christmas present for her two children, he was almost a year old, and had been living on a farm somewhere off the grid in the locals' version of "Lost Nation." It was a serious adjustment for him to go from a free-roaming puppy to a house dog, but that was not his biggest problem. The plain truth was just that he was such a strange-looking mutt. It wasn't so much that extra-long ebony coat, as it was the sight of those pale yellow eyes peering eerily out from under the shaggy white "eyebrow" spots above them. All this, in the middle of a pure black face. The children were delighted, but Emma's cancer-ridden husband had shaken his head.

"That poor mutt looks like the devil," he had remarked from his sickbed.

"Okay, we'll call him that," son Ted had proclaimed. "'Devil.'"

"No! Not 'Devil,'" the young Paula had objected. "We can't call him something like that. Think of something better."

"Okay then, let's call him 'Diablo,'" her older brother had suggested.

The sensitive child thought it over, and decided it was a pretty classy name. In the end, the whole family agreed, even the dear daddy for whom she was so sincerely praying, "Oh, God, please heal my daddy."

It was only after the devastating death of her father ("God is not real," she concluded) that she discovered she had been even further hoodwinked by her very own family. In a rare moment of repentance, her brother confessed the family's collective guilt in deceiving her about their dog's name. "Diablo," it seemed, was Spanish for the word, "devil." Already grieving that her prayers for her father had not been answered, the girl took this betrayal as the final blow. The sensitive little girl morphed into a determined, assertive person, insisting on being in charge of her own life, intent on succeeding in every endeavor, and "...to heck with the fairytale notion of God." From that point on, Paula chose to call the dog, "Blow."

Neither mother nor brother had had the heart to protest.

When they came back in from the greenhouse, Paula put the leash on Blow and took him outside for his last "sniff and poop" of the day. As she walked slowly around the designated area behind the greenhouse, she thought over all the things her mother had just told her, including the bit about the cheerleader scandal.

"Which one of us is she?" she wondered out loud. "What the heck did she do?" Her mind went down the list of EJHS cheerleaders, trying to spot any unusual behavior in each one of them. She concentrated on the five regulars, first, but none of them fit the bill.

Blow tugged her to another section of the unkempt yard behind the greenhouse.

"So that leaves the two subs," she whispered. The first name came quickly: Roxanne Foxx, first sub, and —. "Wait a minute," she said aloud. "Doesn't her dad work for the bus company in Burlington?" She dragged the reluctant dog back into the kitchen. "Hey, Mama, you want to hear something spooky?"

***

Walking out to the barn, Uncle reflected on his bus trip last Tuesday morning. It had been pretty interesting. Not only had he witnessed an intense exchange between Sir William and that agitated couple, but, upon his own boarding of the Shelburne Road bus, he had noticed the absence of Roxie in the seat across from him. Further, he had had barely time to take his own usual seat on the bus, before the spooked bus driver cranked the door shut and took off. People had been running toward the bus, but Bill had gunned the vehicle forward in an early departure, fiercely pulling the bus's steering wheel, to turn left up Main Street, where he had made one stop in front of Strong's Hardware, and then shifted gears, guiding it laboriously up the hill for the right turn in front of Edmunds High School.

Uncle pulled his tackle box out from under the darkened workbench in the barn. It was time to get ready for a great day of fishing. He went over and pulled the string on the light over the Dodge, then went back to the shelf. As he worked to straighten out the mess in the box, he found himself trying to straighten out the mess in Bill Flannigan's life.

Once more, his mind focused on the bus driver's frantic actions. It was like a movie that would not stop. The picture flashed before his eyes, again and again. Suddenly, he corrected that picture: Those were not so much actions as they were *re*actions. The man was running.

The behavior was familiar. A seasoned combat veteran, Mr. Smart recognized all the signs, and as he stood there in the barn, his opinion of Bill Flannigan started to change, right then and there. This bus driver was clearly reacting like a trapped animal, in "fight or flight" behavior. Obviously, the man had suddenly realized he had somehow stumbled into enemy territory, and he was going to have to do whatever he needed to, just to survive. Uncle had seen first-hand that the man's panic had to do with that whispering couple. And there *was* something familiar about them…

But right now, he remembered last Tuesday morning, sliding across the seat to speak to Bill, catching instead, the reflection of the pale face in the rearview mirror. In his haste, the driver had neglected to don his sunglasses, and Uncle had gotten a clear view of the panic in those eyes. Then, at the stop in front of Strong's Hardware, Mr. Smart had watched Bill slip the stylish sunshades on, to hide that wild fear from the world. It had brought forth a vivid memory for the retired Army veteran.

As he stood at the workbench there in the barn, he let his hands fall idle across the tangled mess, remembering a time of abject terror, himself.

"Good frickin' move, soldier. When you're hiding in a gawdim cemetery, you'd better look like all the rest of them frickin' ghosts. Hide in plain sight, boy."

It actually happened in a tiny, remote Christian missionaries' cemetery over there in Korea. In the dead of night he got separated from his unit during a firefight, and there, right in the middle of nowhere, he stumbled upon this small fenced-in area with a half-dozen old headstones. There wasn't time to question the situation; he instinctively threw himself to the ground, face-down over his weapon, just behind one of the stones, barely breathing as the enemy moved cautiously past him. This Abenaki warrior fully expected to die right on that spot, but his ancestral skills came in handy one more time. He was hiding in plain sight, just another war casualty, lying in a crumbled heap, obviously dead and not worth another bullet.

Even after all those years, he could not forget the piercing fear as he waited for those North Korean soldiers' footsteps to fade away to nothing. It was the same kind of fear he had seen in Bill Flannigan's eyes, just a few days ago. There was no doubt, the two of them shared a brothers-in-arms connection.

Now, as Uncle bent over the barn's dilapidated workshop shelf on this following Saturday morning, the situation was still on his mind. Sorting through his fishing gear, one last time before Father Tom showed up in the rattling green Ford, the little man wondered if there was something he could do to help the Air Force veteran.

One thing was clear: the girl was the enemy. For sure, she could shatter his whole life, if she wanted to… and she was the type who could do just that, because she didn't get mad… she got even. That's what her mother taught her. In fact, if he was in *either one* of their gun-sights, Bill Flannigan had to be in a "fight or flight" pattern, and that split-second decision was always made with a deep-down survival instinct, right out there, no unnecessary complications, just sucking in the next life-sustaining breath.

And that brought it all into perspective. Roxie had masqueraded as the gorgeous, helpless child, in order to pull older men into her sexual fantasies. That was what she was doing, and it had to be exposed. The little Abenaki snorted in contempt. There was no doubt in his mind that it was time for the tables to be turned; time for this phony victim to actually be baited and hooked, herself.

A scheme took shape. *"What that young lady needs is to be distracted to a frickin' new target...one that would turn out to be too big to handle. Hail, yes."* The logic was, if she got distracted enough, she would have to leave Sir William alone, and move on. He smiled and went back to the tangled fish line, shaking and loosening and carefully pulling the flexible threads, to rewind them slowly onto the spool. It was slow work, but necessary, for the next fishing season. So it would be with the baiting process for the girl, he finally concluded, but he figured it would also be worth it, in the end.

Uncle smiled to himself as he realized he was thinking like Police Chief Rob Allen. What was it the chief had said? "If there is anything else, please let me know." Suddenly, the man was excited. He felt he certainly could be a lot more help in this situation than he had realized. The trick was to make it happen, and then she would be put out of business. When he had done that, he would go back to show Chief Allen how he had planned it all.

As he slipped the rewound fish line into the box, his mind went back to all the damage this teenager had done to his friend, Alan. It was a type of murder. And now she had Bill trapped and tethered like a poor, dumb animal. That was cruel.

It was like the kid was possessed.

"Well, okay then, she needs to be set up with a new gawdim target, who would lead her down the rose-covered path to her own destruction before she does anymore frickin' harm to anybody else." He flashed his coffee-stained grin. "And I know just the frickin' guy who would be more than happy to do it."

A certain young fellow who worked at Yandow's Market was always looking for a few extra bucks. The boy spent two nights a week restocking shelves and cleaning the freezer area. He was a high school student, and best of all, he had a car. "Which is why he's always looking for extra money,"

Uncle muttered. He stopped and reminded himself, "Just have to make sure he can keep his gawdim mouth shut." Indeed, the plan needed to be carefully thought through. Bill, the bus driver, already had his hands full trying to protect himself; he didn't need any more complications.

As he secured the tackle box, Uncle remembered, once again, the situation he had witnessed involving the intense couple in front of the bus terminal last Tuesday, October 20. Bill Flannigan was definitely under attack by those two. Uncle wondered if they were the girl's folks. "I should have taken a longer look at them," he said. "Maybe I could have seen some frickin' family resemblance."

But something else was bugging him about that unpleasant encounter. It was as though he had a picture in front of him, but he just couldn't identify… something. He was sure it was important, but every time he got close to it, the thing would dissolve as in a ghostly vapor. He needed to get to the bottom of that one, too.

Right now, as he lifted his fishing pole off the hooks on the wall, he was really glad that only last Tuesday, he had bought a small spiral pocket notebook and tied a small ballpoint pen to it… with fishing line, of course. On that day, he started keeping dated records. It would help him keep things in order. He knew Chief Rob was going to like that, too.

***

The Ford pulled into the Thompsons' driveway at the southern entrance, and the tackle box and pole were loaded. At last, the two fishing buddies were on their way to a third Saturday morning fishing adventure. As usual, they headed for the Ladue family's fishing hole on the shore of Shelburne Bay.

It turned out that the fishing was lousy, but the conversation was great. Somewhere around eight in the morning, the two men were just letting their lines hang in the fishing hole, and enjoying funny Army stories by Mr. Smart. The veteran lightly jigged his line as he re-counted an especially entertaining memory.

"Well, we had this frickin' cigarette machine with a big mirror on the front of it, in the snack room, just off the hangar, see?"

"Umm, one that you put a quarter in, then you push-pull the lever and the pack of cigarettes drops out?"

"Exactly. You've seen them in the gawdim bus terminal, or wherever, right?"

Father Tom nodded.

"Anyways, it was in the snack room just off the hangar where the planes were kept. And of course, there were gawdim security guards all over the place. But this one guy, as gawdim green as they come, was assigned to guard the entrance booth between the snack room and the hangar. Nobody was supposed to get into the frickin' hangar from the snack room, without his frickin' permission." He jigged his fishing line ever-so-gently, as he chuckled.

"The trouble was, this flakey kid was just in from the States, where he had been watching a gawdim TV show — not sure if it was *Gunsmoke*, or what, but he was all into the 'quick-draw' fantasy, see?" He leaned forward to look Father Tom in the eye. "And there was a moment where, well, he came into the snack room to get a pack of smokes, and he kind of started making quick-draw moves in front of the mirror. The kid was enjoying hisself so much, he lost his frickin' common sense. He quick-drawed on his reflection… and… would you believe it? He shot the gawdim cigarette machine!" He roared with laughter. "Never even checked the frickin' safety on the gun." Uncle dissolved into a moment of hilarity such as the priest had not heretofore witnessed.

"Security people came forward out of the gawdim woodwork and that poor bah-serd was sent back to the States in a real hurry, I can tell you!" He caught the priest's eye. "You just can't frickin' make this stuff up!"

The fishing didn't get any better, but these two seasoned sportsmen were not about to quit... not just yet, for the camaraderie was finally genuine. Uncle was in rare form, and so he went on to a fishing story which turned out to be... well... quite informative.

"Me and Pooh used to go fishing all the time. My sister, Marie... Pooh's mother... depended on us to get something for supper, more often than I frickin' care to remember." He pushed his long hair back behind his ears. "Sometimes, when it looked like we were coming up empty, we would just go for the gawdim spear-fishing."

"You had fishing spears?"

"Naw, not really." He grinned as he recalled something. "We used an eel spear, 'cause that's all we had. It was my father's." He held up three fingers. "See, there were three points on it. The outside ones were made from some kind of wood. They were sort of like guides, where you aimed to catch the eel in between." He wiggled the middle finger. "But this middle point, that was like a gawdim steel needle. That's what caught the damn thing." A philosophical tilt of his head emphasized his next thought. "We was a couple of kids, doing the best we frickin' knew how." He hunched over, imaginary spear in hand. "See, all we had to do, is stand real still in the low-running parts of the river, and when we got a fish nearby, just nibbling away at whatever, we just frickin' stabbed it in the gut." He leaned back a little on his haunches. "I have to tell you, Pooh was one super gawdim spear fisher. More than once, she speared a two-pounder."

Father Tom shifted his weight on the tackle box. "I can't imagine that little woman having the strength and agility to spear a two-pounder."

Uncle grinned proudly. "I watched her. Her feet would actually raise up out of the water, like a gawdim bobcat on a kill."

The two men observed a quiet moment of unabashed admiration.

"That's quite a picture in my mind," the young priest finally commented. He let another polite pause occur before the next question. "So how did *you* do in this spear-fishing competition?"

"Ahwww, I came in a close second, me." The Indian leaned into a relaxed position on his haunches. His level of comfort had increased since the first time the two of them had chatted uneasily on the porch. It had gotten to the point where Uncle slipped easily in and out of what the Smart family referred to as "Frenchman talk," a dialect fraught with double-negatives and a lot of colorfully expressed bad English. Today, Uncle felt safe enough to ask the question. With a side glance toward the priest, he continued, "So, anyways... how am I doing, me? On the swearing, I mean. Any better?"

Father Tom was caught off guard. He had gotten used to it, and was not sure how to answer the question, so he took time to think about it. "You know, I do believe I'm noticing it less and less." That was the truth, told without discouraging the man.

"Still got a ways to go, I guess," Uncle remarked, looking for something more definite.

"Oh yeah... still a little ways to go."

Uncle stood up slowly, holding the rod with both hands. "So, just exactly how did *he* do it?" Just a little two-handed jig, right there. "Your dad, I mean."

"Ah, yes," the younger man replied. At last he would get to address this issue, and do so as a friend, revealing something important. He stayed seated on his tackle box as he began to share.

"I can't remember a time when my mom wasn't on him about his bad language. Not that she didn't love him, mind you. She was crazy about him. You could see it in her eyes. In fact, she probably would have overlooked this shortcoming in him, if it hadn't been for us boys. I think now, she was concerned that we would pick up on it, and no child of hers was going to talk like that." He grinned. "She had this big, ugly bar of Lifebuoy soap that she left in plain sight, all unwrapped in its smelly glory, right there near the bathroom sink."

"Oh, good old Lifebuoy soap," Uncle laughed.

"We didn't use it to wash up; we had Ivory soap for that. But that odorous monster was there to remind us what could happen if we got too raw with our language."

"So, did you ever have the pleasure?"

"Only because I was curious. Took a tiny, little lick... real quick." Father Tom leaned toward Uncle as if to underline the boys-will-be-boys thing. "You know, like a dumb little puppy." He faked a gasp and a choke.

"A frickin' little puppy-lick!" Uncle twitched with amusement.

"Anyway, none of us actually had our mouths washed out with soap... not even my dad, who certainly..." He stopped short, not wanting to condemn his fishing buddy. "Well, anyway, he had a real hard time controlling that stuff... even after Mom got sick." He paused, and licked his lips. "He tried, because he knew it meant so much to her, that good little Roman Catholic girl." He licked his lips, again. "Then the cancer took her away from us. It was hard for us boys, but it sent Dad into a tailspin like we had never seen before." He switched the pole to his other hand. "Wouldn't talk to anybody for three weeks. Twenty-one days. Didn't even leave the house except for the funeral."

Uncle moved his head in sympathy.

"But when he started talking again, not one swear word came out of his mouth."

The Indian was watching the priest's thoughtful countenance.

"I'm still not sure exactly what happened. I would like to think he did it for God, because that's the real reason we should try to live right." He frowned, then resumed the train of thought. "Years later, I learned about this 'twenty-one-days' thing... you know, how it takes that long to form a habit, and takes that long to *break* a habit. Something about that length of time, where the brain sort of switches and goes into a new mindset."

"Ahwww, hail," Uncle muttered. There wasn't much hope for him, in that case. He couldn't stop talking for a whole hour, let alone for twenty-one days.

"I also think now, that it's possible my dad was doing his own version of penance. Maybe he was taking the punishment for not stopping before she died. But, in the end, he repented — just did a complete mental turn-around, if you will. The fact that the process took the magical twenty-one days probably 'sealed the deal,' as they say." As he turned to see what effect the story was having, he caught the disappointment in the older man's eyes.

"I could never keep my frickin' trap shut that long. Hail, no. I need a frickin' miracle."

"And that's possible," his friend assured him. "But, in my dad's case, he probably had a gradual one. First, he had a change of heart and it changed his mind, and consequently changed his swearing habit. That had to happen, in that order, because it was — and often still is — a *process*, Mr. Smart."

"Like I say, I need a gawdim miracle. I just don't respect God enough, me."

"You respect Him enough to be bothered about the swearing."

"Or I respect Pooh enough... ahww, hail, I don't know." He scratched his head and pushed his hair back behind his left ear. "It's like I'm frickin' just not motivated, me." The long hair slid back into his face and he flipped his head to shake it back from the little brown eyes. With another side glance, he went on. "Now, your dad, he had what the gawdim U.S. Army would call 'serious motivation,' him."

"For sure. Death, or the threat of it, is indeed 'serious motivation.'" Father Tom raised his pole up out of the water, let the reel end slide down to rest upon the ground, and stilled the quivering upright tip of the rod with his other hand, as if to study it for a moment. "So let me ask you this. What would you do about the swearing, if you knew Winnie would be gone to Heaven, just twenty-one days from now?"

Uncle's head dropped forward, a deep shadow passing over his face. For a long time he stood quietly, staring at the water below. Then he slowly began to reel in his line, without saying a word.

The priest sighed gently. "Sometimes we can learn a lot from the experiences of our elders."

It was probably the perfect thing to say to this middle-aged Abenaki.

***

Later that day, after evening chores, the three of them gathered for supper.

"How was the fishing?" Winnie asked.

"Not so… good," Uncle answered slowly.

"Didn't think you cleaned any fish out there this afternoon," Cecil remarked as he spread butter on a warm baking powder biscuit. His hired hand had been unusually quiet since he returned from this fishing trip. "Well, sometimes we come home empty-handed." Uncle nodded. "You going again next week?"

"Mmm…" the little man shrugged his shoulders.

Winnie looked up from her bowl of steaming beef stew, blowing gently at a spoonful just inches from her mouth. "You do something to make Father mad, you?" Her uncle chuckled and shook his head "No." She sipped the liquid off the spoon and slipped the chunk of potato into her mouth. Chewing slowly, she gave Cecil a look that meant "Something's up," then watched her husband make his move.

"Probably pretty damned cold out there this morning, I would imagine."

Uncle looked up and spoke around a bite of tender beef. "Not bad." He picked up his tumbler of milk and washed down the meat. Noticing one last biscuit still in the pan, he looked questioningly, first at Cecil, then at Pooh. She motioned for him to help himself. Smiling, he proceeded to slice it across through the middle, then slather butter onto one of the halves, before maneuvering that same unbroken half gently, meticulously into his mouth.

"So," Cecil persisted, "no fish, but you look pretty happy, anyway."

The fisherman leaned back, savoring the mouthful of biscuit. His eyes twinkled just a little. Cecil could see something was coming. At last, Uncle took another swig of milk, licked his mouth, and put on a big grin. "Well," his measured reply began, "it's like this..." He paused before explaining. "I learned something, from a... dead guy today."

Cecil chuckled. "A dead guy? Like a ghost?"

"Nope. Like... an... elder." The words came forth as though he was thinking them through, even as he spoke.

Winnie tilted her head and lifted her eyebrows. "And what would that be?"

"How... to... fix... something," came the slow, deliberate reply.

"Fix what?" she asked.

"Something... really... important," the man articulated carefully.

Seeing that his wife was beginning to lose her patience, Cecil encouraged the man to speak. "Well, if it's really important, we sure want to hear about it."

The man looked down at his bowl and stirred the stew just a little before lifting a spoonful up to his mouth. As he scrutinized the contents of the soup spoon, he said, "It takes twenty-one" — he swallowed hard — "days." The intensity of his look emphasized the seriousness of this lesson. He slid the stew into his mouth. The other two watched, curious, for they had never seen him quite like this before. At length, he continued in that same strange, halting speech pattern, "This is only the first… day."

Winnie leaned forward. "First day for what, ay?"

He looked surprised. "Haven't you even… noticed?"

Her eyes got bigger. "Noticed what, for Pete's sake?"

Sitting up straight, he slapped the spoon smartly upon the table to emphasize his triumphant declaration, spoken in perfect Frenchman talk: "Your uncle, he don't swear no more, gawdimmit!"

CHAPTER FOURTEEN

Cycles

Despite anything she could dream up, there was no way Paula could exclude the likes of Roxie Foxx from the Boogieman Bike Bash on Halloween night. It was too widely publicized, word-of-mouth being the chief information channel in a normal high school, and by the week before, there were already fifteen participants signed up. Diana Bixby and her boyfriend, Jack, were already rethinking the wisdom of this gathering — a scavenger hunt on bikes — which would originate and terminate at Jack's home, the Wilson Dairy Farm, located on the sharp curve of the Old Colchester Road, about one mile north of Essex Junction. Paula felt a vague uneasiness about this girl being involved in an evening of free-wheeling fun. The cheerleader suspected that "free-wheeling fun" did not mean the same thing to Roxie, as it did to most of the teenagers attending the party. There needed to be some kind of control over each of the three scavenger teams.

Suddenly, she had a brilliant solution: *chaperones*.
Shortly, she came up with the perfect list. Father Tom Ladue loved to bike. He could be one of the chaperones for the party. Then, only two more adults were needed to keep watch over the rest of the gang. To that end, she enlisted the

services of a married couple to help keep watch over the whole bash. They turned out to be none other than their high school teacher, Connie Collins and her husband, Don. Principal Marvin heard of the arrangements and, even though this was not a school district event, seemed to give his approval. "Better than having a bunch of dumb kids turning over outhouses," he was heard to say. And so, the plans for the bash continued.

By Tuesday morning, the numbers had increased to nineteen. Everyone, including the chaperones, was busy in the last-minute tasks always involved in such an undertaking. Because of this event, the three prayer partners met for special prayer at the usual site, the Lincoln Inn's café. Don and Connie were both on lunch hour, so they were glad Father Tom was a little early. All three were excited about this happening, because there was such a need for healthy activities for Essex Junction teenagers. While Halloween was not the praying team's favorite holiday, this was a great opportunity to gather these kids together for some wholesome fun. All three knew that one of an evangelist's best tools was being an example of a good Christian life, and so they were all pleased to have been asked to chaperone this scavenger hunt. Who knew? Maybe just one of these young people would see something in them? Besides that, the Collinses were happy to get back to doing a little bicycling. The trio prayed, ignoring their lunch. At the end of the prayer, Connie smiled brightly at the priest as she reported a second counseling session with Roxie, just the day before, had been a really good one. "We are encouraged," she said. In the end, the rushed prayer warriors departed, each one with a wrapped sandwich in hand, to be consumed on the way back to work.

***

Meanwhile, Uncle was having another interesting morning over in Burlington. He had arrived on time to catch his bus out to the next poker game, and taken his usual seat. To his left, Bill Flannigan was sitting somberly at the wheel. The bus driver barely acknowledged his passengers as they boarded, his eyes moving erratically across the busy scene in front of him. A couple of times, Uncle noticed him looking at all three of his rearview mirrors, back and forth, back and forth. The man was clearly on watch duty, and extremely nervous.

Outside the bus, in front of the orange doors which led into The Harvest, a swarthy-looking man in a Burlington Transit uniform stood guard, his arms folded solidly across his chest. Uncle recognized him as the man who was part of the whispering couple he had seen last week. He glanced around, but saw no sign of the woman who had been with that man only seven days ago. Looking at that fellow more closely, he began to rethink his first impression of those two. Maybe his initial hunch was wrong. Maybe there was nothing significant about this couple, after all.

The time to move out finally came around, and the bus driver threw everything into motion, compelling the bus to once more groan up the Main Street hill, where it made its usual right-hand stop across from Edmunds High School.

And there, behind three other bus boarders, a beautiful redhead slinked onto the bus. She moved toward the front-most seat she could find, and quietly sat down, right beside Uncle.

"You forget your bus pass, you?"

She looked surprised, then pretended to check her pockets, coming up empty. She smirked and tossed her head. "Yup!" Her fingers tapped noiselessly across the top of the ukulele on her lap. Looking straight ahead, she whispered huskily, "So what?"

Mr. Smart focused on the man in the rearview mirror, who was hiding behind the sunglasses again. The man's jaw was set hard, and his lips were a thin, white line.

The bus rambled along under the elms on South Union Street, picking up and dropping off an interesting variety of passengers. Some were students without jackets, while many were Vermonters with enough savvy to know that October 27 was pretty near the end of Indian summer. It was starting to get a little nippy in the mornings and evenings, and there on the edge of Lake Champlain, the wind came up often and sometimes quite suddenly. Because Roxie had ridden in with her mother at the usual early hour of six in the morning, she had donned a rich navy blue pullover sweater, and had pulled its fashionable hood up to where only a few of her luxurious curls were exposed.

Someone from the back of the bus pulled the bell cord to signal an exit at the next stop. Across the aisle, where Roxie usually sat, a young man turned to see who had rung that signal. Spotting the woman who rang the bell as she moved toward the back door, he, himself, rose, turned, and waited for Bill to open the front door. Before he was down the steps to the sidewalk, Roxie was sitting in her usual seat, right where she could talk to the very handsome Sir William. She pulled the hood off and shook out her curls.

Uncle turned his attention to the ads which lined the curved edges of the ceiling just above her head. This gave him an excellent peripheral view of the girl, without actually looking at her. Right at this moment, he saw her watching him carefully. He squinted his eyes, and moved them ever-so-slightly as though trying to read something. Sure enough, she turned to try to make eye contact with the driver. Apparently unsuccessful, she picked up the ukulele and executed a couple of loud chords. Uncle allowed himself to look down at her. With a cocky little smile, she hit one more chord. "Learned a new song today," she said to nobody in particular.

Nobody in particular answered. Uncle looked around to see that there were only three other riders, two of whom were seated almost at the back of the bus, preoccupied with the views from their respective windows.

The third one surprised him. He recognized her immediately. It was one of the waitresses from Howard Johnson's; one who had worked there for quite some time, he reckoned. When he was employed at the Children's Home, he would come down for ice cream or pie, quite often. He remembered her as a pleasant, even-tempered person. But now the thirtyish woman was looking at Roxie, and she was scowling darkly. As the bus approached the Howard Johnson stop, she reached up and pulled the cord. Before the vehicle stopped, the lady navigated forward along the center aisle, coming to a stop in front of Roxie. As Bill cranked the door open, she spoke to the girl. "Your mother know you're on this bus?"

The silver eyes shot wide open. "What?" She glanced past the woman to see Bill lower his head in defeat. Suddenly, Roxie's nostrils flared.

"What?" she asked indignantly this time.

"Does she know you're on this guy's bus?"

Roxie cast a sideways glower, but did not answer.

The woman stepped down toward the exit, twisting a little to look into the girl's face. "Well, she does now." She took the last step down and out the door.

"Aw, for God's sake," Bill muttered.

"Who *is* she?"

"She works with your mom at The Harvest," he answered.

"No, she doesn't."

"Yes, she does. She's new." He shook his head and reached for the crank.

Roxie jumped to her feet. "Wait!!" she yelled, bounding down the stairs. "Catch you on the way back!"

Bill closed the door and proceeded on his route, where he was once more surprised that Mr. Smart did not get off at his usual stop. He lifted his face to the rearview mirror. "You okay, Mr. Smart?" Uncle nodded. "No headache or anything?" Uncle shook his head, again.

Slowly, the vehicle pulled out from the bus stop. The trees between St. Anthony's Catholic Church and the Children's Home had finally all turned color and some were nearly bare. It had been odd to these Pine Street residents, at first, that their area was just that much delayed in the inevitable change of seasons, and yet, after so many years of the same pattern, that which was odd, was now normal to them.

As the Burlington Transit bus approached Home Avenue, Uncle spoke up.

"Used to work there, at the Home."

The reply was courteous. "Is that right?"

"Ay-yuh… right after I retired from the Army."

"Yeah?" The interest perked up. "So, you're a veteran."

"Ay-yuh. Did my frickin' twenty." He leaned a little closer. "How about you?"

The driver corrected the position of the bus before turning onto Home Avenue. "Yeah. Did my frickin' twenty, I can tell you." He steered onto the street.

"Army?"

"Nope, Air Force."

"Few years ago, they were the same gawdim thing."

The driver managed a half-smile. "Don't tell that to any flyboy you run into, now-a-days."

"Hail no, they'll eat your lunch and pop the frickin' paper bag!"

Bill chuckled, just a little, as he drew to at the bus stop at Route 7, Shelburne Road. A woman stood at this bus stop for the Children's Home, her purse held with both hands, in front of her abdomen. The driver opened the door and she climbed slowly up the steps. She was trying hard to stop crying. Her hands shook as she fumbled to get the fare out of her purse.

As she worked to find the right change, Bill suddenly reached out and covered the coin box. "That's okay, ma'am. We had a guy pay for the next rider. That's you!" Her bloodshot eyes briefly caught his gaze, as she murmured a thank-you. "Yes, ma'am. Get settled, and we'll be on our way." He motioned for Uncle to help her. The little soldier stepped up to take the elbow of the weeping woman, steering her carefully to the first front-facing seat. At that point, both men saw that she was pregnant. Uncle slipped back onto his side-facing seat, trying not to look at the softly sobbing passenger.

Suddenly, Bill set the brake and turned to slip out of his seat. He moved toward her as he spoke: "Are you okay, ma'am? Not sick or anything, are you?" He tilted his hat to one side of his head, and placed his hands on his hips as he came to a stop in front of her. There he stood, feet apart, like Superman on a rescue mission. "Do you need me to call for help?" It was as though he had rehearsed this line many times, in his sleep.

The woman reacted to this attention by covering her face with her hands and releasing a loud, tearful wail. Immediately, Bill shifted position, bending forward to give her a couple of comforting pats on the shoulder. She drew a big breath and cried even louder.

"Oh, no," the hero crooned, as the patting hand stopped to give a gentle squeeze. The two passengers spun around in their seats, rising up to stare. Bill raised his left hand and motioned for them to be seated. Then he addressed the woman: "Okay, ma'am, you just go ahead and let loose. Nobody here is going to bother you." He pivoted around and resumed his seat.

The bus headed for the end of the line, where the two passengers got off and headed into Ralph's Diner. Bill followed them, soon returning to the bus with a cup of hot coffee for the lady, who, by then had finally gotten herself under control.

"Thanks," she said. "I… just had to l-leave my kids at the Home."

"Aww, that's a rough one. Sorry, ma'am." Bill patted her hand, then adjusted the route signs and took his seat. The bus continued back into Burlington proper. There was no further conversation between the hero and the pregnant lady. Mr. Smart had watched this brief interaction with great interest. His previous theory was confirmed right there in front of him. He saw very clearly what could have happened if the woman had been prettier, and not pregnant and possessed a flattering, lying tongue. This guy was a frustrated hero. It was what made him feel important. It was also what made him so susceptible. Uncle made a quick note in the spiral notepad.

There were five people waiting for the bus in front of Howard Johnson's, and sure enough, one of them was Roxie. She made sure she got on first, tapping the coin box with her hand and quickly sliding back onto her favorite seat. Uncle wondered if anybody else noticed she had dropped no coins. As the riders were getting seated, she made eye contact with Bill. With a little nod of her head, she reassured him, "Piece o' cake."

Then she spotted Mr. Smart, who had purposely turned his attention toward the grieving mother on the front-facing seat.

"What are you doing here?" she muttered at him, across the aisle.

Uncle pretended not to hear her, keeping his attention on the lady's face. The girl waited until she was sure he wasn't interested in her business, then turned back to Bill. Slowly, the driver pushed his foot against the accelerator, and they moved on toward downtown Burlington. In between stops, she filled him in.

"Her name is Betty, and she had to pick up her final check from Howard Johnson's." She glanced to check on whether Mr. Smart was still preoccupied.

"She has a car, but it's in the garage. So she doesn't usually ride the bus."

She had to wait two stops before she felt safe to make her final statement. It just so happened that Mr. Smart decided to help the pregnant lady down the steps, at that particular bus stop. He stood on the bottom one for a moment, his back turned to the driver, as though to check that the woman was all right. Thinking he could not hear her, Roxie leaned over toward Sir William and whispered clearly, "My mom told her about me. I just said, 'Now don't be mad. I just need to talk to him for a minute.' Then I promised to be good if she wouldn't upset my poor mom. Uh-huhhh!"

When Uncle ascended back into the bus, he saw Bill exhale a long, quivering breath. Before the driver stepped on the gas pedal, he wiped the sweat off his upper lip. Clearly, Sir William was not in control of that young princess.

Roxie got off at the Maple Street stop in order to avoid being seen at the Vermont Transit terminal. She could walk at a leisurely pace all the way to Main Street and catch the Essex Junction bus, one stop farther up the hill toward the university. As his bus pulled out past her, Bill looked back at her reflection in the side-view mirror. His shoulders slumped.

At the terminal, Uncle checked the schedule and saw that he had time to call Pooh to let her know he wouldn't need a ride home. The Sears operator reported that Winnie was "unable to come to the phone at this time." He left a message. Outside the phone booth, the morning was still cool, but quite sunny. He checked his watch and realized he was hungry. If he was quick about it, he could grab a doughnut from The Harvest.

Inside, the aroma of coffee and breakfast foods filled the air. The long diner counter stretched along the left side of the restaurant. A mirrored wall behind it made the small place look twice as wide as it really was. Bustling between the counter and the mirror, a waitress was serving up, scraping dishes, and dipping things into water. Her strawberry-blonde curls hid her face, but somehow she had seen him come in. "What'll you have?" she asked, without lifting her head.

"Just a doughnut."

She wiped her hands on her apron as she walked down to the other end of the counter. "Here, or take-out?" she called back to him.

"Take-out."

She grabbed a napkin, lifted the heavy glass pastry cover, and picked up a large, plain doughnut. He was pulling out a quarter as she came toward him. When he looked up, he connected with a pair of beautiful silvery eyes. The resemblance was uncanny. It was Roxie, twenty years older.

"Fifteen cents," she said, wearily.

He handed her the quarter. "Keep the change."

"Thanks." She managed a little smile.

As he left The Harvest, he muttered under his breath, "That has to be Roxie's mother." His insides felt uneasy. Something was wrong. There was that odd feeling again… something he couldn't quite put his finger on. He set the doughnut down on the window ledge just outside the orange doors, and made a quick note.

The doughnut was gone, and he had licked his fingers clean before getting on the Essex Junction bus. To his surprise, there was hardly any place to sit. The vehicle was nearly full of rambunctious sixth-graders and their chaperones from, of all places, the Essex Junction Summit School. Out for a field trip, their school bus had broken down. There wasn't another bus available for hours, so the decision was made to postpone the trip and get the whole class back to the village on the regular local transit system. The alert Burlington Transit bus driver had made a phone call.

Uncle had found a seat at the very last window on the curb side of the bus, when the whole place suddenly went quiet. He looked up over the bobbing heads to see a swarthy man in the Burlington Transit uniform. He immediately saw that it was the male half of the whispering couple from last week. The man stood at the front, and began to speak to the attentive crowd.

"My name is George Foxx, and I'm Personnel Manager for this bus company. The problem with your broken-down bus has come to my attention. Well, I can't get you back your field trip, but maybe I can make things a little easier for you." Little ears were listening. "I could make this a free bus ride for you. Would you let me do that?" The kids heard the adult chaperones exclaiming in delight, so they followed suit and started clapping and cheering. With a satisfied look on his face, Mr. Foxx waved goodbye and got off the bus. As it pulled out, Uncle took another look at the man, who was still waving goodbye from the sidewalk. "So that's Roxie's father," he said to himself as he scribbled another note.

The Essex bus had to travel through Winooski, so it also headed laboriously up the Main Street hill, making a stop just past Edmunds High School, before the street became Colchester Avenue. It picked up one passenger. She bounced on, dropping her coins into the box before squeezing into a seat near the front. Uncle was pretty sure it was Roxie, but could not see clearly past the crowd. The bus proceeded along Colchester Avenue down toward the Winooski bridge.

The kids started singing, just as they always did on their school buses, and before anybody realized it, they were passing through downtown Winooski. As the coach followed Route 15, climbing the East Allen Street hill, it made a stop to let someone off at the Florida Avenue intersection. Uncle pressed close to the window to see if he was right. Sure enough, as the bus moved away, there stood Roxanne Foxx.

"What the gawdim hail is she doing in Winooski on a school morning?" he muttered. He turned around to watch out the rear window of the bus. She waited for a car to pass, then crossed the highway, and started to run along Florida Avenue. He reached for the little green notebook in his pocket.

***

It was finally Halloween, and the Boogieman Bike Bash was in full swing. The end count was eighteen teenagers, which turned out to be perfect. Since there were three riding chaperones, there could be three teams of six riders, each with their own adult supervisor. With the prize of five dollars for each member of the winning team, the teenagers were more than eager to compete. A kid could buy a lot of things for five dollars in 1952.

At seven o'clock all were gathered in the Wilson's driveway, over in front of the carriage barn, going through last-minute safety checks. Jack Wilson's father, Jessie, went down the list on his clipboard. All bikes had a light in front and reflectors in the back, and all riders had white or yellow shirts which would be visible in the headlights of traffic, coming and going. Each chaperone had a minimal first-aid kit, a wrench and a screwdriver. All scavenger items were to be kept in the booty bag tied onto the bike basket of the adult leader, if possible. Caution was given that the group was to stay together, even if a broken bike had to be left behind. Double-riding was only allowed as an emergency measure. "Finally," the dry-humored dairy farmer said, "Chief Rob was kind enough to alert every house on the route of this scavenger hunt, so there is little chance you will encounter any angry dogs or shotguns." The kids snickered, knowing there were perhaps ten houses on the route, and most of those folks knew each other.

Seeing that her husband was finished, Laura Wilson held up a stopwatch for all to see, and gave the rules for the actual hunt.
"Each team will be sent out separately, five minutes apart. The winning team is the one that comes back in the shortest time, with the most items." A chorus of questions erupted

from the little crowd. The tall, willowy woman smiled and lifted her hand for silence. "Just get all the items you can possibly get, in the shortest amount of time you possibly manage. It's not complicated." More questions came. Again, she lifted her hand. "No, the first team will not have first pick, because all three teams will have a different list of items to find." There was a pause for collective thought, so she pulled three toothpicks from the pocket of her flannel shirt. "We'll decide who goes first, and second, and then third." She cuddled the picks inside her right fist, the tips of which poked out in an even length. "Get into your own group now, and then your adult leader will draw a toothpick. The longest one goes first, the middle one is second, and the short one will be the last to leave." It took just a couple of minutes. Father Tom's group was first, Don's was second, and Connie's was last. Laura motioned the first group into starting position. "Lights on, please." As the group turned on their variety of handlebar lights, she pulled a slip of paper from her other pocket. "Okay, you have to read the list, and then off you go." As she handed them their list of seven items, she lifted the stopwatch high with her other hand. "Your time starts *now!*" She pushed the button and called out the time for her lanky husband to jot down: "Seven-fourteen and two seconds."

Father Tom read the list aloud: "A horseshoe, a black button, a shaving brush, a broken phonograph record, a whole maple leaf, a 1951 calendar, and a pig." He looked at Laura. "A pig? Really?" She chuckled and tapped her wristwatch.

That first group sped off across the road to the southern entrance of the Thompsons' driveway. Father Tom knew to lead them to the back door, and they quickly glided out of sight. The other two groups listened intently to the distant shouting and laughter. After a couple of minutes, Father Tom's entourage pulled up under the maple tree, dropping to snatch up a bunch of leaves. Then they remounted and headed toward the railroad track. The priest held up his hand to slow them down for a careful crossing over the rails, and then they disappeared down the deep slope to the highway.

"Second group, get ready," Jessie ordered. Don commandeered his troops to front-and-center positions. The dairyman looked over at his wife and nodded. "Now," she said. Then he jotted down the time: seven-nineteen and two seconds. Don read the list like the military man that he was: "A hardboiled egg, a bowtie, a dead fish, a corn cob, a photo of Santa Claus, a grocery receipt, and a jock stra—." He looked up at Laura.

"I didn't make these lists," she said, unapologetically.

Don's troops took off for the Thompsons' following the path of the first group, right around to the back door. Connie's team leaned forward, listening for hints of how their predecessors were doing. At one point, there was a huge cheer, and then the group reappeared at the maple tree exit, crossing the road to the edge of the cornfield. After a brief scurry, there was a shout of triumph, and the whole band of plunderers moved over the track and sank out of sight.

"Third group." Jessie was pleased at how well this whole operation was going. He looked up and listened one more time. It was seven twenty-four and two seconds.

Coach Connie grabbed the list out of Laura's hand, to address her team. "Now, listen to me. We can do this, just use your imagination, okay? Use your imagination!" She shook the list out and read it rapidly: "A seashell, a wad of chewed gum, a three-stranded braid of hay, a piece of pie, a movie ticket stub, something that flies, and a s-s-snake." She threw her leg across the slanted bar of her girl's bicycle, and pushed forward toward the Thompson farm, closely followed by Diana and Jack, Paula and big brother, Ted, Marsha, and Roxie Foxx. As the six team members reached the back door of the Thompson house, the coach pulled them into a tight circle. "Don't you see?" she chortled. "We can get all these items together in just one place!" The kids leaned in once more, curious. Her eyes sparkled as she spoke. "All we need is depictions of these things — toys, or plastic renditions, like what they use in science class." She smiled as she knocked on the door. "Other than that, what we really need is a few magazines, and a pair of scissors." The back door opened, and Connie asked Winnie, "Do you have a stick of gum?"

Twenty minutes later, almost all items were accounted for. Paula chewed the gum that Cecil handed her, rolling it neatly in its own paper liner. Cecil also let them have a slender slice of Winnie's fresh-baked apple pie, wrapped carefully in waxed paper. Winnie agreed to loan them one of her plaster bluebirds for something that flew, then gave permission for Diana to cut a seashell from a photo in an old National Geographic magazine over there on the window seat.

"A photograph would be cheating," Connie admonished the teenagers, "but an object cut out of a photo becomes an entity unto itself. That's legal." Then she reminded Winnie of the movie she had attended with April. "The same day as the Burlington Transit picnic in Battery Park." Winnie remembered. "So, what do you always do when you get your stub?" she asked. The little woman grabbed her purse and reached deep into an inner pocket, producing a dull red ticket stub from the Strong Theater in Burlington.

All that remained were the straw braid and the snake. Diana and Marsha were already looking for a picture of a snake, when Cecil spoke up. "What kind of snake do you need?"

Roxie Foxx volunteered to go out to the barn's hayloft, to retrieve the long strands of hay, and help make the braid. Winnie escorted her out to the barn, pulling the chain for the overhead light to illuminate the area, and watched the girl scurry up the ladder in order to snatch a small handful of supple strands, just right for braiding. The two of them returned to the house just in time to see Cecil hauling a long metal rod from the recesses of the little closet in the bathroom.

"What is that?" someone asked.

"It's a plumber's snake," Cecil replied as he waggled the supple object in front of them. "You unclog the toilet with it."

"Ewww," the girls said.

"We'll take it!" the boys said.

By the time Roxie and Connie had fashioned the braid, there were shouts coming from the road. Father Tom's team had arrived back at the Wilson's driveway. It was time for Connie's group to finish up.

They were back at the Wilson Dairy Farm just two minutes later. Jessie's was impressed as he recorded Connie's team's return. It was only seven-fifty, on the mark. Only about thirty minutes had elapsed. The first group had been gone for almost thirty-five minutes. Don's group was still somewhere on route, probably near the creamery. Laura eyed the booty bag hanging on the handlebars of Connie's bike, but decided to hold off on any questions until Don's troops got back. Instead, she invited everybody to have some cider and doughnuts over in the horse-and-carriage barn, while she and Jessie tallied the booty from Father Tom's bag.

This first collection was placed piece-by-piece on an old card table near the farmhouse's back door. The couple checked off each found item, as they went down the list, making a final tally at the very bottom. "Missing one item. Pig." Underneath that, Jessie wrote the time expended: "Thirty-four minutes and fifty-eight seconds."

Connie's group's collection was carefully placed on a large towel which lay on the back steps to the house. As they lined up the items, the couple shook their heads. The final tally read, "One item missing. Seashell. The time expended was thirty minutes and two seconds." Laura folded the towel over to hold the lighter-weight items in place, and looked at her husband. "We may have a problem, here."

Over on the swept-clean floorboards of the old barn, Scottie and Penny, who were in Father Tom's group, sidled up to Jack and Diana. Scottie looked at his watch. "How did you manage to get back so soon, you guys?" he whispered to the other two.

Jack grinned. "Just lucked out, I guess."

"Did you find everything?" Penny inquired.

"Think so..." came Jack's vague reply. He picked up a doughnut. "How do you like my mom's cinnamon doughnuts?"

"They're delicious," Penny said. She caught Diana's eye. "How did your handlebar flashlight work? Did it fall off at all?"

"Nope," her friend replied with a pinched little smile. "That big, ole' sucker just hung right in there." She looked at Jack and chuckled.

Scottie looked at those two, from one face to the other, before he started a slow grin. "You guys are up to something. What the heck did you do, rig the contest?" he joked.

The other three laughed, then Jack changed the subject. Looking around him, he remarked, "Starting tomorrow morning, we put a parade float together in here."

Ten minutes later, Don's band of weary warriors came dragging up the road from Essex Junction. Their faces were red and sweaty. It had been a hard ride. Father Tom led a rousing cheer when the final contestants hit the driveway. As he dismounted, Don saw that Connie's group was already back. "Hey!" he puffed. "How did you get past us?" Laura was approaching him for the booty bag, so he didn't really have time to catch the answer. Jessie came alongside Laura. He reached out and patted Don on the back. "Helluva try, Don."

That told Mr. Collins all he needed to know. He twisted around to call out to his team: "Well, we came in last but let's see how many items they got. Maybe we still have a run at it." The winded kids set their bikes aside and headed for the cold cider.

That evening, the Boogieman Bike Bash was won by Connie Collins's team, but it wasn't because they had all their items. The seashell "entity" was deemed "a piece of paper with printing ink depicting a seashell." Connie ceded this defeat to the judges, Jessie and Laura, since it still left her team winners, based on the shortest length of time it took to scavenge the other six items. All-in-all, the event was considered a success. The dance in the barn afterward, probably put it over the top.

Roxie Foxx spent most of that part of the evening manning the portable record player, talking like a disc jockey and hooting at her own jokes. She started the music with a Decca 78 by the Andrew Sisters, **I Can Dream, Can't I?** because the bicyclists were still getting their second wind. The music echoed off the open rafters of the barn, while the youngsters shuffled in a slow dance over the creaking floor. After she flipped that vinyl platter over and the Sisters finished **The Wedding of Lili Marlene**, however, the group was ready for something with a little more of a beat. She slipped Rosemary Clooney's **Come On-a My House** onto the spindle and lowered the needle. Immediately, the old barn floor vibrated under stomping feet. Even the little tap-dancer, Penny, who had shed her crutches a few days before, was into it. Scottie mostly just stood still and twirled her by the hand as she hit every beat. Their eyes met in the fun of the moment.

Watching that couple dance, Roxie's face suddenly clouded over. She had forgotten that Penny was now ready to resume her cheerleading position. That meant she, herself, would be benched. But then, she smirked to herself, she had been up there in front, for a good portion of basketball season. The victory would have been sweeter, however, if there hadn't been the incident with that jerk, Scottie. She watched him grinning and enjoying himself. Right then and there, she decided she wasn't finished with "that one."

Meanwhile, there was other fun to be had for the resilient redhead. The tall, lanky Ted Donahue, Paula's older brother, sidled up to lean on the old horse feed bin right next to her. "Hey, Roxie! Is it true what I heard about you?" The girl's nostrils flared. He shook his wavy hair. "I heard you know how to jitterbug. Is it true?"

She took a short, hard breath. "Does a cat have four paws?" she wisecracked.

Paula could not believe her brother was even talking to that girl. She shot him a warning look, but he ignored her.

"Well, I just bet I can jitterbug your pretty little socks off," he challenged.

"Oh yeah?" She sized him up, then sneered. "We'll just see about that." She slid a record from its cardboard casing and placed it on the player, then gently dropped the needle. Glen Miller's In the Mood thumped into action.

If there was one thing Roxie could do well, it was *dance*. Having been enrolled in dance classes back there in Albany, New York, the ten-year-old had excelled especially in jitterbug. By her eleventh birthday, she was the lead female performer in a jitterbug special production in that year's dance recital. Her mom, who seldom hung around during lessons, actually had black-and-white glossies of that one.

Now she was in full swing, and delighted that Ted not only could keep up with her, but showed an exciting and inventive style. It was as though they had been dancing together for years. For a while, neither one was aware of anything else but the music and the moves. By the finish, the two were out of breath, and bowing to an appreciative barn dance audience.

The jitterbug over, she complimented Ted with a flat-handed slap on his butt, and morphed back into the wisecracking platter-pusher. She stayed that way for the next hour.

At nine-fifteen, the Wilson hosts stood in the middle of the carriage space to say goodnight. "As you know, we have assured Chief Rob that you would all be off the roads by ten o'clock. Plus, we need to get this dance area ready for the construction of the new parade float, starting tomorrow. If you can help with that, it would be much appreciated. Meanwhile, thanks for a great time. We couldn't have done it without you."

The Boogieman Bike Bash participants left a half-hour later, a trail of bobbing lights moving southward toward the village. As they moved along, their jesting and laughter became more and more distant. At last, silence came upon the curve of Old Colchester Road.

The crackle of a leaf in the driveway indicated the presence of one cyclist who was lingering a bit longer, actually taking a detour through the Thompsons' driveway. She stopped to gaze into the barn for a few seconds, then moved on to catch up with the others.

Someone saw her from the darkened kitchen window of the upstairs apartment.

PART II

~~~

Reality
~~~

CHAPTER FIFTEEN

Faith

"I do not wish to offend anyone, but I believe we have grossly underestimated God Almighty. Do we really think that, when He said, 'Let there be light!' that He immediately thought, '*Oh boy, I sure hope this works!*'?" The folks at Swift Street Pentecostal Church chuckled along with Deacon Peter Foster. They were enjoying this early November service.

"Would God Almighty, have doubts about His own authority, His own all-encompassing power?" Absurdity emanated from his squint. "I think we may all agree that God knows very well, just who He is, and what He can do." He ambled toward the front of the platform, his hands clasped behind his back. "Not only can He create, but the Bible tells us that He *sings* over His creation." The smile was broad. "The last few verses of Zephaniah tell us that our God is mighty, and will save us, and when we are saved, He rejoices over us, with singing!" The preacher raised his hand. "How many of you know that?" To the few who responded, he posed the next thought. "And did you also know that when He saved you by the Blood of Jesus, not only did the Holy Ghost enter into you, but also Jesus and God, Himself?" Those faces, lit by the frosty Sunday morning light of the church windows, froze in place. "Ah…, I see that this is a bit of a surprise to you, but hold on, my friends." This smile was reassuring. "The Trinity is inseparable." He shrugged, letting his hands fall to his side. "Jesus said it, Himself: 'I am in the Father, and He is in me.' Now think about that. When you are really saved, the Holy Ghost enters in, for certain, but so does Jesus and the Father." He wandered back toward the lectern, calling out over his shoulder. "And there's that prayer where Jesus asks that all those who accept Him, be made 'one with' Him, just as *He* is one with the *Father*." He stopped and picked up the glass of water. "So, when we are saved, we become one with the whole Trinity." He took a sip, and continued, still gripping the plain, translucent tumbler. "May I take a moment to address the issue of God-like faith?"

"Now remember, it was not that God simply willed that there be light, it was that He *fully expected* that there *would* be light and, why? Because God Almighty knew the power" — the drink was placed firmly back onto the dais — "of His Own Word!" All eyes were on this preacher as he stood on the platform of Pastor James's church. "Oh, that I could help you all to understand it; we have this kind of faith and this kind of power inside of us." His head lowered, as though listening to a voice.

Suddenly, he leaned back to release rich, rolling laughter. "Yes, Lord!" he exclaimed. Then he clapped his big hands together, and moved lightly down from the platform, to stand directly in front of the first row of the congregation. There, he addressed a little woman in sensible, slip-on shoes and a pale green plaid dress. "Dear lady." The closeness of his deep, melodious voice made her gasp. "May I ask you a question?"

Winnie Thompson's small eyes grew wide. She was speechless. Paralyzed like a deer in the headlights, she regretted that she, a faithful Roman Catholic, had ever agreed to accompany the Collinses to a Pentecostal service. It did flash through her mind that she had done it out of curiosity, probably for the entertainment, and now she was caught and if anybody recognized her in the glare of this unwelcomed spotlight, she would have to recite umpteen Hail Marys after confession next week. But right now, all she could do was stare back at this big man who was hovering over her.

"Is Jesus Christ your Savior?" he asked gently.

She jerked her head, ever-so-slightly, to confirm that.

"Do you believe that He died, rose again, and ascended into Heaven?"

Another quick jerk of the head.

"And you have *accepted* Him as your Savior?" He rephrased the question in order to put the responsibility where it belonged.

This time she moved her head with a full nod.

He looked up at the congregation. "Then this lady has the Holy Ghost inside of her, is that not true?" He paused, taking a couple of steps to his right. With his eyes still on the crowd, he softly reminded them, "John fourteen, twenty-six, my friends, says that Jesus had to leave the earth, so that the Holy Ghost could come. And the Holy Ghost did come, at Pentecost, and then He entered into every person who gave his life to Jesus, after that, to this very day, amen?"

The amens rumbled softly forward.

"Now," he rubbed the little furrow between his eyebrows as though to get the thought into its proper place, "the Holy Ghost is part of the Trinity — the Father, Son, and Holy Ghost. Will you all agree with that?" Heads nodded everywhere. "Three in One, inseparable, working in unity?" More nodding. "Excellent." He turned to step up onto the platform, heading for the lectern.

Winnie turned and whispered to Connie, "Good Lord, girl! Did we have to sit in the very front row?" Connie glanced in amusement toward her friend, then her attention was back on the beautiful black man, and his thundering oration.

"So, we all have the God-like faith, and the power in us, am I correct?" More acquiescent nods moved throughout the crowd. "So then, should we not be able to reach out to minister encouragement, to — dare I say it? — to heal the sick, bring sight to the blind, call out the demonic?" He opened his palms toward the listening brethren. "If we are truly one with the Trinity, then, like the disciples, like the Apostles, we should be doing the same mighty works." He shrugged once more. "Tell me, are any of *them* more saved than *us*? In fact, is your priest, or elder, or pastor more saved than *you*? No! Being saved is being saved, no matter who you are. If you are saved, you have all the God-given power that Peter and Paul and your own church leaders have. In this matter, God is not partial; all saved people are His children, and have these gifts. Can you see that, now?"

Once more he looked out over the crowd, as he took a couple of steps toward them.

Winnie lowered her head. "*Oh, Lord Jesus, please don't let him come down here again.*"

But then, the orator held up a cautioning hand. "Remember, we are speaking of the God-kind of faith, which is *always within God's will.* The Holy Spirit is ready to guide you into all wisdom, and that is always God's will and God's way and *that* is the *only* way you and I can speak things into being. Do we all understand that quite clearly?"

A brave voice spoke up: "Yes, sir!"

"Once you understand that very important rule, you can settle into doing what Jesus commanded you to do the same as He told the disciples to do in the Book of Matthew. Cast out unclean spirits, heal all manner of sickness and diseases, cleanse the lepers. Indeed, preach the gospel and perform signs and wonders." He slapped his hand together to emphasize the last few words. "And I am talking to every last one of you in this congregation."

He watched eyebrows rise all across the room.

"No-no-no! Don't let anyone accuse you of *playing God*. You aren't *playing God*; you are *obeying God*."

Now some of the folks were leaning intently forward.

He looked up. "If you are saved, God's law is already establishing itself in your heart, my friend, through the teachings of the Holy Ghost. So, God's law and God's wisdom are both accessible to a surrendered believer." The handsome face was more intense, now. "We are under the divine covering of God's grace, through the miraculous blood sacrifice of His Son. Jesus died for our sins. His blood paid the price."

He looked around. "Is there anyone here who has not accepted Jesus as their Savior? If so, now is the time for you to do just that. Until you belong to Him, you cannot have this power." He pursed his lips. "Let me just do this, my friend. Let me lead you all together in the Sinner's Prayer. We want to make sure no one leaves here today without the beautiful grace of God over his life." He raised his hands. "So, with every head bowed and every eye closed..."

When the one elderly man was led to the Lord, it was finally time for the actual healing line to form. Pastor James gave the nod, lining up a couple of deacons to serve as "catchers," just in case those who got blessed might "fall out under the power."

Deacon Foster moved forward to the right side of the platform, placing himself at the head of the slowly growing queue of seekers. Rehema took her place close to her ministering husband. By the time the line stretched across the front of the platform, the Fosters and Pastor James were laying on hands and praying with authority over the first few people. A lady fell backwards into the arms of a catcher, who laid her gently upon the cement floor.

This is what Winnie had really come for. She wanted to see these Pentecostals in action. Her eyes never left the faces of

Deacon and his wife; her ears caught as much of the powerful prayers as they could.

She saw some hands suddenly shoot upward, while others trembled in place, and still others fluttered like sparrows at each side of the head. Some folks fell backwards, some collapsed in a heap, some wobbled in place, and others just stood like statues. People were actually showing signs of physical healing. Some laughed, some cried, a couple of them shouted, but most of them just took a little breath and slipped to the floor into some kind of rapture. This little Roman Catholic lady could see that something was definitely happening, here, something quite strange and maybe even wonderful.

Slowly, methodically, the trio speaking this biblical healing power worked their way down to the end of the line. By the time the last person was prayed for, Winnie was sitting on the edge of her seat, her mouth wide open.

A touch on her left arm brought her back to the friend sitting beside her, who, with a smile, said it all. "How about that?!" Winnie closed her mouth and stared at the people still lying prostrate on the floor.

It was time to leave, and Connie looked around in time to see her husband heading for the door, but she, herself, wasn't ready to move her friend along, just yet. There was too much to absorb, first.

The Roman Catholic lady shook her head slowly. "Well," she said, "if I hadn't seen it for myself, I wouldn't have believed it." She looked her friend in the eye. "Did I really see that mole drop off that man's forehead?"

"Everybody here," Connie replied loudly, "saw that mole drop off that man's forehead."

"And," Winnie bowed her head in a moment of unbelief, "that woman all bent over like that. I mean, I could hear the bones snapping when she stood up straight." Her little eyes were wide with wonder. "And the baby with the club foot."

Finally, the two women stood up to head for the exit.

"Excuse me, dear lady." The voice was gentle.

Winnie stopped and looked up into the face of Rehema Foster, the compassionate one.

"May I just have a word with you, for one brief moment?" The glistening golden eyes were fixed steadily on Winnie's guarded gaze. She reached down and clasped the little tan hand inside her graceful black one. "I mean no harm, dear lady. I just have a word from God for you."

Winnie gasped.

"No-no," Rehema reassured her, "there is no need to fear. I bring you a word of encouragement." Connie closed in to hold Winnie's other hand, and stayed at her side. Her friend was glad she was there, but in reality, Connie just didn't want to be left out.

"Compassion" stepped back, drawing the little Abenaki to the side of the exit line, not letting go of her hand, desiring to speak out of the crowd's earshot. Connie pressed in closer, not wanting to miss a word.

"Earlier in the service, when my husband singled you out, you remember that, do you not?" Winnie acknowledged this with one more short jerk of her head. "As he was speaking to you, I saw a picture." Winnie frowned ever-so-slightly. The sweet black lady's eyelids slipped to a soft close, and her voice became melodious.

"I saw a faded teddy bear, sitting on a large golden throne. The well-worn, well-loved bear had a slash diagonally across its chest, and stuffing was coming out. Above the throne, silent, sad birds clung to a colorless rainbow. Because they had no joy, they could not sing, and because their stilled wings could find no updraft, they could not soar. There is no rest, no respite, no release, only helplessness and despair."

She tightened her grip on Winnie's hand. "Now here is what the Lord says to you. He says, 'I will restore the hope and mend the wound. Faint not, and fear not. I am the Lord, your God, your Deliverer. With Me, all things are possible.

Faint not, and fear not, for you will receive a *double portion revelation.'"* She slowly released the small hand. "Thus saith the Lord." She opened the golden eyes again, and smiled. "God bless you, little sister," she said. And then she moved back into the crowd.

***

The inside of the Studebaker was pretty quiet on the ride back to the Thompson farmhouse late that afternoon. Don and Connie sat in the front seat, holding hands and looking softly into each other's eyes at every stoplight. As the light went green, the old bomber pilot turned his attention to the road, letting his wife go back to the mental pictures of the healing service. In the back seat, Winnie Thompson stared out the side window, her deep thoughts interrupted briefly by the occasional rattling of the Flannigans' croquet set back in the trunk of the car. The sun was hanging low over the bare treetops when Winnie said her thank-yous and slipped in through the back door to get supper going for Cecil and Uncle.

"She said she was glad she came," Connie said, as Don guided the car slowly over the railroad tracks, across the highway and down into the gulley of Case Road. He nodded, shifting gears to climb back up the other side of the deep ravine. The couple was headed for the Flannigan house, to deliver the croquet set which had been sitting by the back door of the Collinses' screened-in patio. It had been languishing there at their Winooski home, for the last three weeks.

As they approached the sloping hill ahead, Connie glanced to her right for a quick view of the old Case house, where Shirley Bogue lived. She reminded herself that there was another meeting of the Maple Leaf Sewing Circle next Saturday, right there at Shirley's house. She was looking forward to it, since she had not been inside the place before. It promised to be an interesting experience, since there was some local history there, and especially since this was where the Ouija board activities were going on.

Less than a mile later, Don pulled the car into the Flannigans' driveway. April appeared almost immediately on the front porch. She called her husband to come out from the garage, then invited the visiting couple to join them for supper.

"Oh my goodness!" Connie exclaimed. "We had no idea of doing such a thing. In fact, I don't think either one of us has thought about food for the last four hours. "She looked squarely at April. "We've had quite a day."

"You haven't eaten, then. Good." The blonde lady ushered the Collinses into the delightful antique setting of the small living room. "And you can tell us about your day over roast beef dinner."

Bill came in through the front door a couple of minutes later. He had clearly been working on something that involved a lot of grease. After a courteous greeting, he excused himself and headed for the shower. While he was doing that, Don and Connie related most of what had taken place at the little church on Swift Street. With each additional tidbit of information, April became more amazed. At last, Bill reemerged, all sparkling clean, and definitely hungry.

Dinner was served on an old Duncan Fife dining room table, its inlaid-wood top carefully covered with padding and a genuinely stained old lace tablecloth. The four matching chairs — one carefully reinforced with strategically placed wire — still had their faded green brocade cushions. The whole set filled one corner of the tiny kitchen, and the seating was snug, but nobody seemed to mind, since the meal was great and the conversation was stimulating, to say the least.

Although Bill had missed most of the details, he surmised there had been a healing service at the Collinses' Pentecostal church that morning or afternoon. He only half-listened, making no comments on the event, until the third repeat of the baby with the club foot was brought up. Suddenly, he leaned back and wiped his mouth with the special company-only linen napkin. Then he looked at Don and asked, "Does Cecil know his wife went to this so-called healing service today?"

It caught the other three off guard. They stopped what they were doing and stared at him, then glanced at each other.

"It never occurred to me to ask that question," Don finally answered.

Bill tilted his head in his best James Dean fashion and said, all-too-casually, "Just seems to me that Cecil is not the type who would go for that kind of stuff, know what I mean?" He jabbed at a couple of string beans, lifted them up on his fork, and waggled them in front of his mouth. "He's more the quiet, thinker type, wouldn't you say?" He thrust the beans into his mouth, chewing slowly as he made eye contact with Don once more. Clearly, he was expecting an answer.

"You know, I don't really know Cecil Thompson all that well," the older man replied.

Bill's condescending smirk cut short the eye contact. The movie actor slipped his plate off the table as he called the dog. "Charley! Come here, boy!" April raised her hand to reach for the plate.

"No, no, Bill. Please don't feed him that stuff."

Her husband pulled the plate back from her reach. "Charley!" The scurry of little doggie feet signaled the poodle's arrival. The plate went down to the floor, and the noisy slup-slup-slup of the feeding brought forth a benevolent grin on Bill's face. He kept his eyes on the small bundle of curls as he spoke in his hero voice. "Is that good, boy? Huh?" He laughed. "Good stuff, huh, Charley? Good stuff, huh, boy?" As the slup noises ceased, Bill reached down and picked up the dog, snuggling his face against the wriggling little body, acting every bit the Wonderful Master. "Yeah, yeah, yeah, little buddy. I know. Yeah, I know." As the dog continued to wriggle, its ears suddenly folded down, and it began to make little yipping noises. The three witnesses sensed the dog was in distress.

"Bill, he's not happy," April warned him. Another condescending smirk broke forth and the man kept the lifted dog up in front of him, holding the unhappy animal under the front legs, and leaving the rest of the little body to dangle.

"Us guys have to stick together, right, buddy?" He gave Charley a little shake.

"Right, little buddy?" He put his nose to the little dog's nose and gave him another little shake.

Charley peed a warm stream down the front of Bill's neck.

The hero's face went into shock, and multiple curses escaped his mouth, as the toy poodle was dropped into the middle of the dining room table.

The ensuing scenario could have been straight out of a Laurel and Hardy movie at a Saturday afternoon matinee in the Strong Theater. The short end of the story was that April and the Collinses cleaned up the dog and the mess on the table, while Bill stripped down to wash his neck, then donned a clean shirt.

At the end of thirty minutes, Don stood before the open trunk of his Studebaker, and raised out the croquet set. Bill took the racked set and put it down in the driveway. In the fuzzy light of dusk, he took a long look at his favorite lawn game's equipment.

"Where's the red mallet?" he asked.

"What?" Don moved forward to inspect the racked set. He saw the yellow, green, and blue mallets on one side of the rack. On the other side, the orange and black ones were each in place. But there was, indeed, no red mallet. He moved in closer to the trunk of the car, sweeping his hand across the empty space within. "It's not in there," he murmured. "Maybe it fell out when I brought it around from the back."

Bill's eyes were focused on the bumper of the Studebaker. "Yeah, maybe," he said.

"I'll check it out as soon as I get home," Don reassured his fellow bus-driver. "But don't worry. I will replace this set with a new, complete one, if necessary." He reached out to touch Bill's shoulder. "I will make it good, Bill." Bill's shoulder remained rigid under Don's reassuring pat.

It was dark by the time they got home, but Don still retraced his steps from the back patio to the garage where he had loaded the croquet set into the car. The red mallet was nowhere to be found.

"I sure don't know what happened to that thing," he said to Connie. "I guess we really will have to buy them a new set."

"Oh well," she remarked, "if that's the worst thing that ever happens to us..."

CHAPTER SIXTEEN

Dancing

Scheduling Roxanne Foxx's counseling sessions with Don Collins had been difficult, since there needed to be another female present at all times, and Connie could not always meet the usual appointment times. Both Don and Connie knew there was a six-session time limit, then an assessment needed to be done, determining whether or not the client was responding favorably. The usual procedure was to make the evaluation, and then decide whether to continue the treatment, or abandon the effort. Surely, a client who was "playing" the counselor, was not ready to make the necessary lifestyle changes in order to enter into a healthy new life. That was almost always evident by the sixth session. In Roxie's case, they had barely squeezed two sessions into the three-week period. The third one took place just after the Boogieman Bike Bash, on the following Tuesday evening, November 4.

Before the counseling session, the Collinses prayed that the truth, and the whole truth would be revealed in this meeting with Roxanne. The girl, of course, was unaware of the fact that both Don and his wife were suspicious of her claims concerning the deceased bus driver, Alan Strong. They also knew they had to reinforce that bond of trust between themselves and Roxanne. Thankfully, there was a natural opening into the subject, because minutes after the session began, Roxie had proudly announced she had written a song.

"It's about my dreams. You told me to write a song about my dreams, right?" Seeing the nods of approval from the Collinses, she pulled the ukulele up close to her bosom and struck a couple of soft chords.

Suddenly, she leaned forward.

"This song is between us, right? I mean, nobody else is going to hear this, right?"

"Okay, Roxie, if that is what you want, then that is what you shall have," Don reassured her.

"Swear?"

The couple laughed. "We don't swear," Don said. "But we can promise."

There was a long look from the girl's silvery eyes, moving slowly from the man to his wife, and back again. The statement came forth in a husky, foreign whisper. "I don't trust you."

Don's head bowed, then lifted. "Okay, then we don't need to hear your song."

"What?"

"It's okay, Roxie. We don't want you to feel threatened." His engaging grin emphasized his sincerity. "We don't need to hear your song."

"Oh, Don, she is so talented." Connie's gaze pleaded with him. "Please, I really want to hear this. I'm sure it will be precious." She looked at Roxie, then back to her husband. "This could help us to help her, Don."

The man's eyes focused on his knees for a few seconds, then he raised his head and sighed. "Alright. We'll hear your song, Roxie." He glanced over at his wife. "Maybe it *will* help."

To his surprise, Roxie reached into a pocket and pulled out a white sheet of lined paper. The lyrics filled the whole 8½ by 11 inch space. The Collinses peered more closely as she spread it across her knees where she could read it. Don reckoned there were at least ten verses. He caught Connie's eye and deliberately leaned back, ready to endure an extended concert. Connie hid a smile.

The girl strummed an introduction, soft and sweet, before she started to sing. Both the man and his wife were surprised to hear a melody eerily similar to the old Irish folk song, Molly Malone. At first, the lyrics were quite charming:

"Sweet butterfly me-ee, dear butterfly me-ee,
So fragile and lovely and fluttering free.
Did Heaven decree-ee you lonely to be-ee?
Sweet flutter-high, flutter-by, butterfly me.'

"Sweet butterfly me-ee, dear butterfly me-ee,
Once more you enchant as you dance o'er the lea.
Beguile gracefully-ee, each blossom you see-ee.
Sweet flutter-high, flutter-by, butterfly me.'

"Sweet butterfly me-ee, dear butterfly me-ee,
Go seeking the food-of-the-gods from the tree.
Wing'd goddess, for thee-ee, the blossoms will plea-ee.
Sweet flutter-high, flutter-by, butterfly me.'

"Sweet butterfly me-ee, dear butterfly me-ee,
Drink deep from the nectar and quiver with glee.
When petals fall free-ee, you'll sting like the bee-ee,
Sweet flutter-high, flutter-by, butterfly me.'

At this point, the tone of the song signaled a foreboding descent. It went slowly into thinly disguised decadence, then to derision, and finally into all-out destruction. The last two verses told it all:

"Sweet butterfly me-ee, dear butterfly me-ee,
You've drained all the life in a blind-thirsty spree,

It was quiet in the basement office. Roxie set her ukulele down against the front leg of her chair, and smoothed the notebook paper carefully into a double fold. After she placed it back into her pocket, she looked up. Don Collins was holding his chin in one hand, looking at his wife. Connie was very solemn.

"How did you like it?"

The two adults nodded a cautious approval.

"It's my dream song." She slid one foot forward and slouched down into the chair, quite satisfied.

"The tune was very Irish-sounding… rather plaintive, I would say," Connie offered. "And I like the way you played on the word, 'butterfly.' Very clever."

The gorgeous redhead wriggled in pleasure, then looked at Don.

"I agree, the wording was pretty darned good for a writer as young as you are. How old are you now, Roxie?"

"I'll be fifteen on the twenty-first of this month."

He put on his impish grin. "A Thanksgiving baby, huh?" She tossed her curls in pleasure at the idea of being so special. He leaned forward, arms folded in front of him on the desktop. "So this song is about your dreams?" She nodded. "Very good." He slid back toward the chair again, sitting up straight. "So-o-o…" He looked up in a friendly, quizzical manner. "…have you thought about what this all means? I mean, what is your gut feeling about your dreams? Any ideas on that?"

Her eyes clouded over just a little. "I'm not sure."

He waited for a few seconds to give her time to think about it, then gently asked, "Was this a hard song for you to write?"

"Not really. I think about writing songs all the time." She tapped her fingers lightly upon her knees. "This one just was a little hard on the rhyming. I guess you noticed, all the rhyming was 'ee's.'" Both adults nodded and smiled. "That was hard."

"I'm curious. Why did you make all the rhymes 'ee's'?" he asked.

She hooted softly. "I lo-o-ve the challenge."

"Well, you certainly aced it!" Connie commented. She looked up from where she was taking notes in the back-corner chair. "I bet that's why you're such a good student, liking a challenge, I mean."

Don grinned again. "So, you're a good student, Roxie?"

"Yup!" She twisted her mouth into a prideful smile. "No problem."

"Good at math?"

"Yup."

"All that problem-solving?"

She hooted, again. "Nothing really changes. You just stick to the basics, and it all comes together, no problem."

"Well, I'm impressed."

The session went on for another forty-five minutes. Several important insights were achieved concerning the sadness of not having her dad around when she was little, and some of the ramifications of that situation, but the girl continued to waltz around any explanation of the meaning of her so-called "dream song." Her mother finally pushed the door chime button, and it was time for Roxie to leave. By now, both mother and daughter understood that every counseling session began and ended with prayer, so they stood quietly until the closing prayer was done, then hastily departed to attend to other more important things.

As Connie closed the door behind them, she turned and addressed her husband. "Wow! She sure didn't want to talk about that so-called 'dream song'!"

He stuck his hands into his pockets, a worried look on his face. "And that wasn't even the scariest part."

Roxie had no idea of all the information she had just revealed.

***

The Sadie Hawkins Dance was held on Friday, November 7. Not everybody was comfortable with that, with Thanksgiving break coming up, and there was the little matter of getting ready for midterm finals. Nevertheless, the dance had become a tradition, and this was the best the dance committee could do.

The Sadie Hawkins annual dance was named after a man-chasing character in the *Li'l Abner* comic strip, and based on one of the main social events celebrated by the folks of Dogpatch, Li'l Abner's hometown. On Sadie Hawkins Day, each young lady of Dogpatch tried to catch a husband by overtaking an eligible bachelor in an annual foot-race. If she caught him, the fellow had to marry her.

Young people in educational institutions across America were caught up in the fun of this role reversal, and decided to take ownership of it, in their own way. The theme was altered a bit, and turned into a fun school event where the girls got to ask the boys out on a dance date. Truth be known, many, many teenage guys who would have been turned down if they had asked a girl to a dance, were secretly practicing dance moves in the privacy of their bedrooms, just in case they got asked. Some were actually surprised to be asked. The rest pretended it didn't matter.

Despite all its gender-liberating qualities, this year the Essex Junction High School Sadie Hawkins Dance was still a well-supervised and organized event.

The usual couples attended, since there was no basketball game scheduled, and quite a crowd showed up in the gym. Bales of hay, bundled cornstalks, and a number of small, battered barrels lined the walls. The boys in their "country bumpkin" outfits lay around with straw grass hanging from their mouths, trying to impress their dates. Most of the girls were in pigtails and freckles. The majority of these young ladies sat on the bales, giggling and dangling their tennis shoes from under the legs of their dungarees. One couple showed up as a scarecrow couple, complete with carefully drawn clown faces and straw draping from the edges of their shirtsleeves and overall legs.

Even the local three-piece band, Shake-Down, took the time to dress accordingly before they showed up for this gig, pushing seedy-looking straw hats toward the backs of their heads and wrapping red and white bandanas loosely around their necks. But, even though a guest fiddler had been added, the music wouldn't quite strike the hillbilly/bluegrass mark; it would still have the popular pounding beat of rock and roll. Shake-Down was not intimidated about that, because most of those kids wouldn't know Bill Munro or Ralph Stanley from a couple of holes in the ground, anyway. It was going to be fine.

***

There were two special events to take place during this year's Sadie Hawkins Dance. The first one was a dance contest, with the winning couple being awarded free passes to the ski hill at Underhill, Vermont. "One time only," the poster had emphasized. Even though ski season had not yet started, this was considered an outstanding prize, and would come in handy in just a month or so. Several couples signed up. The duo of Roxanne Foxx and Ted Donahue was one of them. Because of their jitterbug duet up there at the Boogieman Bike Bash, both knew they could probably win. They began to rehearse the first week of November, and pretty soon Teddy was calling her by the playful name, "Shug-ah," a Southern version of "Sugar."

Paula had been disgusted that her older brother was linking up with Roxie, for anything, whatsoever. "That girl has a horrible reputation. Why would you do something so stupid?"

"She's a good dancer."

"She's also only fourteen years old."

"She's very mature for her age."

Paula caught that. "I can't believe my own brother is a drooling pig."

"Hey, I'm a guy."

"Same thing."

While Ted loved to ski, Roxie had no intention of using her pass. She didn't bother to tell him, however, since, as her dance partner, he had been especially attentive the last few days, stopping to chat in the hallway, waving from his black four-door sedan with the wide-whitewall tires, then gunning the engine as he roared out of the school parking lot. Most of the EJHS students were sure that he had the coolest car in the village.

She was pleased that he liked her, enjoying being called "Shug-ah," and it wasn't but a week before the relationship became more involved. One late afternoon, the two of them left the gym after a strenuous rehearsal. Darkness was deepening over the countryside just outside the village, as the two of them shuffled down the sidewalk toward the parking lot.

"Hey, Shug-ah," he said softly, as he reach over and squeezed her hand. "You must be tired. Let me drive you home."

She responded to his invitation with velvety eyes. "You know what? I would really enjoy a nice, relaxing drive." Her lips showed a faint smile. "Are you up to that?"

***

Publically, however, Roxie was careful not to appear too friendly with her dance partner. After all, it was Marsha who had the crush on Ted. The girl had a part-time job at the Donahues' Lincoln Street Greenhouse, and part of the benefits, as far as she was concerned, was having proximity to the company of this handsome fellow with the wavy black hair. Knowing all this, Roxie did not want the ski ticket for herself; she wanted to use it as bargaining material for Marsha. Sometime in the future — Roxie wasn't quite sure yet, just how or when — she might need some help from that girl. A free ski pass to go shushing with Teddy Donahue would be some *heavy* bargaining material. So, Roxie really, really wanted to win that ski pass.

In a "control" move to make sure she won the contest, Roxie had read the sign-up sheet for the dance contestants and concluded that she didn't have to worry about most of the competitors on the schedule. In fact, the final couple listed actually made her hoot out loud. It was Diana and Jack. There was not a dancing bone in their bodies. Both of them were, if anything, lanky and awkward. She knew there was only one serious challenger-couple in the contest, and it was the second team to perform: Scottie and Penny. "The perky little tap-dancer," she muttered aloud. There was definitely a need to manage this threat, so two days before the dance, she cornered Scottie Allen in the cloakroom on the main floor at EJHS.

"Stand still, and act like you're enjoying this conversation," she growled darkly at the surprised freshman boy. She put a phony smile on her face and spoke quickly and intensely: "Ted and I are going to win the dance contest this Friday, do you understand? Why? Because I always win, that's why. I always win, because if I don't, I get real upset. But I don't get mad. No-no. I don't get mad, I just get even. You know what happens when I get even? I talk a lot. About things you have done. Do you understand that, you slimeball?" She pressed closer to his pale face. "I win either way. So listen: if you win, you will lose. Big time. Think about it." She pulled back and tilted her head as the sweet, little murmuring voice returned. "I know you won't let me down." He could not see her face as she walked away.

Scottie informed his older brother of this conversation, that very same afternoon. This time, it was the chief who made a few notes.

***

The second special event of the evening was the unveiling of the Essex Junction parade float. A colorful locomotive structure had been put together in the carriage barn at the old Wilson Dairy Farm. The building, located a few hundred feet north of the dairy barn, had originally been a rather luxurious buggy barn for its era, with stalls for four horses, a large tack room and a spacious area in the very center, which could have housed a large carriage. This carriage area was the ideal site for constructing the lightweight parade float.

On the evening of the Sadie Hawkins Dance, the float was slowly driven by Jessie Wilson from the horse barn to the front of the school. It was mostly hidden from view by the several tarps which protected it from flying pebbles off the dry roads. Only the bright yellow cab of the basic truck remained in sight, so it could be legally and safely driven down the Old Colchester Road to its destination. Jessie drove the float down, with the prearranged understanding that Jack would leave his own Ford truck in the parking lot and drive the float back after the dance. After all, a dairy farmer got up early, and Jessie was no big fan of dance contests. Laura had followed in their car, so Mr. Wilson could ride back home with his wife in order to hit the hay early.

At precisely eight o'clock, one hour after the start of the dance, the local officials representing the float committee — including the high school principal — stood spotlighted on the sidelines of the structure out there at the near end of the parking lot, where they extended various praises and thanks to all those involved. Finally, the two spotlights went out, and after the loosened tarps were removed in the dimness of the night, the bright lights burst forth to illuminate the colorful, playful creation which would represent Essex Junction in the next two major parades in Burlington. The dance crowd, along with a lot of curious village visitors, raised a collective cheer.

And well they may have, for the sight was almost magical.

Though it was not readily identifiable, the small pickup truck was the basic powering vehicle under the outer shape of this cartoon version of an old-fashioned locomotive. The yellow-painted cab of the truck had become the usual raised engineer's cab of an antique railroad engine. A few inches lower, the same bright yellow color showcased the locomotive's cylindrical front, which extended several feet out in front of the hidden truck, like the forward section of a real locomotive. From the pretend engineer's cab, the driver and the dairy princess could look over the front of the engine, out past the train's bell and the red-and-yellow-striped chimney, which stood playfully mid-center on the cylinder of the locomotive's front. But it didn't end there. Way down below the bull-nosed front, a bright blue cow-catcher pointed its sweeping, fan-shaped structure just inches above the ground. Not far behind the sweep of the cow-catcher, small purple engine wheels wobbled in slow rotation against the lower sides of the cylinder, two on each side. Then, farther toward the back of both sides, two larger red wheels oscillated, as though propelling the exquisitely designed coal car just above and behind them.

The happily tilted, bright green coal car not only hid the bed of the pickup, it truly completed the presentation. All four sides were decorated with a glinting gold filigree of swirling lines and delicate, mysterious flowers. An ingenious touch on the float was the array of little, old-fashioned banner ads for Essex Junction business sponsors, which lined the spaces between the wheels and filled in the lower back edge of the float.

Altogether, the striking colors, professional attention to delightful creative detail, along with an artistic acknowledgment of sponsorship, made this float an instant hit with the crowd.

Principal Randall Marvin once more thanked all the volunteers who had so quickly put together this wonderful exhibit for the two upcoming parades. "All that is left to do," he said happily, "is to get the locomotive headlight on the front, and that will be done tomorrow morning in the Wilsons' carriage barn." He looked over at Jack Wilson, who was assigned as parade driver for the float. "It's my understanding that the float will be in place tonight, in order to be ready to work on first thing in the morning… is that right, Jack?" The young man in the scarecrow costume nodded. Mr. Marvin then explained that the Dairy Princess for Chittenden County, Diana Bixby — "One of our own EJHS students" — would be riding in the engine's cab, and that "Shake-Down, tonight's featured band" would be riding in the coal car, making music all along the parade route. A general hum of approval went up from the onlookers.

Over on the crowded sidelines, Paula Donahue nudged her friend, Penny. "Us cheerleaders could have been up there in that gorgeous coal car, if it wasn't for You-Know-Who."

"We don't really know the details," Penny-Pal reminded her.

"Aw, for Pete's sake," Scottie murmured, "we all know darned well, she was messing with that bus driver, in more ways than one."

Diana Bixby blinked her scarecrow eyes and leaned close to Jack's shoulder, listening to her nearby classmates' remarks. She remembered how Roxie had treated her like eavesdropping hired-help at the Lincoln Inn. Yes, she had heard how the girl had talked to her stepfather, but as a newly trained waitress, she also knew she was to ignore that type of conversation and to concentrate, instead, on the needs of the customer. After all, that was where the good tips came from. But this encounter had been upsetting, and now, ironically, Roxie was left sitting in the grandstand while the "nosy waitress" took center stage. Diana smiled. "There is a God," she said aloud.

Jammed closely in the shadows of the crowd behind the dairy princess and her boyfriend, Roxie Foxx began to fume. Not only had she heard Diana's remark, but she had duly noted the lowered voices and glances of her other three classmates before that. She looked up at Ted, but saw no indication that any of it had even registered with him. Quickly, she tugged at his sleeve and pulled him back toward the gym. "We need to get ready for the dance contest."

By eight-thirty, the portable spotlights and the microphone had been brought back inside and re-positioned in their respective places, ready for the dance contest.

The contest judges were introduced. They were the music teacher, Mrs. "Dead-eye" Desmond, and two of her professor friends from the Fine Arts Department at UVM.

With a brief introduction, Roxie and Ted, in 1940's garb, took their places on opposite sides, just outside the black center ring of the varnished floor. Somebody gently dropped the phonograph needle onto Glenn Miller's In the Mood, and suddenly the gym was filled with the low, rhythmic drone of multiple trombones, interjected with short trumpet blasts and the thump of a persistent bass drum... repeated and repeated... as the dance began.

At the first downbeat, Roxie and Ted turned face-to-face, and rock-step, step-stepped their way toward each other, taking command right from the start, with the smooth, balanced execution of this basic jitterbug dance move. Their faces were relaxed and confident, and as their hands touched for a closed position, Ted gave a little wink to his beautiful partner. She smiled as they continued the same step, their hands barely touching. Then he turned his left hand lightly against hers and she slipped easily into a whirl and a wrap, then back out again, the golden-red curls accenting the graceful move of her head. The hemline of her slim '40's-style skirt slapped to a stop just above her knees, as they ended in a promenade position. It draped slowly back down as the two went back to more of the basic step, until Roxie suddenly twirled under her own arm for a smooth inside turn. A couple of beats later, Ted guided her through an outside turn, where she finished the move with her own hand pressing the small of her back in a perfect hammerlock. She shook her padded shoulders just before his light touch brought her back around once more to a side-by-side promenade position. Without missing a beat, the two dancers tapped out the basic step again, then sleekly slipped into an amazing back walk. As they moved effortlessly backwards, they lifted their feet in coordinated dance-kicks, executed on the same beat.

The crowd was impressed.

The well-rehearsed dance continued as the backing-up stopped and the couple performed an impressive eggbeater... a consecutive ducking of their two heads through the continuous overhead rotation of their connected arms. This whirling move brought them forward along the same path of the back walk, ending right back where they had started at center circle.

Now there was appreciative applause.

Wisely, the next moves were back to basic steps, as the two got their equilibrium back. Then Roxie slipped behind Ted, her hand draped forward over the top of Ted's shoulder. Slowly, he reached around and touched her other hand, and she slipped around behind him, dragging her draped hand softly across his shoulders and down his arm. As they finished that shoulder slide move, he guided her into a one-handed face-to-face whirl and tuck, then placed his free hand firmly on the small of her back, supporting her for a perfect Apache dip, backward over his extended knee. For drama, they held the pose for six whole beats.

Finally, he pulled her gently upright, stepping in place as she circled once more around toward his back. But this time, her hand was firmly grasped in his, and she step-stepped back around to his other side, to suddenly drop to her bottom on the slippery floor. He braced as she grabbed his strong fist with both hands and twirled in a double circle, still on her bottom. Then, right on cue, Roxie pulled her feet under her body to make a concentrated push, while Ted pulled her upward. In a second, she was springing two feet up into the air. A shriek went up from the crowd as she landed on her feet. It was an impressive mop-the-floor.

The performance was half-over, and the couple had not missed a move. Keeping time with the throbbing trombones, they resumed the first position and repeated the same foot-stomping dance moves, and this time there were shouts and applause throughout. Finally, the Apache dip was once more holding the audience hostage as Roxie froze in position. But this time the presentation would end differently. Suddenly, Ted tugged her upright, and turned with her as she dropped to mop-the-floor. She spun around twice, then they gripped both hands together, and with one concentrated effort, at the very last beat of the music, Roxie flew high up from the floor... not to land on her feet, but to make a straddled landing upon Ted's extended knee. They held that finishing embrace and waited for the applause.

While this was a legitimate jitterbug dance move, it was clearly an overreach for this high school venue. Out of the silence which followed, a gasp was heard here and there. Somebody said, "Oh, my gawd..."

There was polite applause as the two left the dance floor.

Scottie and Penny were next, doing a tap-dance number. As usual, he stood pretty much in one place, tapping a basic rhythm in borrowed tap shoes, while Penny whirled and did cartwheels between the tapping. The music was **The Yankee Doodle Boy**, from a musical about George M. Cohan... perfect for this couple, who had not only worn matched red-and-white-striped shirts as part of their Sadie Hawkins outfits, but were both bona fide Yankees. It was a pleasant presentation by a well-liked couple. However, the applause was somewhat reserved, probably because folks were still shocked by the unusual ending of the previous performance.

The next two dance contestant spots were quite short, since one had to cancel because the girl had developed pleurisy, and the other couple doing the Charleston had an unfortunate fall right in the middle of the act.

Finally, it was time for Jack and Diana to do their special thing. As they were introduced, it was made very clear that what they would be doing was interpretive dance, a form of dance which told a story or expressed an emotion. The auditorium lights were dimmed to the legal limit. A couple of faint shuffles were heard from the middle of the gym.

Then the spotlight cast a sudden light on a lone scarecrow, loosely attached to a wooden frame behind her. She was lazily waving about in what seemed to be a gentle breeze. Suddenly, she jerked to attention, blue eyes wide open, head up and alert. The music started. It was **Ride of the Valkyries**, a classical piece by Richard Wagner. As the music swelled, the sudden whirr of a large fan was heard from somewhere in the dark, outside the spotlighted area. Much to the delight of the audience, a hard wind began to blow directly upon the lady scarecrow. She valiantly struggled against this destructive force, slipping and sliding gracefully from one position to another, but managing to stay attached to the wooden frame. The audience chuckled as her arms flopped and her loosely attached legs were blown into ridiculous positions, and just when things seemed like they couldn't get any worse, another scarecrow came whirling into the circle of light, slamming down to pin her feet to the ground. Much to the amusement of the crowd, the male scarecrow went through several struggles to get to his feet. He was clearly trying to protect the straw-stuffed lady. Then, just when he seemed to get things under control, the poor fellow was gracefully swept up by the wind and slammed belly-to-belly against the female. As straw flew in every direction, the poor clown tried to peel himself loose, only to be overcome by the wind. The confused looks on their innocent scarecrow faces brought the young audience to a comfortable chuckle again and again. It was like watching two stuffed toys perform an exercise in artful clumsiness.

After several attempts, the repeated straw-body slams were overcome, and the gangly fellow was blown sideways, where he saved himself from being blown into the North Forty by grabbing onto the lady's straw-stuffed arm. There he was caught in a comical dangle, his downward foot nearly leaving the floor, the upper leg nearly straight out sideways from his supple waist. The music soared and receded like the windstorm which had come upon these two fragile persons in the cornfield. It was as though there would be no surviving the onslaught.

Suddenly, when all seemed lost, the wind began to die down, and the heroic scarecrow spun around and around, slipping dizzily down into a tangled heap, once again at the feet of the straw lady. He lay there without moving. The wobbly female lowered her head to observe her woefully fallen comrade. Then, slowly, slowly, she unhitched her arms from the wooden frame and carefully slid down to her knees behind the crumbled male. There she slipped her lanky arms around to clasp her wobbly straw hands across his torn chest. She jiggled him, but got no response. She shook him a little, but his head was limp and flopping. She looked heavenward for a moment, then sadly shook her head as she once again observed her silent friend. As the last long, lingering strains of the music faded, she pulled his limp body back against her, to gently rock him in a tender embrace.

Then it was dark.

The judges took only a couple of minutes to confer. It was Mrs. Desmond who made the announcement, her dark eyes glinting with pleasure. "It is my privilege to announce that the winners of this dance contest are Jack Wilson and Diana Bixby, the very charming scarecrow couple."

Roxie was furious. She insisted that Ted take her home immediately. He tried to talk her into staying for the rest of the dance, but she would not hear of it. "There's no need to hang around any longer with this bunch of losers," she said.

Ted was humming **In the Mood** as he slowly drove his 1937 Pontiac to the Foxxs' modest house in Indian Acres. "I think we were terrific," he commented. "We should have won."

"Darned right, we should have won." Her voice was filled with bitterness. She stared silently out the passenger window as the vehicle wound slowly around a curve and into the driveway of the darkened house.

Ted rolled up his driver's side window against the chilly night, using the ceramic-knobbed handle on the inside of the door, then turned his attention to the sulking beauty beside him. "I hate to see you all upset like this, Roxie."

She responded to the sympathy, sliding easily into the dramatic role of the unappreciated princess. As her head lowered, both hands rose slowly and two sets of pinched-together fingers began to tap softly against each other. She took a long, shaky breath. When he reached over to touch her shoulder, she looked up at him through tear-filled eyes.

"Aw, Shug-ah…" he whispered.

"You know what, Teddy? I just hate those two," she said in her victim voice. "They think they're so special. *They* hang out with the 'in' crowd. *They* give the party. *They* win the dance contest. And now they even get to ride up front in the parade float like a couple of *movie stars*." The tears were running down her beautiful cheeks. "It just isn't fair. It just isn't."

Ted reached over to give a sideways hug. "They're no more special than anybody else… just got lucky, that's all." Roxie leaned closer to lay her head against his shoulder.

"I… I just can't… believe that… right now," she sobbed softly.

He buried his face in the luxurious curls. "Don't cry, Shug-ah," he said, as he pressed a tender kiss on the top of her head. She responded by turning her body to embrace him.

By ten-thirty she had showered and was in bed, the covers drawn tightly around her neck. She heard the car pull into the driveway, and the muffled conversation between George and her mom. A moment later, Marilyn poked her head in to say goodnight, but Roxie pretended not to hear. The weary mother was glad her daughter was home early. She stepped around the sliding door which opened off the dining area and grabbed the last pot of geraniums, placing it safely on the linoleum floor just inside the door. The morning weather forecast had predicted another winter freeze, sometime overnight.

***

At eight in the morning the next day the call came in for Chief Rob. It was one of the few times he had ever gotten a call at home. The word was out: no unnecessary calls to his residence. But here it was. Younger brother, Scottie, was lounging in his underwear on the sofa nearby. When he heard his big brother swear, he sat up to listen.

"How extensive, Laura?" A brief pause. "How the hell did that happen?" The chief glanced over at Scottie, then turned his back and lowered his voice. "What kind of an ignoramus would do that?" The voice on the other end of the line was answering the question. "Where the hell was Jessie when this was happening?" Another pause. "I understand, but at that early hour of the morning… it was freezing. The oil's not even flowing yet… you don't just jump in and rev up an engine like that." He sighed and shook his head. "No, I don't think so. Once you blow a rod, you've got your hands full, especially on a '39 engine." He listened for the final question. "I'm afraid not. That float is not going anyplace… probably ever." He slammed the phone down on the cradle.

"What happened to the float?" Scottie asked.

"Stupid kids, that's what." Rob plopped down into one of the plaid-covered easy chairs. "A couple of young studs, acting like race-car drivers in the barnyard." He drew one hand across his forehead in disbelief. "All that money, and all that work, shot to hell by a couple of teenagers."

"What did they do?"

"Turned it on, and revved it up like a race car for a couple of minutes, then tried to 'lay rubber' pulling it out into the barnyard. Jessie came running from the dairy barn just as the rod blasted through the engine block."

"Do you know who the guys were?"

"Well, Jack Wilson knew better." He leaned forward toward his brother. "Don't let some guy ever talk you out of your good sense, just so you can be buddies." Scottie looked a little guilty, because he knew this was a guy kind of thing, and that it happened a lot amongst his peers. "Anyway, it was mostly this other guy who was doing all the revving and jerking around."

"Who was that?"

"Mr. Cool Pontiac, that's who."

CHAPTER SEVENTEEN

Dullards

The ladies of the Maple Leaf Sewing Circle were gathering at Shirley Bogue's house on Case Road, when the news broke about the ruined float. Someone asked where Laura Wilson was, and it was Winnie who reluctantly gave the details. She was sitting in the overstuffed chair just in front of the back window of the living room, arranging her crocheting on her lap, when the question was asked. The little lady took a minute before she answered, spreading the handiwork carefully over her knees, then turning slightly back to her left, to switch on the metal floor lamp. Gently, she adjusted the yellowed lamp shade on its metal rack, taking time to find the right words.

"It's sad, really," she said to Shirley and the other two guests.

"That's the understatement of the year," Grace Allen interjected. "I was there when my son got the call at eight o'clock this morning." She puckered her lips. "But I don't get to repeat official business, so go ahead, Winnie."

Before the woman could resume her statement, Lily White, who was sitting right beside Grace on the sofa, spoke across the room to Winnie. "I'm assuming you got a first-hand look at this whole thing."

"Well, I heard stuff: the truck engine being revved up, or warmed up... anyway, the screeching seemed to go on forever. Then I heard a roar and more revving, and a huge noise." She picked up her crochet needle and chained a few stitches. "As to what actually happened, Cecil went over and got the details."

Shirley, who had been standing at the top of the two steps which led down into the kitchen, moved over past the phone table to sit on the arm at that end of the sofa. She bent forward to the plate on the coffee table, grabbed a Ritz cracker with a piece of cheddar on it, and began to munch it slowly as Winnie continued.

"It was almost six o'clock in the morning, so Ceese and Uncle were out milking. They didn't hear it, I guess." She turned the work, to start a new row. "It can get pretty noisy at milking time, even in a small operation like we have." The crochet needle jabbed deeply. "I can see why Jessie probably didn't know anything until the float was almost all the way to the dairy barn."

"Yeah," Shirley said, as she licked her fingers.

"Well, the minute I heard all that screeching, I went out to get Ceese. I just didn't like the sound of it, and it wasn't all that light out there. I couldn't really see anything from the parlor window."

"That's right. It was early," Grace agreed.

"And just as he was following me back out through the milking parlor door, we heard a gosh-awful *BAM!* Sounded almost like a cannon." She paused. "Not that I would really remember what a cannon sounds like, I guess. It's been a long time since I visited Fort Ticonderoga."

Grace laughed. "I don't think they do that anymore."

"Well, anyway, Ceese headed right over there—"

A knock on the front door caught everyone's attention. Shirley crossed around the front of the coffee table, where she paused to lean lightly upon the other arm of the sofa, in order to bend forward and peer out the window of the front door.

"It's Connie and April," she announced. "Oh, and there's Anna, just behind them." She opened the door and stepped back to the right toward her bedroom door, giving the ladies plenty of room to maneuver their parcels.

There were greetings, the shuffle of potluck dishes out to the kitchen, and coffee poured, before the three late-arrivers were given the news. Connie slipped onto the front-door-side of the sofa, while Anna and April took a seat on the chairs brought in from the kitchen. These two chairs were placed in the niche in front of the small door which led down to the infamous cellar stairway from which a terrified Laura had bolted, so many years ago. It was just a few feet from the kitchen doorway, and diagonally across from the front corner of the coffee table. Shirley could barely squeeze between them and the coffee table as she headed for another straight chair which had been pulled just outside her bedroom, next to the oil heater.

First-time visitor, Connie, noted the beautiful Victorian floor register located directly above that stove. While its purpose of allowing heat up into the second floor was obvious, the twelve-by-twelve-inch grate still seemed oddly out of place for this humble dwelling. In fact, there was something odd about this whole place, something old and musty and confining. Looking around, however, she noticed that Shirley's lady friends did not seem to be aware of the strange atmosphere in this place. But then she thought, it may have been because their attention was on the details about the destroyed parade float. She turned her thoughts to that issue, joining the other ladies with great interest. Grace brought the new arrivals up to snuff, then Winnie went on with the story.

"Ceese was over there for quite a while. I was just getting dressed to join him, when he got back. Boy, he was madder than a wet hen."

The ladies forgot about the coffee and the snacks on the plate in front of them. Winnie's crocheting lay untouched on her lap.

"It seems Jack and his new buddy, the Donahue boy, had been out all night, doing who-knows-what. Jack was still in some kind of costume when Ceese got over there."

"Are you talking about Teddy Donahue, of the Lincoln Street Greenhouse Donahues?" Lily asked.

"Exactly," Grace said as she folded her arms. "I watched that kid grow up. Who would have thought he would turn out so… irresponsible?"

"I guess they had both been to the dance at the high school last night, then after they dropped their dates off, Ted helped the guys get the float covered, and followed as Jack drove it back to the dairy farm. Once there, he again helped to uncover the float and back it into the horse barn. Jack needed to go back to the school to pick up his truck, took Ted's offer for transportation, and ended up staying out all night. Anyway, that's what they told Jessie, right in front of Ceese."

"What were they doing all night?" Anna, the church secretary, wondered out loud. "I mean, there are just not that many things to do."

"Guys just hang out," Grace explained. "I know. I raised two of them."

"Sometimes they go drinking," Connie said, in her counselor voice.

"Ceese said he couldn't smell anything," Winnie replied.

April peeked at Winnie from her niche, around the end of a small upright piano which was pushed tightly against the wall that separated the upper and lower stairwells from the living room. "So how did they wreck the float?" she wanted to know.

"Jack was late for milking, so he headed straight for the barn, but before he left, Ted offered to go ahead and move the float out, so the men could have it all ready for them by eight in the morning."

"They still needed to put the headlight on the front," Grace explained to April.

"So anyway, Ted offered, and Jack said okay, and that the key was in the ignition, and then Jack headed for the barn." Winnie looked up at the embossed white wallpaper of the ceiling, trying to remember correctly. "I'm not sure if he made it all the way to the barn, or what. All he told Jessie was that Ted revved that cold engine something fierce, and so he turned around and ran over and started to yell... but the muddy barnyard was crusted over with ice, and he fell. When he finally made it back to the horse barn where his buddy was pressing the pedal to the floorboard, the screeching was so loud, Ted couldn't hear him. Jack said he waved his arms to get Ted to stop, but Ted had his head down, watching the gauges or something. Then suddenly, young Donahue shifted the truck into gear and spun out into the barnyard, making a sudden stop over near the dairy barn, and revved the engine again." Her eyes scanned around the room. "Well, of course by then, Jessie had heard the commotion and was just coming out of the barn... when the engine blew a gasket, or something."

"I believe it was a rod. It threw a rod right into the block thing," Grace said, with great authority.

"Anyway, it sounded like a cannon." Winnie picked up her crocheting and looked closely at the stitches. "Just like a bloomin' cannon."

At that very second, a thunderous shake struck the living room ceiling, causing all six women to jump in their seats. Instantly, Shirley left her chair, pounding across the room in front of Winnie's chair, and on past the other end of the piano. Without hesitation, she grabbed open the door to the upper stairway, and yelled, "What's going on up there?"

"The twins must be home," Lily whispered to Grace.

"What do you mean, 'The dresser tipped over'?" Shirley listened to the muffled replies, then turned to the ladies. "Hey, make yourselves comfortable. I have to fix this." With that, she pounded up two steps to the landing, turned right, and stomped up the stairs.

The ladies chuckled and got busy with their various projects.

By one o'clock, the forgiving needle-workers had convinced Shirley to let the twins come down and join them for lunch. Connie, who had never met them, immediately noticed they were not identical twins. Oh, they had the same pale skin and blue eyes, but Peter had a thick, bushy head of sandy-colored hair, while Paul's dark-black hair lay heavily against his scalp, like a slick skull cap. The whole group headed for the kitchen to dish up lunch. With amusement, this student of human behavior observed how the two ten-year-olds stood politely in line, hands holding their paper plates out flat in front of them, while their eyes targeted certain desirable eats.

The drop-leaf table was fully extended and draped with a faded "forties" floral print tablecloth, upon which the potluck offerings had been carefully placed. It stood in the center of the kitchen, a humble, but inviting feast. As the ladies moved slowly around the table, Connie slipped in just behind the twins. She smiled as the boys watched every spoonful of certain delightful dishes rise and plop goodies onto the person's plate in front of them. They anxiously assessed the size of the remains in the bowls from which those all-too-generous portions had been taken. Two sets of eyebrows remained raised in concern until the twins reached their turn in line. There, they stood tall to strain forward, digging deeply to fill their plates with the same plopping spoonfuls, eyes sparkling and mouths curled in delightful relief. Connie bent forward to murmur into their ears, "There ya go, guys. Plenty for everybody." They turned to meet her knowing gaze. She winked, and they rewarded her with a couple of tight-lipped little-boy grins.

"I can't eat another bite," April moaned, forty-five minutes later.

"Well, I haven't tasted that cherry pie you brought," Connie remarked. She looked at the twins, who were sitting politely on the floor beside her seat on the sofa, patiently holding their empty plates, in hopes of refills. She bent over and winked at them, once again. "Shall we try one piece?"

The twins, who had already had two cookies, looked to their mother for approval.

"Oh, Shirley, we only live once," Lily chided.

Shirley gave the boys the nod, and they followed Connie into the kitchen.

As she was serving up, Peter got very brave.

"Thank you… um, ma'am." He looked a little embarrassed, and stepped back.

His brother moved up to receive his serving. Once the slice was on the plate, he moved back to stand beside Peter, and took a big breath. "You're sure a nice lady," he said, stretching his neck, trying to look tall and impressive.

Mrs. Collins, the counselor, rose to the occasion. "Thank you, gentlemen." She reached over and cleaned the knife on a paper napkin. "My name is Mrs. Collins." The boys stood stiffly in acknowledgment. "But I would really like it if you would call me 'Miss Connie.'" She saw two sets of shoulders relax.

Encouraged by this exchange, the now-apparently more forward of the twins, Paul, went for the whole prize. He looked at the piece of pie, then up into the kindness of those large, gray eyes. "Miss Connie, do you like whipt-cream?"

"Oh-h-h, yes… you bet I do," she chuckled as she cut her own little slice of the cherry pie. Picking up her fork, she turned to see the two boys still holding their plates out in front, as though this mission was not quite completed. A warm tug stirred within her mothering soul. These darling young boys were waiting for a dollop of whipped cream on their slices of cherry pie.

She lowered her voice to ask. "Where is it?"

Two sets of blue eyes identified a pink Tupperware bowl, centered inconspicuously on the table. It had not been opened, and probably for a good reason. In this household, such things were not to be used frivolously. Whipping cream was expensive and to be enjoyed only on rare occasions. Surely, this was to be the *coupe de grâce* for the day's dining experience.

Connie would have to be very, very careful. She kept her voice low, but her attitude casual. "My, did your mom make this as a special treat today?"

Peter nodded, but it was Paul who spoke. "We watched her." He glanced at his brother, then back at her. "She said we could have some, but not until all the ladies got theirs first."

"Oh, I see," she replied. She reached for the bowl and peeled the lid off to peek at the luscious white cloud inside. "My... look at that. I sure would like to have some of it... but do you know what? I really can't have that today, and do you know why?" She shook her head sadly. "I have had too many calories already. If I eat this whipped cream, I will most certainly put on another three pounds." She could see that the hopeful pair had no idea what she was talking about, but that didn't matter. They were waiting to see what she would do. Sure enough, she picked up the spoon that had been set out right beside the rosy-colored plastic bowl, and poked it gently into the creamy delight. There, she paused as though she had just had a big idea. "Hey-yy," she said as she lifted a heaping spoonful from the bowl, "how about I just give you two guys *my* share?" Before the boys could answer, she shook a nice mound of whipped cream onto Paul's piece of pie. Their eyes glinted as she dug in once more and dropped the same amount of delectable sweetness over Peter's slice. "Now, doesn't that look good?" she whispered. "But let's eat it right here at the table." She was already clearing a spot on the pantry-side of the table, just out of sight of the living room crowd. In a moment, three chairs were in place, and the trio sat down to dig into their pie.

"Ummm," Connie commented as she took the first bite. She licked a bit of sweet cherry off the side of her mouth. The boys were savoring the whipped topping. Miss Connie settled into a more relaxed posture and threw the question out there.

"So, the dresser tipped over, huh?" The boys nodded, keeping their attention on the creamy topping. "What were you doing, building a fort or something?"

"Nope." It was Paul, again. "It just tipped over," he asserted, as he licked the back of his fork for escaping topping.

"Oh, maybe you were just leaning against it, or something," she suggested.

"Uh-uh," Peter murmured through his mouthful. "It just tipped over."

She cut another bite. "Maybe one of the dresser's legs broke. That would make it topple over, that's for sure."

Both boys waggled their heads, denying the possibility.

She laughed softly. "So you were just sitting there… or what?"

"On the floor, playing with the wee-jee board," Paul murmured, concentrating on the dessert in front of him.

Connie stabbed at the bite, then withdrew her fork and started to cut it into a smaller portion. She moved the fork slowly as she spoke. "Is that a fun game? I don't know how you play that one." She put a small bite into her mouth and chewed slowly.

"It's easy. You just move the glass around, and you get to talk to people." Peter spoke the words before he even had time to think about it. Now Paul was giving him a hard look. Connie deliberately looked away toward her plate. Peter lapped his tongue across his bottom lip. "We're not supposed to tell people."

"Ahh, I see," she said. "Thanks for sharing with me. I won't tell." She looked up suddenly. "Unless you say it's okay..."

The boys looked relieved.

"Um, do you mind if I ask... to whom were you talking today... I mean, just before the dresser tipped over?" The boys looked at each other, their forks poised in midair. "I promise not to tell... unless you tell me it's okay."

"Mom would be mad, if she knew..." Paul was truly the leader of this team.

"Oh well, that's alright. I don't need to know... unless it was somebody who could actually tip the dresser over on you and hurt you."

"Beng wouldn't do that," Peter objected.

She thought she heard him say Bing. "Bing? Are you talking about Bing Crosby, the singer?"

The boys gave her a blank stare. They did not know who she was talking about.

"So, is this a nice guy, or what?" She was trying to be casual, wiping her fork handle with her paper napkin, as though to get a clean grip for the next bite.

Both boys snickered. She looked up, surprised. "Oh-oh! Am I being silly?" Her head took an apologetic bow. "Sorry, I don't mean to be silly." She covered her mouth with both hands, in embarrassment. When the boys looked sympathetic, she continued, "I guess you'll just have to explain it to me, fellas."

Peter bent forward and whispered, "It's not a guy... it's a kind of ghost... sort of."

"Oh my goodness! Not really. You're teasing me..." she said.

"No, I'm not teasing you," the boy replied.

Paul needed to take command. "It's something we don't talk about to other people, Peter." He made one last cut into the bit of remaining pie. "Beng would not try to hurt us. It likes us. It helps us." He put the bite into his mouth and chewed hard.

"What about the tapping? Can we tell her about the tapping on the walls last night?" the bushy-headed one inquired.

Connie took a quick breath, then tried to be nonchalant. "Bunch of kids banging on the outside of the house walls, probably. Some of them just don't have enough to do on a Friday night."

"Nope, I don't thin—"

"Peter!" Paul whispered to his brother. "You need to shut up."

"How's the pie?"

Connie wasn't sure how long Anna, the church secretary, had been standing in the living room doorway.

"Great!" Connie replied. "You should try some, right, gentlemen?"

The boys sopped up the last of the whipped cream-drenched pie, said polite thank-yous, and went back upstairs. In a couple of minutes, the group was reassembled in the kitchen for a round of dessert. As the ladies tasted the various sweets, Connie slipped back into the living room, pretending to work on her embroidery. Shirley poked her head through the kitchen doorway. Noticing Connie's knitted brow, she asked, "Have we done something to upset you, Connie?"

She looked up in surprise, then quickly answered, "Oh, my goodness, no. I was just trying to get some more work done before I have to leave."

There was a curious stare at the needle-worker. Connie averted her eyes and whipped the embroidery thread around her needle to make a perfect French knot, as she made her excuse. "I had dessert with the boys," she said. "It was delicious!"

"That's nice, but we would still enjoy your company, Connie," Shirley said coolly.

The upset woman just couldn't bring herself to go back out to socialize in that kitchen, even though Shirley seemed a little put out about it. As it turned out, in less than thirty minutes, everyone was back in the living room. Striving to hide her concern, she finally looked at her watch and mentioned that it was time for her to leave. With a polite glance to the others in the room, she paid a brief visit to the bathroom, across the room, to the left of where Winnie was seated. When she came back out, Shirley was standing in front of the piano.

"Are you really leaving, already?" the pudgy woman asked.

"I am. But it was fun. I'm blessed that I got to come at all," Connie said lightly. She looked directly at her hostess. "I have a counseling session I have to monitor, in just one hour." She walked across the room and picked up her craft bag, which was snugged under the arm of the sofa, actually blocking the entrance to the front door.

"I'm just betting," Shirley folded her arms, "that would be Roxie's four o'clock appointment today." There was a brief, uncomfortable moment for the ladies.

"And just why would you bet me that, my friend?" Connie replied as warmly as she could, but she was looking at April, who, to her great relief, was also packing up her things to leave.

"Because my Marsha went to the movies with her today, and will be waiting upstairs in your living room while Roxie does the counseling thing." She grinned grandly back at Connie. "Then the girls will take the Essex bus back home." Satisfied that she had established her inside-knowledge advantage, she motioned the perplexed counselor back into the kitchen to pick up her now-empty casserole dish. "Thanks for the macaroni and cheese," Shirley said. "It was great."

By the time she dropped April at the house, Connie was still fuming.

"Do you want to come in?" April asked.

"Thanks, but I don't have time."

"So what's going on with you?"

"Some people are completely clueless," Connie exclaimed, as she started to back out of the driveway.

April, thinking her friend was referring to the destroyed float, called out, "But we don't really know what happened!"

And, that was so very true.

CHAPTER EIGHTEEN

Buddies

When Ted left Roxie's house on the night of the Sadie Hawkins Dance, he drove his Pontiac sedan back to the school parking lot. The next twenty minutes passed slowly, and though it was getting very cold, he sat patiently, deep in thought. At ten o'clock, the crowd began to leave. He watched as the students, then the band, and finally the staff, moved out into their various vehicles. A few parents arrived to take the younger people home. Across the parking lot, a couple of scarecrows were enjoying a goodnight kiss, then Diana got into her parents' car for her ride home. Jack strolled back toward the school, avoiding the last group of walkers as they clamored toward the street.

Several minutes later, a strong voice directed the covering of the float for its return to the Wilson Dairy Farm. Mr. Marvin, the principal, was shouting out directions, when Ted approached to stand on the other side. Randy Marvin spotted him. "How's it looking on that side?" he called out.

"It's good."

"Keep going, Jack. Not too fast."

The dark-haired senior checked it out. Sure enough, Jack Wilson was on the other side of the float, drawing the canvas carefully over the front of the locomotive.

The three of them became a team. In another twenty minutes, things were secured and the float was ready to move out. Jack would return along the same route by which the float had been driven to the school, via Summit Street, to avoid the steep Prospect Street hill. Chief Allen had assigned a patrol car to escort it down Pearl Street, around the traffic circle, and all the way over the train crossing in front of the creamery, then Jack would continue slowly up Old Colchester Road to his home. There in the school parking lot, the principal waved at the police officer, and thanked the young men, before he made a beeline for home.

Jack headed for the cab of the engine. As he was stepping onto the running board, Ted came alongside.

"Need any help, Jack?"

"I've got it, thanks." He climbed onto the seat and closed the door.

"Wait a minute," the older boy signaled him. "Isn't that your truck over there?"

"Yeah. Mr. Marvin said I could leave it overnight," Jack replied as he started to roll up the door's window.

"Oh, man… you don't want to do that," Ted's dark head shook slowly as he spoke. "That's a good way to lose a couple of tires." Seeing Jack freeze in that sudden thought, he continued, "Why don't I follow you home, then I can bring you back here and you can get that truck back where it's safe?"

The Wilson boy considered the offer, but declined. "That's too much trouble."

"No-no! No trouble at all." He grinned and shrugged his shoulders. "Hey, I have nothing else to do. Let me save you a couple of tires, man."

By the time the two young men had the float backed halfway into the barn, it was nearly midnight. Jack let his dad know he had a ride back to the school to pick up his truck. The tired dairy farmer turned over and grunted into his pillow. His son went out to find Ted just removing the tarp from the front of the locomotive.

"Why did you do that?" he asked.

"Just making it easier for you in the morning," Ted answered. "All you have to do is drive it a little farther out of the barn, and you're ready to go." He smiled as he slapped the scarecrow on the back, and opened the door to his car.

Jack got into the Pontiac. He leaned back onto the soft tan upholstery of the passenger seat, and felt the surge of the straight-eight engine as Ted put the pedal to the floor. The car went skidding out of the driveway, heading south toward the Junction.

Someone was watching from the shadows of the parlor across the street, a half-smile on his Abenaki face.

***

"Wow-w-w," Jack said in a low voice. He watched as Ted reached up to turn on the small, oval-shaped radio on the dash. There was some electronic crackling.

"Local stations are off the air," Ted said, matter-of-factly.

"Really?" Jack leaned forward, reaching for the dial. "May I?"

"Go for it," laughed the driver.

Jack turned the dial knob slowly past the familiar numbers, only to get more crackling, this time accompanied by whistling and howling noises. "You're right. Both WCAX and WJOY are off the air." He turned the knob again, stumbling upon a far-distant, high-pitched voice from out of nowhere: "Welcome to Dubya-Dubya-Vee-A, Wheelin', West Verginya, home of the Gra-a-nd Ole' Ah-pree," the hollow voice cried through the crackles.

Both young men laughed out loud. But they left the dial right where it was, because it was the only thing they could pick up. By the time they got back to the high school parking lot, some guy was singing Your Cheatin' Heart, accompanied by the strong twang-twing-twang of a guitar and the raw scrape of a mournful fiddle. Ted brought the sedan to a stop right next to Jack's old truck. The farm boy sat still.

"Wow, this sure is a nice car." He couldn't help asking, "How does a guy get a nice set of wheels like this?" He felt a need to lighten the question, and leaned just a tad to his left to ask the guy jokingly, "Steal it, or what?"

The answer was unexpected.

"Inherited it, man." Ted stroked the steering wheel. "This was my dad's car."

"Aw, jeez… I didn't mean anything by that remark. Sorry." He watched his companion lower his head and run his fingers through the wavy black hair. "Aw, jeez," he apologized again, "I forgot about that, Teddy."

Ted looked out his driver's side window, then back down at the steering wheel, before he replied: "That's okay, Jack." He turned and looked at his contrite passenger. "I'm real glad you like the car." He nodded in approval. "My dad would be real pleased." He pulled the key out of the ignition, hefting it lightly a couple of times in his right hand. "Tell you what, mister, would you like to take it for a drive?"

Jack's scarecrow eyes registered his surprise. "Are you kidding me?" He looked more closely at the guy now sitting in the driver's seat. "Are you kidding me?" he asked, again.

"Hey, do you think you can handle a real car?" The look on Jack's face gave the answer. "Great," Ted laughed, "but first, let's get rid of the rest of that straw hanging on your arms and legs."

They headed down through the five-cornered traffic circle of Essex Junction, where they made the half-circle in order to turn off at Maple Street. Jack moved carefully along, learning the feel of the vehicle as they proceeded farther out to where Maple Street became what locals called, the "River Road." The car moved on into its own headlight path, past a few darkened buildings, until there was nothing but the bare trees lining the banks of the Winooski River. There on the right, the river water glistened like a twisting serpent under the cold, clear sky. It was an area where, at that time, Chittenden County traffic ordinances were seldom enforced.

Ted instructed his driver to make a left onto a side road, where they pulled into a half-acre of cleared land, now vacant, but used in the past for a school bus turn-around and temporary storage of county vehicles. There on the hard crust of frozen dirt, Ted took the wheel and launched into a demonstration of what this classy car could do. Then he turned the keys back over to Jack.

The farm boy in the scarecrow outfit had driven tractors and all the rest of the farm machines, but this was a whole new experience. He threw himself wholeheartedly into the lessons. There were exercises on double clutching, speed shifting, dead-starting, entering and exiting a curve, and — most importantly, slouch-sitting. A guy had to look cool.

Jack had no idea that driving a car could be so much fun; he was having the time of his life. He laughed as he popped the clutch, squirreled tires, and came to screeching stops toward the edge of the road. Then there was the fine art of using the steering wheel knob to turn the driver's wheel. This was best utilized for executing small circles in the middle of the road. He grabbed the knob, which was a red rose surrounded by a globe of clear plastic, and twisted the wheel to one side as sharply as possible, while stepping on the gas. At first he made careful circular turns, but before long, he was making real professional doughnuts. Finally, Ted put his hand on the young driver's shoulder. "Better quit before we do some damage."

Jack was exhausted. "Awwwh, man… This was a blast," he said to his new buddy. "But I am done here. I need to get home and get some sleep."

Ted took the keys and drove easily along this same road toward Essex Center, where they could get a cold soda before heading back to the village. As he observed the icy landscape outside the car window, Jack suddenly realized he was on the old school bus route he had traveled for so many years, as a grade school student. Because he lived outside the village of Essex Junction, he had not been allowed to attend school in that school district. Not until he reached ninth grade, had he been a student at EJHS. Those early years had been long-forgotten, but now, as Ted drew up and parked in front of the Merle Wood's Country Store, a whole lot of memories came flooding back.

Before the headlights were turned off, they illuminated the bright red Coke machine which stood just outside the main door of the store. Jack got out of the car and stood looking at it, now a dull red in the glow of the night lighting which shown out from the store windows. It was covered with a thin, white frost. Underneath, the white paint on its dome top was as rubbed and faded as the rest of the machine. There on the patchy-white background, even the swirly style red lettering, Drink Coca Cola… in bottles, had parts of the letters missing. More memories flooded his mind: the musty smell of the inside of the store, the dusty walk up the hill to the old academy which had been converted into a junior high school, the racket of rowdy kids on the school bus each morning and afternoon…

A heavy shiver brought him back to reality in the piercing cold night air. Maybe a cold Coke wasn't all that great an idea. Ted was already dropping a dime into the slot, so the young man sauntered over to watch as the bottle came crashing loudly into the chute opening. Ted picked it up and hooked the top into the elongated oval opener located just up to the right. The cap flipped off easily, but missed the narrow receptacle beneath, landing on the ground. Ted ground it flat with his foot and turned to catch his friend in mid-quiver.

"Damn! It's freezing out here. We should have brought heavier jackets," he said. Jack nodded, rubbed his arms, and looked around for something. Ted laughed. "Yeah… me, too. Sudden cold will do that." Neither one of them could see much beyond the shaft of light from the store, but they knew there had to be a bush out there somewhere.

Suddenly there was a low, scraping sound.

"Hey!" It was a screech, bordering on a whine. "What do you guys think you're doing?" Although surprised, Jack recognized the voice. He grinned and turned toward a window he could not see.

"Hey, Mr. Wood! It's me, Jack Wilson."

"Who?"

"I tried to steal a candy bar when I was in the seventh grade."

"You and fifty other kids."

"You called my folks. They said it was okay to make me sweep the floor in your store."

A little snicker came forth out of the darkness. "Ay-yuh… you were the first one, and it worked with most of the rest of them."

Jack shook off another shiver as he ignored Ted's amusement. "Yessir."

"What's wrong with your face, kid?"

Jack laughed and tried to wipe some of the clown paint off. "School dance contest."

"Who's that with you?"

"Ted Donahue, sir." He grinned. "He's a real troublemaker."

"I can just imagine." The boys waited while Mr. Wood blew his nose. "So what are you up to?"

"Just took a ride in Ted's car," Jack replied, as he shoved his freezing hands deep into his pockets.

"That it?"

"Yessir."

There was a rough snuffling as the storekeeper finally cleared his nasal passages. "Do you guys have any idea what time it is?" Both youngsters looked at their watches. "It's three o'clock in the morning, for Cry-sake." The guys exchanged shocked looks. "You need to get your sorry butts back home."

"Yessir, Mr. Wood," Jack said. "We just got a Coke, and we were kind-a looking for a place…"

"Don't you do that in front of my store, buster. I'll have you doing more than just sweeping floors, if you do." He sniffed one more time. "See that light down the street? That's Ely's garage. They don't lock up their restroom at night. That should take care of your problem."

Ted finally spoke up. "Thanks, Mr. Wood. Sorry we woke you up."

Not long after, the two frozen adventurers slipped back into their respective seats. Ted started up the Pontiac and turned on the heater. They sat there warming their hands in front of the heater fan for a couple of minutes, then Ted put the car in gear, and they purred off toward Essex Junction.

The car choked and sputtered and ran out of gas about a mile down the road.

"Oh, crap," Ted said, as the vehicle came to a stop at somebody's driveway entrance.

Jack looked around. "I don't believe this."

"We should have been watching the gas gauge. I don't believe this, either."

"No, I don't believe where we're stranded."

"What?" Ted looked down the driveway toward a two-storied, white colonial house. "Nobody's awake or anything. We should be okay here for a little while... you know, until we figure out how to get some gas."

Jack laughed incredulously. "Nah, you don't understand. This is my old school bus driver's house. Mr. Nichols gets up at four in the morning to take care of his animals before he heads out for the day. He usually goes fishing on Saturday." He rubbed his hands from the center of his face toward his ears. "He's going to spot us in this driveway by... what? The next hour or so?"

There were about fifteen seconds of silence, then Ted grabbed a navy blue plaid blanket from the back seat. As he threw it over their knees, he smiled.

"Perfect!"

It was five forty-seven when the Pontiac followed Jack's truck into the Wilson driveway. Frost covered the trees and shrubbery around the neighborhood, and there in the midst of it all, Jessie was heading for the barn. He turned to see the vehicles crackle to a stop. In frustration, he beckoned his son to get to work, then stepped carefully across the frosty farmyard toward the dairy barn.

Ted rolled down his window as Jack approached him. "Oh, man, I'm in big trouble," the young dairy farmer murmured.

"Hey, I've gottcha covered, buddy. Go ahead and get to the milking." He looked around. "That float needs to be out and ready for the volunteers to put the light on in just about two hours, right? I can make that happen, even though we got delayed." His breath made a little cloud as he called out to Jack who, by then, was crunching through the ice across the barnyard. "Just tell me where the key is. I'll take care of it."

***

Roxie had figured it out pretty quickly. Georgie Porgie would manage to change Sir William's bus route. She had sneaked into the bus barn and checked the roster for the week, and there it was. North Avenue. While this no longer allowed for her to connect with him because of her Edmunds High School ukulele lessons, she knew she could still ride his bus, if she planned it just right. So, on the Saturday morning after the dance, she called Marsha and invited her to the movies. The girls met in front of the Unitarian Church at the head of Church Street, where Roxie informed her friend that she really had other plans, and needed some help.

"Now, don't get mad," she demanded. "I just want to take a ride on Bill's bus for a little while. I just need to talk to him."

"Hey, I don't want to get into trouble," the girl murmured. "I don't want my mother feeling like she needs to keep an eye on me all the time, like yours does." She grimaced a little. "It's not bad enough she has me to look after. She has the twins, as well, and they're a handful."

Roxie wasn't listening. "All I need is for you to do this just once. That's all." She saw the irritation on Marsha's face. "All I want is a chance to talk to him. That's all. And you're the only one I trust to help me." The irritation softened a little. "Marsh, if you will just help this one time, I will owe you one." The pale blue eyes looked up. "I just need…"

A sudden thought hit her. She stepped closer, lowering her voice. "You really need to start living up to your spiritual name, Loyal." The blue eyes blinked twice as that thought sank in, and then the countenance softened. "Alright then, come on," the conniving beauty commanded.

Roxie led the way west along Pearl Street, almost in a dead run, and talking all the way. They turned right on Battery Street and reached the bus stop at the North Entrance of Battery Park, just a couple of minutes before the bus came whining up to it. Roxie peered through the windshield at the figure of the driver. It was Sir William.

"Remember, just agree with me," she cautioned her friend.

The bus door swung noisily open and two heavy, Italian-speaking ladies came down the steps before the girls could get on. Roxie stepped aside to let the noise disappear, then deliberately slipped into the doorway to make eye contact with Bill. Once she established that special visual connection, she moved slowly up the steps. There was a little, triumphant smile on her lips as she handed him a dollar bill. He managed to look away in order to make change, but she still sought more intense eye contact before she even *began* to deliberately drop the money — one coin at a time — into the machine. "*They can't keep us apart,*" her eyes told him. It was a delicious victory for the princess, and she was savoring every moment. But for Marsha, who was not making eye contact with anybody, it was exceedingly embarrassing. Finally, Roxie turned to steer her friend to the usual side-facing seat.

That's when she saw that the whole front half of the bus was full, and most of those folks were staring curiously.

The beautiful redhead quickly recovered from the surprise. With a shake of her curls and a cute little hoot, she merrily led her friend down to an empty seat near the back door. Once seated, however, she went into the finger-tapping mode. When she looked up several minutes later, she suddenly realized that the large rearview mirror over the driver's seat allowed the handsome driver to see every single passenger. Furthermore, Sir William was periodically glancing back at her. She could still be in charge.

From that point on, the girl became an entertainer. Using her DJ voice, she made one loud comment after another, pretending to be a misinformed tour bus guide. Marsha accommodated her by being the perfect audience. Even the tense Sir William smiled a couple of times. It was a good cover for what she was really up to — moving forward into a newly vacated seat, at every opportunity.

"And now, if you will look to your right, you will see the entrance to Ethan Allen Park, where Ethan had some farmlands, and shared Thanksgiving dinner with the local Indians." She scooted forward to a single empty space, leaving Marsha to fend for herself. "Mrs. Allen did all the cooking. As you can imagine, she was irate." She paused for the next line. "Oh, wait. No, that was Ethan's brother," she called back to Marsha. Somebody laughed. "*Her* actual name was Fannie." She raised a hand. "No, wait, that was the daughter's name. Now I ask you, what kind of a name is that for a young girl?" Another pregnant pause. "*Fannie...* sort of brings to mind a very interesting mental picture." More people laughed.

A couple more stops left her favorite seat completely empty. She slipped gracefully onto the side closest to the front stairwell, reserving the other end of the vacant side seat by putting her hand on it. With a toss of her head, she signaled Marsha to join her. The skinny blonde came wobbling up the aisle and sat down hard beside her friend. From there the real task for the day commenced.

"How did you like my tour guide, Sir William?"

He glanced back at the three other passengers, then replied politely, "Very good." The bell signaled a de-boarding for the next bus stop. Roxie waited for the man to leave by the back door. As that exit closed, she noted the presence of two teenagers seated together on the very back seat. The boy and girl were head-to-head, talking intimately. It was safe for Roxie to make her move.

"Sir William, this is my friend, Marsha."

The bus driver nodded an acknowledgment.

"I wanted her to meet you, because I have told her so much about you, *and* because she didn't believe me when I told her you were so young." She gave her friend a small punch in the arm. "Didn't I tell you?" Marsha nodded, looking closely at

Bill. "So, take a guess." She grinned at her buddy. "How old do you think he is?"

Marsha pretended to think about it, then said shyly, "Probably in his early thirties, right?" Roxie hooted in delight. "Right?" the other girl asked, again. The silvery eyes glinted in pleasure. She could see that Bill was enjoying this.

"Of course you are right," the young schemer assured her. "See? You thought I was in love with a really older man. Now you know better." She poured a love-sick gaze all over the good-looking bus driver. "I *am* in love with him, that's for sure." Her whole body rocked slowly back against the seat. "I don't know what I would do without him."

Bill's lips sealed into a grim line.

Roxie ignored that. "I almost won the dance contest last night, didn't I, Marsh?"

"Well, you and *Ted* almost won it." She lifted her voice to tell the bus driver that Roxie and Ted should have won it, "...hands down."

Roxie smiled, very proud of herself. "We did the best jitterbug *you* ever saw, my friend."

"That's right. You two had to practice a lot. I watched you at the gym, whenever I could. Yeah, you two should have won." She leaned toward Roxie. "I was really jealous of you dancing with that handsome guy."

Suddenly, Bill's interest piqued. "So, you finally caught yourself a handsome fella, princess?"

Immediately, the pretty redhead assumed Sir William was jealous. This pleased her very much. She gave him a teasing look as she spoke: "Oh-oh! Do I see a little green monster on your shoulder, sir?"

"Nope. I'm real happy for you," the man said as he slumped slightly forward in the driver's seat.

But Roxie wanted to believe that he was jealous. It made the whole relationship more exciting than ever.

***

As the two girls left the bus stop at Florida Avenue, Roxie was reassuring her friend that there was no romantic interest between Ted and herself. Walking to the Collinses' house, she emphasized it, once and for all. "I am in love with Bill. Ted is just a good dancer. That's how it is." Marsha seemed to be peaceful about that, and while Roxie went downstairs for her counseling session, she sat down in the living room, to flip through magazines. But then, she had another idea. Why not sit out in the covered patio and enjoy the fresh air at the same time? It seemed like a good plan, and as fate would have it, it was the perfect thing to do, for she had no clue what was going to happen down in that office.

"How's it been going this week?" Don asked.

The girl shrugged. "Pretty good, I guess."

"Just 'pretty good'?"

She shrugged again. He didn't move. Connie sat down quietly in the corner.

The fingers started to tap, ever-so-gently. Finally, she spoke up: "I've been having bad dreams." The tapping continued as she dropped her hands to her lap. She glanced up. Mrs. Collins was writing in her notepad. Mr. Collins was staring at the top of his desk, listening.

The polite silence encouraged her. "I'm scared," she said in her victim voice. She saw the man close his eyes and nod understandingly. His wife paused her pencil, but kept her eyes on the notepad.

Roxie stopped tapping and rocked her body gently, pushing her heels and toes rhythmically against the floor. "In my dreams, somebody is chasing me," she whispered, "and I can't get away." Mr. Collins opened his eyes to survey the top of his desk, again. Otherwise, the couple did not stir, apparently waiting for her to continue. She took a big breath.

"I… I think I know who it is… finally." She paused for a reaction, but they were very quiet, waiting for the answer. "I can't believe it," she said, with a sob in her voice. "I can't believe he's doing this to me." She wiped a tear from her cheek.

The counseling couple still sat quietly waiting.

"Don't you want to know who is chasing me?" she asked, tearfully.

Don looked up. "In your dreams, or for real, or both?" he asked gently.

"What?" The girl was thrown off track. She drew her hands back up under her flexing nostrils, where her fingers started tapping again.

His gaze was steady. "Remember now, sometimes people and objects can just represent something. Things are not always what or who they seem to be, in a dream."

There was a brief, blank, silvery stare. The eyes moved sideways, first one way, then the other. "Well, there's no doubt about it. I know who was chasing me in the dream." She looked questioningly at the two unresponsive faces. "Don't you believe me?"

"Why wouldn't we?" Don asked quietly.

Suddenly, she went into a fierce rant. "But I know for sure. It's my stepfather! No, it's nobody else. It's *him!* And he's chasing me and chasing me, and then he's catching me, and he's laughing with his stinky breath against my face, and then he's touching me… over and over and over… and I can't get away… I can't get away… not ever… o-o-oh, my God…" She gripped her thighs, dissolved into tears, and dropped to the basement floor.

There, she cried, twisting in terror, murmuring in agony, then crying some more, and twisting some more. The two counselors did not touch her nor console her, but let her go as far as she had the energy to go.

It took about five minutes.

Finally, as she lay there exhausted, Connie came over and took her hand. "Are you ready to get up and be honest with us?" she asked.

"What?" the spent actress whispered.

"We have important work to do here, Roxie. We have no more time for drama. You only have a couple more counseling sessions left. After that, we either can help you... or we can't." Mrs. Collins helped the wobbly young girl to her feet, settling her into the counselee's chair. She handed Roxie a tissue and waited for her to blow her nose and wipe her face, then she retreated to her corner station.

"Are you *ready to get real*, missy?" Don Collins inquired.

The puffy-eyed girl put on a pout. "I don't know what you're talking about."

"Well, suppose we take for example, what just happened here in the last few minutes," Don said. "Number one: you stated that you've been having bad dreams. I can believe that, because you certainly have something troubling you. No problem there.'

"Number two: you named your stepfather as the sexual menace who has you trapped... in *the* dream, you said... not in the *dreams*." He tapped his pencil against his cheek. "So, are we talking about one dream, or is this attacker in all of your bad dreams?"

Roxie couldn't answer that, so he continued. "In addition to that irregularity in your story, you suddenly lost all control in a dramatic display of the ultimate victim." An incredulous look came over his face. "Really? In a real scenario, such information is put forth pretty clearly and simply by the child, when she is comfortable enough to talk about it, without all that drama to make sure everyone in the room believes her." He leaned forward and looked her in the eye. "You are trying too hard, kiddo. Real trauma needs no drama."

The beautiful face turned to stone. "I should have known you wouldn't believe me."

Don focused once again on his desktop, then he tilted his head and looked her in the eye once again, determined to keep the train of thought.

"But you changed George Foxx from a dream-world villain to a real-world sex offender." He glanced quickly at the ceiling, then back at the girl. "'I can't believe he's really doing this to me,' you said." He leaned slightly toward her. "You wanted to set up your big, convincing scene... which was number three: as I pointed out just now, you went into hysterics far beyond what the usual victim would go. In fact, those people are usually traumatized and quite guarded when it comes to their emotions."

Connie spoke up, "In other words, you overacted. It just wasn't believable, especially since I saw you do the exact same thing when you 'accidentally' tripped Penny during cheerleader practice."

"That *was* an accident, Coach, and you know it, because you saw it," Roxie retorted. "Where do you get the nerve to..." She stopped, suddenly realizing that she was actually "telling off" one of her teachers. She folded her arms and sat up straight. "You two are so off-base," she proclaimed. "I don't know why I am even coming here."

Don ignored that, to go on. "Number four: your arrogant attitude as you sit on that chair right now, suggests very strongly, that you have no intention of addressing your problems. In fact, you are expending an amazing amount of energy in an effort to convince us that you are the innocent victim, and everybody else is to blame for all your difficulties." He took a big breath. "In other words, you have been a performer, an actress, and a scheming deceiver since you came into counseling."

Roxie glowered at them. "How can you two even call yourselves counselors?" Her eyelids lowered as she emitted a low growl. "*You* are the wicked ones. *You* are the deceivers. Your job is to *lie, lie, lie* to young people like me."

"Our job… no… our *ministry*, is to help people to see what God intends for them to be while they are here in this world, and even beyond that," Don replied.

"Roxanne, God does not intend for you to be a deceitful, scheming person," Connie said as she put down her notepad. "He has much, much bigger plans for you. In fact, very specific plans for *you* and *you only*."

Suddenly, the girl sat rigidly in her seat, her eyes glazed over, no expression on her face.

Connie rose and moved slowly toward the unresponsive child. Her words came forth softly and tenderly. "You are not meant to be a deceiver, nor a manipulator, Roxie. You are meant for much greater things." She came close to the girl, reaching out, intending to place a comforting hand on the stiff shoulder. "We just need to admit to and address these awful things that are destroying your li—"

The girl's fist slammed into Connie's stomach before she could finish the sentence.

By the time Don reached his doubled-over wife, hysterical laughter was coming from Roxie's mouth. It shrieked through the small room, rattling off the walls and drowning out the husband's spontaneous prayer: "Jesus, Jesus, Jesus…"

As he lifted Connie in an embrace, he could hear the girl's weird laughter morph into choking, then into snorting, gagging noises.

"Jesus, Jesus, Jesus…"

Miraculously, Connie drew a breath. Ron choked out a prayer. "Thank you, Lord."

Shortly, Connie became aware of Roxie convulsing on the carpeted basement floor.

She looked at her husband. "Take authority!" she whispered intensely.

Ron leaned in closer to his wife. "Are you okay, babe?"

"Let go of me, and take authority right now!" she said, hoarsely.

He looked at her, making sure she was safe.

"Don!" she croaked, "Do it *now!*" She reached around to peel his arms loose, pushing him toward the gurgling sounds on the floor.

When he turned back to the girl, he couldn't believe what he saw. A purple mass of pulsating flesh had replaced what had been a beautiful young face, only minutes before. He recognized the demonic presence, and at that moment, his earthly based panic turned into a holy, righteous anger. He looked into the hideous face, dropped down beside her, and held his hands over both rotten-fleshed cheeks, as he spoke a supernatural command: "In the mighty Name of Jesus of Nazareth, I command you to back off and stop hurting this child right now!" He clapped his hands together just inches above her face as he continued. "Let go of her right now. Let go of her body right now." He clapped again. "You cannot tell me '*No.*' I have the authority of the Name of Jesus. You *must* obey this command." He clapped hard above her face one more time. "I do not send you to the pit, but I do command you to let go of her right now, at this moment, and you must do that. You *must* back off, right *now.*"

Roxie's legs were lifted up off the floor; after they slammed back down, her body was still.

Don and Connie moved in closer, looking for signs of life, and were relieved to see the girl was breathing. They prayed quietly, watching her slowly recover. At length, Roxie opened her eyes, and blinked.

"What am I doing on the floor?" she whined. "My heels hurt... and my face."

"Let us help you up," Connie offered.

"What happened?" the girl asked in a scratchy little voice.

"That's what we would like to know," Don said, as he helped her to her feet. "Here, get your balance. Take a seat."

Roxie rose up, but did not sit back down in the chair. Instead, she stumbled toward the stairway door, coughing, sniffing, and confused.

"What happened?" she asked, again.

"What do *you* think happened?" Connie asked.

"I don't know," Roxie said, shakily.

"Roxie, we need to know if you remember anything from the last few minutes," Don insisted.

The girl's eyes narrowed. "There's something wrong here. I've had enough. I'm not coming back here."

"You don't mean that," he said.

The girl glared at him. "Yes, I do. Something is wrong here."

"Tell us what you think is wrong. Can you do that?" Connie was pleading.

"All I know is that I have to get out of here and never come back," Roxie growled.

"No, Roxie, you can't do that," Connie replied.

"We'll see about that," the teenager croaked.

"Roxie, you don't understand," Don said. "You can't stop counseling now. You don't have any choice."

"Says who?"

"Roxanne, you are this far," — Connie's thumb and index finger measured out a tiny space — "from being removed from your parents' supervision, and your home, by social services." She stepped cautiously toward the teenager. "You are already on record with the authorities as being inappropriately involved with bus drivers who are thirty or forty years older than you, and being instrumental in the suicide of one of them." She leaned closer. "Are you listening, young lady? You are in *trouble!*"

Roxie coughed and hooted at the same time. "That's what you would like me to think."

"Well, you may want to think about *this*": Don folded his arms as he moved between his wife and the girl. "If you are removed from your household, you will become a ward of the state of Vermont. Do you know what that means?" He paused just long enough to make his point. "It means you will be taken to the Children's Home here in Burlington, or, if you continue to behave like a juvenile delinquent, to a much stricter place, the Weeks School in Vergennes."

"What's that?" she asked suspiciously.

"That's a detention center for juvenile delinquents," Don answered. "You won't even be allowed to brush your teeth without supervision."

She grabbed the doorknob. "I don't believe you," she hissed.

"You had better listen, Roxie," Connie murmured.

"Because, if the Weeks School doesn't get you under control, the state can declare you mentally unstable, and commit you to the psychiatric hospital in Waterbury." Don took a breath. "It can take years to be released from that place."

The redhead's face twisted, still stinging.

"Roxie," Don pleaded, "God has a better plan for you. He really does." His voice cracked as he continued: "Please take a minute to think this thing through."

Her hand clasped the doorknob for what seemed like a long time. Then she turned the handle and stomped up the stairs.

The Collinses followed her up into the living room. Marsha heard them come up, and came in from the patio. They watched the shock register in the pale blue eyes.

"Roxie! What happened to your face?!"

Her beautiful friend reached up to touch her blazing cheeks, and shot a look of pure panic straight back to her loyal friend.

"Help me, Marsh! Help me get out of here!"

The Collinses spoke almost in unison: "Oh no, Marsha. No, it's not like that at all... No, she just had a bad time for a few minutes... No, we would not hurt her, for anything in the world..."

But it was too late.

***

Ted was sitting in his car in the parking lot of the new IGA grocery store, located just to the right as the Vermont Transit bus passed and then drew to a stop a block later. He stood out close to the curb of the road, strained forward, and watched as Roxie stepped off the bus and started to walk the few blocks to her home in Indian Acres. He had driven by her house only a few minutes before, noting that there was no car in the carport, and apparently no one home. It was a good time to make the call. He waited for ten minutes, then headed for the phone booth in front of the store.

She answered on the fourth ring.

"Hey, Shug-ah."

"Oh hi, Ted."

"You having a nice day?"

"Not really."

He laughed softly. "Well, that's about to change." He laughed again. "I have some good news for you, Roxie."

"I could use some good news right about now. What is it?"

"Your movie star couple won't be riding the float in the parade next week."

He heard her draw a quick breath before she asked, "What happened?"

"I did it for *you*, Shug-ah."

"What?" She took time to digest that. "What did you do?"

"Nah-nah-nah-nah," he teased her. "I want to see your face when I give you the details." She was silent. "I really went out on a limb for you, Roxie. I really did."

"Wow," she said, without the exclamation point.

"Do you want the details?"

"Yes. Yes, of course I do." She drew a breath. "Where are you?"

"A hop and a skip behind your house, over in the IGA parking lot."

She thought about that. "Do you know where the path is?"

"Yeah, I've already checked it out. It ends up right in your back yard."

"Leave your car there; we have nosy neighbors." She took another big breath. "Come to the sliding door in the back."

"You've got it." He moved closer to the phone's mouthpiece. "I did this just for you, Shug-ah."

"Well, if that's true, I'll just have to give you a great, big hug."

He hung up the phone and stood there in the booth, thinking about what she had just said. Then he murmured to himself, "Yeah… oh, yeah… I'll take some more of that."

CHAPTER NINETEEN

Painting Pictures

On Sunday, November 9, Father Tom was quite surprised to see all four members of the Bogue family at the eleven o'clock Mass. As he stood shaking hands with the exiting parishioners after the service, he could see the apprehension in Shirley's eyes all the way down to where she stood at the end of the line. Further, as he greeted the last few people, he noticed out of the corner of his eye that all three of her children, instead of running outside to join the other youngsters, were hovering close to her side.

When her turn came to shake his hand, she still kept back from the door where the priest stood. He moved back inside a bit, to reach her extended hand. He was surprised when she gave it a little tug and pulled him even farther back from the entrance. She looked at him with worried eyes and spoke in a low voice. He moved closer, to hear her repeat it.

"We're a little scared at my house." She still kept her voice down.

"I can see that," the priest answered. "What's happening?"

She looked around. "Is church over yet? Is there another Mass this morning?"

"That was the last Mass for this morning." He sensed that she and the children needed some privacy. "Shall we just slip over here to a back pew for a minute?" He motioned the nervous family toward the bare wooden bench. He smiled inwardly as each of the children dutifully crossed themselves before slipping into an orderly line onto the bench. The twins followed their big sister, sitting together in the middle. Shirley sat on the other side of them, wringing her hands over her lap.

Father moved into the pew in front of them and sat half-turned to face the little family, his arm looped over the back of the bench. "What can I do for you folks?"

Shirley swallowed hard, preparing to speak, but it was Paul who spoke up: "We got ghosts!"

"Have you?" Father Tom said, carefully. Seeing Peter nod in agreement, he asked, "And how do you know this?"

"Exactly!" Marsha snapped, folding her arms defiantly. "All we know is somebody's knocking on the walls. It could be some darned fool boys from school, for all we know."

Shirley lifted a hand to signal for silence, then turned back to the priest. "It isn't just knocking on the outside of the house walls, it's coming from all sorts of places. Sometimes in the middle of the living room ceiling, or a wall dividing two rooms."

"Well, clever pranksters have been known to do some pretty odd things," Father Ladue suggested. "If we are talking about real ghosts, however, there is usually a reason why they would suddenly show up. So, has this happened before?"

Thinking he was addressing her, Shirley answered. "No," she shook her head. "It's never happened before."

"Yes, it has," Peter murmured. Turning to his brother, he said, "Tell him."

"Um… it happened once when Peter and me were… um… playing with the wee-jee board."

Shirley nearly rose off the seat. "*What!!?*" She turned to glare at the twins. "That can't be true. You can't even get to that board; it's locked up in my top dresser drawer." Both boys sat stiffly still, elbows tucked close to their bodies. "So what are you talking about? Are you lying to a *priest*? How could you play with a Ouija board that is locked away, and the key is on my person at all times?"

Peter nudged his brother. Paul glanced over at his tight-lipped sister, then looked down at his knees. "We made our own," he said.

Father Tom saw that this was going to get complicated. "Well, we probably need to get together and talk about this, don't you think?" He tried to be a little more encouraging. "It still could be nothing more than a prank. Tell you what, I'll ask my policeman friend to take an unofficial walk around the outside of your house, just to check things out. Would that be alright with you, Shirley?" The woman nodded in approval. "But I also think we need to address the possibility that there are some supernatural things going on, and if that is so, we need to take action immediately, for your own protection." He stood up to face them squarely. "I need to know how many rooms there are in your house." He watched as each of the Bogues ticked off the numbers on their fingers.

"Seven," Shirley said.

"Wait. Does the pantry count?" Marsha asked.

"We should cover it, as well."

"Does the cellar count?" Peter piped up.

"I would certainly think so," Father answered. He moved out of the pew. "Wait here," he instructed them.

In a few minutes he returned, a box of Bibles in his arms. "There are ten Bibles here," he said. "Open each one up and lay it on a table or wherever, in each room of the house." The three youngsters' eyes showed doubt, but Shirley nodded enthusiastically.

"I remember that now, Father. Devils are repelled by the Word of God."

The children seemed appeased by her words, so Father nonchalantly escorted the family out to their car, placing the box of Bibles in the trunk. Before they left, he reassured them that he and his off-duty policeman friend would be coming by before too long, maybe even this afternoon. The family seemed a lot more relaxed as they drove away.

But Father Tom could hardly wait to get to a phone. When he finally made the call, he was relieved to hear Rob Allen's voice. "Hey, Chief, is this your day off?"

At two o'clock the two men were walking a careful circle around the old Case house. They started from the front porch, going toward the west side of the house to pass by the windows of Shirley's bedroom. There were no dragged trails in the tall grass, and no signs of disturbance at the slanted cellar door entrance. Robbie Allen bent to look closely for possible scratches from someone walking or climbing on the wobbly wooden door. The layer of dust on the unpainted surface was undisturbed, so the men abandoned that idea and continued around the corner to the area behind the house.

A soft breeze moved over the tips of the dried grass, but there were no signs of human presence. The two looked back at their own trail, to double-check. It resembled the wake of a small boat. Father Tom looked at Robbie. "Nobody's been out here." He looked over at the unpainted woodshed which stood only a yard or so from the back of the house. Its roof was one long slope toward them, so they could see the whole thing from where they stood. There were no signs of activity on it, either.

"Probably should keep on checking the rest of the way. Somebody could have been operating out of this shed," Tom said. With a small move of his hand, he motioned the more-experienced Rob to walk ahead of him. A noise at the living room window caught his attention, and he turned to see the twins, both with their noses flat against the glass. In the background, he could barely make out Marsha's form. Their priest smiled and waved.

He followed Rob's path around the black rot of the north side of the shed. Apparently, there had been no disturbances there, either, since Rob was now turning the corner to check out the wide-open east side of the small structure. When

Father Tom caught up with him, the off-duty policeman was standing and staring into the shadows of the old storage space. The remains of a wood pile lay in shambles on his left. A few empty tin cans and a broken garden rake lay against the far back wall directly across from him. As Father approached, Rob took several steps forward into the shed, turned to his right toward a walled-off space, and gingerly pulled open a dilapidated wooden door. It creaked as he peeked inside.

"What's that? A storage cabinet?" Tom asked.

Rob pulled his head back out and laughed as he closed the rickety door. "Nope," he said. "It's an old, built-in outhouse." He slapped the dust and cobwebs off his hands as he came back out into the daylight. "And there seems to be no unusual stuff going on out here." He motioned his head toward the front of the house. "Probably should check out the back porch. It leads into the kitchen, right?"

Father Tom nodded. "I believe so." He kept his eye on the ground as he moved forward, passing Marsha's bedroom window before coming to the porch. The chief was right behind him, taking care to check around the roots of the old crabapple tree growing a dozen feet or so from the littered back porch. He looked upward through the bare, tangled branches. A few miniature apples still clung to their life source, for a little while longer. The chief squinted. No wires, no strings, nothing.

Robbie caught up with Tom after scrutinizing the dead flowers along the underside of the front kitchen window. Again, no signs of tampering, no newly chipped paint on the old house's shingles. He shoved his hands into his jacket pockets. "Well," he said to his fellow-detective, "nothing here, my friend. What do you want to tell them?"

He had no sooner spoken, when the whole family came quietly out onto the front porch. They stood there, waiting.

Father Tom took a big breath, and let it out slowly. Then the question came quite naturally. "Marsha, you seem to think this knocking is just a mean trick by, I think you said, 'high school guys,' or something like that?"

She stepped forward, almost relieved. "Yeah," she said, her thin arms akimbo to stress her position on this situation. "I would almost bet my life on it."

"Well, you don't want to do that," the priest cautioned her, "but maybe you can help us identify the rascals who possibly would do such a thing." He watched her slowly draw her arms behind her, but she did not move backwards. That was a good sign. She was thinking, ready to prove her theory.

"Before we started the inspection today, when my friend and I were interviewing you, you all were not quite sure when the knocking began." He looked at the rest of the family. "Am I right?" Encouraged by their collective nod of agreement, he continued, "Even so, would it be pretty accurate to say it began to *seriously* occur as of last Friday night?" They all wobbled their heads as they weighed the question, then agreed. "So, what was going on in the neighborhood that night? Anything special?"

"This is not a very social neighborhood," Shirley said. "I doubt that anything spooky was going on around here, at all." She turned to her daughter. "Unless there was something going on at the high school, where somebody might want to scare you and your family." She shrugged her shoulders at the two men.

Marsha had been standing very still. Suddenly she blurted it out. "The Sadie Hawkins Dance!" She moved down toward the man she knew as the Chief of Police. "Maybe you should check out *that* situation."

Chief Rob Allen suddenly remembered yesterday's eight a.m. phone call. He zipped his jacket closed over his midriff and looked into the girl's pale blue eyes. "I will," he said.

"Now," Father Tom was ready to wrap things up for the day. "I hope you have destroyed the cardboard Ouija board, guys." He was looking at the twins.

"I cut it into shreds," Shirley volunteered. "And that glass will do nothing but hold something to drink, from now on."

The priest turned his attention to her. "Best that you get rid of the genuine article, as well." She pressed her lips together and checked out the porch floor. "Meanwhile, let's just keep those open Bibles in every room, until we get this thing figured out, alright?"

The two men walked back down to the road where the church vehicle was parked.

"What do you think?" the policeman asked the priest.

"*Not* a pretty picture."

A half-hour later, at the rectory, Father Joe asked him, "How did it go this afternoon at the Bogue household?"

With a sigh, the freckle-faced priest replied, "God is in charge."

"O-oh," the older man said, "that bad…"

***

"What the hail were you thinking?" Uncle confronted the young man. He had been waiting a half-hour for Ted to come to work, out by the back door of Yandow's Market. "You were supposed to get into that girl's favor, not destroy the gawdim community float!" He coughed loudly and vibrantly, in the cold of the nine o'clock air. Eventually, he asked the question again. "What were you frickin' thinking?"

Ted shuffled in place as he chuckled. "Hey, don't worry, Mr. Smart. I've got it all under control." He picked up a broom, getting ready to do his Sunday night work inside the store. "By destroying the community float, I am '*In-like-Flynn*' with the lovely Roxanne Foxx." He wiggled his broad shoulders. "She thinks I am willing to go to the moon for her." He grinned. "She thinks I am her perfect patsy," he chuckled. "And the benefits…" He sniffed a male sniff. "… are unbelievable!" He tossed the broom handle straight upward and caught it on the downward drop, before opening the back door. "Don't you worry about a thing. It's all good."

"Wait just a frickin' minute," Uncle raised his voice a bit. "How about letting me know what the hail is 'all good'? What about the five hundred dollars you blew with that gawdim stupid trick? You think the dairy farmers and the float committee are gonna let you get away with that, you?"

The handsome young man leaned backwards out the door to reply. "There's a meeting with those folks tomorrow night. I'll make my case, and don't worry, I will charm their socks off. I won't have to pay a cent… you just watch."

"You'd dimwell better hope so, 'cause you're not getting one cent more than what we agreed on. My hard-earned savings won't take a frickin' hit like that." He turned to leave with a parting shot, "And don't go gettin' any more gawdim wild hairs."

***

The float committee, along with Jessie Wilson representing the local dairy community, met as usual on the second floor of Lincoln Hall. As the chairs were dragged up into a semi-circle, a few interested visitors took seats on the sidelines. One of them was Police Chief Rob Allen.

The man from Yandow's Market pulled a single chair across the floor, centering it in front of the half-circle of the committee. Immediately, eighteen-year-old Mr. Theodore Donahue walked determinedly in from the sidelines. His EJHS senior sweater was neatly buttoned over a spotless white shirt. There was a slick crease in his navy blue trousers, which ended just above his navy blue socks and shiny black loafers. As he took his seat, his demeanor was that of a sincerely repentant teenager. Over the next few minutes, frequent eye contact with the committee telegraphed the shock and shame which this young man was experiencing. He pulled back his gaze, again and again, to stare at the floor in front of him, in obvious defeat... what he had done was so, so, so stupid... and he really knew it... and he really wished it all had never happened. Indeed, the committee members were already assessing the young lad who was sitting dejectedly in front of them, long before Randy Marvin even called the meeting to order.

"You understand, Ted, that we are not here tonight to condemn you?" the high school principal stated. "Rather, we would like to have an explanation of what happened last Saturday morning."

"Yessir," the young man answered.

"Our first concern is why you have insisted that your friend, Jack Wilson, not be blamed for anything that happened on that morning. Why have you insisted on this, before agreeing to come before this committee?"

"Jack is a fine young man," Ted said, glancing over at his joy-ride buddy. "He had no idea that I would do something so stupid. It was the last thing on his mind." He wiped a shaky hand across his brow. "I will never be able to make it up to him, and his family." He hung his head. "I am so sorry for what I have done to them. They don't deserve it... they really don't."

The whole committee sat quietly, then Mr. Marvin continued: "You realize, son, that you have cost a whole lot of other people... not only time, but money... by your reckless actions." The boy hung his head, again. "So, what do you intend to do to make up for it, Ted?"

The young Mr. Donahue raised a brave, determined face toward the committee. "Well, sir," he said in a firm, decisive voice, "I will be joining the Air Force next spring, right out of high school. At that time, I intend to repay the whole five hundred dollars to the float committee, at so much a month, until it is all done." He leaned forward and looked them in the eye. "I *really need* to do this. Otherwise, I could never live with myself." He sat straight up on his folding chair. "I am asking you all to allow me to make this thing *right*."

At the end of the hearing, the committee agreed to write the whole blasted experience off. The sincere young man had certainly learned his lesson, and there was always next year for another float. Finally, as the evening drew to a close, Mr. Wilson expressed a new respect for this young guy who had the gumption to protect both their son's, and their family's, reputation. There were man-hugs and moist eyes, before they closed the meeting.

Ted Donahue relaxed. He was *"In-like-Flynn"* once more, and it was *"All good."*

But Chief Allen was waiting at the foot of the stairs as the two joy-riders came down. "Talk to you two guys for a minute?"

The three of them stood to one side, but Jessie Wilson moved in to listen.

"Mind telling me where you were out driving on Friday night?"

"Not at all, sir," the senior student replied. "We went out along the River Road, and then into Essex Center. We ran out of gas there, but got some help and came back home along Route 15."

"So, you *were seen* in Essex Center?" The two guys nodded. "About what time, would you say?"

Ted laughed. "Merle Wood reminded us that it was three o'clock in the morning." He thought for a second. "Then, your old school bus driver —" He turned to confer with Jack.

"Mr. Nichols," Jack interjected.

"Mr. Nichols… got us back on the road shortly after five." Ted tugged uneasily on his white shirt-collar. "Something wrong, sir?"

The officer looked down at his shoes for a moment, then jerked his head back up. "Nope!" But he cautioned the two young men. "You guys take it easy, though. We have too many bad endings to these joyride stories."

Mr. Wilson extended his hand to the chief. "Thanks for your good work," he said, with a vigorous handshake.

"Yessir. That's my job."

Chief Allen waited for the stragglers to leave, then locked up. As he headed for the parking lot, he found himself murmuring uneasily. "So it wasn't those two making mischief up on Case Road on Friday night. Either something scary is going on at the old house, or the whole Bogue family is lying." As he slipped in behind the wheel, however, he realized there was something else that was really gnawing at his policeman's gut.

Back at home, Robbie Allen asked his brother, in casual conversation over a bowl of popcorn, "Do you know Teddy Donahue?"

"Who doesn't?" came the reply. "He's one of those guys the girls all go gah-gah over."

"What are you talking about? Is he a Casanova, or what?"

"Nah." The younger brother popped a handful of the fluffy white stuff into his mouth. He spoke between slurpy crunches. "He's just one of those handsome phonies... an 'actor' kind of person. Been in a lot of school plays. Never know who you're talking with at the moment... kind of weird, ya know?"

"Would you say he's pretty clever?"

"At what?"

"Making himself look good, for whatever reason."

"What? Um... I don't know. He's just kind of a weird duck." The younger Allen turned his attention back to Monday night television.

"That weird duck sure knows how to paint the perfect picture," Rob muttered to himself. "Just a little *too* perfect."

He tucked the daily paper under his arm and headed upstairs. "That young man has *got* to have some kind of agenda."

***

About ten o'clock the next morning, November 11, April stepped back from her oil painting of Haystack Rock on the Oregon coast. As she swiped her sable brush through a damp paper towel, she knew this special creation was finally finished. She smiled as she dropped the brush into a jar of turpentine, then leaned back against the opposite wall of the small living room. It was good.

No, it was better than that. It was pretty near perfect. Further, it was a special Christmas gift for their younger son and his wife, who still lived in Bill's home state, not far from the endlessly breaking waves of Cannon Beach.

She slipped down into the comfort of a nearby chair, and closed her eyes. In a moment, she would open them, hoping to get a fresh look at the artwork she had just finished. Until then, it was important to release the last glimpse, the last visual, and come back with a whole, new perspective. She needed to focus on something else for a few minutes.

"*The watercolor class in the lower floor classroom area at the Fleming Museum, there near the main UVM campus.*" She smiled quietly. It was going to be so much fun. A great teacher… and maybe some new friends. Maybe some couples who would like Bill. Maybe there would be a husband who would invite him to… something… that Bill would really be interested in, like…

Her mind went blank.

She scrunched her eyes even tighter. "*What the heck does Bill really like, anyway?*"

It came to her immediately. Huskies. Especially the ones with the pale silvery-blue eyes. She smiled softly. Probably because his mother, who had walked out on the family when he was only three, had had those beautiful silvery, shimmering eyes. She had heard stories from the family of how devastated he had been. So, maybe he would meet someone who had a passion for silvery-eyed Huskies. This concept offered many possibilities — a club, or an organization where he could pour out his heart, find healing, be a buddy, a member of something really meaningful.

Because, after all, he really did not have a hobby. He liked to read, but that wasn't his obsession. No, what he really liked was to tell stories, to be admired, to be special, like most people, but more-so, much, much more-so. Indeed, he did not seem satisfied with the normal needs of a guy, just to be admired and respected. No, it was more like he needed to be *revered*. And that was the bottom line. She could not even *begin* to count the times she had seen him bend over backwards to help people, even to the *extreme*. In fact, even at the expense of his own family.

Yes, Bill could play that "hero" role very well, and seemingly sincerely, but only for a short time. If somebody pressed in for the long run, he got stressed — really stressed — for, like any other human being, he was not able to keep up this act. Eventually, he would fail to maintain the performance, exposing his phony persona. It was a humiliation which, over the years, continued to leave new painful scars on his struggling soul. He had even sought that "hero" role through military service, but that had ended badly, as well. In addition, these futile attempts to be a superhero had undermined his marriage. He could not maintain the picture of the perfect husband and father. When that happened, he withdrew into the shame-filled depths of what he considered to be failure to be a *real man*.

Still, he could not seem to let go of the need to be a larger-than-life personality. And so, once again, here he was, playing the part of the "knight on a white horse," trying to rescue this beautiful child princess from some vague, unconfirmed peril. April feared that his desperate, insatiable need for self-affirmation was about to destroy him, once more. She wondered how to stop this vicious cycle of failure, before he plunged into a place of no return.

"If we could only go into therapy," she had suggested once. But he had thought that was insulting. It had driven him even further away, emotionally. He concluded that his own wife considered him a "loser." Furthermore, he felt that such a move would harm his military career, so it was never an option. The façade was in place, and it would stay there, as long as he could "fake it."

The phone rang.

Avoiding the view of the painting, April picked it up and heard Connie's urgent request. "I have five minutes to make this call, so I am going to cut right to the chase. Could you please meet with us at our prayer-meeting lunch at the Lincoln Inn today?"

"Um, maybe. If I get my stuff ready to go at five o'clock. I have a class starting this evening at the Fleming."

"Our meeting will be at noon in the café," Connie said. "I think you need to be in on this. What time is your class?"

"Six until nine."

"Oh, that gives you plenty of time. All the rest of us have meetings by one o'clock." She had a second thought. "Don has the car. He could pick you up, if you could be at the Susie Wilson bus stop at eleven forty-five." She went on to talk about the plight of the Bogue family... something about needing to close ranks... the usual counselor's heart brimming over with encouragements and cautions.

April's thoughts wandered back to her project. Her conversation with Connie faded into the background as she opened her eyes and looked at the painting. To her great delight, it was an absolutely gorgeous meld of color and motion, conveying both a spiritual and earthly message to her family. "Oh, thank you, Lord. Thank you, Lord," she whispered. The joy was surprisingly personal and overwhelming, almost bringing her to tears.

At the urgent sound of Connie's voice, she suddenly refocused. "So, is it alright for Don to pick you up at eleven forty-five?"

"Sure, Connie," she said softly. "I'll be at the Susie Wilson bus stop."

"On the Essex Junction-bound side, right?"

"Right, Connie. At eleven forty-five."

CHAPTER TWENTY

Possessions

Don was on time, and the group gathered in the large corner booth in the back of the Lincoln Inn Café at precisely eleven fifty-five. In addition to the regular three, April Flannigan and Chief Rob Allen were present. The waitress took orders for coffee and sandwiches, and the conversation began immediately after a short prayer, just one minute past noon. Father Tom began.

In the next three minutes, he related the happenings from the eleven o'clock Mass until the finish of that afternoon's investigation. He was able to give great detail, with little correction or opinion from the chief, so the others were well updated by the time he finished. "After a lot of prayer, and some more research, I have personally come to the conclusion that there is a genuine haunting going on there, and it is probably the result of the use of a Ouija board, and the lack of Christian education or influence, not necessarily in that order."

The Collins couple nodded in agreement, then turned with great interest to hear what the chief had to say.

"I hope you all realize that this is all off-the-record, since there has been no formal police complaint, and because of that, I prefer to give just my own personal opinion. Of course, if there is any criminal activity involved, it would be the business of the Chittenden County law enforcement guys, and my involvement would be that I did a friend a favor, and used my experience to help him determine whether this situation should be reported to those county officials." He looked around the table to ascertain that everyone understood his position, then leaned back into the tucked vinyl of the booth's backrest. "From a non-religious point of view, it appears that either the whole family is scheming and lying, or there is some clever weirdo trying to scare them into *his* scheme." He leaned forward, again. "There has to be a motive... a destination... a goal, involved in such activity. All that knocking isn't for *nothing*. There is a reason for it."

"Excellent!" Don commented. He made eye contact with Robbie Allen. "There certainly *is* a reason for it." He never even blinked when he asked the next question. "Got a theory for us?"

The chief replied immediately: "Who would want to get that family to leave that house?"

The waitress arrived with their food. They all sat in silence as she called out each order and placed them before all five customers. It was still quiet after she left, until Don asked the blessing. Then the silence was broken only by the rustle of paper napkins and the clink of large restaurant spoons against the thick cups.

All five took bites and sips and kept their eyes upon their meals, until April finally spoke up. "Wasn't that place where that odd lady, Mrs. Case, had all those cats in the cellar?" Connie nodded affirmatively. "Well then, other than them, did Mrs. Case have any close friends?"

Somebody chuckled.

"Not according to Winnie. You heard her, April. Remember? At her house last month?" Connie turned to explain to the chief. "We have a sewing circle called, The Maple Leaf—"

"Right," he smiled. "My mom is a member. Gracie Allen...?"

"Oh, my goodness… of course." She smiled. "We love her. She's so funny."

Don got back to the business at hand, addressing the chief once more: "Any clues?"

"Well, there were a couple of guys out and about on that Friday after the Sadie Hawkins Dance, but they seem to have witnesses that they were nowhere in the neighborhood. Plus, there were no other complaints from the general area of Case Road on that particular evening." He paused. "I tend to lean in the direction of trouble inside the Bogue family. Maybe somebody wants to get *out* of that old, smelly house." He tapped his coffee cup lightly with his left digit finger. "My first thought was that it was the teenage girl who's making all that scary noise."

Father Tom spoke up immediately. "I thought about that, myself. But it would be quite a trick to tap on walls all over the house, without anybody seeing her moving rapidly from one room to another, even in the middle of the night. I walked up those stairs and they are old and creaky. The doors squeak, also." He looked at the ladies. "Imagine two terrified ten-year-olds lying wide awake in their beds up there, and knocking occurring from all different directions. Surely, they would have to see some movement. Yet, when Chief Rob and I interviewed them, they were especially definite about seeing nothing… only hearing."

"When did you interview them?" April needed to be reminded again.

"Just before we made our inspection of the house, inside and out," the priest replied. "We talked to Shirley and Marsha at the same time."

"What struck me about Marsha," the chief remarked, "was her stubborn reluctance to believe there were any ghosts. She kept insisting it was probably pranksters. If she was scared, she certainly wasn't showing it."

"Is it possible that she wants to keep this problem 'in the family' for some personal agenda? Like, for instance, do you think she might be setting up a situation because she wants to leave that place?" April asked.

Before Rob could answer, the priest spoke up. "I am certain she has a personal agenda, Mrs. Flannigan. But does she want to get free of an old, smelly house, or is there something in that house that she doesn't want to lose? Could it be possible she wants to direct attention away from any supernatural activity in that dilapidated, one hundred-year-old homestead? Maybe she actually does *not* want to leave. Maybe she just wants *us* to leave, to butt out."

"If that were the case," Connie quickly interjected, "she would have to be in close contact with whatever it is that is doing all that knocking. It doesn't sound like she is too upset about it."

"The question then would be," Don proposed, "does she know the source of the noise? And if she does, why would she blow it off so casually?" The others stopped to think about that. "And if she is in cahoots with those people who are tapping on the walls, is she hiding the identity of a couple of pranksters, or is she concealing a relationship with supernatural beings?"

"That is a real possibility," Connie suggested, "and I think Father Tom has already touched upon it." She looked around at the others as she said it: "She could be spiritually linked up with the so-called 'ghost.'"

"You mean she could be possessed?" April's eyes went wide.

"Maybe not possessed. More like *op*pressed. You know, deeply under the influence of a demonic being." She took the leap. "Its name is 'Beng,' by the way."

The priest caught her eye. "That's exactly what Anna, our church secretary, told me."

"I *thought* she had overheard me talking with the twins," Connie said with relief. "That makes me feel better, because I promised the boys I wouldn't tell anyone that they were conversing with that thing."

Both April and the chief snapped to attention. "Conversing?!" they exclaimed in unison.

"That's what they told me," Connie asserted. "And you just heard Father Tom... Anna heard them say that, also." She lifted her cup of coffee. "I can also tell you that this information just sort of slipped out during my conversation with them. They said their mother would be mad if they told anybody about Beng." She took a sip of the warm brew. "I believe they are telling the truth."

At the end of the next ten minutes, it was well-established that there was demonic activity in the Bogue household, and all of its family members were fully aware of that fact. Still, Chief Robbie Allen did not want to believe it. Connie looked at her husband, and together, they decided to drop the bomb.

"We had a counseling session just a few days ago with a close friend of Marsha Bogue. During that session, a demonic presence manifested itself in her body. It was very real and very powerful." Father and April nodded, ready to listen, but Chief Rob's attitude became even more doubtful, and he dived into his sandwich, pretty much trying not to be impressed by all the hocus-pocus. Nevertheless, Don continued, "This young lady has been a regular visitor to the Bogue household, and is known to have participated frequently in Ouija board activities with both Marsha and her mother, Shirley."

"Shirley, herself, gave us that information at the same Maple Leaf meeting last month." Connie tilted her head to one side. "Of course, she told us it was innocent fun, and that the drinking glass-pointer moved by the vibrations of their fingertips. Not one word about Beng."

Rob Allen wiped his mouth with the paper napkin, apparently now very much interested. He eyed the old ceiling of the café for a second, then brought his gaze down to meet Don's, once again. "Soo-o-oo, are you saying this friend..." — he leaned in closer — "... a young girl, right?" Don conceded this with a nod. "You're saying this young girl is *actually possessed*?"

"A physical manifestation like that can only happen if the demon is in charge of the body," Don asserted. Secretly, he hoped he was being accurate, but this was the best answer he could think of at the moment.

"So, what did you do about this... incident?" the policeman wanted to know.

"I took authority over it."

"Oh. And how do you do that?"

"I commanded it to back off, in the Name of Jesus."

Chief Allen looked to the priest for verification. "Is that how it works?"

"Actually, yes. That's exactly how it works. Christians have power over demons, because they are under the Blood Covering, and have that authority to issue commands to them. Furthermore, the demons *have* to obey those commands." He added a qualifier. "Sometimes it takes a little while, but they eventually must obey a command issued in the Name of Jesus, by a real Christian. Mind you, I mean a *real* follower of Christ."

"Well then," the chief said sourly, "maybe we all should know who this little witch is. She could be doing real harm to that whole family."

"More likely, she and the whole Bogue family have already come under the influence of demon powers," Father Tom replied softly.

The policeman looked at his watch. "It's getting late. I need to get back to the desk." He looked solemnly at the counselor couple sitting across the table. "It would be a big help if you could tell me who this young lady is."

"That would be unethical," Don replied.

Robbie leaned back once more, the fingers of his hands laced together upon his chest. He stared quietly past Don's head to the wall behind for a few seconds, then brought his eyes back to the elfin face. "Does she have curly red hair?"

The elf smiled. "I refuse to answer that question on the grounds that my answer may tend to incriminate me."

The chief nodded appreciatively. "I need to get back to work. Thanks for the update… and 'mum's the word,' so don't worry." He slid out of the booth. Just before he left, he threw the offer over his shoulder: "If there's anything I can do to help, just let me know." He walked quickly out to pay his bill.

"Do you think he'll keep his word?" Connie asked Father Tom. "Keep this information to himself, I mean?"

"We'll just pray the fear of God into him," the priest smiled.

"Do you think he guessed who our client is?" she asked her husband.

"Oh yeah. I could see it in his face." He leaned closer to give her a hug. "How many curly haired, redheaded teenage girls has he seen at our house, right after one of our counseling sessions with her?"

"You're right. Only one."

"Oh… dear… God!"

The three prayer partners turned toward the small voice at the far inside of the booth.

April Flannigan's face was as white as chalk.

It took the rest of their noon hour to reassure the lady that she had been invited to this meeting for a very specific reason. That she might be armed and able to bring about not only the rebirth of her marriage, but help save this tormented girl.

Her husband, they explained, was under the control of more than just a wayward teenager; he was in mortal danger of losing his very soul. But because April, herself, was saved, she had the power over that evil thing which was bent on not only his destruction, but the destruction of his whole family, even into the next few generations. This was not to be viewed as a moment of disaster... it was the start of a battle for a whole new beginning, for a wholesome and fulfilling relationship between her and Bill and the Lord. If she could get a good grasp on that reality, then she would surely make it through this journey. All she had to do was to realize who she really was in the Lord, and then act accordingly.

It was probably the most powerful thirty minutes in the short history of the three prayer partners' ministry. Had there not been ample prayer and praise before this encounter, it probably would not have worked. As it turned out, when April was dropped off at the Susie Wilson bus stop, she was actually hopeful.

"Remember," Don said as she got out of the car, "look at Bill the same way God looks at him: a precious soul entrapped in an evil situation. You are his way of escape right now. Remember that, okay?"

Years later, she could not remember the rest of the afternoon. She had walked into the living room in relative peace, then suddenly, the world blew apart. It had been surreal, filled by screams and pounding fists and stunned silence. Sometime in that space of time, there was a call from Connie. Something about being a brave soldier, making dinner, being pleasant. She had stopped crying by then, and had placed a cold washcloth over her eyes.

By the time Bill drove in at four o'clock, she had warmed up a roast, and laid out a nice table setting for him. She greeted him with a kiss, encouraging him to sit down and enjoy the meal. After some small talk, she picked up her watercolor supplies and left for class in the woodie.

She didn't make it past Ethan Allen Air Force Base before she started to cry again. It was only four-thirty. That gave her some time to pull into the back row of the Fanny Allen Hospital parking lot, where she once again let the horrendous flood of self-pity rush through her whole being. It was as though she was trapped in a smothering tunnel, and there was no escape. None. There was no air, but she was not able to die, only to writhe in horror and panic. She was surprised by beads of sweat rolling from her brow as she gasped and struggled and prayed frantically, "Jesus, Jesus... please, Jesus..."

Suddenly a sweep of fresh air passed in front of her nostrils and she sucked it in, deeply, deeply. Then she passed through the tunnel, into a strange, wonderful peace.

"This can't be real. This can't be it," she thought. But the respite was welcome, and she felt encouraged to "do it God's way." She decided, "Nothing else has worked, so this has to be it."Once that was done, she started to follow instructions. She started praising God for the restoration of her marriage, her home, and her family. It went against all she was feeling, just below the surface, but she pushed ahead, *hard,* and at five fifty-five, she took her place in the watercolor class.

***

Back at the little stucco house, at that very same hour, Bill Flannigan answered a knock at his back door.

As he turned the key in the lock, Roxie pushed the door open and slipped inside. "Hurry up and close the door!" she cried. Helping him to do so, she landed securely inside his embrace, then turned her lovely face up to his, moving in for a passionate kiss.

He drew back. "For God's sake, Roxie..." His voice reflected his shock.

"I don't want to hear about God," she murmured. "I want to hear how glad you are to see me." She moved in for the kiss again, but Bill drew back once more, pulling her arms from around his neck.

"No, please, Roxie," he pleaded. "This isn't right. This is my *home!*"

She dropped her arms, her head down, and leaned back against the door. The sultry voice came from deep in her throat, vibrating throughout the little kitchen.

"I know, I know… but… I can't help myself… you know how it is with me. When it comes to you, I just can't help myself." She caught a short breath. "You know that. You know what we have between us."

Slowly, the atmosphere in the room became heavy and fragrant. She lifted her angelic face in order to make bewitching silvery-eyed contact.

He turned his face away, trying to avoid the spell he knew was there.

"Look at me, Bill. Look at me."

***

At nine forty-seven, April pulled the car into the garage. She collected her art class supplies and tried to slip quietly into the house by the back door, which oddly, was unlocked and standing ajar.

Charley barked an unusually shrill welcome, circling and bouncing against her knees, almost too anxious to be picked up.

She laid aside her school supplies, and swept the little dog into a hug to quiet him. Her efforts were apparently successful, since there was no response from the darkened bedroom.

She put the car keys on their hook near the back door, so Bill would be able to get them on his way for his next day with Burlington Transit, then poured a cold drink from the ice tea pitcher in the refrigerator.

About a half-hour later, she went to lock the back door, but the key was not in the keyhole. She glanced at the row of keys on their hooks on the varnished key holder plaque, and there it was. That was definitely odd. She lifted it off the hook and inserted it into the keyhole, where it belonged. Then she locked the door.

Wearily, she headed into the bathroom to get ready for bed. At the bathroom door, she nearly fell over a pile of soaked towels, some of which were draped over the hamper to her left… the rest which had been left in a heap upon the floor, right in front of the door.

"Oh my gosh," she thought, "there must have been a plumbing problem." She went back into the bedroom and shook Bill awake.

"Honey, what happened in the bathroom? There are wet towels all over the place."

Bill suddenly sat upright in the bed. "What?" he asked.

She repeated the question, adding, "Was there a leak or something?"

"Oh yeah," he replied groggily. "But I fixed it. It's fixed." He flipped the cover back over his head. "Go to bed," he muttered from underneath the little red patchwork quilt.

April stared at the lap quilt, which was normally out on the front porch. She wondered for a moment just how it would have found its way into the bedroom. "Had to be some reason he was out on the porch." She went to peek out the living room window. "What the heck…?" She opened the door and stepped out to get a closer look. There, at the front step to the porch, the rocking chair lay on its side across the porch entrance at the top of the stairs from the front sidewalk. The only time she did that was when Charley was to be kept from leaving the porch and running around the neighborhood. She picked up the rocker and put it back in place. "He must have forgotten to put it away when he let Charley back into the house." Assuming Bill had brought the lap quilt in for some reason at that time, she proceeded to get ready for bed. Tonight, she would surrender everything to the will of God. Without doing that, she would not rest. It had been a long day, to say the least.

As she slipped into bed beside her husband, she noticed that the bedding was damp. "Oh, poor guy. He's had another one of those nightmares where he wakes up in a cold sweat," the woman surmised. She reached over and wrapped her arm across Bill's body, snuggling in close to his rigidly turned back. Very quietly, she whispered the Lord's Prayer. It was the only one she could think of.

Within seconds, a supernatural peace flowed over the Flannigans. They relaxed and slept.

CHAPTER TWENTY-ONE

Bait

Thanksgiving was just over a week away, and still there was no snow. Some folks were beginning to wonder just how much of a hunting season there would be. The only "hunters" who did well in this situation were the ones who had been putting out apples, drawing the deer to a familiar feeding place, and then picking them off as they innocently reached for one more rotting piece of fruit. It was generally considered cheating, but was still a common practice. Some folks thought it was only being smart, insuring a meat supply for the winter. Others looked the other way, hoping for a nice venison steak dinner at the neighbors' sometime over the long, icy season.

Because of the lack of snow, the ski hills were not yet open. The ski club at EJHS, however, was organized and ready for that first outing. Equipment was being swapped and waxed, and there was an air of eager anticipation. Meantime, the members of this club cooled their heels with other endeavors. In the shadow of the old Essex Junction train station's covered platform, one such student was meeting with a business partner.

"So, how's it going? You making any progress, you?" Uncle asked the young man who was sitting beside him on one of the benches. A Friday night train had just moved noisily out, southbound, and there was no one else still out there near the tracks.

Ted smiled and reached for one of the man's French fries. "Still laying the groundwork, but it's all coming into place." He bit into the salty potato stick, and chewed it slowly, then swallowed. Uncle waited impatiently for the next sentence.

"The first thing was to get in good with the 'in' crowd, and that seems to be working." The high school senior licked his lips, then wiped them dry on the back of his hand.

"The Wilson family's favor really got that ball rolling." He seemed to be quite proud of that accomplishment. He looked over at the tan-skinned fellow next to him. "I've been invited to a couple of things, but I don't bring her with me. It's too soon for that. In fact, they keep asking me why I'm even seeing her. Know what my favorite line is?"

Uncle could have cared less. He took a swig from his brown paper bag.

"I almost always say, 'Roxy can be sweet and kind, if you treat her right.'" He grinned. "They look at me like I just got off the boat... all innocent... stars in my eyes." He chuckled. "And that's what we want, right?" He reached for another fry, but Uncle moved the little greasy paper cone out of his reach.

"Get your own gawdim fries," he muttered.

Ted laughed, then got back to the subject. "Anyway, I need to work on that one a little longer."

"How long is this frickin' thing going to take, ay?"

"As long as it has to, Mr. Smart. We want this to work, don't we?"

"Ay-yuh, but you don't get paid 'til the job gets done, Buster."

Ted stood up. "That's fine, sir. Meantime, I'm off to work on it. Got a hot date on this happy Friday night."

"Treat her right."

"Ooh, yeah," he grinned again.

Uncle looked up into the young man's face. "Every date counts; time's growing short."

Ted moved in to whisper, "I get to meet her folks tonight. How about that for a little progress?"

"Hope they like you."

"Oh, they're gonna *love* me! I'm a high school kid, and I don't drive a public transit bus."

Mr. Smart slipped another fry into his mouth as he watched the youngster stride around to the right, then out of sight behind the train station's waiting room.

"Probably one of the best frickin' lures I've ever used," he thought happily.

***

Ted arrived to pick up Roxie at about seven o'clock. Marilyn opened the door and was pleased with what she saw. At last, her girl was dating a high school boy, and he was good-looking, to boot.

"Hi," Ted said shyly. "I'm Teddy Donahue, and I'm here to take Roxanne to the Edmunds High School dance, in Burlington."

Marilyn smiled and motioned him inside. "Nice to meet you, Teddy. Just have a seat. She'll be right out." She moved to the kitchen off the living room and called to her daughter, then came back in, to slip into the small easy chair near the sofa where he had stiffly settled. "Getting a little cold out there, don't you think?"

"Yes, ma'am."

"Maybe we could get some snow."

"Oh no, ma'am, it's too cold to snow." As though suddenly realizing he was correcting the lady, he looked down at his loafers, then reached down to brush something off. When he came back up, his face was red.

"I guess you native Vermonters know things like that. Hope I'm not making you uncomfortable, Teddy."

"No, ma'am." He seemed to relax awkwardly back into the sofa.

"Roxanne tells me that you live right here in town."

"Yes, that's right. My family has the Lincoln Street Greenhouse." He looked like he needed to explain where it was. "Um, that's right past the Brownell Library, just off the traffic circle." He nodded as though to reassure her of the accuracy of his directions.

"Oh sure, I know where that is."

Ted stood abruptly to his feet as Roxie entered the room. She was gorgeous in a luxurious pink angora sweater which stretched softly down over her bosom to gently touch the top of her navy blue wool skirt. She swirled around in front of her mother, as if to get approval, then slipped over to pull a Navy pea coat out of the closet near the front door. Immediately, Ted was at her side, helping her to slip into it. She kept her face hidden from Marilyn as she shot a sultry look toward Ted, then grabbed a dark pink scarf and a pair of navy blue gloves from the top shelf. Looking into the full-length mirror on the inside of the closet door, she gave a word to her mother.

"Okay, Mom, we'll be back before midnight."

"Eleven would be better. Your dad will be home by then, and you know how he worries about you."

"Eleven it is, ma'am," the young man assured her.

Roxie lowered her head again, to conceal the smirk. Then they were out the door. As the car moved out of the driveway, Marilyn felt a great sense of hope. "Roxanne is finally getting into a normal relationship. God knows, I'll take that," she said to herself.

And she did… hook, line, and sinker.

The next morning Roxie was due to have her next counseling session with Don Collins, but woke up complaining of a searing headache. She staggered to the breakfast table, then left it, to head for the bathroom. After a few minutes in there, she came out, all wobbly, and fell into her bed. Her mother tried to take her temperature, but Roxie refused to cooperate, hiding her head under the covers and moaning to be left alone. There would be no counseling today. Apparently, the poor girl had the flu.

***

Don and Connie were furious. They felt it was obvious Roxie was faking illness in order to avoid the next counseling session, and yet, without the girl's cooperation, there could be no further progress. In desperation, they called their prayer partner, Father Tom.

"How's your schedule for the next couple of days, including today?"

"I'm no longer fishing with Mr. Smart on Saturdays... at least, not until ice fishing starts. I'm back to my usual schedule for Saturday Confession, so today would not work." He thought for a moment, then suggested they meet on the next day, Sunday afternoon.

"Would it be inconvenient for you to join us for a barbecue at two o'clock at our house?"

The priest was delighted. "I'll clear it with Father Joseph," he said.

Connie made a quick trip to the Winooski IGA on the way home from church, and picked up a couple of things for the barbecue. By the time Father Tom arrived, everything was ready, so the three of them sat down at the picnic table inside the screened-in patio at two-fifteen, that Sunday afternoon. The sun was shining brightly across the dried grass of Saint Michael's green area, and it was a warm sixty degrees, quite balmy for the sixteenth of November. The three of them were comfortable in just light sweaters.

"I don't think she realizes what is going on," Connie commented. "Her folks certainly don't see it." She dished up some baked beans for the priest. "And that's another problem. How do we break the news to *them*?" She whacked the spoon smartly twice against the casserole edge. "They probably won't even believe us."

"It will be hard to convince the parents — or even Roxie, herself — about the demonic influences right now. I think the parents would have to see the manifestation, themselves, before they would believe it," Father Tom said as he scraped a mouthful of beans up off the sturdy melamine plate. He chewed softly and smiled. "You made these, right?" He looked at Connie.

She laughed. "They're from the freezer, I have to confess. Made them two months ago." She poked her fork into the hamburger on her plate. "Now, *this* is absolutely fresh!"

Don shook some catsup over his hamburger before his closed it inside the bun. "So, we can't actually deal with the girl as to the reality of demonic activity?"

The priest shrugged. "Probably not. Her parents would have to be aware of and convince her of the fact that there is demonic possession involved."

"Wow… demonic possession," Connie murmured. "I still can't quite fathom that concept, right there in Essex Junction." She squashed the potato salad into the flat of her plate with the back of her fork. "Nobody will ever believe us."

"Regardless of all that," Don concluded, "something has to be done." He leaned back in his webbed chair. "That demon has to be removed, one way or another." He waved his fork at Father Tom. "And we have to make sure it doesn't have a chance to re-occupy the body of Roxanne Foxx."

"Ay-yuh," the priest agreed. "There's the danger." He dropped his fork and looked directly at Don. "If we remove it, and she doesn't know how to keep it out, it could come back in, with seven more." His head lowered in concern. "She could be seven times worse off than before." He looked over at Connie. "I'm sure you know that's in the Bible."

"Lord God," Connie said, "and we're talking about a demonic spirit of *lust*, here." She pressed on the top of her hamburger bun with the fingertips of both hands, then drew back and looked up into the gray corrugated roof of the screened-in patio. "Not only could *she* be destroyed, but she could take every sexual contact, and then *their* sexual contacts with her." She turned to her husband. "What is that Bible verse about becoming spiritually one with a prostitute?"

"First Corinthians six, sixteen through eighteen," her husband replied.

"'What? Know ye not that he who is joined to a harlot is one body?'"

"Umm," she mused, "what does that mean, again?" She leaned forward. "I really need to know this, for sure, for sure."

Her husband continued with the quote:

"'... for two, saith he, shall be one flesh.'"

Connie no longer was interested in the food. She sat back in her chair. "So, God *is* telling us that a prostitute and a customer are joined in a spiritual union when they have sex."

"Uh," her husband stopped to think about how to delicately inform his wife, but there was no escape. "That's what it says," he stated.

Connie looked at Don, then at Father Tom. "Oh, Lord God, what is April up against?" Tears welled up in her eyes. "Oh my dear God. How can she stand up against such a fierce stranglehold?" Her eyes closed for a moment. "Not only does she have to fight what's in that girl, she has to fight what is now in her husband."

"Thank God she's a Christian," Don said.

"'Greater is he who is in me, than he who is in the world.'"

He smiled at his wife. "*She* doesn't have to fight anything. She has the Holy Ghost inside her. That's Who does the fighting, right, babe?"

Connie let her head roll back in relief. "Of course. That's exactly right." She took a minute to wipe the wet from the creases of her eyes. "I lost it, for a moment there." She gazed through the screen wall of the patio, out across the yellow grass. Finally, she sighed and relaxed, then turned to the priest. It was time to get down to business.

"So, Father Tom, Don and I lured you here by promising a winter barbecue, but you're smart enough to know that there's no such thing as a free lunch." The priest smiled around a mouthful of hamburger. She nodded toward Don. "You ask him."

Don wiped the catsup off his mouth and looked at his freckle-faced friend. "Guess there's no easy way to do this, so I'll just ask you right out. Does Holy Family, your church, have access to an exorcist?"

Father Tom held up a wait-a-moment index finger while he finished chewing and swallowing, but his head was bobbing affirmatively. "I thought this might come up today," he finally said, "so I have had time to think it through." He took a quick sip from the bottle of Coke in front of him, licked his lips, and leaned forward. "We actually do. We have people specially trained for this. Trouble is, in our particular case, there is a heap of paperwork and clearances before it can be approved. After that, believe it or not, there is a long waiting list." He sat back in his chair again. "But I think I have a better idea, anyway." He ran his fingers through his auburn hair as he asked, "What about your black preacher, Deacon Forester, or whatever his name is? He's into that sort of thing, from what you've told me. You said he had a healing and deliverance ministry, didn't you?"

The Collinses sat still, surprised.

"Deacon Foster... I guess we just never thought of that... did we, babe?"

"Never even once."

"Don't know why it wouldn't work..." He glanced at her to see if she might have a cautionary word. She shrugged her shoulders and nodded in agreement. He went on to address the priest. "It would probably be alright, but we would have to get the two of them back down from Canada." He smiled faintly. "Thanks for the idea."

Father Tom bowed graciously. "And that's probably the best I can do for you. Officially, I can have no part in this. I can only operate under the aegis of the Roman Catholic Church."

"Of course," Don said. "I'll contact Pastor James this evening, and see how to go about this. Meanwhile, my friend, you just keep saying those *'Our Fathers.'*"

CHAPTER TWENTY-TWO

Blankets

The absolute silence woke Cecil Thompson. He lay there for a couple of minutes, listening. No wind, no rustling leaves, no early morning twitter of wintering birds, not even the swish of traffic from the other side of the railroad tracks. It was a complete, long-lasting quiet.

Suddenly, he realized he had experienced this engulfing silence before. He rose quickly from the bed and drew the nearest side of the pulled-down window shade away from the window to peer out into the darkness. There, the lovely, deep blue landscape outside the window panes revealed an old, familiar story. It was the first snowfall of the year.

"Wow. About time… the eighteenth of November, for Pete's sake."

He went through his morning routine more quickly than usual, and was standing out on the sheltered back porch, puffing on his first Camel of the day, when Uncle came bursting out, boots on, and ready to shovel a walkway to the barn. The little Abenaki grabbed the snow shovel he had stashed near the back door the night before and got right to it.

"Hey," he called over his shoulder, "the white man is such a frickin' amateur when it comes to the weather. I knew before I got into bed last night." He flashed an ivory grin back toward the smoker on the porch. In ten minutes, there was a nice path to the milking parlor door. Cecil put his cigarette out on the metal jar-top ashtray on the porch rail, and went out to milk the cows.

Inside the house, Winnie woke up from another night of troubled dreams. Since the Sunday morning service out at the Collinses' Pentecostal church, she had been struggling once again with her perspective on all things spiritual. First, there was the sudden reality of a God who actually cared... cared enough to heal actual diseases and Who even talked to His children through people like Rehema, and through the Bible... yeah, even through the Bible. "Imagine that," she whispered to herself. "And all that time as a good Roman Catholic, I never got that. I never understood that." She had certainly heard about miracle healings, but had not personally witnessed any. This was a whole new perspective on who God really was, right now, today.

In addition, on this particular morning, she was wrestling with reports which she had heard concerning their rental up there on Case Road. Something about weird tapping noises, and open Bibles in every room, all this related to her by Shirley, who was beginning to make threats about leaving that "haunted" house. Father Tom had been up there, checking the placing of those Bibles throughout the little dwelling, to stave off demonic spirits. Demons in the old Case house? Did that mean there could be demons right there in her own house, as well? And how did that line up with those miracle healings? And a message from God? And ghosts making noises? At this point, things were almost overwhelming.

It was as though yet another world had suddenly invaded the old confusing ones in which she had grown up — Abenaki and Christian. That was unsettling enough, but what made it *scary* was that this additional new world was becoming more and more real. The idea that ghosts or spirits or demons... or whatever... could actually be in the same room with her, gave this little lady a persistent case of the creeps.

Though her head was swimming in confusion, she automatically started to get ready for work. She slipped her feet into well-worn moccasin slippers, pulled her old pink chenille robe on and moved out of the darkness of the bedroom. As she walked through the shadows past the dining room table, a hazy, cool light to her right caught her attention. She stopped and smiled, delighted by the familiar glowing winter scene neatly framed above the window seat.

"Well, now we're getting back to normal," she whispered as she walked slowly over to gaze out the wide window. She estimated maybe four or five inches of snow on the ground. The five-thirty train would have no problem whizzing along the track on its way to Essex Junction. Beyond that track, straight ahead, the tan ribbon of Case Road had disappeared under the pale blue blanket. Her gaze moved up to the far horizon of the hill just past the old Case house, where tips of snow-covered branches were lightly tinted with the pink and purple of an early morning sunrise.

She stood there as long as she dared, but this was a work day for her, and Uncle had to be dropped off there at Sears, on his way to the bus station for the ride to his Tuesday poker game. She was washed and dressed by the time the electric pot had heaved it's last sigh, leaving the kitchen filled with the aroma of fresh coffee. As she poured a cup, the sound of Ceese's tractor signaled the plowing of the driveway. He would get that done, then clear the Old Colchester Road curve out front, and continue all the way over the railroad tracks and down the slope to the new Colchester Road. That would get Winnie onto a county-plowed highway, all the way to her job.

Uncle came in, stomping and wiping his feet, just about the time she was giving a final stir to the oatmeal. He called to her from down the back hallway.

"I won't bother with the front walk. It's not that gawdim cold out." He slipped his boots off as he finished his weather report. "Most of this stuff will be gone by noon. That's how frickin' warm it is out there."

She peeked at the round thermometer just outside the window over the sink. It read only thirty-four degrees. "You're probably right, you" she answered. "Well anyways, we're having oatmeal with maple syrup dripped on top, your favorite." His grunt of approval made her smile. That was familiar, too. Getting back to the preparation of breakfast, she stepped into the narrow, open pantry which was located underneath the back stairway up to Uncle's apartment, and grabbed a jug of maple syrup. Pulling the cork, she poured the amber syrup into a small metal creamer.

"Oh darn," she muttered, as a hairy lump plopped into the little pitcher. "It's got a 'mother' on it."

She had removed the fungus and poured the whole quart of syrup into a pan for a thorough three-minute cleansing boil, when the phone rang. Uncle was just passing by to double-check the front walk, so he stopped and picked it up. He was a little surprised that Teddy Donahue would call him at this phone number, and at this early hour, but figured it must be important, so he listened intently.

"Got some news for ya, Mr. Smart."

"Okay..."

"Our little femme fatale is about to take a long vacation from her nefarious activities."

"Okay..." He checked to see if Pooh was listening. She was busy stirring boiling syrup.

"She'll be 'out of commission' until at least next summer. Your friend, Bill, should finally be off the hook."

"Okay..." Pooh was washing the little creamer in the sink, splashing and rinsing and clanking. "So what happened?" he almost whispered.

"She's P.G."

"What?"

"Pregnant." There was a little pause. "She's 'with child,' Mr. Smart."

"You sure?"

"Yup. Told me, herself." Another pause. "Mad at me, of course."

"Why you? You're not the only one."

"The only other one is Mr. Flannigan, and he got fixed two years ago."

Uncle watched Pooh go down the back hall to drop a dish towel into the laundry sink. "How do you know?"

"She told me, herself." He chuckled. "Said I was the father, like it or not."

Cecil came stomping in through the back door, and there was a conversation going on between him and his wife, something about tracking snow in from the outside, so Uncle continued the conversation, speaking in a low voice.

"This is not what we frickin' planned," he muttered. "This involves a kid, gawdimmit. That is not how this was supposed to happen."

"Look, Mr. Smart, you asked me to get this girl off Mr. Flannigan's back, and into some kind of jail time. That's what you wanted. Well, I have delivered. You owe me a thousand dollars."

Uncle looked over his shoulder, making sure he wasn't being heard. "Listen to me, you frickin' jackass. You better not let that girl kill that baby. That's murder, pure and simple." He looked down the hall one more time. "That's what these girls *do*! They abort." He spoke through gritted teeth. "You get your frickin' thousand dollars, alright, but not until that poor little baby is born and in a safe family." He hissed the final words. "I should-a known. I just should-a frickin' known."

On the other end of the phone line, Teddy Donahue hung up.

Uncle did not hear the second hang-up click of the phone in the greenhouse.

"Marsha," Mrs. Donahue called from the behind a huge collection of poinsettias, "Did you get the *Free Press* yet? We need to get that ad changed, young lady!"

"Not yet. Somebody was on the phone in the house."

"At this early hour? What the heck for?"

Marsha did not answer, asking instead, "Should I try it now?"

"Of course, but call the number I gave you, not the 'business-as-usual' one."

"Yes, ma'am," the girl replied.

The woman felt a pang of guilt. "Hey, Marsha… thanks for coming in so early today. I know that wasn't easy, what with having to walk in all that snow, in the dark, and everything."

"Yes, ma'am," the skinny blonde responded. But as she picked up the phone, her mind was on other things.

A very upset Marsha reported the conversation to Roxie during school lunch hour. The beautiful redhead was livid, but instead of offering any explanations, she stomped off the school grounds, cutting classes for the rest of the day. Nobody seemed to notice or even care.

***

"Bill, I can't find the key to the back door," April said softly. "Did you put it away someplace?" At seven o'clock that same November Tuesday morning, when she went out to find the snow shovel in the back of the garage, she had noticed that the door had been left unlocked.

There was an extended silence from the bedroom. At length, there was a huge sigh, and he replied, "What are you talking about?"

"Our back door is unlocked, Bill." She was careful not to accuse. "That is scary to me." She paused, then continued: "We need to find the key, so we can lock our door at night, right, honey?" She tried to walk nonchalantly into the bedroom as she offered the next excuse. "Maybe we dropped it. Did our Charley pick it up?"

Bill rubbed his eyes and cursed the small poodle. "We should get rid of that little pest."

By the time the two of them had left the house that afternoon, the key still had not been found. Although it was a bit unsettling, April pushed that situation to the back of her mind and concentrated on putting one foot in front of the other, and letting God do the rest. She dropped Bill off at work just before three for his swing shift, with the understanding that she would meet him after her class, which ended at nine o'clock. Much to her relief, the class ended on time. April cleaned up her workplace, brushed snow off the woodie, and headed for the St. Paul Street bus terminal.

When she climbed onto his bus, it was a little after ten, and it was still snowing lightly. The bright lights of City Hall Park had faded into golden globes behind the feathery downfall. Soon, the bus was moving along through the winter streets of Vermont's Queen City. From where she sat right behind Bill, she could look out the windows across the aisle at the seasonal sights passing by. Christmas "candle" lights in Victorian windows — soft blue, or white, or gold, and even a few joyful red blinks of color, alternated with winsome lines of multi-hued bulbs entwined around the posts and railings of verandahs, and, here and there, the lights on front lawn evergreens twinkled softly from under a thin covering of snow. The bus moved slowly through unplowed fluff, passing one historic house after another, each one a lovely glowing symbol of the upcoming holiday season. It was almost magical.

As the evening passed, the snow continued its silent, persistent fall.

There were few passengers on the bus, so the two of them were able to chat and enjoy the peaceful panorama, for the better part of his final run. Then April drove the station wagon behind Bill's bus, back to the bus barn on Winooski Avenue, and helped him to do the clean-up. She waited in the car for him to sign out, and then he was there, sliding into the driver's seat of the woodie. Before he turned the key, he reached over and squeezed her hand.

"That was fun, April. We should do this more often."

She felt a glimmer of hope.

At a few minutes past midnight, the weary couple arrived back home on Susie Wilson Road. There were three inches of new-fallen snow on the driveway. Bill was parking the station wagon in the garage when April unlocked the front door and stepped inside. Charley, who had been yipping hysterically before she even got the door open, leapt into her open arms, his eyes rolling wildly. She hugged him closely, wondering what was wrong, and then she looked up.

She couldn't believe her eyes.

The bedroom door was blocked. Her lovely oil painting, which normally sat just to the right of the doorway on the narrow shelf of a large easel, had fallen to her left, and closed off access to the bedroom. The easel, itself, had also fallen, but somehow had landed on its side, its long, top panel wedged between the wall and Bill's heavy easy chair on that same left side of the doorway. The wooden structure crossed the front of the painting, actually bracing it into an almost immovable position.

She gasped, then moved slowly toward the barricaded doorway, noticing that not much else had been disturbed in the room. She looked at the dog. "Charley! Did you do this?"

But then she saw something that made her know he had not: the whole lower edge of the painting which touched the floor had been scratched, and scratched repeatedly. They were Charley's scratch marks, the same as when he was scratching to dig out a mole in the yard. She had seen them many times, and she knew that when he dug like that, he was in a frenzy. She leaned carefully over the three-foot height of painting into the dark of the bedroom. Charley growled softly. She dropped him gently onto the bedroom floor as she reached around the doorjamb and flipped the wall switch on. As light flooded the room, she looked around slowly. Charley stood trembling on the other side of the painting, the hackles straight up under the curls on his back. Carefully, he moved to sniff at the edge of the bed ruffle, the floor under the bedside table, then back to the scent around to the tall wooden stool near the doorway.

"What is our bathroom stool doing out in the bedroom?" she wondered out loud.

Bill came in, looked at the mess, and swore. "What happened?"

"I'm not sure," she said as she stepped back to look at the disarray again. Charley yapped from the bedroom. The bus driver loosened his tie as he observed the scratches and the wet oil paint paw prints on the floor. "Was he out *here*, or in *there* when you came in?"

"Out here. Obviously, he was trying to get into the bedroom." She waited.

"What for?"

"I don't know, but there was something in there he really, really wanted." She waited, again. Then she got brave. "Or somebody was egging him on. Remember, the back door was left unlocked." Suddenly, the man's handsome jaw went hard. Charley yapped again.

"Get that mutt out here, so he'll shut up," Bill growled.

She tried to reach over the top of the painting, but could not reach low enough to pick up the little guy. "I can't."

Bill moved his easy chair, releasing the top of the easel. In a few seconds, the easel was once more leaning against the wall where it had been before, and the painting was back up on its shelf. Charley ran out, skirting around the angry man, and headed straight for his doggie bed near the back door.

April grabbed a rag still damp with turpentine and began to wipe the paint off the floor. "Better let the dog out, Bill," she said, trying to sound matter-of-fact.

The man pulled the back door open and Charley made a beeline for his favorite shrub, only to find it sitting in pretty deep snow. Still, with a shivering tilt, he managed to answer nature's call. Bill stood on the small back step and purposely looked around. He didn't have long or far to look. There, from the back step, a trail of footprints, almost invisible under the new snow, led out to Case Road.

Charley made a hasty retreat back into the warmth of the house, with Bill right behind him. The shivering poodle pounced and pawed at his blanket before doing his little circle dance and plopping down. It was when he plopped down that the back door key flipped out and rattled to a stop on the kitchen floor.

Bill picked up the key and swore, again. "That stupid mutt had the key all this time."

April looked up. "Well, I don't know where he could have had it, because I emptied that whole little bed out, just this morning."

Her husband looked at the key, then gazed out the kitchen window toward Case Road. "Well, we won't keep it in the door anymore. We'll keep it in the drawer with the potholders. That should solve the problem." He locked the back door, dropped the key in the drawer, and headed for bed.

As she washed her hands in the kitchen sink, the artist allowed herself to mourn the loss of her beautiful painting. Not that she couldn't re-do the damaged part, or even do a whole new one, but who would be so nasty as to tease a little dog and purposefully ruin a painting by April Flannigan? She was sure it was something very evil.

But, even so, it needed a tall wooden stool to climb back out of that bedroom.

***

The next morning, while Bill was out shoveling snow from the driveway, April made a call.

"Good morning. Essex Junction High School."

"Yes. This is Mrs. Flannigan. I would like to leave a message for Mrs. Collins, please."

Surprisingly, Connie called within the hour. Bill was getting dressed for work, so April kept her voice down. "Do you have the Studebaker today?"

"No. Don is picking me up at four o'clock, though. What do you need?"

"To tell you something scary that happened last night. It could take a few minutes." She paused to think a second. "Would you two like to have supper with me? Bill has a swing shift today."

"Um, well, we do like to make the Wednesday night Bible study. But that's not until six-thirty. Sure, that would be nice, but please don't fuss. We like soup, you know, right out of the can."

It just so happened she had given Bill a steaming hot mug of Campbell's tomato soup to warm him up, after all that shoveling that morning. More than half of it was left over. So April added another can and made some grilled cheese sandwiches, and the three friends sat down to share this meal at four-fifteen that afternoon. Don said grace, and then looked expectantly at his hostess. "Well? Tell us your scary story, young lady."

"Take a look at my painting," April said as she motioned to the artwork leaning against the wall just behind her dining room chair. The couple moaned in dismay. "Yeah, and this is what we found when we got home last night."

She went on to describe the whole experience. Don and Connie exchanged meaningful looks several times before she finished. "So I… I…" April was surprised by her own sudden gush of tears. "I just f-feel so… violated… *again!*"

Connie reached over and patted her hand. "And so would anybody else." She looked over at her husband. "It's adding insult to injury."

"That's true. But April, you are in some pretty distinguished company, I can tell you. Take a look in the Bible. There is a lot of abuse of God's people, most of them more famous than you and me." He lifted his soup spoon and moved it gently to emphasize his point. "But there is a word of encouragement for us all." Both ladies paid attention. "In the Book of Romans, chapter twelve, verse one:

'I beseech you therefore, brethren, by the mercies of God, that ye present your bodies a living sacrifice, holy, acceptable unto God, which is your reasonable service.'"

He dipped the spoon into the soup and stirred it slowly. "Now, what does that really mean?" A warm spoonful of tomato soup later, he continued: "Means you and I are to surrender *everything* to God. Trust Him, trust Him, trust Him." He leaned toward April. "You are not the only woman in the world that this has happened to, and certainly not the *last* one this will happen to. We need to keep it in the proper perspective." He laid the spoon down, perfectly aligned beside the knife at the right side of his bowl. "Now, I know that sounds pretty hard-hearted, but let me ask you this. How much are you willing to go through, to save your marriage, and even more, to lead your husband to Christ?"

April shook her head in disagreement. "I'm sorry, but I don't see how the tormenting of an innocent little dog amounts to a sacrifice on my part. The only sacrifice is to endure the thought of what happened to him. She teased and teased and tormented him!"

Don looked over at Charley, who was lying quietly in his bed, even though his big brown eyes revealed how very, very much he would like to get a tiny morsel from that table. "He's a cute little fella," the man said with a smile, "But that cute little fella is — at heart — a fierce hunter. You know that? He's an animal who was created to hunt, April. That's who God created him to be." The man turned back to the table, where he picked up the last half of his grilled cheese sandwich. "Sometimes hunters succeed, and sometimes they don't. But failure doesn't mean the hunter is being tormented. It only means he has to go on to the next hunt." He smiled gently at his friend. "*He's a little hunting dog*, April. Once you understand that, she can't use this tactic to get to you. After all, she drove him into a hunting frenzy, just to destroy what she thinks *you* are — a dog-lover and a darned good artist." He held up a forefinger. "Oh, and her biggest competitor for the latest bus company door prize, Bill Flannigan." There was a crumb to be brushed off his lip before taking the next bite. "And this *is* a contest to her, April... a stupid, teenage contest... and in her mind, she does *not* lose... not ever." He took a small bite off the sandwich, chewed twice, then spoke out of the corner of his mouth. "And, by the way, she plays filthy-dirty because she has a demonic spirit in her. Just remember that, will you?"

"Um, I'll try." She looked over at Connie, whose hand was still resting gently over hers. The women exchanged a sisterhood look.

"You know what, hon?" Connie said. "You have, in effect, been a living sacrifice for this guy, working around his warped ego for many, many years to keep the peace in the marriage and the family. Why not utilize this same mode of operation, but for a better, higher reason?" She pulled her two hands together under her chin, lacing the fingers together. "Why not *really* become a living sacrifice, just like Jesus did;

give your whole self, in order to save your husband and your marriage, ultimately, for the glory of God?" She tilted her head to one side. "In fact, you could even get a 'new' husband out of this deal."

"Oh my goodness," April whispered, as the overwhelming reality of her situation set in. "I actually have to die — to my own needs and my own rights." She looked defeated. "I don't think I can do that."

"Praise God, you don't have to do that on your own," Don said. "This is something we can only do by the power of the Holy Ghost within us." He stood up, getting ready to leave. "Thank God, April, that you belong to Jesus. He knows how to turn you into a regular Holy Ghost warrior."

Before the Collinses backed out of the driveway, Don prayed a mantle of protection over the Flannigan household, in the Name of Jesus. "And Lord, it would be a whole lot easier for April, if she could finally understand that You have her back."

It was a prayer which would be answered in an amazingly surreal manner.

***

Roxanne Foxx's fifteenth birthday was the day after Thanksgiving, the twenty-first of November, which happened to fall on a Friday. Since both George and Marilyn had to work on that holiday (Thanksgiving travelers kept both the bus company and the conveniently located restaurant busy every year.) the family of three planned to celebrate the next day, making Roxie's birthday dinner also Thanksgiving dinner. The teenager was pleased with this arrangement. Secretly, she planned a special present for herself, which involved asking Ted Donahue to join them for the double celebration. George and Marilyn were more than pleased to have the young man come for dinner, and so Roxie made the phone call to Ted, early on Wednesday morning.

"You're not mad at me anymore?"

"How could I stay mad at *you*? We mean too much to each other."

"Aw, Roxie, thank God. I've been missing you already."

"We need to work this out together," she murmured.

"Yeah, Shug-ah, that's right." His voice was warm and tender. "We're in this together, right to the end."

At five o'clock that Friday evening, Ted leaned forward on his elbows and gazed across the dinner table at the beautiful mother of his child. He knew it would only be a matter of time before her folks would know it, and then things would probably change drastically between him and them. In the meantime, he needed to make sure nothing happened to the baby. He was going to make Roxie feel like a *real* princess. He gave her a mischievous wink. "It's still pretty early. Let's help clear the table, and then go take in a movie. What do ya think?"

Marilyn laughed. "I can handle this; you two go ahead. You should be able to make the six o'clock show."

Before they left, Ted turned and thanked the Foxxes for a great meal.

"You are certainly welcome, Ted," the charmed lady answered. "Please come again."

Once the car left Indian Acres, Roxie slid close to her suave driver. "Forget about a stupid, old movie," she cooed. "Let's take a nice, long drive."

***

At eleven o'clock that night, Marilyn shook George awake. "What?!" he growled.

When she turned on the bedside lamp, he saw the panic on her pale face.

"She's not home yet. I checked all over the house."

"Not again," he moaned as he slid out of bed.

A forty-five minute search-around-Essex Junction later, he returned to the house. "Didn't find her, but ran into Chief Rob Allen, out on patrol. He made a few calls. All we can do is wait."

Robbie Allen was familiar with Ted Donahue's vehicle, so he began his own sweep of the local lovers' lanes, but turned up nothing. He pulled back into the parking lot at Lincoln Hall, intending to call the other two officers at home. Just as he started to get out of the patrol car, something came to mind.

"His joyriding buddy, Jack Wilson." He slid back onto the seat. "Yeah, he might know where this guy would take a girl... especially a girl like Roxanne Foxx." This time he got out of the car, and went inside to call the Wilson household. By the time Jack got to the phone, it was twelve-fifteen, and it was snowing again.

"I can't think of any place like that," he answered sleepily. "He's pretty respectful of her. I don't think he would tell anybody that."

"Okay, son. Thanks."

Jack's head had barely slid back into the hollow of his pillow, when he had a sudden thought. *"Maybe I do know a place."* He pulled on some warm clothes and paused at his parents' bedroom door.

"Dad," he whispered. He saw Jessie's head lift from the bed. "I need to go help Chief Rob." His father's nod gave him permission, and he was on his way down the River Road a few minutes later.

The snow was coming down steadily, but he managed to find the left turn that led to the open area where he had learned to spin doughnuts in Ted's sporty Pontiac.

And there it was. Ted had pulled the black car as far to the back of the lot as it would go, and indeed, casual passersby would not have seen it from the road.

"Aw jeez, Teddy," the young man muttered, as he noticed movement in the car. "This could be embarrassing." He turned off his headlights and let the truck idle for a minute, and then decided he would be better off just reporting the sighting. Having made that decision, he headed back to the village and pulled into the lot at Lincoln Hall. He was relieved to see Chief Robbie just coming out of the building.

"Jack!" The Chief of Police was surprised.

"I found them," the young Wilson said.

The chief followed Jack's truck out to the site, where he parked the patrol car so that his headlights fully illuminated the Pontiac. The dairy farmer stayed in his truck and watched as the policeman walked purposely up to the driver's side of the car and rapped smartly on the window. The chief paused a moment, then peered inside the car. A swear word escaped as the officer turned the handle and opened the door. The limp body of Ted Donahue slid into his arms. Quickly, Chief Rob heaved it back into the driver's seat and felt for a pulse. Even as he was doing that, he spotted the unconscious Roxanne Foxx, her torso lying under a blue plaid blanket. He stretched hard to reach over to feel her neck for a pulse. Stepping back outside the car, the chief turned and ran back to his vehicle. Jack turned off the engine and jumped out of the truck, just in time to hear the chief calling for an ambulance.

"How many people?" the question crackled over the police radio.

"Two kids," Robbie answered. "Both still breathing."

"Are they hurt?" Jack asked. The chief motioned him to go back into his truck, and kept up communications on the police radio.

In a matter of five minutes, the siren and flashing lights of a Chittenden County Sheriff's car announced the arrival of Max Duncan. He jumped out of the car.

"That was fast," Robbie commented.

"Just settled a domestic disturbance right up the road," the sheriff replied. "So, what do ya have here?" The two officers walked toward Ted's car as Rob spoke.

"Two injured teenagers. Don't know what happened yet. Thought you would want to check that yourself."

The older law officer carefully opened the driver's door, peering at the unconscious young man. He stopped short, then grabbed a flashlight from his belt, shining it slowly across Ted's deeply discolored throat. "Hmm. Looks like this one's been chopped in the throat."

Rob bent around to try and see. "Chopped?"

"Some kind of karate chop, more than once, I would guess." He lifted the teenager's arm gently up into the lap of the limp body, then carefully closed the door. "He's breathing, though. Must be the cold kept the swelling down." He looked down at the snow-covered ground. "Any footprints when you got here?"

"Uh… no, no, what you see are mine."

"Alright then, you stay where you are. I'll make one set of prints around the front of the car, to keep the crime scene as clean as possible." He proceeded around the hood, careful not to leave fingerprints, even though it was snowing, then stopping to open the passenger side door.

Roxanne was sloped gently against it, so, after checking her breathing, he lifted her up to set her farther toward the center of the bench seat. As he did so, his hand felt the dampness and he looked down. She had been sitting in a pool of blood. The seasoned law officer could not contain the gut reaction and he dropped her roughly on the seat, causing both of her arms to slip out from under the blanket. Once more, he stopped and then pulled out the flashlight. As he moved it slowly up and down the wrists and outside edges of her hands, multi-colored bruises glistened in the beam of light.

"Looks like this young lady was fighting for her life," he said. He moved the light toward the floorboard where it exposed a rumpled navy blue pea jacket. "Had her coat off," he commented. He flicked the beam around and quickly located Ted's jacket tossed carelessly into the back seat. "Him, too."

Chief Allen was intently studying the scene, not moving from where he stood just outside Ted's car door, when the sound of an ambulance siren broke his concentration. He quickly walked back to his vehicle, where Jack was standing.

"What happened?" the youngster asked.

"Don't know yet," Robbie answered. "But you'd better get home. Sheriff Duncan will probably contact you later for a statement."

"Are they both hurt?"

"Ay-yuh."

"Was it robbery?"

"Not likely."

"But who would attack a couple of kids making out in a …?"

The chief was beginning to lose patience. "I don't have any answers for you, Jack. All I can say is, thanks for showing us this location. It was a big help." He put a fatherly arm around the inquisitive fellow and steered him gently back to his truck. "Tell you what, sir," he spoke diplomatically, "I will keep you updated as soon as I have any information."

Jack got into his truck, but just before he closed the door, he leaned out and whispered hoarsely to the chief: "Somebody has to be pretty darned sick to do something like this."

It was one-forty in the morning as Jack's truck disappeared back onto the road. The chief brushed the snow off the collar of his police jacket, then turned his thoughts back to the violently beaten couple in the Pontiac.

"Pretty darned sick… or pretty darned mad," he mused.

CHAPTER TWENTY-THREE

Revenge

"I'm sorry, Mrs. Donahue, but at this point, all we can tell you is that your son has received several severe blows to his spinal cord, delivered from the front of the throat, not only destroying his vocal chords, but making him completely paralyzed over his entire body. All he can do is to move his eyes and his eyelids... at least at this point." The doctor was sympathetic, lowering his eyes to give this grieving mother a moment to digest this shocking information. "Of course, he might surprise us all, but that doesn't look promising. The fact that he can be helped to breathe somewhat normally with the oxygen tube, helps a whole lot. And please understand, he seems to have normal cognitive ability, that is, he can think just as clearly as you and I at this point." He reached over and touched her hand. "He can communicate with you by blinking and rolling his eyes. He knows to blink once for 'no' and twice for 'yes.' That is a miracle in itself. So, please keep that ability going in him. That is crucial to his recovery, at whatever level that may be."

As soon as the doctor left the room, Emma Donahue collapsed in grief, into the arms of her daughter, Paula. In the bed, Ted's eyes reflected the shock, as a large tear escaped from the corner of his right eye, rolled down his temple, and dropped to the sheet beneath his head.

Just a few doors down the hallway from Ted Donahue's room in the Fanny Allen Hospital, the parents of Roxanne Foxx learned that their daughter had received a severe pummeling in the abdomen, which resulted in a miscarriage. The pregnancy was quite new, and her prospects for a complete recovery were therefore quite good. George and Marilyn sat near Roxie's bedside, holding hands. It had been two days. Roxie was clearly traumatized, barely able to speak, dissolving into tears from the pain one moment, staring blankly into space the next. Even though things were getting better, there just seemed to be no more words.

A tap on the doorjamb broke the silence. The couple looked up to see Sheriff Duncan step quietly into the room, followed by the Collinses, who had arrived at the same time as the sheriff. Connie reached over and hugged Marilyn, who once again began to weep. "They wouldn't let us come in for a couple of days," Connie explained. "But today we finally got permission."

Marilyn dried her eyes. "Thank God you're here. I was afraid they would bring in a social worker."

"No," Don said firmly. "You're covered, just because we have been counseling with her for several months." He looked over at Roxie. "How's it going, young lady?" The girl's eyes narrowed and she turned her face from him. Don took a big breath and let her know he wasn't going away. "As you can see, Sheriff Duncan is here with us, Roxie. He has to ask you a few questions. That's his job. Now, as your counselor, I am here to protect you and help you in any way I can." The pretty face turned back to view the law officer suspiciously. Her mouth froze with apprehension. "Just remember, whatever you tell this gentleman can be used as evidence in a courtroom, should there be some kind of legal action. So, tell the truth, but you don't have to say anything that could make you *responsible* for what happened." Her parents nodded appreciatively as Don issued that warning.

The sheriff removed his hat, tucking it under his arm, and reached for a small notebook from the pocket of his jacket. "I don't want to take too much of your time, Miss, because what you have been through has been pretty rough, I'm sure." He pulled a pen from an inside pocket and flipped the notebook open. "Can you tell me what happened to you and Mr. Donahue last Friday night?"

"We went for a long ride and ended up in our special spot. We were just going to make out a little," she whispered.

"Did anyone else know you were going there?" the man asked.

"No, I don't think so."

"Is this place used by other couples?"

"We never saw anybody else there."

He scribbled in the notepad, then looked up. "Did you notice anybody, a car or anything, following you that night?" She nodded negatively. He paused, then took a breath. "So, when did you first see your attacker? Outside the car window, or what?"

"I never saw anybody." She pulled the thin blanket toward her chin. "We were just messing around, and then I blanked out."

"So, maybe Mr. Donahue hit you?"

"Maybe." She seemed to think about that a moment. "But I don't remember."

The sheriff changed his tactics. "The doctor just showed me a picture of what shape your abdomen is in. Somebody pounded you repeatedly, so much so, that you had a miscarriage. That had to hurt. Surely, you remember *that*."

"I don't understand what happened. I just blanked out and woke up here in the hospital. *I* want to know what happened." Suddenly, Don and Connie exchanged knowing looks. They had heard her ask that question, before.

Sheriff Duncan continued. "Well, maybe you could tell me how Mr. Donahue sustained such severe blows to the neck that he is now paralyzed."

The girl's eyes grew wide. "Paralyzed?"

"She wasn't told that yet," Marilyn objected.

"I'm sorry. But that is a fact." He looked the girl in the eye. "Are you saying you did not see that happen, either?"

Roxie looked down toward her feet, before she replied in a cold, even voice. "I did not see that happen." Don and Connie exchanged a long, dark look.

The officer sighed. "Well then, do you know anyone who was mad enough at you to do something like this?"

This time, she took a lot longer to think about the question. Finally, she spoke up, even though her voice was shaky. "There are some people who don't like me, that's for sure. But I don't think any of them are strong enough to do this so I really can't say. I need to think about it then I will get back to you, if that's okay."

"Her pain meds are kicking in," Marilyn whispered.

As he flipped the notebook closed, Sheriff Max Duncan offered one last possibility. "Is there the chance that someone had been hiding in the back of the car, maybe on the floor?"

"I doubt that," a strong voice answered.

Chief Robbie Allen was standing in the doorway. Sheriff Duncan turned to inquire, but the chief answered before the question got asked. "No footprints in the snow. I was first up-close on the scene, and I think both you and I can attest to that. There were tire marks, but no footprints, remember?"

The sheriff put his hat back on, thanked Roxie for her cooperation, and headed for the doorway. As he passed Chief Robbie, he signaled for him to follow. Once out in the hallway, he asked what the chief was doing at the hospital.

"Networking," the man replied. "I have a working relationship with Connie Collins. She's the counselor at EJHS, and right now, that student body needs all the help it can get. This whole thing has been a big shock."

Sheriff Duncan eyed Robbie Allen. "Just so you remember, this case is in my jurisdiction."

"Yes, sir."

Once the sheriff had disappeared down the hall, Chief Allen returned to the room to speak to the Collinses. "I just needed to touch base with you two, if you have a couple of minutes."

"We should probably step outside so we don't disturb her," Connie suggested.

The Foxxes rose from their chairs. "We need to get back to work. Thank God she is doing so much better today," Marilyn whispered.

"They said she could probably come home soon," George murmured. "We'll have to have someone to stay with her for a few days."

"Have anyone in mind?" Don asked as they stepped softly out into the hall.

"Not yet." The burly man looked concerned. "She probably won't be a good patient."

"I might know someone who could handle her," the counselor grinned. "Let me get back to you."

The Foxxes hurried away, and Chief Rob Allen turned to the Collinses. "What the heck do you think happened last Friday night?"

The two made eye contact again before Don answered. "Probably the same thing that happened in our last counseling session with her. There was a glazing over of the eyes, an attack, and then she couldn't remember a thing."

"So, let me get this straight. The kid has another personality? I've heard of that before."

"More like, 'The kid has a demon,'" Don said.

"Aw, come on." He looked at the two of them. "This is bogeyman stuff."

The three of them ambled toward the front entrance as the conversation continued.

Back in the hospital room, Roxie opened her eyes and checked to see if she was alone. She stared at the ceiling, trying to remember what had happened, right after she confronted Ted about his thousand-dollar deal with Mr. Smart. She had not yet pulled the cigarette lighter and nail polish remover out of her coat pocket, had not yet caused the "accident" which would have permanently disfigured his handsome face. No, the only thing she could recall was the horrified look in his eyes. The rest was a mystery. For a long time, she stared upward, trying to figure it out. Finally, the drugs clouded her reasoning, and she concluded that somebody else had handled the problem, and that was just fine with her. She closed her eyes again, emitting a huge sigh.

"Paralyzed…"

Slowly, a wicked smile crossed her countenance, and she gave a little hoot-laugh. "That's even better!"

Meanwhile, just a few miles away on Case Road, Marsha Bogue lay uneasily upon her bed, her tear-filled eyes focused on *that* ceiling.

***

Uncle couldn't believe his ears. "That gawdim stupid kid… paralyzed."

Winnie paused, then went on to finish the rest of the story — at least, what she and half the village of Essex Junction thought was the rest of the story. The word was that the couple was "spooning" out in the woods just off the River Road, and were viciously attacked by an unknown person. Both were so badly beaten that they ended up in the hospital. Roxie was going to be okay, but Teddy Donahue had injuries so severe, he was paralyzed from the neck down. Law officers were combing the countryside, but there were no leads. One thing that had everyone baffled was that the attacker's footprints were nowhere to be found in the snow. It was the scariest thing local residents had heard in a long time. "These young people need to stop doing such foolishness… out in the woods at all hours," she concluded.

Uncle gazed at her, once again amazed at the innocence of his beloved niece. She was, indeed, a good little Catholic girl — one who had no clue what girls like Roxanne Foxx were all about. He looked toward her from the barn's workbench. "That poor, dumb guy, Pooh. Hanging out with…"

From where she was leaning against the old Dodge, Winnie could not see the sudden expression that crossed Uncle's face. The early winter sun was dropping, casting shafts of light through the old boards of the north wall behind him. All she could see was his silhouette. But his sudden silence did pique her curiosity. "You okay, you?"

"Ay-yuh." He laid down the pliers he had been working with, and turned toward the milking parlor. "We'll be done out here in a few minutes. What's for supper?"

It was when he laid his head down on his pillow that night, the full force of what he had done finally hit him: Ted Donahue was paralyzed because of the plan hatched by the two of them, to "shame and defame" Roxanne Foxx, once and for all, and clear the reputation of Alan Strong and, hopefully, Bill Flannigan.

He turned over in the bed, wrestling with the guilt. Something had gone terribly wrong with the plan. The pregnancy, of course. And now the baby was dead. It just was all wrong. Roxie's levels of credibility and respectability had not suffered further damage one bit. Instead of getting the girl off Bill Flannigan's back, it opened the door for more sympathy-getting, probably prolonging the relationship, instead of ending it.

He turned over again. "*I should never have involved a young kid with wild hormones, to begin with. I should have found a way to fix her wagon, myself. I should have…*" The thought made him sit straight up in bed. *"I should have asked Father Tom what to do."* He swung his feet out and down from the bed, letting their soles rest on the frigid floor. He sat and pondered the situation until both feet got too cold. Still, he did not want to crawl back into the restless warmth of the blankets. After turning on the floor lamp which stood beside the bed, he looked around, knowing he had a pair of slippers somewhere. When the man spotted Pooh's hand-knit slippers across the room in the bottom of the closet, he picked his way over a couple of piles of clothes on the floor, then reached down to pull the bright red footies out from under a girlie magazine.

But he never picked up the slippers. Instead, seeing the photograph of the scantily clad model on the front cover, he froze. Slowly, he bent down and picked it up, stepping back toward the bed, to bring the glossy picture closer to the lamplight.

There it was, in living color. His jaw dropped. Now he knew the reason he had had such an uneasy feeling when in her presence. It was a young Marilyn Foxx, silvery eyes and all.

He sat down heavily on the edge of the bed, staring at the photo. Then he remembered to check the date. Yes, it was about thirteen years old. It almost embarrassed him that he had kept something like this, hauling it from military base to military base, for so many years. And yet, here it was. He opened up to the first page, hoping to find the photo credits, and they were there: "Photographer, Bernie Sage; Model, Bettina Silver."

He chuckled. "Bettina Silver, my butt." He looked back at the cover. "Must have been her stage name, or whatever they frickin' call it." Then he had another thought. Quickly, he began to turn pages, checking for any further information he might get on Bettina Silver. He was shivering from the cold as he folded the last page over, but he still had nothing more. Nevertheless, he felt that he had something he might be able to use against Roxanne Foxx. Just what it was, he wasn't sure. He put the magazine on the floor beside the lamp, turned off the light, and crawled back into bed. Maybe he didn't have to ask Father Tom anything, after all. Maybe he needed to get this information to Chief Rob Allen. Better yet, maybe he had a chance at a whole new plan, and maybe this plan would make up for that dumb kid getting paralyzed. With one last therapeutic shiver, the little Abenaki snuggled into his pillow, a smile on his lips.

"Revenge, rightly done, could be oh-so-frickin'-sweet," he thought, as he slipped slowly into dreamland. Uncle had no intention of letting God take care of this.

That attitude would eventually be challenged, suddenly and violently, on a dark, rainy night.

CHAPTER TWENTY-FOUR

Disclosures

On Sunday morning, November 23, a string of expletives poured forth from Bill Flannigan's mouth as he slammed his fist upon the top of the dining room table. "I am so sick and tired of the messes that one gets herself into. First, Alan's suicide, now this 'Ted' guy being paralyzed. What's next? What the hell is next?"

The man was clearly terrified.

Surely, there would be an exposure. There would be questions about this under-aged girl's activities and her "friends" for the last few weeks, and months, and maybe even before that. Sir William had been a big part of her life, in more ways than one, and it was almost certain that all of that would come under the scrutiny of a law enforcement investigation and ultimately, into the judgment of the general public. His life-long dream role of "Bill Flannigan, Superhero" was about to be shattered. The hero he had tried so hard to be could very possibly now be reduced to a nationally known police profile of a filthy, low-life "predator."

April rose from her seat at the breakfast table and grabbed a clean dish towel. She ran cold water over it and twisted it as dry as she could. Slowly, she placed the folded cloth across the back of Bill's neck, as she had done so many times before. In a few minutes, she thought, he would recover, and get on with another flawed attempt to be the handsome hero. As she held the cold towel in place, she was once again gripped with an old, familiar fear, but this time there was a whole new twist in the process.

All that they had endured for a very, very long twenty years in the military — the many physical and emotional separations, the lack of a loving father in the home, the frequent uprooting and relocations, the stress which enveloped the children every time they entered a new school's social structure, the adjustment to an unfamiliar local culture, the challenge of making a new housing situation feel like a real home — all of these difficult experiences which had been endured for the final promise of a secure retirement income were now all for naught, all sacrificed for the ego of a phony hero who was supposed to be, but never really was, the protector of his own household.

As she held the cool towel against her husband's sweaty neck, April came to the realization that Bill's obsession with being a hero, especially to Roxanne Foxx, could very well, finally destroy every last bit of a peaceful retirement. Only God knew what would happen to them, now.

"I need a lawyer," Bill said.

The fear of complete disaster grew stronger. "I think maybe you do — no, *we* do." She recognized that this had to be a family thing. "But where do you begin to look, without drawing a whole lot of attention?" She lifted the towel and turned the cooler side to his neck.

"I've been thinking." He moved his head from side-to-side, trying to ease the pain in his temples. "I have some old Air Force buddies who worked in the JAG office at Fort Ethan Allen when I was stationed there."

"Lawyers?"

"Yeah. One of them retired and went to work for some bigwigs in Montpelier. John Courtney. Do you remember him?"

"Barely," she said. Then she remembered something. "Wasn't he the hotshot who investigated those child predators over in Shelburne?"

"Yeah, that's the guy." He reached back and gently pushed off the towel. "I think he's exactly the one I need."

"Oh, Bill, I don't think of you as being in that category. You are more the target of an obsessed teenager. That's the truth. You're not a criminal."

He stood and turned to give her a gentle hug. "There are some people who would not agree with you. This is a touchy situation. I have not been very smart."

The hug was another little glimmer of hope for April Flannigan.

Suddenly, he let go of her and headed out the door.

"Where are you going? It's your day off."

"Montpelier."

"Shouldn't you call first?"

"Called him already. He's meeting me at one o'clock. I need to deal with this."

"Shouldn't I… be with you?"

"No. That wouldn't be a good idea." He gently pressed his teeth to his lip. "You're going to have to trust me on this, April. It could be very…" He shook his head, not wanting to speak the words. With one decisive tug, he closed the door firmly behind him.

***

"I think she did it," Scottie said as he reached for Penny's mittened hand. The two of them were walking down the newly shoveled sidewalk from the Strong Theater toward the Hotel Vermont. They were followed by their double-date partners, Jack and Diana.

"Nah, I don't think so," Jack offered. "She's way too fragile to deliver a blow like that."

"I agree," Diana said, curling her arm through her date's folded elbow. "I'm told there were at least two hard karate chops."

Scottie talked back over his shoulder. "Hey, she had bruises on both wrists and the outsides of both hands. He got chopped, sitting right there beside her, and somebody pummeled her in the belly. Nobody else was in the car. What does that tell you?"

"Somebody else *was* in the car," Jack and Diana said almost simultaneously.

Scottie pulled Penny gently to a halt and turned to the couple behind him. "So, where did that 'somebody' go? Remember, there were no footprints in the snow."

Penny spoke up. "Maybe he got out of the car before it snowed."

The other three looked at her. Finally, Diana said, "Wasn't there already some snow on the ground that day?"

"Maybe, but maybe not right there where they were parked," the petite one answered.

The foursome continued a few feet farther, then proceeded to enter the Bixby family car, which Diana's folks had agreed to let Jack drive, since his truck was too small to carry four passengers. In a few minutes, they were crossing the Winooski Bridge. Suddenly, Scottie had an idea. He loosened his arm from around Penny and called out from the back seat.

"Why don't we stop and see him?"

"Who, Teddy?" Jack was surprised.

"Yeah. We're going right past the hospital. Why not?"

"Do you think they would let us in?" Penny sounded doubtful.

Scottie checked his watch. "It's only three forty-five, still visiting hours. If he can have visitors, we should be able to see him for a few minutes."

The white-capped lady at the nurses' station got a serious look on her face. "I don't know. He doesn't need a lot of ruckus right now."

"We understand that," Penny whispered politely. "It's just that we thought, if there is no one else there at the moment, we could step in and give him a quiet word of encouragement." She blinked sorrowful eyes. "We want him to know we are all thinking of him."

The nurse's face softened, then she looked at the young men. "No loud male noises, do you understand?" Jack and Scottie nodded obediently.

As they followed the bustling white uniform down the hall, Scottie asked softly, "Can he talk, ma'am?"

The nurse stopped. "Oh, yes, I need to tell you that. No, he has no vocal chords working right now. He can only blink his eyes... twice for 'yes,' and once for 'no.'" Then she took them to the door of the room. "Remember... be very quiet."

The youngsters were in no way prepared for the sight of Teddy Donahue in that hospital bed. There were tubes and machines all around his upper torso. The body lay heavily immobile, covered only by a thin, white blanket. His eyes were closed, making the pale face look like a death mask. A ghastly dark discoloration covered his swollen throat.

The collective gasp awakened the patient, and the eyelashes fluttered over the dark eyes of a frightened, trapped animal. Jack reached over and grasped Teddy's limp hand.

"Hey, buddy." He could do nothing more than just stand there with a grim look on his face.

"Hi, Teddy," Penny bent closer. "We just wanted to come by and let you know we are praying for you."

"That's right," Diana whispered. "And for your mom and Paula, too."

"We aren't allowed to stay too long," Scottie spoke softly. "But we wondered if there was anything we could do for you." He glanced quickly at the other three. "For instance, Ted, did you see who did this to you? Maybe we can get some justice, huh?" He repeated the question. "Did you see who did this to you?"

To their amazement, the young man's eyes blinked twice.

"Yes?!" Scottie wasn't sure what he saw, but the others were nodding in agreement. He turned back toward the dark eyes. "Somebody you know?"

The eyelids blinked twice, again.

The four of them bent forward as Scottie was about to ask the next question.

"What the *hell* are you kids doing in here?"

They turned to see the tall figure of Sheriff Max Duncan standing in the doorway.

"V-visiting our friend, sir," Jack stuttered.

The sheriff regarded the wide-eyed look on the two pretty girls, and drew back a bit. "You get permission to come in here?"

"Yessir," Scottie was thinking fast. "Just to give my friend a man-hug. He kind-a needs one, don't you think, sir?"

The officer moved toward the door, looking for an official reason to oust these kids. "Nurse!" he called down the hall. When there was no response, he turned around and barked out the impatient order, just as Scottie came back up from the man-hug. "Get yer tails outta here. This is official sheriff department business. You," he growled at Scottie, who was staring into the eyes of his friend, "that's enough. Get lost."

Scottie arrived home from the double-date earlier than expected. Gracie was just leaving for the Christmas pageant rehearsal at the church.

"Robbie home, Mom?"

"Just went to pick up milk at Yandow's. He'll be back in a minute." She smiled. "Leftover turkey in the refrigerator," she said as she went out the back door.

For once, the high school freshman was not interested in food. He paced the kitchen floor a few times, then came out into the living room, where he stood impatiently peering out at the driveway. When he saw the car pull in, he turned an expectant eye toward the back door. Robbie came bounding in, just as the younger brother reached the doorway between the living room and kitchen.

"Hey, kid," he addressed his younger brother, "what's going on?"

The youngster stood in the doorway, watching Robbie pull open the refrigerator door.

"Just saw Ted Donahue in the hospital."

The big brother placed the milk on the shelf and closed the heavy door before laying a consoling hand on Scottie's shoulder. "That must have been a shock, kid. Not a pretty sight."

"Yeah." He looked down at his feet, then back up, eyes filled with a knowing glimmer. Rob spotted that, and drew back.

Cocking his head to one side, he asked, "So, what's *really* going on, mister?"

"You know he can't talk, right?"

"Yeah. But he can blink his eyes 'yes' and 'no.'"

Scottie nodded, then went on to the details of the visit. Near the end, the police chief needed to know: "Did the other kids know he recognized his attacker, Scott?" The younger Allen nodded. "They need to be quiet about that. It could blow the whole case."

"Okay, I'll call all three as soon as I finish telling you the rest." He cleared his throat. "It was almost over, when that sheriff showed up... you know... Max Somebody."

The chief winced; that was not good. "Bet he kicked you all out."

"Well, that's sort of what happened, but when the other guys were kind of involved with that little matter, I gave Ted a man-hug."

Rob guffawed. "Since when do *you* give man-hugs?"

"Since I need to whisper a question into someone's ear," the reply came through a self-satisfied grin.

The Chief of Police folded his arms. "And what did you ask, kid?" He was trying not to show approval.

"I asked, 'Was it Roxie?'"

Robbie Allen leaned forward. "And what did he do?"

"He went like this," Scottie Allen replied. Then he slowly and deliberately blinked his eyes… twice.

***

"Mama?"

Shirley Bogue looked up from reading in bed to see her daughter standing in the bedroom doorway. She was barely visible in the lamplight, but obviously shivering under her flannel nightgown. "I thought you were asleep, Marsha." The girl's head was bowed. Motherly instinct sounded an alarm, and Shirley closed the book. "What's wrong?" The head moved slowly from left to right, but the words did not come out. Shirley pulled the covers back and patted the side of the bed. "Come here, kiddo." Slowly, Marsha slipped in beside her mother, and pulled the blankets over her legs. Shirley pushed a pillow behind her daughter's back, and waited. It was the Sunday night after Thanksgiving.

"I've done something awful, Mama," she whispered.

"What, you?" the mom responded. "Nah, not you. You're a sweet little gal. You wouldn't hurt a flea."

"Well, I just got so mad." The voice was starting to choke up. "I wanted to punish both of them."

"Who?"

"Ted and Roxie." She covered her face with both hands, inhaling and exhaling tremulously.

Shirley was astounded. She had heard the news about the vicious attack, and was as shocked as anyone else, but never once had she thought her own girl would have been involved. "W-what are you talking about, Marsha? What do you know about all that?"

The words came between sobs from behind the hands. "I… set… it all… up, Mama. It was me. I set it up. I'm so sorry. I'm just… so sorry."

Shirley reached an arm around her girl. "Now, wait. Wait just a minute." She pulled a tissue from the bedside table with her other hand. "Here. Blow your nose, and get yourself together." Marsha obeyed as best she could. "Now you tell me just how you so-called 'set it up.'" The girl blew again, folding and pressing the tissue around her red nose. "I don't think you even know people who would do such a thing. You're a *nice kid*, Marsha. Now, you calm down and talk to me."

Marsha sniffed, then told her mother all that she had overheard on the greenhouse extension phone. Shirley's mouth scrunched up in disgust as she learned of the plot between Ted and Mr. Smart. Roxie had been up to no good — and for a long time, at that — but this was a bad thing, just the same. Winnie's uncle had some sort of battle fatigue… a lot of people knew that, and so she could see where there was some sort of excuse for his behavior. But she was indignant about the nerve of that young kid, doing what he was doing, and for money, on top of that. Still, she needed to hear what Marsha's part was in the actual attack.

"Everybody's talking about the fact that here were no footprints in the snow. I know there weren't and I know why, Mama."

"Okay…"

"The attacker couldn't leave any."

"Because...?"

"Because it was not a person." She turned her bloodshot eyes toward her mother. "It was Beng."

"Beng?" Shirley was incredulous. "Our Ouija board 'Beng'?"

"Yeah, Mama. I asked it to punish the both of them."

The woman sat straight up in bed, looking at the wall across the room. "Uh, no, Marsha." She shifted her weight in the bed, and smoothed out the blankets across her own legs. After a little pause, she turned abruptly to look her daughter in the face. "Okay, now tell me, Marsha, why do you think that attack was done by Beng?"

"Mama, I'm so sorry." Her voice was barely audible. "I've been in touch with it for a while — I don't know how long — and I have asked it to do a couple of things for me, and it has done them."

"Like what?" But then she had a sudden thought. "How did you get in touch with this Beng person? I have the only key."

"I made another cardboard one, just like the twins did."

"Oh, no." But then she got back to the former question. "So what do you think Beng has done for you?"

"I got an A on my algebra test." She looked down at her knees. "You know how bad, really bad, I've been at algebra."

"Well, yes, but you *have* been studying more."

The pale blue eyes brightened. "And you know how I've been trying to get into the ski club? That's where all the popular kids are." She got a little smile on her face. "Well, I am getting all the equipment I need — skis, ski boots, ski poles, all of it, Mama, from the special 'ski closet' at the Congregational Church!" She bent forward. "Mama, I never even asked them." She shook her head. "It had to be Beng. It *had* to be! That's the only one I asked."

A sad look came into Shirley Bogue's eyes, and she leaned her head against her sweet daughter's. "Aww, kiddo," she moaned, as she slammed into reality, "I wish it could have been all that simple." She planted a kiss on the girl's head. "I need to do some confessing of my own," she murmured.

Over the next few minutes, this lady with the rough edges laid it all out for her daughter.

"First of all, kiddo, there is no 'Beng.'"

This time, Marsha sat straight up in the bed. "What?!" She stared at her mother. "But we talked with it... him... whatever... so many times... you and me and Roxie... and even the twins, Mama." She wrinkled her nose in disbelief. "How could that be? You've got to be kidding!"

"Nope. Not kidding."

"But the pointer answered all our questions, all that time," the objection came.

"Yup, and I was manipulating it every inch of the way," the embarrassed Mama admitted. "Wow, do I feel stupid. But, please understand, at the time, I felt so powerful."

"What do you mean, you were manipulating, whatever?" Marsha wiped the end of her nose on the crunched-up tissue. "Beng is real. It answered so many questions. It was right every single time."

"Naw, that was me, baby, every single time, just feeling so important."

"But it knew my spiritual name, 'Loyal.'"

"It fit you so well," her mother commented.

"And you were 'Seeker.'"

"Yup. It fit *me* so well."

"And Roxie was 'Passion.'"

"That girl's head is full of sex, sex, sex. Of course she wanted to hear that."

Marsha had to admit that was true. "But what about the ski club?"

"I submitted your name through Gracie Allen. She and Lily White saw to it that you got what you needed." She reached out and patted her daughter's hand. "I have been so, so stupid, my girl, trying to be a 'big shot.' I guess this damned divorce has affected me more than I thought."

Each of them retreated momentarily into their own thoughts. Finally, the mother turned to her daughter. "So, you see, kiddo, Beng is not, and never was, *real*. So you had no effect on that mess last Friday, other than that you let Roxie know about the phone call." She patted her daughter's hand again. "So now stop blaming yourself for something you never did. And," she, herself choked up this time, "I am so, so sorry for the grief I have caused you." She gave Marsha a long hug. "Please forgive your bungle-butted mama for exposing you to all that guilt. I only wanted to have some fun. It was so wrong, and I am so sorry, my girl." There was a sob. "You're a sweet kid, and don't you ever forget it."

A couple of minutes later, Marsha stood once again in the dimmed light of the doorway. "There were still no footprints in the snow." Shirley shook her head, unable to answer the mystery. "And, Mama, what about the tapping on the walls?"

"I… I really don't know, kiddo."

"I wonder… could it be that the twins have contacted something?"

"I… I really don't know. We'll just keep those Bibles open."

Shirley put her book away for the night, turned out the light, and lay awake for a few minutes longer. Finally, she decided, since she was on the late Monday shift at The Harvest, she would do two things in the morning. First, she would take a heavy hammer and smash the Ouija board into smithereens. Then she would ask Marsha to stay far, far away from Roxie Foxx because, if there was one thing Shirley knew for sure, it was that this girl was *big* trouble.

What Shirley did *not* know was that, in the Romani language of Indo-European gypsies, "Beng" was the word for "devil." Further, she did not know that demons have always had assignments in all areas of the world. All they have ever needed was an invitation from some clueless human being,

and they were more than happy to come tap-tap-tapping at
the door.

CHAPTER TWENTY-FIVE

Busted

On November 25, Roxie was released from Fanny Allen Hospital under strict orders for bedrest for at least two weeks. Arrangements were made for Connie Collins to drop off and pick up all school assignments, so the girl would be able to keep up with her studies. Meantime, her parents hired a visiting nurse to be present at all times while they were at work. Marilyn was determined her darling girl would have a full recovery, both physically and emotionally. In pursuit of that goal, she agreed to take the advice of Don Collins, who assured her that he knew the exact person who could keep Roxie in line, and on a healing curve.

Early the next morning, as Marilyn prepared to leave for a day shift at The Harvest, the visiting nurse's firm knock announced her arrival. Roxie heard her mother answer the door, and the ensuing murmur of pleasant voices. Curious, she sat up carefully in bed — a painful process, which took a couple of minutes. Still, she needed to be at an "in charge" position, so she pushed on, pulling a pillow behind her back to help her sit up straight, then leaned gingerly back against it, trying to look regal. The chit-chat drew closer as the ladies made their way from the living room.

"Ow-ow-ow!" Roxie whispered, as her abdomen exploded with pain. She lay back farther onto the pillow and closed her eyes, panting shallow breaths, and hoping for quick relief. "Oh my gosh, Roxanne!" she heard her mother cry out. "What are you doing?!" But Roxie's eyes remained tightly closed against the increasing pain. She felt the pillow slip out from behind her shoulders, replaced immediately by a strong supporting arm, which slowly lowered her flat onto the bed.

"Ow-ow-ow-ow," she said out loud. Then she inhaled and her loud moan filled the little bedroom. Her eyes closed even more tightly, as she stretched and recoiled from the overwhelming pain.

Somebody was bustling near her bedside. Then she felt the cold wipe on her arm, and the sudden poke of a needle. After one more sobbing cry escaped her lips, something like a white light broke through, and slowly the pain subsided. She took a short breath, exhaled a moan once more, and then, quietly… quietly… her body rested in a blessed peace.

Finally, Roxie took a pain-free breath and opened her eyes… to connect with the golden gaze of a sweet-faced Negro lady.

"Hello, Roxanne," the lady said. "I will be looking after you for a while. I'm your visiting nurse, and my name is Rehema Foster."

Roxie gave her mother a worried look.

"It's alright, honey," Marilyn reassured her. "She comes highly recommended." Seeing the question on her daughter's face, she added, "…by the Collinses."

The girl moaned again, but this time it was a different kind of pain.

***

Mr. Raymond René Smart laid the large grocery bag gingerly upon the desk of the Chief of Police, being careful not to let the folded-over top edge come undone as he did so. After some real soul-searching, he had concluded Chief Rob was the one he needed to contact about this new discovery concerning Roxanne Foxx's background. The meeting was taking place after regular work hours, even though Lily was still laboring at the switchboard out front. Outside, it was already getting dark.

"I take it, this is the item you talked about on the telephone, Mr. Smart?" The tan-skinned gentleman nodded in agreement. Robbie looked at the paper sack. "May I open it now?"

Uncle looked around, locating a couple of nearby windows. The shades were not drawn down, so the wintery blue and gold of the traffic circle was clearly visible. The little man glanced back at the officer and had a second thought.

"People can see us in here," he concluded. "Maybe you should just open the frickin' top and take a look inside, without taking it out of the bag."

Curious, Robbie reached for the paper sack. He let it slip down between the desk and his knees, before he unfolded the top in order to see what was inside. He frowned, then shot a startled look toward the man. "Is this who I think it is?"

"Gawdim right." He jerked his head in confirmation. "Her mother."

"Awww, crap," the policeman lamented. "No wonder..." He closed the bag, running his fingers along the same crease that had kept it closed before. After a quick check to see where Lily was, he turned back to his informer. "What do you know about this?"

"Not a helluva lot," Uncle replied, with a quick shift of his slender shoulders. "Went through the whole gawdim magazine, and got nothing but some kind of a frickin' stage name... uh... Betty Silver, or something like that."

"Where did you get this? It must be ten years old, at least."

"Hauled it around during my Army time." He crossed his legs, then uncrossed them. "That thing is only a part of my gawdim stash... like a lot of us sorry bah-serds... it was all we had." Suddenly he held up a qualifying hand. "That, and the frick—." He corrected himself: "...and the... the Rosary. Please excuse my religious-osity right here, but I *am* a gawdim believer, sir."

Robbie leaned back in his desk chair, rocking the springs under the seat ever-so-gently. "This could work either in our favor, or against it." He continued to rock as the facts jostled about in his mind.

His vision shifted vacantly toward the windows, not really seeing the deepening azure scene blinking into view between the flashing gold of the five-cornered intersection's traffic light.

There against the background of blue snow, the golden beam from the traffic light beacon flashed around the circle. A brief yellow glow highlighted the low piles of shoveled snow along the sidewalks which encircled the intersection. Then, each time the beam blinked out, a brief, fluorescent purple filled the rectangle frames of the chief's office windows. It was almost hypnotic.

Robbie drew back from the conversation, slipping slowly, deeply into his own thoughts. He did not notice the headlights of a small truck outshining the yellow gleam of the pulsating traffic light. Nor did he notice the nondescript vehicle move around the right-hand side of the circle, its small reddish tail lights being pelted by freezing clumps thrown upwards from the back tires. Before he came back to reality the battered truck had crept into a slow exit onto Maple Street. Instantly, the golden flashes resumed a rhythmic piercing of the sapphire glitter of this early winter evening.

"Um... I'm going to have to get back to you on this," Chief Rob suddenly said. "Meanwhile, is there anything else we need to talk about?"

The Abenaki warrior, who had been waiting patiently, looked down to make a quick assessment before he reached for the notepad in his pocket. "I'm not sure there's anything that will do any frickin' good in this," he murmured, "but here are some things I have been taking notes on for a few weeks." He slapped the little green spiral pad onto the chief's desk. "There might be something in there that could help get this frickin' show on the road."

Just then, Lily approached her boss's desk. "Ed is taking over, so I'm heading home, Chief." She pushed a strand of hair back from her face. "Anything else I can do?"

"Not tonight, Lily. I'll let you know tomorrow." He smiled gratefully. "Thanks for fielding all those calls on this attack in Essex Center."

"Anything new?"

"Naw, afraid not." He waved her on. "Get home and get rested. This could be a long haul."

He waited until she was out the door, then opened the small notebook. There were roughly a dozen scribbled notes, each on its own page. He skimmed across them, glancing up in surprise at the insightful comments, several times. At the very last entry he came up with a question.

"This note about Florida Avenue in Winooski... can you tell me more about that?"

"She got off the frickin' bus, on a school morning, mind you. And then she took off like a shot down that street."

"That's where she goes to counseling. At the Collinses' house." He glanced up at the ceiling. "But not on a Tuesday morning." He looked directly at Mr. Smart. "Reason I know that is, even if Mr. Collins was at home and available, that couple is a real team, and they have a standing policy of never having two people of opposite sex alone in a counseling session... and I do mean *never*." He closed the notebook. "Furthermore, on a school-day morning, Mrs. Collins is at her job at EJHS." He added another thought as he tapped the little green pad lightly on the top of his desk. "Maybe Roxie needed to make an unscheduled visit to the Collinses' house."

The River Rat had a relevant idea. "Maybe she was out fishing for one gawdim thing or another." His eyes suddenly sparkled. "She sure looked like she was on a frickin' hunt."

The officer rose to the challenge. "What do you suppose she would be hunting, Mr. Smart?"

"Some poor gawdim fish who's trapped in a shallow pool," he barked a little laugh as he spoke. "Easy pickings, if you get my drift."

Robbie made a mental note: "*That would NOT be the way she would operate. She would work with more stealth, and more purposeful tracking.*" He gave Uncle no clue of what he was thinking, practicing the poker face technique he was taught in the police academy. Still, he was puzzled at the advanced mode of operation of this very young girl. "*That just isn't normal.*" He turned back to the Rat. "Any idea at all, why she would need to visit that neighborhood? I mean, was she simply passing through, do you think?"

"That little snot *never* simply passes through *anywhere.*" He lifted his shoulders as he leaned toward the chief. "She was hell-bent-for-frickin'-leather, mister. I can tell you that." He sat back in his chair. "She was on a hunt, I'm telling ya."

"Okay... okay, Mr. Smart. She was definitely headed for a target."

"Yes, sir!"

"Can you even venture a guess?"

The man was flattered to be asked. "Well," he answered with great aplomb, "it was either a frickin' *thing* or a frickin' *person.*"

The Chief of Police's brow wrinkled ever-so-slightly. "So, she was on her way to do something important. I get that." He blinked once, very slowly. "My question is, what was so urgent about that task that she would risk being late in getting back from her ukulele lessons?"

"Well..." The hunter was enjoying the hunt, himself. "My guess is that she was on the scent of something. You know, another gawdim kill — another trophy."

"A trophy?" The many months of amateur detective training prompted a suspicion that there was a special meaning in that remark.

Mr. Smart's head moved sideways with a small jerk. "She loves to win. She hates to lose. She gets gawdim frickin' even with anybody who beats her out of that win."

"Aw, for Pete's sake, man. She's a fourteen-… no… fifteen-year-old girl!"

He lifted his shoulders and hunched toward the Chief of Police once more. "You've gotta put it together, mister." The little Abenaki warrior made piercing eye contact with the law officer. "That kid is always involved in some kind of a frickin' contest. For Cry-sake, she just added another one to her frickin' list of victims, that poor, dumb Ted guy." His voice trailed off. Suddenly, he lowered his eyes and bit his lip. The policeman picked up on that as he watched the man slip back in his chair.

The chief waited just a few seconds.

"So," Robbie seemed to be studying the little notebook in his hands as he casually inquired, "do you know Teddy Donahue, Mr. Martin?"

***

Jack let the truck engine idle as he gave one last warning to the two girls. "As far as anyone knows — other than the sheriff and the nurse — none of us four even visited Ted at the hospital." He looked into Diana's eyes. "We have to keep quiet about that, *and* the fact that Ted indicated he knew the person who attacked him and Roxie." Penny shifted in her seat next to the door, to peer around Diana. Jack saw the question in her eyes. "Don't even go there. We do *not* want to know who that is. That's why Scottie wouldn't tell us." He took another big breath. "If that person found out that we know their identity, we could all be in big trouble." He turned his head to take a long look up and down Maple Street, where he was parked in front of Diana's house. "The safest thing to do right now is, like Scottie said, act like we don't know *anything*." He grabbed his girlfriend's hand. "And really, we don't. All we have is two blinks of Ted Donahue's eyes."

"That's not enough?" Diana whispered.

"Not nearly enough." He lifted her hand and held it against his lips for a couple of seconds. "You know, he could be 'out of his mind,' for all we know." He puckered a small kiss on her knuckles. "Right?"

"Oh… right. I hadn't thought of that."

"Neither did I," Penny said.

"Sure… sure. We don't really know anything, *for a fact*." He lowered his sweetheart's hand and released it, as he leaned across to reassure Penny. "We just visited our friend, to encourage him. That's all we did."

Penny opened the door and slid out of the truck, preparing to go just around the corner to her own home. She was expecting a phone call from Scottie, who had been recruited to help his mother do some early Christmas shopping after school. But before she closed the door, she paused. There was one last question. "So, what happens if that sheriff comes and starts to question us?"

"The four of us?"

"Yes, Jack. What do we do then?"

Diana watched her hero closely as he pondered the answer. Finally, he gave the only reply he could honestly make. "Well then, ladies, I guess we do the right thing."

"And what is that, Jack?" Penny queried.

"Never lie to a cop. We really do not know who did it."

"What if they ask if Scottie knows?" Penny was worried.

"Tell the cop to ask Scottie." Then he quickly added, "And call Scottie right away, because he may need some legal advice. He could be in danger."

CHAPTER TWENTY-SIX

Confession

On November 29, Shirley Bogue watched her twin boys ride away for a day with their father, then loaded herself and her daughter into the old car for the two-mile trip to Essex Junction's Holy Family Catholic Church. It was finally time to make Confession, no matter how long it might take, and this *was* a Saturday morning.

When her turn came, she approached the confessional, her head covered with a slightly soiled lace scarf. She pulled the short, heavy curtain closed behind her, and knelt down on the carpeted step to confess her sins. A nervous sweat moistened her brow, and spread a sticky film across her tummy. With a single swipe, her fingers removed the drops above her upper lip. She inhaled the stale air inside the little booth. It had been way too long since she had done this but oh, how this needed to be done, right now.

She waited until she was sure she could hear the soft movement of the priest on the other side of the screen, and then she crossed herself, speaking out loud: "In the Name of the Father, and of the Son, and of the Holy Ghost. Amen."

She was relieved to hear the familiar voice of Father Tom pronouncing a blessing over her. When he paused, she took up her part once more, speaking as best she could remember them, the first words of the ritual. "Bless me, Father, for I have sinned."

"Yes, child. Please go on."

"I haven't been to Confession for several years, Father."

"I am glad you are here today. This is a good thing. Remember First John, one, verse nine: 'If we confess our sins, he is faithful and just, and will forgive us and cleanse us from all unrighteousness.'"

"I don't know where to start," she said sadly.

"Just start with that which is heaviest on your heart."

It was the exact encouragement she needed. In a few minutes not only had she told of the deception at the Ouija board; she had confessed to the stress she had caused in her children with the invention of the phony character, Beng. Further, she repeated the conversation she had had with Marsha about the overheard phone call and the girl's efforts to put some kind of hex on Ted and Roxie. "And there is still a tapping sound, Father, if we remove the Bibles. We tried it." There was a shivering in her voice. "I don't know. What have I done?"

"It is serious, but God is bigger." The priest was silent, apparently assessing the situation. "I think penance for this should be that you restore the trust of your children, in all that you do and surely, you need to alert the authorities of the plot between Mr. Smart and Ted Donahue and of your own deception about the Beng person, and of the tapping which is still occurring in your home." He paused again. Then he spoke. "I certainly would recommend that you bring your daughter in to Confession, as soon as possible. There is a lot of guilt in her, right now."

"She's next in line, right behind me," Shirley assured him.

"Excellent." He turned his attention back to the sacred ritual. "You need to read the Gospel of St. John to your children. That will complete your penance."

She was surprised. It was supposed to be Hail Marys or Our Fathers, not reading a book of the Bible to your kids. But then, she remembered who was sitting on the other side of the screen — no ordinary priest, that was for sure. There was an awkward moment, and then she remembered it was time for her to make the Act of Contrition. She crossed herself and said the words as best she could remember: "Father, forgive me for my sins. I am sorry from the bottom of my heart that I have offended You. Help me as I try harder to do better. I am at Your mercy, dear Lord."

The priest pronounced absolution over her "In the Name of the Father and of the Son, and of the Holy Ghost."

"Amen," she said, with great relief.

By eleven o'clock that morning, Shirley and Marsha were seated across the desk from Chief Rob Allen. Half an hour later, he bid them goodbye and hurried back into his office to turn off the hidden tape recorder. Ed was busy at the flashing switchboard out front, so Rob quickly put the recorder back into his locker, then sat down at the desk to think.

"So much for the existence of a real bogeyman…" he mused. But then, something else occurred to him: "Mr. Smart needs to be notified that Roxie knows about the plans between him and Ted. He could very well be her next target." He shook his head. "'Could be?' More likely, 'Will be.'"

It had to be handled carefully.

Meanwhile, he wasn't going to talk to anybody about this visit from the Bogues, not even Sheriff Max Duncan.

***

Mid-afternoon of that same Saturday, Connie Collins received a call from Principal Randy Marvin.

"Just a reminder of the teachers' meeting Monday at seven a.m."

"Oh yes, sir. I am ready."

"Good." He paused, then asked hopefully, "Do you think we did any good for these kids this week?"

"Absolutely. I am so glad you had us teachers meet last Monday morning, Mr. Marvin. We needed to have some answers and reassurances for these young people, not to mention a few warning words about hanging out in isolated places."

She could almost see him working his lips before he asked the next question. "Any changes for Ted and Roxanne? Health-wise, I mean."

"Well, as you know, she is at home, recovering. Bedrest for another week, at least. As for Ted, it doesn't look too promising. They are transferring him to Burlington, to the Bishop DeGoesbriand Hospital, very soon. You know, they have the University of Vermont Medical School right nearby. That should present a more hopeful situation. Meantime, he is paralyzed and cannot talk."

Mr. Marvin sighed deeply. "Hopefully, our interaction with EJHS students this past week will help avoid a repeat of such a tragedy." He took a breath as though to ask another question, then stopped short. "Very well, Mrs. Collins. I look forward to hearing from all of you at the meeting."

Connie hung up the phone and stepped out of the kitchen into the hall which led to the two bedrooms. At the first door, she peeked in to check on her napping husband. To her surprise, he was sitting up on the side of the bed.

"I guess you must have heard the phone ring," she said.

"Yup," he said, as he scratched his midriff with both hands.

She stepped just inside the door, leaning back against its frame. "It was the principal, reminding me of the—" She stopped when he held out one hand, inviting her to sit down beside him. As she did, he drew her close to his side.

"You know what, babe?"

"What?"

"It was a good thing, taking time to watch over your students like that, but I have to say, we can warn them all we want, and there will still be couples out there, parking at the edge of the woods." He shook his head slowly. "It's all those raging hormones in kids who don't really know the Savior."

"Still, we have to try." She leaned her head lightly against his shoulder. "My goodness, you would think something like this would scare the devil out of them."

"Yeah. Trouble is, they didn't actually see *this* devil at work that Friday night."

She sat up straight and they looked each other in the eye, both having the same thought.

"That's the problem, babe."

"Right. They would wake up in a hurry, if they could see what we saw at Roxie's last counseling session."

"Yeah, that's for sure."

The couple went into deep thought, then suddenly shook their heads "No" in unison. "No way we could ever do that, Connie."

"Right."

"Got to be a better way."

"Right." She rose slowly from the bed and wandered thoughtfully back out into the little kitchen.

She had made a ham sandwich for a five o'clock snack before he finally shuffled in through the hallway door.

"Hey, babe. I have an idea."

The huge gray eyes relayed her concern. "It had better be Holy Ghost-inspired," she quipped.

He pulled a small chair out from under the dropped-leaf kitchen table. "Roxie has to be aware that there is something wrong."

"Maybe. No... very likely. She is at least vaguely aware that these obsessive, overwhelming emotions are out of her control. Remember the **Butterfly** song?"

"You're right," he said, as he sat down. "You know what I think? I think it's time she *really* faces the music. She's guilty of letting these lustful demons do terrible damage. This stuff has to stop."

Connie slipped the sandwiches onto salad plates. "And it won't, until she gets smart enough and strong enough to recognize them, get rid of them, and keep them out for good."

"Now listen, we both know she won't believe *us*, so no sense in *our* trying to inform her. She needs somebody else, somebody she trusts, to tell her the truth." He flung his hands upward to clasp them behind his head and leaned the chair backward to balance on two legs. "Now, who would that be?"

Once again, the couple stopped talking and looked at each other in agreement.

"Her mother," Connie said, as she placed the snack on the table. "Now please stop abusing that poor chair."

***

Miles away, April looked across her own kitchen table at her handsome husband. He had just come back from his second meeting with his lawyer friend in Montpelier. A cup of steaming coffee was warming his cold hands against an eerie chill which filled the inside of the small stucco house. They both watched his fingers working around the sides of the hot drink, avoiding the eye contact that was way too painful. She had turned off the radio, in order to hear every word he was about to speak. Now she was waiting… and waiting…

"Are you hungry?" she finally asked.

He shook his head "No."

"Is there anything else you need?"

"No. No, thank you."

She took a brave breath. "Okay then." A ladylike clearing of the throat preceded her next question. "So, how did it go with Mr. Courtney? Is he doing a good job for you?" She quickly corrected herself, "...for us?"

Bill's head was lowered, but the words seemed to relay relief. "John is doing an excellent job. He's..." The eyes made contact for a second, then averted toward the floor. "He is right on top of things." The cup was raised to his lips, but still too hot, so the weary man blew softly on it. "But it was still a... hard... meeting."

"Alright then." She fixed her gaze upon the tabletop directly in front of her. "Can you share *any* of this stuff with me? I mean, I'm so left out, here. It doesn't seem right."

He set the cup down, but kept his eyes on it. "I know. It isn't right. None of this stuff is right. I've done a lot of dumb stuff in my life, April, but this is the stupidest thing I have ever, ever done." She heard the crack in his voice, and moved slightly as if to get up and give him a hug, but an inner voice told her to sit still, like a good soldier, and just listen.

"I could be in big, big trouble," he finally whispered. "Multiple felony charges."

"Wh-what does *that* mean?"

He was still whispering. "Labeled as a predator, prison time, loss of my military retirement pay." His head fell forward into his hands, and he inhaled deeply before his shoulders began to shake with overwhelming grief.

She hastened around to his side of the table to wrap her arms around him, her body folding over his bowed form. "That's *not* you, Bill! That's not who you are and not who you *ever* wanted to be." She embraced the convulsing shoulders tightly. "No!" she asserted. "This is *not* who you are."

Slowly, he came upright from the table, pressing April back toward the coral-colored counter behind her.

"I know that. I know I am not a predator. But, I'm guilty as hell, April, because I was the adult." He turned to face her. "I thought I was crazy-in-love. Do you understand that?" He was looking at her, now. "She was the beautiful, silvery-eyed girl of my dreams, and she was absolutely *crazy* about me. She swore she couldn't live without me. She pursued me at every opportunity. We had a fairytale relationship. We couldn't wait to see each other, every single day. We made eyes across the room, across the bus aisle. I couldn't wait to be with her, after work, on my days off, whenever we could manage. All we wanted, was to be with each other. It was the happiest, happiest time of my life. Are you listening? It was the most fulfilling, happiest relationship I have ever had, in my whole life." He stared, waiting for her to retaliate.

The full brunt of the pain went straight through her heart.

Then something surreal happened.

Suddenly, strangely, she seemed to be outside of her body. There was no warning, just an awareness that she was elevated toward the ceiling and watching the exchange between Bill and herself down there in the kitchen. She saw her own blonde hair moving with the conversational shake of her head, the soft gold of her clothing creasing and smoothing with the movements of her body. She could clearly see the hang-dog look on Bill's face, and even caught the scent of his aftershave. But she was still, somehow, removed from the presence of those two people.

Her attention was drawn to the fact that April was swallowing hard, then that her head was tilting slightly to the right, as the next question came forth. "And how do you feel about her right now, Bill?"

His eyes watered up. "If I could, I would take her down south and marry her. Today."

There was a pause while she swallowed hard, again. "And that would make it all okay, do you think?"

He shifted his weight and looked at the floor. "It would be a start. I need to do *something*."

"She would never stay with you, Bill. That's not who she is."

The reply was an unearthly snarl. "You don't know what you're talking about." He turned toward the bedroom. "I just need to get out of here. This is never going to work. I need to start over, and I don't want to take a whole lot of garbage with me. I want *out*, April."

Suddenly, compassion flooded the wife's continence, as she watched the hang-dog look spread from his face, across his sloping shoulders, and down his buckling backbone. "Oh, Bill, you are just so tired. You're exhausted." High above, she heard her own thought very clearly. "*You're like a wounded animal.*"

She saw herself reach out and gently touched his arm. "Look at you. You need to back off and give yourself some breathing space." She guided him toward the bedroom. "Why don't you just concentrate on getting some sleep? Have a nice shower, and crawl in for a few hours."

At the bedroom door, she stopped and turned to speak softly into his pale face. "You know, we don't want to do anything too hasty, here. I mean, we haven't really given John Courtney a chance to do his magic, have we? We need to let him do his job, Bill. After all, he's really very good at it."

As the shower was running, she slipped back down to where April was sitting quietly on the side of the bed. "*I can't believe how well you handled that,*" she thought to herself. "*But you caught that wounded animal thing, didn't you? And that was the clincher. A wounded animal drags itself away from further danger, where it can lick its wounds in peace.*" She hugged her shivering body for a moment. "*And there is no reasoning with a wounded animal. It's like the brain freezes into survival mode, or something.*" She got up and began to pull the covers back on the bed. "*Better to be wise than to be panicked at this point. Better to be calm and trust in God.*" She reached over and gently fluffed the pillows. "*Got to trust Him. Got to...*"

The shower stopped, and she knew it was time for her to slip quietly out of the way. Before she closed the bedroom door behind her, she whispered a little prayer. "I can't do this without you, Lord. I am so *terrified*." The sob interrupted only for a second. "But this whole thing is in your hands. That's how it has to be. Just show me what You want me to do."

It was probably the most profound lesson this woman would ever learn.

CHAPTER TWENTY-SEVEN

Contacts

It was suddenly December… the second day into it, in fact. The usual meeting of the prayer partners was taking place in the corner booth of the Lincoln Inn Café. Once again, there were two invited guests, Chief Rob Allen, and April Flannigan, and for a very good reason. The Collinses had some news.

"We've already contacted the Fosters. Rehema is a nurse, you know, and so we have her in place at the Foxx residence, to take care of Roxie whenever both parents are working." Connie was keeping her voice low, so she was enunciating carefully. "The Fosters are staying with our pastor over there on Swift Street; Deacon Peter has been conducting healing services on the weekends. Meanwhile, Rehema has been filling us in on any goings-on at Roxie's home, which might be helpful, especially for Deacon, who will do the actual exorcism, eventually."

"We say 'eventually' because this has to be a process." Don ticked them off on his fingers. "First, the parents have to witness the demons in action, then someone — probably the mother — will have to inform the girl and prepare her, then Deacon will explain how she will need to keep those things out, and then the actual exorcism will be performed."

"And now we have the perfect setting," Connie said. "In the privacy of the home, where the girl is disabled to a point where she is unable to throw a tantrum and run out the door."

Father Tom shifted his weight on the booth seat. "It does present one problem, it seems to me, and that would be the time element. Remember, she has only one more week of bedrest."

"That's true," Connie agreed. "And they have now allowed her to lie on the sofa out in the living room for a couple of hours a day. She gets to watch some TV, and talk on the phone."

"We actually have only until next Sunday," Don said. "And her parents both need to be there."

"If they will even agree to do that," the chief interjected. He leaned back in the chair at the open end of the booth. "I personally don't feel like they will believe you. I know I still have some doubts, myself. If it weren't for the knocking on the wall…"

"Yeah, we know," Don grinned. "Bogeyman stuff." He saw the troubled looks on the faces of the others. "Actually," he spoke as the grin disappeared, "this is real, and it's serious. I shouldn't be flippant about this matter, at all."

April licked her lips nervously. "I couldn't agree with you more, Don. It is so bad that Bill and I have hired a lawyer." She looked around at the inquiring expressions. "This girl has slowly, but surely, snagged our whole family into a deadly trap. And I doubt she has any clue as to what she has done to Bill, to me, to our boys' families, to our collective future. We are going to have to live with this for the *rest* of our lives. *Think* about that! There will be no release, no reprieve. The consequences will be there for as long as we live." She shook her head. "It is just hard to believe."

"What does your lawyer have to say? Anything we can help you with?" Don asked.

"He hasn't said anything to me, directly, but I get the feeling he is looking for a way to discredit any charges against

Bill, on the grounds that this was a relentless, obsessive pursuit of a vulnerable, war-damaged man... a sitting duck, so to speak."

"And he is not the first one," Connie said.

Father Tom tilted his head back, thinking out loud. "And that ended with a suicide." He blinked and looked across the table. "Then there was the break-in at your home," he said to April. "Pretty obvious who did all that damage."

"What break-in?" the chief asked.

"A few weeks ago, I think. Bill admitted just a couple of days ago that she had stolen the key to our back door during one of her... visits... to our house."

"Did he confront her?"

"I don't think so. He's afraid of her."

"Any damage done?"

"She barricaded our little dog from the bedroom, using a large oil painting I had just finished, then stood on the bedroom side and teased him until he had scratched almost all of the paint off the bottom edge of it. Then, she left it all for me to find. Charley was still all wild-eyed when I found him."

"That's not normal," Connie murmured. "That's just plain hateful."

"Well, I can understand why Bill wouldn't want this to be an official matter, but it would have helped if I had been let in on this."

"Sorry, Chief, but it's kind of hard to keep your head on straight when all these weird things are happening," April said.

"What weird things?" The policeman was out to get some answers.

"I can give you one," Connie offered. "She deliberately injured another cheerleader, so that she could be out there in front, instead of warming the bench as first substitute."

Something clicked in the back of Chief Robbie's mind. "I heard about that. Guess she got pretty nasty when somebody threatened to expose her."

"I don't know anything about that." Connie looked questioningly at the others.

"Doesn't matter," the chief said. "It's enough that *I* do."

Don leaned forward and spoke softly. "If we are adding it all up, we need to include this attack on her and Ted Donahue. A baby died, and a young man ended up paralyzed. That's as bad as the suicide, maybe worse." He looked around the table. "This is not normal behavior for a young girl. Now, Connie and I have seen the manifestation of an actual demon. It *is* a demon... at least one, and maybe more than that — we won't know until we go after it. I honestly believe we need to go ahead with the exorcism." Connie was nodding in agreement.

"I think you should, too," April stated firmly.

"All I can do is, pray for you... you know that," Father Tom said. "But, yes, something needs to be done about all that evil."

Chief Rob Allen pushed his chair back and picked up his check as he rose. "Well, good luck with that."

"You probably should be there... you know, so you can see for yourself," Don said.

"I'll let you know if I change my mind," the officer said with a grim smile.

The other four watched him stride all the way out into the front hall, where he turned to the right, out of sight.

"Whew!" Don exclaimed, as he looked at his relieved wife.

"What's that all about?" the curious priest inquired.

"We were really, really concerned that the chief would put a hold on this."

"Yeah," Connie said. "He could have done that, you know. He's Chief of Police in the town where this ritual is going to take place." The priest nodded in acknowledgment. "But we had to take a chance. It could have been much worse if we had gone ahead with it without telling him, and then something had happened to the girl."

"But now, he's been informed. That makes him an accomplice," Don stated. "He'll figure it out, and I'd be willing to bet you a nickel he's there on Thursday at four o'clock."

April looked up from her meal. "You have it scheduled already?"

Oh yeah," Don grinned. "Connie and I got together with her parents last Sunday night."

"And they agreed to do this?" Father Tom asked.

"Yeah. They don't yet understand this whole procedure, but these are two desperate people. They really, really want a normal child in the household."

***

Chief Allen knew he needed to warn Mr. Smart that he was on Roxie's list, but since she was pretty well under the weather for at least another week, he decided to just catch him at Yandow's on the coming Friday afternoon. In the meantime, there was another decision to be made.

He closed the door to his office, having instructed Lily that he was not to be disturbed "…unless the building is on fire." What he needed to do had to be accomplished before daylight started to fade. At twilight, the inside of his office would be clearly on display from outside those windows, and everybody knew, those windows were *never* closed off by window shades. It had been a promise he made to the city fathers when they hired him: complete transparency at all times. He weighed the situation carefully, then decided there was only one way to handle this.

The clock behind his desk showed one o'clock already, so he hurried to his locker and pulled out three items, slipping them into an empty cardboard box from the supply room. At the end of five minutes, he stepped back out of the office, a taped-shut box in his arms, and went directly to his squad car.

After he had placed the thing in the trunk of the vehicle, he went back in.

"Hey, Lily," he said, nonchalantly, "I've decided to work on that paperwork at home for the rest of the day. I'm way behind, and I don't want any interruptions unless there's an emergency. I really mean that."

"Sure thing, Chief," she whispered as she covered the dispatcher's mike with her hand. "Don't worry, we've got both officers on duty today. You should be fine."

He drove the squad car directly home, and unloaded the box into the empty house. With great care, he toted the precious cargo upstairs into his room and set it carefully on the floor beside his at-home desk, then settled into the old desk chair which had belonged to his father. There, he took time to channel the wide road of obvious choices into a narrow path of moral alignment.

In the end, he decided not to involve the local and state authorities because there was so much more to this situation than what inflexible regulations and one-size-fits-all solutions could ever successfully remedy. This was no place for red tape and endless paperwork, as a troubled child aged quickly through a bureaucratic system fraught with one entanglement after another.

"The kid, no matter how mean she was, would never have a chance, and all those families would be shattered beyond repair," he thought. *"This whole thing needs to be approached from a different angle."*

He pulled out the tape recorder and set it upon a small table beside the desk. Then he inserted the typing paper — layered over carbon paper so he would have a second copy — into his father's old typewriter, rubbed his hands together, and pushed the "Play" button on the tape recorder. Over the next two hours, with the exception of one short break, he transcribed the entire contents of his interviews with Mr. Smart and Shirley Bogue. Because he used only pseudonyms, he felt free to use the exact language and inflections of all those involved. Further, he included dates and times of day for each segment. When finished, he made a note on a separate piece of paper, that the actual persons had not given permission to use these interviews for court documents, and would not be revealed without a court order. The point was clearly stated: *This material is intended to expose the actual situation surrounding the activities of one Roxanne Foxx. It is not intended for use in any legal action, since the identities of the witnesses must be protected.*

Then, to protect himself, he inserted a handwritten note, asking that certain individuals not be informed as to where all this information originated.

There was a slam of the back door, and a stamping of snow-laden feet on the rug just inside, on the kitchen floor. Robbie knew his brother was home. He leaned back once more in his father's chair. It was a good feeling. All of the tapes had been transcribed. Now, he just needed to get back to the office and borrow the department's new-fangled Polaroid camera to photograph the notebook pages and the magazine cover.

With any luck, he could have this stuff in Flannigan's lawyer's hands by the weekend.

***

Earlier that same day, Rehema Foster brought a steaming bowl of homemade chicken rice soup to her patient, who was reclining on the sofa in the Indian Acres home of the Foxxes.

"I don't want that. I'm sick of it," the girl snapped.

"You need to keep things quiet in your digestive system, sweetheart."

"Stop calling me 'sweetheart.' I've had enough of your mush, Rehema. Just stop it."

"Oh, child," the lovely black lady responded, "we all need some loving-on, sometimes."

The girl glared at her. "Says who?"

"Says the Lord, child."

"And that's another thing… stop calling me 'child.'" She hooted softly. "I am *not* your child… don't you *get* that yet?"

The woman brought the metal TV tray closer and placed the fragrant bowl, along with a paper napkin and a soup spoon, upon the tray's painted floral pattern. Then, she slowly drew forth from her pocket, a two-inch-square slice of zucchini bread, loosely wrapped in waxed paper. Roxie watched as her nurse unwrapped it and placed it right beside the soup bowl. The girl's eyes grew wide, as she saw that it was covered with a layer of peanut butter and honey.

Then her nostrils flared in distain.

With a persnickety sniff, she glanced up at her waitress. "Well, that's more like it." It disappeared in one sloppy mouthful.

The nurse smiled down at her. "Now," she said softly, "if you eat that tiny little bowl of soup, I will find a couple more of those delightful morsels."

"How about I just get up off this sofa and go find them for myself?" came the arrogant answer.

"Oh my child, you may surely try… but then you will be injured so badly, you will have to eat chicken rice soup for another two weeks… *at least*." She gently folded her long, black hands together. "Surely, that is not what we all want to see happening here."

Roxie reached for the bowl.

"I hate your guts, you old, black, stupid excuse for a nurse…!"

"I know, sweetheart. Now eat your supper. Your folks will be home soon, and I will be out of your hair."

The girl lifted her soup spoon and splatted it down, sending the liquid out into a two-foot diameter. "Yeah, that's right. That's right. And that's not the only thing I want out of my hair." She pushed the TV tray as hard as she could, sending it and its contents all across the living room. "I want all of it… the wheelchair… the oxygen tank… the needles… the pills… out of my hair!"

By the time the Foxxes got home from work, the living room was cleaned up, and Roxie was asleep in her bed, thoroughly sedated for the night. George took a short trip down the hall, then got back into the car to drive Rehema out to her Swift Street hosts' home. About the time they were headed out on Shelburne Road, the small talk was over, and he took the opportunity to speak to her in private.

"So, your husband is a deacon, huh?" She nodded to affirm that. "So is that why he can exercise demons?"

She smiled, but did not correct him. "Not exactly," she answered. "He can do that only because he is a Christian." Out of the corner of her eye, she saw the doubtful look on his face. "He has the power of the Blood of Jesus, and the permission to command devils to back off and even come out of someone, in the Name of Jesus."

This time, he actually turned his head to cast that doubting look directly at her. "So, okay… I consider myself to be a Christian. So am I able to do that, just like him?"

"Actually, all Christians are supposed to be able to do that. They just don't know it, or just don't know how, or maybe they just don't have the faith." She clutched the purse on her lap with both hands. "It's like receiving a beautiful gift, unwrapping it, and then never taking the gift out of the box."

The man seemed to want to move on. "So, uh… do you really think Roxie has a demon inside her?"

"After having her as my patient for a week or so, I would guess that's a real possibility." She turned to reassure him. "The Collinses have actually seen the thing manifest, and I believe them, since their pastor has great confidence in those two."

George sighed. "Still gives me the creeps."

The car moved along. Finally, as George turned left onto Swift Street, he glanced warily over at his elegant passenger. "Uh… hope I haven't made you mad, or anything," he said.

"Not at all," she answered.

As he slowed down to find the freshly shoveled driveway, he seemed to seal the deal. "Okay then, I guess we'll be doing this thing on Thursday afternoon." A moment later, he was holding the car door open for her.

"There you are!" Deacon Peter Foster called from the doorway of the house. "Won't you come in, Mr. Foxx?"

"Uh, thanks," George replied as he helped Rehema gently over the packed snow to the doorstep. "… but it's been a long day… and Marilyn is alone with the girl… so I guess I should get back home as soon as possible."

He put the car into reverse and backed carefully onto Swift Street, then proceeded slowly up the slippery slope. With his attention on the driving, there was a brief break in his train of thought. Once he reached the crest of the hill, however, the whole situation just seemed to overwhelm him. Deceit and injuries and a pregnancy, and now, demons. He shivered and mentally reached for a more manageable overview… a more practical side to this whole thing. As he turned right out onto Shelburne Road, he suddenly asked himself the sobering question. "How can I protect my job?"

***

Later that same night, April Flannigan stepped off the bus at the Susie Wilson Road stop, and walked carefully through the tire tracks in the snow, all the way to her driveway. It was just about ten o'clock, but the art lessons were really helping her keep some balance in her life. As she put the key into the front keyhole, she heard the telephone ring inside. Quickly, she opened the door and stepped across the rug, snowy boots and all, to answer it. Charley was yipping a little welcome, so she dropped her bundles to pick him up with one hand as she lifted the receiver with the other.

"Hello?"

"Oh, hello, Mrs. Flannigan." She recognized the chief's voice.

"Yes, Chief. And you probably should feel free to call me 'April' by now, don't you think?"

"Oh, sure. So, April, is your hubby at home?"

"No. Anything wrong?"

"Nah, nothing like that. I really only wanted to talk to you. I just have some stuff your lawyer might be interested in looking at."

"Really?" Her heart skipped a beat. "Something helpful, Chief?"

"I really think it might be... *very* helpful." He switched the phone to his other ear and looked out the office windows at the flashing light. "So, he's not home?"

"No, not at the moment. He doesn't get off until almost midnight."

"I see." She could hear him take a big breath, and then let it out slowly. "Ah-hh, let's see... say, April, you don't happen to know when he'll be meeting with his lawyer again, do you?"

"As a matter of fact, they are scheduled to meet in Montpelier tomorrow, around noon, I think."

"Alright." He seemed pleased. "Now I need to ask you a favor, ma'am."

"Oh?"

"Please allow me to drop this material off to you... say, in a half-hour?" He did not wait for her to answer. "I feel this information needs to get to your lawyer as soon as possible."

"Well..."

"It's just some paperwork in a manila envelope."

"Well..."

"April, listen to me. I know what they can do to him. I'm a cop. I really think this information could save his butt."

"Well, alright then. A half-hour, right?"

He was actually there in twenty-five minutes. As he handed her the envelope at the front door, he admonished her about letting *anybody* except the lawyer know where she got this information. "Not even your husband. It could get a lot of people into big trouble," he emphasized.

After he left, she saw that the envelope was not sealed shut. Only the cord wrapped around the button kept it closed. She looked at the clock. Bill would not be home for over an hour.

Thirty-five minutes later, she started to rewrap the cord, but stopped. Stepping over to the kitchen sink, she dampened a paper towel and moistened the seal on the envelope. After pressing it securely closed, she rewrapped the cord around the button, then she hid it in her underwear drawer. As she slid the thing closed, she made up her mind. She most certainly would not let Bill know she had this. He would *never* allow all this stuff to be made public about the "love of his life." No, she would have to deliver it herself.

Early the next morning, she was out of the shower and dressing before Bill even got out of bed. He sat up, still half-asleep.

"You want something to eat before you go to Montpelier?" she asked as she put on the last touch of makeup.

"Nope." He threw the covers back and drew himself into a sitting position on the side of the bed. "Guess I'd better get moving," he spoke through a yawn.

While he was in the shower, April went out to the garage and hid the envelope under her passenger seat. Then she took Charley out for his morning walk. When she came back in, Bill was getting into his coat. She locked the back door and reached for her purse and gloves.

"Ready?" she asked him.

He looked surprised. "Am I dropping you off someplace?"

"Nope. I'm going with you."

He stiffened. "No, you're not."

She walked over and patted him on the arm. "Listen, Bill, we're in this together, and we're going to fight it together." She pulled the door open and motioned for him to go through. "No more Lone Ranger heroics. That's just *one* of the new rules."

"What do you mean, 'new rules'?"

"We are a team. We will work through this problem together. That means the rules need to change... just a little." She gave him a reassuring wink. We can do this, and do it very well."

"The hell you say," he objected darkly.

"Okay, mister, tell you what. I'm getting into the car, right now. If you want to go to Montpelier, you're gonna have to take me with you."

He took a menacing step toward her. Although she held up an authoritative hand, she spoke kindly. "No-no-no. You don't want to add *domestic violence* onto everything else you have done, honey."

He fumed all the way, but they made the noon appointment. John Courtney was a slightly built, young-looking individual, with a big office in an old brick building. They had not been seated for more than a few minutes when April pulled the manila envelope from beneath her coat. Bill's face turned red with anger, but the little lawyer promptly opened it and commenced reading immediately.

Bill glared at her and muttered, "Why didn't I get to look at this before we got here?" April raised her eyebrows as though to say, "Be patient," then leaned back into her chair, to watch Mr. Courtney's face.

At the end of ten minutes, the lawyer looked up and signaled them to be patient. Five minute later, he sat back up in his desk chair and grinned at his old Air Force buddy. "Hey-y-y-y, you certainly married well, my friend."

The very next morning, a phone call came into George Foxx's office at the bus barn. A couple of bus drivers seated at a break table saw him through the glass window which separated the two rooms, as his face turned pale and he sat down heavily at his desk. They could not, however, hear the conversation. When George turned his back toward the window, they lost interest, and went on about their business. Neither one of them was there when George Foxx came out of his office, sweat dripping from his face, and heading toward the restroom.

When he returned, he scanned the empty break room, then reached down into the bottom left-hand drawer of his desk. After one more visual check, he lifted a flask to his lips and drank deeply. Quickly, he tapped the top back on and returned it to its hiding place. Then he slumped over his desk, head in hands, and whispered softly.

"Keep the authorities out of it. Keep Vermont Transit out of it. Just get the kid straightened out, and stay low-profile. That's the best thing for *everybody*."

He lifted the phone and called home. Marilyn answered. He made it short and sweet: "Keep Roxie away from, and I do mean *completely* away from the Flannigans. They have a lawyer. If she so much as *hints* that she has had relations with him, they are going to hit us with everything that kid has done. I could lose my job, Marilyn." He paused, for emphasis. "And she would be taken away from you." Another dramatic pause. "Are you understanding what I am telling you?"

He heard the phone hit the floor.

"Marilyn? Marilyn?"

"Hello?"

He was relieved to hear Rehema's melodic voice. He repeated briefly what he had told his wife.

"Alright, Mr. Foxx. I will take care of her. You can discuss this when you get home."

"We'd better hope this exercise thing works tomorrow night. We need to get that girl under control. Otherwise, we could end up between a rock and a hard place."

Both George and Marilyn had managed to get all day Thursday off from work, enabling them to get some special home treatment for their daughter's on-going "shock" brought on by the "attack." By three-thirty that afternoon, Don and Deacon Foster arrived, followed by Connie, who walked over from the high school. Rehema, of course, was already there, ostensibly to help Marilyn change out Roxie's bed and medical equipment. Marilyn made a big deal out of the fact that the dedicated nurse would come and do that, even though it was the Foster's wedding anniversary. So, when these people arrived, Roxie was not suspicious, since the word was that the two couples were meeting to celebrate with a lobster dinner at the Lincoln Inn. "I love lobster. I'm jealous," Roxie had pouted.

Since there were a total of seven people present, it had been agreed beforehand that the first step of the exorcism would take place in the living room. When there came a tap on the dining room's sliding door just before four o'clock, the total climbed to eight. The Essex Junction police chief, in nondescript winter clothing, stood outside. "I'm Chief Rob Allen," he whispered to Rehema, who had opened the door. She looked out to see where he had walked through the back yard from the hollowed-out snow path down to the IGA. "Thought I had better get in on this," he said.

"Oh yes, sir, but you need to stay out here until she is quieted. This would not make sense to her."

"Sorry. You could just signal for me to come in," he suggested.

"Excellent," she whispered. Then she went and stood in the doorway between the living room and the kitchen. Things were about to begin.

Deacon Foster was chatting amicably with Roxie from his chair located close beside the sofa, where pillows supported her in an upright position.

"Well, how are you doing, young lady?" His voice clothed the room like heavy velvet. "Are you getting enough rest?"

The others in the room fixed their concerned gaze on the beautiful victim.

Roxie responded to the special attention of this captive audience. Her words came out as more of a sigh than a spoken statement. "I… am… so… tired."

"Of course you are," he agreed. "This whole thing has been very draining, and you are so young. What a pity." He looked up at nothing in particular. "I wonder if I could give you some help on that."

"What do you mean?"

"There are ways to find peace, Roxanne, where you can get a full night's rest, while your body heals." He leaned just slightly toward her. "Did you know that the body heals when it is asleep?" He turned toward Don. "Is that not true, Brother Don?"

"Absolutely," Don agreed, with a slow, wise nod.

"Of course," the deacon mused, "…not everybody can do this. It takes a special discipline, like that of an athlete, to focus and learn how to do this." He smiled gently. "Are you, by any chance, active in sports?"

"You bet she is," Connie interjected. "She is one excellent, excellent cheerleader. You should see her out there!"

Roxie got a pleased smile on her face. "It just comes naturally," she said.

"Well then," the beautiful black man sat up straighter in his chair. "You probably could do this very easily." He leaned toward her. "Are you interested in giving this a try?"

The girl looked at her mother, who shrugged her shoulders. "What do we have to lose, Roxanne? You need a healthy sleep." She looked at Deacon Foster. "Would it be alright if I watched this? I could use a little more sleep, myself."

A low, sonorous laugh came forth from his throat. "Of course. In fact, you can *all* stay and witness this. It will not do any harm to our lovely patient, and it may do a lot of good for the rest of us." He turned to Roxie. "Is this alright with you, young lady?"

The drama queen was all too willing.

"Then just lie back into those pillows, and do what I tell you, Roxanne."

She relaxed into the cloudy fluff surrounding her.

"Very good. Now close your eyes... that's right. Close them softly, Roxanne, no need to pinch them tightly... just close them gently... ah, yes, that's right. Now take a deep breath, and let it out slowly." He waited until she had done that. "That was very good. Now, we are going to do this again, but as you let the breath out slowly, relax your shoulders." He watched as she exhaled. "Let those shoulders just fall... just fall... toward the floor. That's right." Those in the room watched her neck and shoulders slowly loosen. "How sweet is this release, Roxanne. How restful and how pleasant." He waited for her to finish the exhale. "Now repeat this one more time, and as you exhale, look for a soft, golden light. It may not be there yet, but start looking for it, because it is coming... it is coming." The girl's hands slipped open, completely relaxed. Deacon Foster leaned closer. "Keep the breathing going now. Keep it going." There were two more deep breaths before he spoke again, this time, almost in a whisper. "Very good, Roxanne. Very good." He looked up at his wife and nodded for her to start praying.

This was the signal she had been waiting for, even though her husband was not aware that Robbie Allen was waiting outside the sliding door. As Deacon continued to coax the girl into complete release, Rehema moved softly toward the door and quietly opened it, just enough for Robbie to slip inside. As she closed the sliding door, she held a finger over her lips and pointed to the sofa where the girl was. They both stood perfectly still and watched, from twenty-four feet away. The lovely black woman prayed softly.

Deacon Foster's voice was smoothly encouraging the girl into a deeper release. Her body was now as limp as a wilted rose. It was time.

"Roxanne," he whispered, "…can you hear me? Please nod your head, if you can hear me."

A slight nod indicated that she could.

"It's time to fall asleep. So now, you need to say these words after me." He bowed his head. "Are you ready to say these words after me?"

Another nod.

He moved close to her ear and spoke the words, slowly and deliberately: "JEE-SUS is LORD!!!"

The girl bolted upright, her eyes opening wide, then glazing over. For a few seconds, she did not move.

And then it happened.

The roiling purple face, the coughing and struggle to breathe.

Marilyn cried out and moved toward her daughter, but George grabbed her, even though he could not believe what he was seeing either.

"Devil, you will not harm this girl… I command you in the Name of Jesus!"

The flesh rolled once more in violent waves across the girl's face, as she noisily sucked in one last, laborious breath.

"Stop tormenting that body, I command you, in the mighty Name of Jesus!"

The countenance of the girl seemed to settle down a bit, but the mouth was moving unnaturally. Suddenly, a deep, gritty sound came out: *"SHUT UP!"*

"In the mighty Name of Jesus, I command you to identify yourself!"

"SHUT UP!"

"I have the authority here, *not you*. You *must* obey my commands, in the Name of Jesus." The preacher's voice was returning to full volume. "Identify yourself, Devil!"

A deep growl came from somewhere in the throat of that beautiful girl. There was a hard, short cough from her, then the rumbling voice filled the little living room. *"We are 'Stronghold,' and we have permission to be here."*

The deacon stood up, hands on his hips. "And just who gave you permission?"

"Her lover," came the responding roar.

"Which one?"

There was a long, low grating laugh. *"The witch."*

"What witch?"

Bright beams of headlights flashed across the living room windows.

"Somebody just pulled into the driveway!" Connie exclaimed.

Robbie Allen disappeared out the back door. Rehema dropped a towel onto the floor to wipe away the melted snow of his boots.

In the living room, Deacon Foster commanded the demons to hide themselves, but not to harm the girl. He placed his hands on her face and commanded instant restoration… just as a loud knock rattled the door.

Don saw that George and Marilyn were too stunned to answer it, so he, himself rose from his chair to take charge. He caught the signal from Deacon Foster, and waited as the man of God whispered, "Bow your heads, people. We are praying."

The knock was repeated, insistently. As Don moved forward to answer it, the group began to recite The Lord's

Prayer. Don waited until they reached "...Thy will be done, on earth as it...", whereupon, he carefully opened the door.

Don poked his head outside, softly whispering to the one who had been knocking. "Yes?"

It was Sheriff Max Duncan.

"Oh, it's you, Sheriff." He stepped outside onto the front step to join the law officer, leaving the door open just enough for the man to hear the praying in the room behind him. He leaned close into the man's face to softly ask the question.

"What can I do for you, sir?"

"I'm actually here to talk with the Foxx family," Sheriff Duncan announced, as he stepped back down to the sidewalk. "Are you George Foxx?"

"Oh no, sir. If you remember from the hospital, Roxie's father is a lot taller."

The sheriff suddenly remembered. "O-oh yeah. You're the one who informed her of her rights. Sure. You're her counselor, right?"

"Right... but right now, we are having a little prayer meeting in there," he motioned inside with a nod. "Roxie has had a very hard day. She needs prayer and a good night's rest. This is really not a good time to be interviewing the family." He reached for the door. "You know... the parents are more than willing to cooperate. It would probably be easier for everybody, if you made an appointment with them for another interview. That would be so much appreciated, sir." He turned to go back into the house, where a soft chorus of **Nearer My God To Thee** filled the room. "But thanks for your dedication to this case." He stopped and looked at the sheriff straight-on. "I mean that sincerely, Sheriff. Keep up the good work."

Just as Don came in and closed the door, Roxie woke up and looked around in bewilderment. "What happened?" Deacon Foster looked at his wife.

The first step of the exorcism was over.

Twenty minutes later, over an anniversary dinner of Maine lobster, the Fosters and the Collinses reached some surprising conclusions.

"I am sure her parents are now looking at the whole situation with different eyes," Don remarked, as the salads arrived. He waited for Diana, the waitress, to finish the placements and move toward the other side of the Lincoln Inn dining room. Then he leaned toward the center of the table where the four were seated. "It was quite a shock."

"It sure was," Connie agreed. She turned to Rehema. "Thanks for all those prayers over that girl."

"Peter and I agree there always has to be some preparation. And today, those evil vibrations were very, very strong."

"And they will continue to be," the preacher said. Then he leaned forward, himself, his elbows resting on each side of the table setting in front of him. "In fact, after tonight, I have a deep sense that those demons — 'Stronghold,' they call themselves — have been in that body for quite a long time."

The Collinses both stopped, salad forks in midair. "How do we know that?" Don asked.

"Well, sir," the deacon's answer took on that pleasant mixture of American English and British accents... the same one that slipped in whenever he was in teaching mode. "First of all, they have a good deal of strength, and are working as a team. That usually takes a rather long time. Otherwise, there is obvious damage to the mind, soul, and body of their victim, and that could mean they might be more easily detected."

The counselor-couple hardly had time to weigh in on this statement, before the teacher continued.

"Secondly, they entered, probably not all at once, but progressively, mostly through sexual encounters... again, more than one." As he moved some lettuce around on his plate, his fork picked up soft glints of light from the wagon wheel chandelier above the table. "Now, let's add it up. After all, the girl is only fifteen years old." He let the couple think about that for a minute, while he worked a hefty bite of greens onto his fork. Before he slid them into his mouth, he put the next piece of the puzzle out there. "Now, correct me if I am mistaken, but did you not tell me, Don, that her mother was worried that her daughter was starting to be sexually active... just over the last year or so?"

The couple looked at each other, then nodded in agreement. "I was there when she made that statement... or something very close to that," Connie said.

Deacon Foster chewed and swallowed. "I think something happened, probably when the child was much younger, that the mother never knew about." He looked sternly at Don. "Do you recall any reference to just exactly when she started having trouble with her little girl?"

Don and Connie again exchanged glances, then mentally went off to ponder individual memories of that particular counseling session.

Rehema leaned slightly toward her husband, quietly asking him to pass the salt. His large hand grasped the rather petite glass shaker, as he asked, "How is your salad, my dear lady?" She smiled and nodded approval.

"I think it was when she was being bratty to the second husband," Connie suddenly spoke. She looked at her husband for confirmation.

"Yup, I was thinking the same thing." He turned to the deacon. "Do you think that could have been the start of it?"

"How old was she at the time?"

"Well," Don tried to figure it out in his head. "I would say between five and seven years old."

Deacon Peter waggled his head. "It could have been." He took another bite of his salad, then reached for the salt, himself. As he shook the crystals over one side of his generous salad, he went on. "But we need something more concrete." He pursed his lips for a second, then spoke again. "Perhaps we will get more information in the next few counseling sessions."

"If we can get her to keep those appointments," Don said.

"I think perhaps we don't have to worry about that anymore," the teacher smiled. "Judging from the revelation which those two parents had this evening."

"Oh, yeah…" Don replied, "they will see to it."

"Instead, I suggest *we four* turn our attention to another factor in this process."

"What is that?" Don inquired.

"Finding that lover," the deacon said.

"What lover?" Connie asked.

"The witch."

CHAPTER TWENTY-EIGHT

Danger

Friday happened to be a busy day at the Essex Junction Police Department, but by three o'clock, the chief was able to get away for a break. He chose to walk down Main Street toward Yandow's Market, taking time to watch for slippery spots on the sidewalk, while at the same time keeping an eye out for Mr. Smart's usual arrival at that grocery store. As he reached the corner of the old brick Brownell Block, however, he spotted the man across the train tracks, just leaving the store, paper sack in hand.

"He's early today."

The chief walked slowly to his left, heading for the train depot. Glancing back, he saw Mr. Smart making his way to Al's French Fries. Nonchalantly, Robbie strolled slowly down Railroad Avenue past the Tip Top, then across the street to enter the historic train depot. Only one person was in there, and she was reading a magazine. He stayed out of her range of vision, and took a seat to wait for the village's "drunken Indian" to show up. Soon enough, the man arrived shortly and took an outside seat under the cover of the loading platform. Chief Allen waited for just a little bit, then went quietly out to where Uncle was sitting.

The man looked up from his French fries at the approach of footsteps, automatically moving the paper bag closer to his thigh. He immediately recognized the chief. Surprise, and then confusion swept across his face.

"Afternoon, Mr. Smart."

"Afternoon, Chief."

"Mind if I sit down for a minute?"

The man moved over on the bench. "Nope." He tried to grin. "Free country, ay?"

"Ay-yuh," The officer's voice seemed friendly enough, but Uncle was still a little uneasy. "…last time I checked," Robbie said as he took a seat.

There seemed to be a little awkwardness. Then Uncle remembered his manners. "French fry?" he asked, as he held the fat-stained cone out to the chief.

The officer smiled a "No, thank you." He patted his hard abdomen. "Have to watch that stuff." His gaze took in the old village cemetery across the train tracks. "That place sure looks forlorn in the wintertime," he commented. Uncle took the scene in, but said nothing. At that point, the chief gave himself a gentle reminder to not speak of any scary spiritual stuff. He was still struggling with the demonic encounter of the afternoon before. Right now, his attention needed to be on the task at hand.

"I need to update you on a couple of things, Mr. Smart," he said, as he took off his official chief's hat and placed it on the bench seat between them. "Um, I guess you could say I have good news and bad news." He turned to speak more directly to the tan-faced gentleman. "Good news is, Bill Flannigan has hired a lawyer."

"That gawdim girl charging him with something?"

"Nope. He's just making sure she doesn't."

"Smart move." He shoved a French fry into his mouth.

"I took the liberty of forwarding the information you had on her — anonymously, mind you… they don't have either one of our names — to that lawyer. I believe it will be a big help. I had no time to consult you on this, Mr. Smart, but I did feel that you would certainly want to do everything you could to start clearing the reputations of not only those two bus drivers, but Ted Donahue, as well." He was encouraged by Mr. Smart's nod of approval. "At the very best, no charges will be made against any of them; at the very worst, we don't get to exonerate Mr. Strong, but we prevent any further damage to the lives of the other two." He paused. "Is that all okay with you, sir?"

Uncle sat upright, his dignity restored by the "Sir."

"Gawdim right, it is." He watched the chief sigh in relief. "So… what's the frickin' bad news?"

"Oh yeah. This is really unfortunate, Mr. Smart, but Roxie knows about the agreement between you and Ted."

Uncle's little eyes went wide. "How the hail did *that* happen?"

"Remember when he called you at home? Her friend, Marsha, was on the phone extension out in the greenhouse. She heard the whole thing, I guess." He twisted uncomfortably on the bench. "Confronted Roxie with the fact that she was pregnant, having had relations with Ted — I guess there was some rivalry for his affections, there." He paused. "Anyway, Roxie knows, and I think you should be aware. This kid can be vicious. God only knows what really happened to Ted out there in the woods."

"Why do you say that?"

Robbie thought carefully before he answered. "See… Ted wasn't aware that Roxie knew about the scheme you and Ted had going. He gladly went out to that secluded place with her."

"But… weren't they *both* hurt in that attack?"

The official hat was placed back on the head, and Chief Allen stood up. "Yeah, well, we don't know what happened out there. All I can do is to warn you that this is one very, very sick girl, Mr. Smart, and you are now in her crosshairs." He turned to leave, with the final word over his shoulder. "Just be careful, sir."

***

Uncle woke with a start the next morning. There had been a bad dream — not terrifying, but just on the edge of a nightmare — and he could still feel the slush under his Army boots from where he was running for shelter from the bullets. He sat up in the rumpled bed, to reorient back into the present. As he looked around the room, it suddenly struck him that it reflected his current lackadaisical style: things had gotten sloppy since he left the military, and he hadn't much cared. But now things were going to be different.

Slowly, he slipped out of the bed and padded out across the cool linoleum of the kitchen floor toward the little bathroom. When he opened the door, he was greeted by his own image in the medicine cabinet mirror. He stopped and took inventory.

"Older. More tired. Bad eyesight." He leaned forward, both hands on the sides of the sink, and noted the increased silver across his five o'clock shadow. Then he looked deeply into his own eyes. "Well, old man, you better shape up. You're in gawdim enemy territory again."

A few minutes later, coffee was perking in the plain metal pot on top of the two-burner hot plate. He dressed warmly, because there was ice rimming the inside of the kitchen window. For just a few minutes, he sat and sipped on his backwoods coffee — made with just a pinch of salt — while he slid deeply into thought. Finally, he put down the cup and reached for his barn shirt. Even though it was still his day off until three this afternoon, he needed to keep busy. Today he would help Ceese with the milking, anyway. Besides that, he needed a little extra time off next Tuesday. There would be less card-playing and more talk out there in the small house down the street from St. Anthony's. Two of his poker buddies would be especially interested in this Roxie situation. He knew his cousin, Michael "Tall Tree" Smart, and Pooh's father, Chief Leroy "Raven's Wing" Smart, would give him wise advice.

***

A cool morning sun bathed the front door of the Foxx residence on the very same day. The Collinses and Fosters were arriving for an early Saturday counseling session with Roxie. As they carefully made their way up the icy sidewalk, Rehema was praying softly. The girl had no idea they were coming.

The door opened before they even knocked. "Good morning," Marilyn said, as she stepped back to allow them entrance. Directly in front of them, Roxie was reclining once again on the sofa. Her nostrils flared and the silvery eyes snapped with suspicion. "What are *you all* doing here?" She looked at her mother. "Mom?"

Marilyn raised her hand to signal a 'calm down,' as the four visitors stamped snow off footwear, then entered with gracious smiles and greetings toward her. George stood up from his recliner, gathering coats for Marilyn to hang in the guest closet by the door.

"My goodness, it's cold out there this morning!" Connie exclaimed.

"Only thirty-one degrees," George announced.

"I believe it," Don said, ushering his wife toward a chair.

Deacon Foster took the same seat where he had ministered to Roxie a couple of days before. He smiled tenderly at her. "And how are you feeling today, young lady?"

"A-about the same," she replied. But she was watching all six people taking seats. It looked like they planned on being there for a while, and that made her uneasy. Again, she warily addressed her mother. "Mom??"

Marilyn deliberately turned to Rehema. "So… going to a big healing service today, huh?"

The woman nodded, but it was her husband who elaborated. "Oh, bless my soul, Mrs. Foxx, this promises to be a humdinger." He caught Don's eye. "How many folks are expected, Brother Don?"

"Over a hundred, we think."

"Over a hundred, praise the LORD!" he exclaimed as he refocused on the girl. Suddenly he leaned toward her. "It's in Jericho. Do you know where that is?"

"Yeah, we have a guy on our basketball team who is from there."

"And so you know that we had to come right through Essex Junction to get there… and we thought to make a special point to stop and talk with you a while." He leaned back. "Have you ever been to a healing service, Roxanne?" She shook her head 'No.' "Oh-hhh," his voice was nearly a song. "What a shame! It's a wonderful thing to experience! You should do that, sometime." Other heads were bobbing in agreement. He looked at George and Marilyn. "I don't suppose we could talk you folks into coming with us…?" He turned abruptly back to the daughter. "Who knows… she might even be healed, right there on the spot."

Roxie's eyes went narrow and she focused on her hands. The fingertips drew together and began tapping, tapping, tapping.

"What do you say, young lady?" He was almost whispering, now.

Suddenly, the girl's face grew hateful, as her voice dropped to a deep growl: "No-oo!" The man pulled back, reaching into the inside of his jacket.

Marilyn tensed up. "Now, Roxanne, please be polite…" She was stopped short by an even more hateful glare, accompanied by a rumbling vibration from the throat. "R-Roxanne—," Marilyn stopped again, seeing the glazed look which was slowly creeping across her child's eyes. "Oh no, honey. Oh no…"

"**You shut up! Just shut *up!***" the voice deepened and the face was starting to turn a hideous purple.

In a flash, the deacon produced a mirror in front of Roxie's face, revealing the grotesque transformation that was taking place, split second-by-second. She shrieked in horror at the sight of putrid, purplish puss seeping forth from the skin, dissolving her nose, her cheeks, her mouth. But Deacon Foster would not allow her to push the looking glass away.

"Who *is* that, Roxanne?"

She heard herself hiss, felt herself swat hard at the mirror, but the man-of-God dodged it and put the horrific reflection right back in front of her face. "*Who* is that ugly thing you see, child?" Her terrified scream came forth like a rising siren, growing in intensity until it reverberated off the ceiling with such intensity that hands whipped upward to cover eardrums. They stayed there, until the volume slowly dropped, eventually reducing to a low moan. Then Roxie turned her face away, pulling up a pillow to hide from the filthy sight.

"Is that you? Is that you, Roxanne?"

"No-oo!" she moaned into the pillow. "That's not me! That's not me!"

He leaned closer. "Then, who is it?"

"A freak! An ugly freak!" Her voice cracked. "That is *not* me! It's *not!*"

The silence which descended upon the room was broken only by her distraught sobs into the pillow. Deacon signaled for continued quiet. Nobody moved for a good five minutes, until the sobbing had diminished.

Finally, the deacon resumed a melodious speech. "Now, child, that was pretty frightening, was it not?" She did not reply, holding the pillow over her face. "It is very shocking to know that one has that kind of thing inside oneself." He laid the mirror face-down on his knees. "Look here, I have put the mirror down. You don't have to look at it any more, if you don't want to. I think maybe you have seen enough of that evil thing."

She raised her red face up out of the pillow. "What... what are you talking about?"

From there on, the conversation got right to the nitty-gritty: The deacon explained that, somewhere in her short fifteen years, she had an encounter which left her open to evil beings. They were the root of all those deep, uncontrollable emotions. They were the basic cause of most of her bad behavior, and the resulting disruption in the Foxx family.

Roxanne looked to her mother for some kind of support.

"It's true, honey. George and I both saw those bad spirits last time these folks were here."

Deacon continued to explain that, as scary and powerful as they seemed to be, these evil things could be overcome and removed. There was every reason to believe she would never have to see an image like the one she had seen this morning... never again... but it would require her whole, undivided cooperation, or they could come back to torment her all over again... only this time, there would be even more of those evil things.

"It is very important that you have time to think about your situation, Roxanne," the gentle black man concluded. "Only with God's help, can you keep those things from coming back into your body and soul. You have to understand very clearly that there is a risk of even worse suffering for you, and that the only way to insure that you will be safe, is to surrender your life to Jesus Christ. Then, and only then, you will have the Holy Ghost to help you." He stood up. "Think it over carefully, child... very, very carefully."

He then turned to speak to Marilyn and George. "Now, it is very important for you two to realize that you also have no power to control the demonic influences in your daughter.

That is because you do not have the protection of the Blood of Jesus, and therefore no help from the Holy Ghost to even protect *yourselves*. I tell you, Mr. and Mrs. Foxx, that these evil spirits can see and hear what is going on right now, and they saw and heard all that went on last Thursday. I honestly believe that, if it had not been for the prayers of this group," he motioned to his wife and the Collinses, "those demonic things could have caused you to have been injured in your sleep, or worse, in just the last two days… and you know your family member, your sweet daughter, was the person through whom they would have acted, do you not?"

The parents sat white-faced before him.

"I will conclude with this one statement: God is love, personified. He does not force anyone to love Him. We each have to decide that for ourselves. And at some point in our lives, we will have to do just that. I'm only showing you that you have no power, no protection from evil, on your own." He let them think about it. "Now, you can either reach out in full trust, or you can go forth into your own failure… and fail you will." He moved a little closer. "Any time you two decide you want God's loving protection for both yourselves and for Roxanne, just let me know. I would be happy to lead you in a prayer of repentance, and surrender to Jesus Christ."

George shifted his feet a little. "Uh, I need to think about it, myself. I got baptized when I was a baby. I figure that covers it."

"But have you ever accepted Jesus as your personal Savior?"

"Uh, I think … anyway, I need to think about it." He glanced at Marilyn, who was looking hard at her beautiful girl. Then she got up and went to kneel at the sofa beside her daughter.

"Honey," she whispered, "we need to do this, or you won't be safe."

"But, Mom, I need to think about it, too."

"But, how will we even *sleep* at night, Roxanne? We don't know what might happen."

The beautiful redhead saw the fear in her mother's eyes, and reached out for a hug. "Okay, Mom, if it will make you feel better."

Three minutes later, the two had recited the prayer after Deacon Foster. Connie and Don hugged them both, but Rehema Foster stood back and watched, without a word.

Before the foursome went out the door, Deacon Foster took time to remind Marilyn that she could control any evil uprising in her girl, by using the phrase, "In the Name of Jesus, I command you." He made sure she repeated that phrase out loud, *three times*; then the little group departed.

The Studebaker wound around the Essex Junction intersection and exited to head for Jericho.

"Well, step two of the exorcism has been accomplished," Don happily proclaimed.

"Yes, Roxanne has been made aware of the demons," the deacon agreed.

"On top of that," Connie exclaimed, "Marilyn and Roxie both got saved."

"We hope so," Deacon Foster said quietly.

"What does that mean?" Connie asked.

"All we can do is lead them through the prayer, Sister." Rehema's words splashed a little cold water on Connie's fervor. She let her husband finish the statement.

"We lead them in the prayer, but we don't always know whether they were sincere. I think we will have to stand back and wait on this one."

CHAPTER TWENTY-NINE

Gaslighting

It was a couple of hours after the Collinses and Fosters left for Jericho that Roxie woke up from a nap on the sofa. George had gone out to gas up the car, and had slammed the front door as he reentered the house. She blinked, then glared at him before she turned over carefully for a few more winks. The morning pain pill was still working, dulling her senses in the process.

George pulled off his heavy jacket, gave it a little shake, then hung it up in the guest closet. He paused in front of the full-length mirror on the inside of the door to smooth back his hair, then crossed the room toward the dining area. Marilyn met him in that doorway.

"You told her yet?" he whispered.

"Not yet. She's been sleeping."

"Well, we have to do it *today*, Marilyn. It's really important. That phone call from the lawyer was no joke, let me tell ya."

She nervously pressed both hands together, as though in prayer. "I know. I understand. I was just waiting until the right time." She looked helplessly at her tall, dark husband. "And the truth is… I just don't know, George. How do I do this?"

The guy answered with a guy answer. "Just tell her right out and out. No more fun and games with Bill Flannigan. No contacts with him or his wife, and no trespassing on their property." He shrugged his shoulders. "That's it. Simple."

"Maybe you should tell her," she suggested.

"No problem." He turned and spoke in a loud voice: "I'll tell her the very minute she comes in out of the foggy-foggy dew." He moved over toward the couch.

"No—! Wait, George!" she moved quickly between him and the girl. "I... I think maybe I *should* be the one to do it."

He was raising his voice, now. "Then *do* it, Marilyn! We can't waste any more time."

"Do what?" the sleepy voice came from the sofa.

Marilyn shot a frantic look at the man, then turned to her daughter, a weak smile on her face. "Well, you sure slept hard, there, little lady." She bent down and helped Roxie get back into sitting position. "Are you feeling better, honey?" she asked lightly, with a little tilt of her head.

"Eh-hh," she replied. "I'm tired of this pill stuff. All I do is pass out."

"I know, sweetheart, but on Tuesday we see the doctor. Maybe, by then..."

Roxie noticed her stepfather standing a few feet away, his hands shoved deeply into the front pockets of his uniform's pants. She eyed him suspiciously. "You look like you're waiting for something," she murmured.

George shifted his weight, then backed off and sat down heavily into his recliner. Roxie looked back at her mother, who was fussing with the afghan covering her beautiful daughter's legs. "So what is it you have to do, Mom?"

Marilyn slipped onto the sofa beside Roxie. One silvery gaze met the other. "Roxanne, George has received an upsetting phone call from a lawyer." She paused, trying to get the right words. "He has been warned that he could lose his job... but worse than that," she cleared her throat to keep her voice steady, "we've been informed that the authorities could take you out of... could take you away from me." The tears were welling up in the mother's eyes.

Roxie sat up a little straighter. "What lawyer, Mom?"

Marilyn went on to explain, little-by-little, in a shaky, but determined manner, the whole situation. At the end, Roxie's eyelids were lowered, and her nostrils were flaring, but she was sitting very still.

"We're at the end of our rope, honey."

Slowly, she lifted her gaze back to her mother. "Yeah." There seemed to be no fight in that reply. She sighed deeply. "I guess we need to make some changes, Mom."

"You really mean that, Roxanne?"

She leaned back into the pillows as she answered her mother. "Aw, crap. I'm just so darned tired of all of it, Mom. I can't do this anymore." She opened her arms for a hug. "Let's start all over, okay?"

"Oh-hh," Marilyn sighed as she reached forward to wrap her arms around her darling girl. "I am *so* glad to hear that."

After a long, reassuring embrace, she drew back, regaining her composure. "So, it's time for a little lunch. Guess what? I got some lobster over at the IGA yesterday. You can have a lobster roll sandwich!"

"Really?" Roxanne squealed, in her little girl voice.

"Really."

As Marilyn rose and went into the kitchen, Roxie froze under the icy stare of her stepfather.

"And you are to stay away from that poor little dog, too. Understand that?" he said.

The nostrils flared again. "Understand that," she said, as she lowered her head back onto the pillows and closed her eyes.

George Foxx noted the steely set of that young jaw, and sat there for a while, thinking and watching.

When he finally left for work, there was a sense of relief to be out of that house, but fear was still churning down deep in his gut. He wasn't at all sure that girl had meant one, single word of that prayer with Deacon Foster. Only time would tell.

The December meeting of the Maple Leaf Sewing Circle was being held at Gracie Allen's home over there on Main Street in Essex Junction. The ladies had been asked to arrive somewhere around nine-thirty in the morning, since the weather was not cooperating at all. A snowstorm was predicted by WJOY radio to hit in the early afternoon of this deceptively sunny Saturday.

Lily White was the first to arrive, bent on helping her best friend to set up before the rest of the group arrived. She put her meatloaf into the oven and turned the temperature knob to two hundred degrees, then went right to work, sweeping up the debris around the back door, where Gracie's two sons had been faithfully stomping winter off their boots. At a quarter-to-nine, Gracie descended the stairs from bathroom-cleaning chores. She called out to Lily.

"Hey, girl! Are those potatoes done boiling yet?"

"Turned them off, and drained them already. You want butter on them, or what?"

"Yup, and a little garlic salt, as well." She was checking cushions for popcorn when the door buzzer signaled another arrival.

"I had to take the bus," April said. "Bill has the car today, and Connie is at a healing service somewhere." She pulled her boots off and slipped her feet into a pair of crocheted slippers. "I couldn't haul a casserole on the bus, so I brought cookies. They're good, though."

By nine-thirty, the rest of the group had arrived. Laura Wilson rode in with Winnie, as did Shirley Bogue, who had trudged through the snow of Case Road to the Thompson farm. Anna had also walked, carrying a Tupperware full of green salad, but she lived only a few blocks away, just like Lily. After coffee and tea were served, the six ladies settled into their crafters' fellowship routine. Winnie started the conversation which always accompanied the flurry of handiwork-in-process.

"Can you believe Christmas is only a few weeks away?" She looked up briefly. "What's everybody doing this year?"

"Oh my goodness," Gracie was quick to respond. "We are going to have the greatest Christmas pageant over at the church this year. Aren't we, Lily?"

"Oh yeah. I am *so* looking forward to it." She flipped something around on her lap, then looked up at the ladies. "You would not believe how cute those kids are."

Gracie nodded. "Not only are they cute, but the music is super-special." She dropped her handiwork for a moment. "You know, every family in the world should attend a Christmas pageant."

Shirley pulled a red ribbon of embroidery floss through her redwork project. "I would like to go," she blurted out. "Now that I've started back to church again, I'm really wanting to take my kids to see cool stuff like that."

"Good for you, Shirley," Anna sang out. "And don't forget, we have midnight Mass on Christmas Eve."

"I've been to that a couple of times," Lily said. "Talk about drama… it was so intriguing, with all the chanting and the incense and all."

"Do you mind if I ask why you decided to start going to church again?" It was Laura speaking, rather shyly.

"That damned tapping in the walls, that's why." Shirley saw Winnie's slight flinch. "Sorry, Winnie, but it's the truth." She poked the needle into the fabric and looked up again. "Just can't figure it out. Father Tom told us to keep open Bibles in all the rooms. It seems to work, but whenever we try to stop doing that, it's not long before it comes back again."

Lily was curious. "Just exactly what does it sound like?"

"Um… sort of like somebody has a stick, and taps it on a certain spot, then moves to some other place, or another room, and taps it some more. It's really creepy. My kids are scared to death." She bit her lip. "Sorry, Win."

"When did all this start happening?" the police dispatcher wondered.

"Aw, I don't really know, but Father Tom seems to think it might have had something to do with fooling around with that Ouija board." She corrected herself. "No, wait. He thought maybe it was the twins. They made their own board from cardboard, can you believe that? Who would ever have thought..." She pulled the floss through the cloth and held it in place for the next stitch. "Anyway, Father thinks maybe they might have contacted somebody or something in — what did he call it? Oh yeah, 'the supernatural.'"

"Oh boy," April cautioned, "that could be big trouble."

Laura laid down her practice piece of hand quilting, a serious look on her face. "You say the tapping sounds like a stick being struck on the wall?" Shirley nodded a confirmation. Laura looked even more thoughtful as she followed through with the next question. "Aren't the walls in that old house made with lath and plaster?" She looked at Winnie, who hesitantly verified that. "So, it would sound a lot like somebody tapping a cane on a porch deck, wouldn't you say?"

It took a couple of seconds.

"Oh... my... goodness," Anna whispered.

Lily stared at Laura a couple of seconds more. "Na-a-ah, I don't believe that."

Laura picked up her quilting again. "Just a thought. I mean, that *is* my main memory of that old lady." She squinted at the last three stitches. "But you would have to believe in ghosts, I guess, to have that happening now." She pulled the thread out of the tiny quilting sharp she was using, then poked the tip of that small needle under the last stitch and pulled it out. "As for me, I happen to believe they are very real."

"So do I," Anna volunteered. "Only they happen to be fallen angels and demons."

Laura did not press the issue. After all, it was a little far-fetched, thinking the woman, or *something* would actually be haunting the house. The subject changed, since it was nearing lunchtime.

"Where is Scottie today?" Anna asked, as the ladies sat down to meatloaf and mashed potatoes. "We always enjoy a little conversation with him, whenever we come over here."

"The ski club went up to Stowe today," his mother informed her.

"Wow, that's great. But I bet not all of them could afford *that* trip."

"Right. That one costs quite a bit more," Grace agreed. "At any rate, I hope they have sense to come back before the weather gets nasty."

At one o'clock the ladies started to pack up. Shirley looked at her watch. "This is good, 'cause we have to pick up Marsha from the greenhouse. She came down with us, to get in a few more hours. And, heaven knows, Mrs. Donahue could use all the help she can get right now, what with all that's happened with her boy."

She suddenly realized the ladies were all giving her "the look."

"Oh, sorry. Didn't mean to bring that up." She dropped her redwork into her bag, then stopped, as though hit by a sudden thought. "Nope, I'm not sorry." She stood up and faced the other five. "Something bad has happened, and I'm not going to pretend it didn't."

"Well, there are a couple of us here who really cannot discuss the case, hon," Gracie reminded her. "So, that's why we've been avoiding it."

"That's all well and good," the woman countered, "but there's something weird about *that* situation, too. It's like we have stuff happening all around us, and no natural explanations for any of it, for Pete's sake." She pulled on her coat and turned around to face the ladies again. "Somebody better get their head out of… the sand."

"What do you mean by that, dear?" Gracie really wanted to know.

"Probably has something to do with denial, or the lack of prayer, or something like that, for Pete's sake."

Anna stepped up to help this inarticulate saint. "Well," she laughed sweetly, "you're right on the money with that one, Shirley. More people in Chittenden County should be on their knees over this stuff." She opened the door to leave.

"Don't hold your breath," Laura remarked, as they walked out into the falling snow.

***

That evening, a collective sigh of relief went forth, that the ski club made it back to EJHS safely, even though it was dark and the bus had traveled most of the way back in nearly four inches of fresh snow. Parents chauffeured their youngsters home as quickly as possible, because another two inches was forecast before the night was over. There were cars sliding off the main roads, and the village, itself, had already had a couple of fender benders.

Little wonder that the Collinses and Fosters accepted the invitation to stay overnight at the Jericho parsonage. The couples actually enjoyed some private time with the local pastor and his family, and then the four left early on Sunday morning, to make the ten o'clock service out on Swift Street. By the time they passed through Essex Junction, Route 15 had been plowed, and they were able to travel more efficiently. They barely made it to the service, just off Shelburne Road.

But they had not had enough time to stop by the Foxx residence, where George was spending his day off taking care of a very quiet Roxanne. The television was on, broadcasting a sports show, but Roxie still wanted to go out into the living room, rather than to be cooped up in her little bedroom. The day before, Marilyn had once more moved the telephone to a TV tray right beside the sofa, so her girl could call any of her teachers, in case there were questions on school assignments.

For most of the morning, the beautiful patient snoozed, then dutifully practiced sitting up straight with her feet on the floor, as the doctor had ordered… an exercise she was supposed to commence three days before she went in for her first follow-up. When George brought her the lunch Marilyn had prepared before leaving for work, the girl thanked him and ate every bit of it. As the afternoon approached, she took the pills he brought her, without complaint. Then, as the game ended, she told her stepfather that she was fine, and he could even go take a nap, if he wanted.

"Nah, I'm supposed to be here if you need me," he spoke through a yawn.

"Tell you what… you know that cheerleader whistle I have on my dresser? Just bring me that, and if I need you, I'll blow on it." She smirked. "Nobody can sleep through that!"

He pondered that, briefly, then went and got the whistle. As he handed it to her, he warned her. "Don't blow on this unless it's necessary. It will probably hurt your gut."

"No problem. I probably won't even need it."

"Okay. Need anything else before I go lie down?"

"Nope. I'm going to be real sleepy, here, in a few minutes."

She waited quietly, until she heard the snoring. Then she reached for the telephone.

"Number, please?" The operator's voice sounded as near as the phone itself.

"Eight, four-seven-one-one."

"Thank you."

She could hear the phone ringing at the other end. After the third ring, someone picked it up.

"Hello?"

She recognized April's voice. Quickly, she brought the mouthpiece close to her nose and started to breathe heavily through her nose.

"Hello?" April answered again.

Roxie smiled to herself, but kept the heavy breathing going. A few more seconds passed, and the girl was having a little trouble trying not to laugh.

There was a click as April hung up her phone.

An explosive, snorting laugh escaped as she hung up, to be immediately checked, as she listened to see if she had been heard by her stepfather. The rhythmic rattle of his snoring from the bedroom down at the end of the hall reassured her that she had not.

She waited for ten minutes, then picked up the phone. Again the operator connected her with the four-seven-one-one number.

"Hello?" April answered again.

Delighted, Roxie commenced breathing, as heavily as before, but this time she made soft little moans between breaths.

April uttered a disgusted grunt and hung up. At that, Roxie gave a barely audible hoot-laugh. She lay back against the pillows for a whole half-hour, before she made the next call.

"Hello?" the voice was a little apprehensive.

This time, Roxie covered the mouthpiece, and stayed quiet. April stayed on the line for a short time, then hung up.

The redhead put the phone back on its cradle and smothered a gleeful laugh with one of her pillows. This was even better than she thought.

She heard the toilet flush. George was up. The clock on top of the television read four o'clock. Quickly, she lay back against the pillows, dropped her chin, and closed her eyes. When she heard him enter the room, she opened them sleepily.

"Good. You're awake," George noted. "Still got that whistle?"

She pretended to look for it. "It's right here, somewhere... yup, right here."

"Okay, I can't wait too much longer to shovel out the driveway, or your mother won't be able to get in. You gonna be okay for a little while longer?"

She yawned. "No problem." She let her lids droop partway over her eyes, keeping track of him as he came and went, getting ready to go out. At last, he stood at the sliding door and reached outside for the snow shovel. She laughed inwardly as he trudged through the living room with it... something Marilyn would have objected to, for sure. At the front door, he glanced over at her. She opened her eyes wide and waved him out the door.

He had shoveled all the way down to the end of the sidewalk, and was starting on the driveway, when she picked up the telephone again. Twenty minutes had passed since her last taunting call.

April answered cautiously. Roxie held her hand over the mouthpiece and snickered quietly. Then she heard the thud of April's phone being laid down. She listened intently. There was a softly spoken word or two, and she knew immediately that Bill was now home. Quickly, she hung up the phone.

The fun was over for today.

***

On Monday, both George and Marilyn had to work, so Rehema took the early bus to Essex Junction and arrived at seven-thirty, just in time to see them both off. The morning was filled with breakfast, bathing, and gentle exercises which, to the nurse's relief, were all accomplished without strife. In fact, the patient seemed in good spirits and ready for a pleasant day. "Only two more days," she chirped at her lovely helper, "until I see the doctor."

"And you started your exercises yesterday like a good girl?"

"Yup! Nothing to it." She allowed Rehema to fix the pillows behind her on the sofa. As the nurse started to move the phone and tray out of the way, however, she made a strong objection. "Don't do that! I need to talk to one of my teachers." She cast a threatening look at the woman. "Don't you *dare* mess me up on that!"

At nine in the morning, Rehema went into the girl's bedroom to change the bed and wipe up the floor. No sooner had she left the room than Roxie reached for the phone and asked for the four-seven-one-one number.

A breathless April answered, obviously in the middle of morning chores. Roxie covered the mouthpiece and waited. Sure enough, April hung up after a brief pause. The girl leaned back. "Good morning," she murmured with a snorting little hoot.

The next call was made about two hours later, while Rehema was supposedly fixing something in the kitchen. Suddenly, the lovely black woman walked in while Roxie was holding the phone by the mouthpiece. Roxie jumped, but then acted like she was waiting for someone to come to the phone. As Rehema was crossing the room, April had hung up again, so the girl slammed the phone down. The woman turned around at the sound of the phone being clacked so hard onto its cradle.

"Is something wrong, Roxanne?"

"Aw, I have to call back in an hour or so."

The compassionate lady noted that would be closer to the teacher's noon hour. "Now, that makes sense, don't you think?" She was placing a dry rug down on the floor just inside the front closet, to catch the drips off winter boots. Noticing a smudge on the bottom of the door's inside mirror, she pulled a soft cloth from her pocket and began to wipe it off.

"Yeah, ri-ight." The nurse's back was toward her, so Roxie felt free to cast a disgusted smirk toward the lady, at the same time, shaking her head incredulously at what she obviously considered to be a *clue-less dingbat*. Then, with a disdainful roll of her eyes, she looked away.

She didn't realize Rehema caught the whole thing, reflected in the closet door's mirror.

For a little while, the nurse was busy in the kitchen, moving back and forth near the door between her workplace and the living room. Once, in passing, she saw Roxie on the phone, again with her hand covering the mouthpiece. She paused and watched as the girl listened intently, then hung up.

"Did you get through, child?"

"What?" She had been unaware of the woman watching her, so great was her concentration. "Uh, no… I mean yes, but she's going to call me back." The nostrils were flaring. "Whatever you do, stay off this phone. I need to get this call."

"Well then, we may as well enjoy our lunch." Rehema disappeared from sight and then reappeared with another TV tray, which she placed beside the one with the phone on it. "I have a special surprise for you," she sang out. Roxie did not seem to care. A worried look covered her face.

The nurse companion bustled into the kitchen, returning with a half-sandwich and a tall glass. As she placed it on the tray, she smiled. "Look, Roxanne. A lettuce-and-tomato sandwich, and" — she made a big flourish with both hands — a lovely strawberry milkshake!"

Roxie drew back in disgust. "You *know* I hate lettuce and tomato sandwiches! Take it away!"

"Oh, of course! I knew that, didn't I? Well then, just enjoy the milkshake." She picked up the half-sandwich. "I will have this for *my* lunch."

The nurse sat down across the room and took a lady-like bite of the sandwich. Roxie picked up the milkshake and stared at it. As she got ready for the second bite, Rehema asked, "Is there anything else you would like to have, Roxanne?"

"Nothing you can get, that's for sure." With that remark, she took a long draw on the straw of the creamy drink. It was cold, and she coughed just a little, but it was undeniably delicious. She wiped her mouth with the forefinger of her left hand, then took another, smaller sip.

Less than an hour later, Roxanne Foxx was down for a nap in her own bed.

Rehema Foster went out into the living room and lifted the receiver on the telephone. No operator asked for a number, but there was definitely something coming through. She could hear movement and a radio in the background.

"Hello?" she said. Then she tried again, a little louder. On the third try, the sound of the other phone being moved came through the line. There was a brief pause, then a woman's voice said cautiously, "Hello?"

"Oh, hello, ma'am. This is Rehema Foster speaking. I am sorry to bother you, but I believe our telephones were connected, and something has happened where they never were disconnected. Am I correct?"

"Y-yes… that is correct." The lady went on to ask quickly, "Did you call me earlier?"

"No, ma'am, I did not, but I believe my patient may have mistakenly called your number."

"Your patient?"

"Yes, ma'am."

Again, there was a hesitation, but the woman finally put it out there: "May I ask, is your patient's name… Roxanne?"

"Oh my goodness, ma'am… that is correct." She waited long enough to get the information she needed.

"Well, my name is April Flannigan. Does that mean anything to you?"

"I… I believe I know that name, yes."

"Well, Miss Foster, your patient has been calling me now for two days. At first she was doing the heavy breathing thing, and then she switched to the dead silence thing."

"Oh, my-my. I am so sorry, Mrs. Flannigan. I will try to take care of that. Does your husband know?"

"He doesn't believe me."

"Oh. Well, I think it would be important for Roxanne's counselor, Mr. Collins, to know about this. He will give you very good advice, I am sure."

"I will do that, right away."

"Excellent. And again, I am so sorry, Mrs. Flannigan."

When Don answered the phone, she was brief and to the point.

"Oh darn, April. I'm sorry to hear this, because we had hoped..." He decided to keep to the problem at hand. "Whatever you do, don't do anything that will cause George Foxx any more pressure. The man is right on the edge, as it is. Let me handle this, alright?"

"Well, okay, but somebody has to get her under control."

"I agree. But we have to be careful not to involve social workers, or we could lose the opportunity to do the job right: God's way. Otherwise, she may never overcome this demonic thing." He went on to emphasize his point, and then the conversation ended.

April Flannigan hung up the phone. After thinking it over for a short time, she made a call to the Essex Junction Police Department, asking to speak to Chief Allen. As soon as he came on the line, she cautioned him to keep this information to himself, so that there would be no interference from authorities with what their lawyer was trying to do.

"But I thought you should be aware of this," she said.

"I'm listening."

The hateful behavior was reported, and then the call was over.

Chief Allen slammed the phone down on its cradle, and rose angrily to his feet. Agitation overcame professionalism, as he began to pace back and forth in front of his desk. On the fifth pass, he suddenly stopped to stare at the floor.

"I swear… somebody's gonna *kill* that kid."

CHAPTER THIRTY

Changes

Winnie needed to find the powdered sugar. She was in the pantry, which was located through an open doorway from the kitchen into a small area under the back stairway up to Uncle's apartment. On the other side of the uninsulated panty wall, Cecil and Uncle were finishing washing up at the laundry sink before breakfast. Even though she was separated from them by the hallway and the bathroom, she could hear the hum of their conversation and the shuffle of their slippers as they moved along toward the kitchen. There was no deliberate effort to hide — she was just standing there, trying to remember where she had stashed that seldom-used tin of sugar — but the little lady was completely concealed from their view as they came into the aroma-filled room. She heard them stop, and there was a little space of silence.

"She must be back in the bedroom." It was Uncle, speaking in a low voice.

"Good, because I want some details on just why you can't be here for milking tonight, and I have a pretty good idea, you don't want to talk about that in front of her."

There was the scrape of a chair being pulled out from the table. Uncle spoke up again, still keeping his voice down. "Aw, it's that gawdim girl again."

"What did you say her name was?"

"Roxie… Foxx, I think. Yeah, that's it."

"What about her?"

"She's mad as hail at me."

"What for?"

The little man snickered softly. "Thinks I'm on to her and her frickin' tactics." Another scrape of a chair. "And she's gawdim right. I been onto her for quite some time, me."

"So what's the problem?"

"Just want to make sure she doesn't add me to her list of those other three poor bah-serds."

"Tell me again… who are they?"

Winnie could hear the sigh that came just before he lowered his voice even more. "Those two gawdim bus drivers and that Ted guy." She heard Ceese grunt in acknowledgment. "I just need to spend a little time with my cousin and my uncle, after the poker game."

Impatience infused his boss's words: "I suppose I have to let you do this, after you coming in early on Saturday morning." There was a little belch. "…for all the good it'll do…"

There was no graceful way for her to get out of this, so she dropped a heavy jar on the old pantry floor. "Darn!" she exclaimed softly. Then she poked her head around the corner and peered out at the breakfast table. "Oh good. Ceese, can you help me get this tin down off the top shelf?"

She ignored the suspicious looks all through breakfast, never letting on that she had heard a word. It was in the car, just as they moved through the Essex Junction traffic circle, that Uncle informed her that he would be late getting back from his game, and would come home on the bus.

"It's okay with Ceese," he added.

She steered the car up the gradual hill past Lincoln Hall. "As long as you cleared it with him," she said.

***

Early that afternoon, Rehema arrived at the Foxx residence, so Marilyn could work the swing shift at The Harvest. Roxie was in her room, doing gentle stretches, getting ready for her doctor's check-up the next day.

"I'll take over, Mrs. Foxx. You go ahead and get ready to go."

Marilyn was pleased. "I could make a couple of stops before work!" And so, she said an early goodbye and was out the door by one o'clock.

Rehema quickly moved the phone and the tray away from the sofa, replacing them with a kitchen chair. Then she went in to check on her patient.

The girl's eyes sparkled as she exclaimed, "Look! I don't have to use the wheelchair anymore!" She stood up slowly and took a few careful steps toward the door.

"Wonderful!" Rehema offered her arm for support and Roxie gladly took it, as the two of them made it slowly out to the sofa. Before she even sat down, however, the redhead came to a wobbly stop.

"Where is my telephone, and why is there a chair there?"

"O-oh," Mama Rehema sang softly. "I have a surprise for you. Now turn around and sit down slowly, child." She guided the girl into place, then lifted her feet and covered her legs with the afghan. "How's that? Are you comfortable?" the melodious voice continued. As Roxie nodded, the nurse took a seat in the chair.

"Now then, Roxanne, you and I must have a little talk."

Over the next twenty-eight minutes, Rehema Foster had to rebuke the devils twice, to keep them from surfacing and harming either herself or the girl. In between, Roxie was fit to be tied, shrieking denials over and over, throwing anything she could get her hands on, and threatening disaster for the woman of God who clearly had outwitted her. She kept it up, until her nurse reminded her that she had to pass a physical check-up the next day, or she could be bedridden for another week. After that, the young patient sat and fumed, eyes snapping with hatred, and nostrils flaring in defiance. In addition, she could not seem to stop twisting the thin silver ring on the little finger of her left hand.

In the end, however, a bargain was struck. Rehema Foster would not tell Marilyn and George about Roxie's malicious phone calls to April Flannigan, if the girl agreed to have a counseling session with Don Collins, right there in that very same living room, on the upcoming Saturday morning... a session which would be witnessed by Mrs. Collins, Deacon Foster, and herself.

"Please understand, however, that if you make contact with the Flannigans at any time before that counseling session, I will *personally* inform your parents about *all* of it."

A low growl rumbled from the girl's throat.

"As for you, Stronghold, I bind you, in the Name of Jesus. You will *not* surface until you are summoned by a child of God. Now, BE SILENT!"

***

Winnie had forgotten that Uncle wasn't riding home after work with her. She laughed at herself, for briefly wondering why he wasn't waiting in the car at five-fifteen, as usual. Now, driving across Church Street from her Cherry Street parking spot, she decided — on a whim — to turn left onto North Winooski Avenue, and take the Intervale Avenue route toward the Winooski Bridge. It had been a while since she had traveled this street which wound slowly along the high cliff up over the flat expanse of the interval. She had followed this route many times before. The snow crunched under the tires of the old Dodge as it moved along, heading around a familiar curve.

There, a wave of nostalgia overtook her. Just ahead, she spotted the wide space of the unofficial overlook where she had so often stood dreaming about all the activities the Abenaki tribes had carried on down there. On another whim, she steered the car into a snowy parking spot against the curb, got out, and walked across the street to the edge of the drop, so that she might once more view this ancient site. Below and to her left lay the location of the aboriginal campsite, now a faded memory of another era, its fertile floodplain fields long since claimed as Ethan Allen farmlands. Somewhere even farther out there in the distant darkness, the actual Ethan Allen farmhouse stood as a historic landmark, opened to tourists only through Vermont's warmer seasons. Now, no doubt, it was boarded up, silent, and covered with snow.

From the depths of the deep violet landscape, the lonely whistle of a train echoed mournfully across this flat valley the Abenakis identified as a *pasohono*, "… a place of flood lands." She could not see the train as it snaked its way across the darkened landscape toward the Burlington depot, but she *could* just barely make out, directly below, the Winooski River in the moonlight, flowing down from the partly frozen waterfalls which rushed under and around the bridge in Winooski. She watched the glistening movement, lost for a few minutes in thoughts of her early childhood. This was not the Missisquoi River near which she had grown up over there in Swanton, but it was a definite, riveting reminder of her own past.

"Mother, why did you name me 'Winona'?" she had asked the question, haltingly, since she was still trying to learn the old language. "I am told that is a name from the western tribes of the Iroquois. Am I a lost child of the Iroquois?"

"No, little one," Marie "Yellow Flower" Smart had replied in the ancient tongue. "You are 'the firstborn daughter,' whose great-grandmother was of the Sioux tribe." A soft smile had crossed her ruddy face as the two had huddled together in the fishing boat. "You are our beautiful bridge of friendship between the Iroquois and the Algonquin."

"I am a bridge?" The little girl was confused.

"Firstborn Daughter," the loving mother had replied, "you are only one of many." Then she had drawn closer to speak softly into her child's ear. "We were all here before the white man ever made his way across our lands. We have that common thread. We do not forget that."

Winnie shivered gently as a frigid wind blew up from the interval below. *"That shared, long-ago culture,"* she thought sadly, *"is dying."*

Decades of war, devastating disease, broken treaties, and political manipulation had long since reduced both the Iroquois and Algonquin Indian confederacies to feckless meetings around the white man's varnished tables. What was left of them were loosely associated remnants of American indigenous peoples, strung out across those lands, each struggling through its next challenge, its next attempt to maintain its identity. Indeed, it seemed to her, perishing ethnicities took an agonizingly long time to die.

She wrapped her coat tighter around her knees against still another chilly blast.

The woman was determined not to spend her whole life waiting for that inevitable demise. It would certainly come, and life would go on. There would be no going back, no way to fix it. Any romantic illusion of herself as a bridge, in any sense of the word, was ridiculous. Things had gone too far already.

She bent forward and looked far off to her right, through the distant fog of a ground inversion, to where the old

Winooski Bridge was now barely visible. That distant ghostly structure had stood there as long as she, herself, could remember, through season-after-season, night-after-night, glowing softly under its own street lights. No doubt, someday it would be gone, as well, replaced by another connection stretched over the river. One thing was for sure: it would never, ever again, be the familiar, old Winooski Bridge. That link, like most worldly ones, was also temporary.

Her feet were getting cold through the soft rubber overshoes which were snapped tightly over her sensible two-inch-heeled shoes. Still, she stood in the freezing slush only a few feet off the sidewalk, staring once more down at the purple plain below, trying to compose a mental picture of those long-ago seasonal encampments of teepees and campfires and little tan-skinned children, running innocently amongst the many activities of their community, times she imagined that had been filled with happy laughter, flutes, and drums.

"I don't need to do this anymore," she reminded herself. Then she returned to her car, where she turned up the heater, and headed toward Winooski.

***

It was as she was actually driving over the Winooski Bridge that she remembered the thing that happened at Cathedral High School.

"Oh yeah, *that's* where all the frustration started."

Her father, Chief Raven's Wing, had decided to send his daughter from Swanton to live with relatives in Winooski, in order that she could attend Cathedral High School, just a few blocks west from Sears and Roebuck's location there in Burlington. There was some kind of tuition that had to be paid, but the man, who was only one of several Abenaki chiefs in the state of Vermont, had broken stride with tradition on this particular issue, determining that his only daughter would be attending a quality high school in the Queen City, and strictly in Roman Catholic doctrine. She never was sure just why he had that strong conviction, but it was what it was, and so she donned the school uniform one fine fall morning, to start the journey.

The freshman year had gone well. She was a model student, doing well in all classes, but especially in religious studies. That first year, the nuns who were her teachers happily expressed on her report card that there might even be a bright future for her in the Church. The chief had been quite pleased, although he was not of the opinion that his daughter would actually enter a convent.

However, somewhere in the middle of the sophomore year, something changed. Her report card reflected lower grades in general, but — alarmingly — there was a drastic drop in her religion classes.

Before long, the relatives pinpointed the problem: it was a renegade Abenaki lad who had landed a lucrative job at the Wilson Meatpacking Company, and was living high and wide, running around in a flashy car, looking for lovely company. He made his move one lazy November afternoon, from where he had parked his car in front of that very same Catholic high school. Before long, the little sophomore was under the spell of this flamboyant young man.

In December, Chief Raven's Wing had shown up unannounced, to pick up his daughter after school, at the start of Christmas break. "We will have some time together," he had said, as they shared some odd-tasting tea at the home of those Winooski relatives.

Three days later, she awoke on the St. Francis Reserve in Canada. The kind native women explained that her father had brought his precious daughter out of danger, carrying her by night through the woods and rivulets over the Canadian border, meeting another Abenaki chief who drove the two of them northward and into "the safe place." Once satisfied that his daughter would be comfortable in that chief's household, Raven's Wing had returned immediately to Swanton.

At first, she cried. Then she sulked. A couple of weeks later, with the encouragement of the local priest, she tried to see her father's point of view.

She spent the rest of her teen years there, amongst the descendants of those indigenous peoples who had escaped the troubled times in America, so many years ago. Some were Abenaki, many were not, but nobody seemed to be bothered by that. It was a place of refuge for the disenfranchised. While she, herself, did not feel abandoned — for she understood that her father loved her and wanted to protect her — it was still a time of painful separation from those with whom she had grown up, back there in Swanton. She missed the warmth of the many riverside Abenaki homes. She longed for the comfort of familiar voices coming from familiar faces, and the reassuring sights and sounds and aromas. She especially missed her mother, "Yellow Flower," who had watched over her and Uncle… a dear lady who had died way too young.

And she did, indeed, miss Uncle, her only "brother," Raymond René Smart, the man whom her own people called "Shining Waters." Not only were these two close Abenaki children no longer looked after by Yellow Flower, but now they were not able to look after each other, as they had in their early childhood. It was a loss deeply felt by both of them, and the many letters over the next few years never really did fill the gap.

Eventually, her experiences at the reserve resulted in a strained relationship between father and daughter, for the distant love of a father just did not make up for the endless hours, days, and years of separation from him and the family. Further, the strict Roman Catholic ethic on the reserve clashed with her own more laid-back Abenaki traditions, creating a confusing life-foundation for this young woman. There emerged, from deep in her soul, a fierce desire to figure it all out. However, the more she sought answers, the more frustrated she became. For a while, she soothed the turmoil by throwing herself whole-heartedly into helping the young people on the reservation who needed compassionate, sisterly care — the outcasts in their culture: racially mixed children, and other abandoned offspring. Seeing the energy being expended in this spiritual search, the clergy urged her to enter a convent, but something just did not feel right about that. Instead, she switched directions, spending long hours wrapped up in duties which allowed her opportunities to meditate and pray. Finally, after five years of spiritual searching, she rejected the inconsistencies of the two cultures, and settled it all with, "I was born into a dying culture, but now I choose to stop dying. Starting with this day, I am born again." Shortly thereafter, she returned to Vermont, ready to make a life for herself as a white Christian, whatever it might take. Winona "Firstborn Daughter" Smart was barely twenty-one when she arrived on a bus in Burlington, quite vulnerable and definitely dependent on her new faith.

She turned to the local church immediately, becoming a member of the Cathedral of Immaculate Conception parish, located, like Cathedral High School, right there at the edge of the old Italian district, somewhere between Sears and Roebuck and Battery Park. The ladies of the church took her in, found her a family to live with, and set out to help her find a job. At the end of five long, determined years, she had gone from sweeping floors at the dime store, to a sales clerk position at Sears.

"Then, along came Cecil Thompson... and there was my *new* safe place," she smiled, as she steered the car around the curve past Saint Michael's College. In a few minutes, she thought she would be back in her Essex farmhouse, eating and enjoying the company of both Cecil and Uncle.

Once again, she had forgotten that Uncle would actually be absent from the table.

***

Indeed, it would not be until the next evening, after chores, that she would get to talk to him. Of course, she would have to be careful in her conversation, but she was curious as to what advice her father and cousin had offered, concerning the girl.

"So, how did your poker game go, yesterday? Did you come home broke, you?" She was passing him a glass of milk to go with his dessert of apple pie and vanilla ice cream.

He smacked his lips and grinned before he took a sip. "Nope."

She watched him dig into the pie, allowing the ice cream to melt into the crevices.

"Well, that's 'a help to the community,'" she quipped. "I doubt you would keep going, if you lost too many of those little copper pennies, Uncle."

"Hah!" he laughed.

"Still, there has to be more than that... than just playing penny poker." She looked at her husband for support. "Must be the pow-wowing, I think."

"Hah!" Uncle laughed again.

"I think she means, it's the enjoyable company," Ceese murmured through a delicious mouthful.

The little warrior slipped his fork under another bite. "Ay-yuh, it is definitely frickin' good company." He was still chewing as he came to the happy conclusion. "We get along good, you know? We stick together like a bunch of burrs on a gawdim hound dog." He nodded to emphasize the point. "We help each other. We learn from each other... all kinds of frickin' things."

She slipped it right on in there. "Really? Like what?"

"All kinds of things," came the reply.

"Like for instance... what did you learn last night?"

He put down his fork, and stared at the wall, sorting through the possibilities. Finally, he got a mischievous grin on his face. Leaning over to tease his niece, he let the cat out of the bag. "Like for instance... us gawdim Abenakis know how to out-*wokw ses* the *wokw ses*...!"

Cecil looked inquiringly at his wife.

She smiled as she interpreted: "...how to out-fox the fox."

Then she rose to clear the table, satisfied that her father and cousin — and probably a few other Abenakis, were on the alert. And really, they all knew how to hide in plain sight... just like they were doing right now.

"Okay, so that part of our dying culture is still not dead," Winnie thought, as she picked up the empty plates.

She was a little surprised about how relieved she felt about that.

***

Very early on the following Saturday morning, Roxie got up. Quietly, she went out into the kitchen and carefully slipped a one-gallon clear glass storage jar from its special low cupboard space where Marilyn kept it, and took it, inch-by-inch, into her bedroom, softly closing the door behind her. There, she pushed the jar under her bed, alongside the newspaper and the scissors, then slipped back between the still-warm sheets, to think through her plan once more.

When she was satisfied that all was in order, she arose once again, drew the newspaper and scissors out from their hiding place, and brought them to her little dressing table, just beside the headboard of the matching bedstead. After spreading the paper over the top of that table, she put the scissors down upon it, and pulled open a side drawer, to slip out her hairbrush, which she also placed on top of the paper. Next, she drew forth the large jar and quietly unscrewed the white tin cover, before placing the transparent container on the floor between the bed and the dressing table bench. Finally, Roxanne Foxx sat down and took a long look at her beautiful self in the round mirror.

She was ready.

CHAPTER THIRTY-ONE

Escape

It was the Saturday before Christmas. Two things were on the day's schedule for the Foxxes: a morning counseling session for Roxie, then decorating the Christmas tree which George had brought home the night before. Marilyn rolled over in bed, smooched a light kiss on her husband's shoulder, then started her day. She showered and dressed before going up the hall to wake her daughter. The doting mother opened the door, then gasped.

"Roxanne… oh my gosh… what have you done?"

The girl was sitting at her dressing table, and she was almost bald. Only a thin layer of reddish fuzz covered her skull. She gave a cocky waggle of the head and hooted loudly, "Uh-huuuh! You should see your face!" Then she held up the glass jar, which was stuffed with the shorn tresses.

"Don't worry, Mom, you can still see it, whenever you want." Once again, there came a long, hilarious hoot.

Marilyn was not smiling. She stepped forward to inspect the haircut. "Oh, for Pete's sake, what a mess. There are long straggles all over the place."

Roxie handed her the scissors. "Yup, but I figured you wouldn't want me to go around looking like that, so-oo... have at it!"

"I should leave you this way," her mother threatened. But both of them knew she wouldn't.

When the others arrived for the counseling session, the drama queen was once again in her glory, seated at the center of attention on the sofa, with a whole new "thing" going on.

"Whatever made you cut off all that beautiful hair?" Connie was baffled.

"I'm taking my life back, that's what. What do *you* care?" came the snarky answer. Immediately, the atmosphere in the room turned tense.

"Hey!" George snapped. "Watch your mouth, girl."

Silvery eyes scowled from beneath lowered lids. "Don't call me 'girl.'"

Deacon Foster changed the subject. "Well, Roxanne, thank you so much for allowing us to come and talk with you, once more." He ignored the amused look, turning to Don. "Shall we get started?"

Before her counselor could speak, Roxie answered the question: "Not if you're still hiding mirrors in your britches, mister." She stared intently into the deacon's concerned look. "We aren't going to have any more of *that* stuff... do you understand me?" Hearing her mother draw a shocked breath, she turned to her. "No, Mom. Those are scare tactics. I've been to enough movies to know how that works." She looked back at the deacon. "I don't know how you did it, but you had me for a few minutes last time." She hooted and rolled her eyes. "Like I really have demons inside me. Oh, pul-eeze."

"Whoa, just a minute there, Roxie." Don shook his finger at her. "You forget that we all have seen them... every single one of us in this room is a witness that they are real, and they are—"

"Oh yeah? Well, how about *this*? How about it's something the whole bunch of you cooked up, just to keep me in line, huh?"

The group went into stunned silence.

"Yup, I knew it." Her voice was dripping with disdain.

Don cleared his throat before he jumped into this little game. "Well… and I suppose we all cooked up that fact that you have a lesbian girlfriend."

The girl's mouth dropped open.

"That's right," Connie said. "And guess who told us?"

Still no comment from the quivering mouth.

"*They* did." Having answered the question, Don sat back in his chair and waited. The mouth stopping trembling and slipped into a hard line, and that's when he went for the critical information. "Who is she, Roxie?"

Suddenly the eyes went narrow again. "Where did you *ever* come up with something as stupid as that? You don't really expect me to fall for that one, do you?"

Don was out of the game, but Deacon jumped right in.

He caught the nodded signal from Rehema, who had been silently praying. It was time for him to speak up. "My dear girl, we happen to know that this is true. There is really no point in your denying it."

"It is *not* true," Roxie asserted. "No such thing has ever happened to me." The anger was simmering just below the surface. "So, no bunch of demons ever said such a thing."

"Oh, young lady," the beautiful black man sang out, "…not only did they say such a thing, but we can prove it." He had her attention. "What if they told us something about this lady that we could not possibly have known? Would you believe us then?"

"Like what?" came the suspicious reply.

The big man stood up and stepped toward the sofa where she was sitting. "We know," he said in a low, steady voice, "that she is a witch."

Roxie's face went white.

The deacon sat gently down beside her. "Now, Roxanne, it is important that you tell us about this witch. We need to know more about the situation, so that you can get out from under whatever power she has over you. And believe me... she *does* have some sort of spiritual hold over you. It is a power which must be broken, and it must be broken with your complete cooperation. Do you understand?"

The fuzzy-haired head drooped. "I guess."

"Very good." He leaned forward, elbows on the knees, to press his folded hands against his lips for a second. Without looking at her, he went on: "So please tell us who she is."

"I... I can't."

He kept his eyes to the front. "Oh." He sounded disappointed. "And may I ask why?"

"She's... mad enough, *already*." Her fingers were tapping together, down there on her lap. "And I really don't want to make it worse."

"I'm sure you don't," he said with sympathy. "Perhaps you can make it up to her, by correcting this offense which has caused a problem between you." Now he turned to engage on a more personal level. "My-oh-my, whatever did you do to cause all those bad feelings?"

The fingers were raised to about six inches in front of her face, tapping, tapping, tapping, as she seemed to regain her composure. "I... cost her a who-ole bunch of money."

"O-ooh yes. Money," he hummed. "That can cause a lot of serious trouble."

He leaned back, folding his arms loosely. "Paying back a lot of money would probably be very nearly impossible for a youngster like you... no matter how much you would like to have your friend back. In fact, your dear friend — what was her name...?"

Unfortunately, the pause was too long after the question. The game was over.

Now she was mad. She stood straight up off the sofa. "Oh no you don't!" She focused her fury upon the deacon. "You want to know the name of my dear friend, mister? *Fine.* I'll tell you what... let's just call her 'my dear friend, Lezzy.' Everybody understands that name, right?" The nostrils flared white. "Yeah! Let's go with that, because it just so happens that my very dear friend *is* my very dear Lezzy. She's *my* 'Dear Lezzy'... and I'm not apologizing one bit for that!" The defiant words were delivered with spittle into the wincing face of the godly gentleman. "You got that? Huh?" Another hoot escaped. "And that's all you're gonna get out of me on *that* subject."

But she wasn't finished.

She whirled around to address the rest of those in the room. "Somebody asked me why I cut my hair. Well, I have the answer." She moved closer to Rehema. "I've already told *you*, but now," she whirled around again, "let me inform the rest of you. I am so tired of being questioned and tormented by you people. I am tired of pills and wheelchairs and nosy, hovering helpers. I want it all out of my hair. I'm serious." Her hands went to her hips as she proceeded to take charge. "I am done with being an invalid, done with being kept away from my friends, done with people interfering in my life, and I am *done, done, done* with any more of this stupid counseling crap!" She reached up and ran her fingers through the stubble on her head. "I cut my hair, because I want all that stuff out of it. It's symbolic, okay?"

No one said a word.

Emitting a short, snotty hoot, the girl hobbled toward the kitchen door, where she turned back toward the six of them, for one last shot. "Now, if you don't live here, get out, and let me have Christmas with my folks."

In the few minutes that followed, there were apologies and hugs and manly slaps of reassurance upon the backs, and then the two couples left.

That was the last time Roxie ever saw Deacon and Rehema Foster. The lovely black couple returned home that night, then left three weeks later, for a long-term mission assignment into the deep, dark recesses of the African continent, returning to Canada only for brief periods, for the rest of their lives.

Obviously, if there was ever to be an exorcism in Roxanne Foxx's case, Deacon Foster would not be doing the honors.

***

Chief Rob Allen grabbed the leash from its hook near the front entrance to the Essex Junction Police Department's front desk. It was near closing of his Monday shift on December 22. Lily smiled as her boss stomped out the door, fully intent on a final confrontation with the Donahues, concerning the latest escapades of the Traffic Circle Terror.

"Here, Blow! Here, boy!" Robbie called out across the snowy intersection. The dog looked up, recognizing a friend, and came bounding over, his tongue flapping happily in this moment of delirious freedom. The officer rubbed some snow off the ebony ears, laughing as genuinely as he could muster. "Hey, boy. Hey, guy. Got snow all over ya..." He quickly snapped the chain onto the dog's collar. The woefully ugly dog jumped up to lick his face.

"Aw, jeez..." For five minutes, Robbie Allen walked the bedraggled mutt around the sidewalks, eventually leading him to the back door of the Donahue home. Behind him, the lights of the greenhouse glowed faintly through the opaque structure as he rapped sharply on the worn door. Emma opened it.

"Oh no," she said, "not again."

"Ay-yuh," Robbie said. "...again."

"Aw, Chief... it's been so insane around here." She stepped back. "Come on in. We need to talk."

As he entered, he saw Paula seated at the opposite side of the kitchen table. When she looked up, he was arrested at the sight of weary eyes, set deeply above hollowed cheeks. This was not the perky little cheerleader he had seen at the EJHS games over this last season. Slowly, the fervor of his mission subsided.

"We in trouble again?" Paula asked, as Emma unhitched the dog.

"Um... just don't want any more stuff happening to you folks. You've had enough already, God knows."

The three of them watched as the big dog flopped heavily into his bed beside the kitchen stove. Then Emma motioned an invitation for the chief to sit down at the table.

"I'd offer you coffee, but we're just about out," she apologized.

"Hey, too late for that, anyway," he laughed lightly. "I've had my ration for the day." He rubbed the top of one knee, looking around in the chilly kitchen. "How's it going for you two?"

The two exchanged a look.

"Getting through it," Emma said.

"Barely..." Paula was not looking at him.

There was a long pause, but finally, Emma spoke up. "Chief, you're head of the Essex Junction Police Department." She took a big breath. "I assume you have heard from Sheriff Duncan... that our Teddy has told, by the blinking of his eyes, that Roxie was the one who attacked him... and, possibly, her very own self."

The chief clenched his teeth, to suppress his reaction. "I did not know that you were aware of this development in the investigation," he answered, truthfully. "I am so sorry... I know this has to be hard for you."

"I can't wrap my mind around that girl having that kind of strength," Emma said.

"Well, you're certainly not alone on that one," Chief Allen conceded. He quickly changed the conversation to the matter of Blow chasing cars in the intersection.

At the end of the conversation, it was agreed that poor pooch would be adopted out, preferably to a farm family in the Lost Nation area, where he could run wild and free.

It was neither realistic nor practical, but it worked for the moment. The chief issued no ticket.

When Robbie got back to his office, the night shift was on. Still, he knew he had to notify Bill Flannigan's lawyer that the authorities were aware that Ted was pinpointing Roxie as the perpetrator of the attack which left him paralyzed, and her injured to the point where she had had a miscarriage. Whether or not social services would believe his testimony was questionable. One thing was for sure: Roxie, if caught, would not go down alone. She would take the Flannigans down with her, April being part of the collateral damage. The only possible exoneration for Bill was the demonic possession situation. Rob Allen was not sure about the demon thing, but knew this troubled girl could ruin lives, and so he went into action.

He called Don Collins, in order to keep himself from any accidental phone contact with Bill. April needed to get the information to their lawyer, and this was the safest way to reach her. Robbie was sure this was going to come down to legal actions on both sides of the situation. Eventually, Sheriff Duncan would find out about Mr. Courtney, and the police chief wasn't taking any chances that his own name would come up in the investigation or negotiations.

Don was clearly surprised. "Chief! You've known all this time, it was Roxie? Wow! I guess the rest of us just never thought about Ted blinking his eyes."

"Yeah, who would have thought? Anyway, social services is bound to get in on this now, Don." His voice was serious. "I think it's important their lawyer is alerted. Mr. Flannigan is gonna need a good, solid reason for clemency."

***

The next morning, there was a knock on the door. George Foxx answered it, since Marilyn had taken Roxie in to Burlington for her final medical check-up. He was in a hurry, because he would be hopping the bus to get to work, so when he opened the door, his heart sank.

It was Sheriff Max Duncan. A woman stood behind him, and behind her, a deputy shivered and shoved his hands into the front pockets of his jacket.

The conversation was short. They were after Roxie. She was wanted for questioning. Social services was investigating. Where was she?

George answered honestly, and the three of them hurried to the car, headed for Burlington.

He stood there for a minute, before he picked up the phone. The receptionist at the doctor's office handed the phone to Marilyn.

"They're coming for Roxie," he said.

Roxie had followed her mother to the desk, curious. She watched the face pale, and moved closer.

"No, they can't take her away from me... but she hasn't done anything... what do you mean she is wanted for questioning? What? They're coming here? Right now?" She was crying now. "Do something, George, for God's sake!" The receptionist sought to assist her, bringing her a tissue, but the weeping turned into panic. The nurse came out from the treatment room and took the wailing woman back where it was more private. The receptionist explained to George and hung up. Suddenly, Marilyn and the nurse came back out.

"Roxanne!" the mother called out into the crowded waiting room. There was no answer. People just sat there, staring. She looked at the receptionist, who bustled down the hall to check the restroom. The woman was back in an instant, shaking her head "No."

"Roxanne!" Marilyn's panic went up another notch. Frantically, she ran to the second-story window and looked down on College Street, just in time to see the girl crossing to the other side. She knew it was Roxie, because she recognized the new navy blue watch cap, bought just a few days ago to cover her bare head, and carefully chosen to coordinate with the Navy pea coat she was wearing.

Suddenly, the girl glanced back toward the building, spotting her mother in the window. She came to a halt and pointed to herself, mouthing the words, "I'll be fine." She gave her mom a "thumbs-up," blew her a kiss, and then disappeared into an alley.

When the sheriff and his entourage arrived at the doctor's office, he was furious to learn the girl had bolted. "Your husband warned you?"

By then, Marilyn had calmed down, considerably. "No, he called to prepare me. He knew I would panic… and I did. Just ask these ladies." She motioned to the receptionist and the nurse.

Sheriff Duncan glanced around at the rest of the people in the room. "Any of *you* see that girl leave?"

At first, nobody answered, then a little boy spoke up. "We was watching *her*," he said, pointing at Marilyn.

"I could charge your husband," he started to say. But it would not have helped.

The girl was gone.

CHAPTER THIRTY-TWO

The Law

Sheriff Max Duncan finally got around to interviewing Jack Wilson exactly five weeks after the young man had spotted Ted's Pontiac on that dreadful night. It was the day after Christmas, and the humble kitchen at the Wilson farm was still bathed in cinnamon and nutmeg from leftover wassail. The lawman was reserved as he questioned the now-eighteen-year-old under the watchful eye of his folks. Declining the offered cup of coffee, Max started by asking if Jack had seen any footprints when he first found the car.

"I don't remember any. Anyway, it was snowing."

"Could you see anyone moving inside the car?"

"Actually, yeah… which is why I decided not to, you know, get any closer."

"My report says you got there about the same time I was in the area on a domestic disturbance call, so that would…" He scribbled in his notebook, then looked up at the lanky lad. "You and Ted good buddies?"

Jack shrugged and nodded, at the same time. "I guess."

"Any reason why somebody would want to hurt him?" The young man waved a negative answer. "Any reason somebody would want to hurt the girl?"

"Um," he mused, "I know she had a lot of issues with a lot of people."

"You got a girlfriend?"

"Ay-yu-uh," came the wary answer. "What does she have to do with anything?"

"She friends with Roxanne Foxx?"

"Not really."

"Why not?"

"Uh, well... they just aren't the same type, you know?"

"'Not the same type'?" The sheriff looked Jack straight in the eye. "You talking 'guy talk,' here?"

Jack's face flushed and he avoided looking at his mother. "Yeah, I guess."

"You and your girlfriend ever have a fight about Miss Foxx?"

"Uh... no..."

"You and *Ted* ever have a fight about Miss Foxx?"

After several more leading questions, Jessie Wilson sat up straighter in his kitchen chair. "Just where are you going with this, Sheriff?"

Max Duncan folded his notebook and stood up. "Just checking all the angles, sir." He reached for his hat, placing it carefully over his balding head. "We have an extremely baffling case here. I hope you realize the seriousness of your son's position in this case."

"What are you talking about?" Laura looked worried.

"It is my understanding that Ted destroyed a parade float, which made Jack look pretty stupid. And Jack could have been the last person to see those two victims still moving. That's pretty compromising information," he bluffed. Then the sheriff glared at the pale fellow. "If you know something, you'd be wise not to hide it. Do I make myself perfectly clear?"

***

Fifteen minutes later, the sheriff was in the living room of the Case house, talking with Marsha, while her mother sat close to her on the sofa. The tall lawman stood to one side, close to Shirley's bedroom door, his eyes constantly moving as he asked questions.

"So, I am told that you are Roxanne Foxx's best friend. Is that correct?"

"Who told you *that*?" her mother asked.

"I am asking your daughter, ma'am," the sheriff said, sternly. He looked at Marsha for an answer.

"Well," she murmured, "we were, sort of, I guess… but not anymore."

"Why not?"

Marsha glanced at her mother, who nodded for her to answer. "Well, see… she gets into a lot of trouble. My mother doesn't want me to hang around with her, any more."

"She gets into what *kind* of trouble?"

Again, the glance toward her mother. "Just a lot of stuff. She lies a lot."

"What does she lie about?"

The thin teenager twitched uncomfortably. "Uh… just a lot of things. She gets caught, and she lies herself out of it." She looked sincerely at the man. "She's a really, really good actress."

"Is she, now?" He stopped his note-taking to pay special attention. "Really makes you believe her, huh?"

"Yeah, she's really good at that." Max noted the agreeing nod of Shirley's head.

"Can you give me a good example of how she has done that?"

Marsha had to think about that, but Shirley was quick to remind her. "Like pretending she had no interest in Ted Donahue, remember? She *swore* they were only dance partners."

"Wow… lied about that, did she? Bet that made you mad, Marsha."

"Hey. Made *me* mad," Shirley proclaimed.

"Well, nobody could blame you for that."

The conversation only got better from there. When the sheriff left there an hour later, he had a whole new list of information. He drove over the hill and parked just a few yards from the intersection of Case and Susie Wilson Roads.

"So, this is where Roxie's boyfriend lives," he said. Right then, he decided not to bother interviewing the other kids who had been at the hospital visiting Ted. There was a lot more to this case than a sick girl who would pound the life out of her own belly.

***

Once he got back to his office, Max made another note to himself. There was a list of phones to be monitored. This girl may be hiding, but she would surface sooner or later, and probably through her most obsessive mode of operation... the telephone. Both Jack and the Bogues had made remarks about that.

He smiled. The telephone operators there in Burlington were experts at checking on targeted numbers — after all, they plugged in and unplugged every phone call in the district. Not only that, but they could listen in on each and every conversation.

It was only a matter of time, and sure enough, just a week later, on the second day of January, a call went through to the Flannigans. It originated from a public phone booth, at five minutes after seven in the evening. The operator who listened in on the call, reported that the caller did not respond to the female who answered the phone. There had been only the background noise of cars and voices, such as that on a busy street. The call had lasted thirty seconds, and the phone booth was quickly identified. It was near the Bishop DeGoesbriand Hospital.

The next morning, the Burlington Police Department put out an alert to all Chittenden County law enforcement agencies that someone had entered that very same hospital during early evening, pulling an oxygen tube from, and slitting the throat of, a paralyzed patient. Emergency surgery failed to save the young male, whose name was being withheld, pending notification of the family.

Armed with the evidence of these two events, the Chittenden County sheriff's department asked for the cooperation of Burlington police to pinpoint any further surfacing of a certain troubled runaway, who had connections with these circumstances. Slowly, over the next few days, the noose closed. By January 5, the search for Roxanne Foxx was nearly over.

***

Very early that next Monday morning, Connie shook Don awake. He turned toward her, his eyes still closed. "What, babe?"

"I've got it," she exclaimed.

"Uh-huh. Good." He swished his tongue around in his dry mouth. "Whatcha got?" He wanted to get back to the dream.

"No! Listen to me, Don." She patted his face to get his attention. "I know who the witch is!" She waited for him to comprehend that. "And I know where Roxie is!"

He drew his body around toward her, trying to focus on her face in the dusky light of the bedroom. "Okay…"

"She's… honey, wake up, and listen. This is important."

There was a cloudy moment for the gentleman. Finally, he repeated it: "Important?"

"Yeah," she laughed. "We should have seen it." She reached over and turned on the reading light which was hung over the headboard, then tugged on his pajama top to help him sit up inside the soft flood of light.

"Look at me, sweetheart." She tugged at the top again. "Are you with me, here?"

Don blinked, then tried to focus.

"It was Alan Strong's suicide note, Don!" Her tone was intense. "Remember? The police officer asked her who 'Lizzy' was." She waited for him to recall.

"Yeah," Don responded, not quite sure where she was going with this.

"The note was *not* addressed to 'Dear Lizzy'... it was addressed to 'Dear Lezzy'!" She waited for him to get that part, then continued. "Remember how she said Alan called her that, just to be hateful, because she hated that name?"

Don finally sat straight up in the bed. "Oh my goodness." He looked at her. "She's right next-door, and I bet she *does* have Roxie with her... and Mindy is a... witch!"

There was not a whole lot of time spent on what was the right thing to do. They contacted their trusted law enforcement friend, Chief Robbie, who, having accessed the notification of the violent attack that killed Ted Donahue, immediately informed the proper authorities of the tip-off.

By three in the morning, on the sixth of January, Mindy Strong was under arrest for contributing to the delinquency of a minor, and Roxie was in the custody of social services.

It was a victory laced with mixed feelings.

At five that morning, Don received a call from Robbie. "You need to notify the Flannigans. Their lawyer needs to be aware of this."

"Already done," Don reassured him.

CHAPTER THIRTY-THREE

Moving On

A hearing was scheduled to be held at the Chittenden County courthouse, a handsome Redstone building just a block off Main Street in Burlington, for the fourteenth of January. But on the Friday before that, another meeting took place in a quiet room at the Hotel Vermont. Attending was John Courtney, some Vermont Transit officials, a couple of social workers, and certain legal staff members from the courthouse. At the end of the day, it was agreed that, in order to spare a lot of people a heap of embarrassment, there would be no formal charges against Bill Flanagan. In exchange for this leniency, it was also agreed that the man would resign his job and leave the state of Vermont.

By the time of the *official* hearing, there was only the matter of dealing with the problem of Roxanne Foxx, and the decision as to whether there would be charges filed against Mindy Strong. As usual, that hearing was open to the public. When George and Marilyn entered the courtroom, they noticed a few familiar Essex Junction faces. The high school principal was one of them. Father Tom Ladue sat a couple of seats away. The couple took their place on the front row, hoping Marilyn could get at least a hug from Roxanne.

But it was Mindy Strong who made the first appearance. As she walked in and took a seat directly in front of the Foxxes, Marilyn gasped.

"Oh... my... G—!" She touched George's arm. "That's Roxanne's old dance teacher, from Albany."

"That's Alan Strong's widow," he corrected her.

"*What?!*" Her nostrils flared with fury. At first, she was too angry to speak, but then it came out. "Well, I can see now, why she never showed up at any of the Vermont Transit activities, that... that *witch!*"

They sat there, almost within touching distance of the woman who had seduced her very young daughter, listening, but not listening, to the entire proceedings. By the time the judge decided to prosecute, Marilyn had pretty much figured it all out. Mindy had followed them to Vermont, from Albany, in order to keep in physical contact with the beautiful Roxie. Alan had been a meal ticket, and a hapless pawn in her scheme to maintain an ongoing relationship with the gorgeous redhead. The very thought of such things happening turned Marilyn's stomach. She sat there, seething in righteous indignation. Her only consolation lay in the vow she made to herself that one day, given the chance, she would finally get even with that loathsome woman. Oh, would she *ever*.

Suddenly, Mindy was leaving the courtroom. A few moments later, Roxie appeared, accompanied by a couple of adults. She spotted her mother and went for a hug as soon as she got to the chair. Her mother's eyes filled with tears at the sight of her girl, shaggy-haired, and wearing jail clothes that were hanging loosely off her slender form.

The judge was a kind, but firm man. Carefully, he asked the girl a few questions, letting the two caseworkers fill in wherever necessary. It seemed to be going well, until Roxie got to the part about the demons.

"Are you hearing voices?" the judge asked.

"No."

"Then how do you know you have demons inside you?"

"Some people saw them."

"I see. And have *you* ever seen them?"

"Kind of… in a mirror, once."

The gentle demeanor gave way to a serious frown, and there was some shuffling of papers in front of the man. He looked up to address the two workers.

"I feel there needs to be an extensive evaluation in this case. So I am recommending transfer of your charge to the State Hospital in Waterbury, for that very reason. There will be no further action until we get the results of this evaluation." He then spoke to Roxie. "Young lady, we feel it is in your best interest to spend a couple of weeks or so at a special hospital, where you can talk with people who understand where you're coming from. You have been through a lot of trauma, and we want to help you get your life back. I'm sure you would like to get your life back on track, wouldn't you?" Roxie nodded. "Very good. Then we will see you in a few weeks."

That very afternoon, Roxanne Foxx was transported by a couple of men from the U.S. Marshal's Office to the State Mental Hospital. She chatted calmly with them through the whole trip. When they got her checked in, she thanked them and shook their hands.

Three days later, she tried to run away. The girl never even made it off the hospital grounds. It turned out to be a lot longer than two weeks, before she saw that judge again.

***

The news of legal decisions concerning Roxanne Foxx traveled quickly through the network of Chittenden County law enforcement. Max Duncan got the details early on the morning of January 15. It was not the happiest Thursday of his career. He got on the phone with Chief Allen, over there in the village, making it clear what he thought about backroom politics and slick lawyers.

"Yeah, I heard," the chief said. "Kind of leaves us lowly law officers up in the air about some things… especially that attack on those two teenagers."

"Well, we didn't have all that much to go on, anyway."

"Really? You're a pretty sharp guy, Sheriff. I thought sure you would come up with something pretty quickly."

"Yeah, well, I think what stumped us all, was the lack of footprints in the snow. What did *you* think about that?" The chief was curious.

"Well, if the girl really did it, she wouldn't have been outside the car. Aw, who knows? I haven't figured it out yet. But I did have a question for *you*."

"Sure." Rob braced himself.

"You know Ted Donahue told somebody that Roxie had attacked him?"

"Ay-yuh. Us 'law ah-siffers' have a pretty good grapevine, as you know."

The sheriff wasn't laughing. "You figure she was the one who got to him at the Bishop Degoesbriand?"

"I think that could have happened."

"Or… maybe it was that woman she was hiding out with."

"I guess we'll find out at the trial."

"Yeah. Well anyway, I was wondering how in the world a little gal like that could haul off and almost kill a guy that big. And then — what? — beat her own belly like a drum? It's just not possible." He took a breath and asked the *real* question. "Something going on I don't know about, mister?"

"Well, there's a reason why she's in Waterbury." It was a cautious reply.

"Ay-yuh. She doesn't seem to have it together — no real friends, hanging out with older men, parents can't control her. What a mess."

"Yes, sir."

"Tell you what I'm gonna do," the senior lawman said. "I'm going to put this one in the refrigerator. If you can help clear this up, I would appreciate a call."

Sheriff Max Duncan hung up the phone and swept the two paperwork copies into separate manila folders, knowing it would take months, maybe even years, before he would have any answers. He walked over to pull open a file drawer, where he found the letter "D," for Donahue, and dropped the first folder in just behind it. The second envelope was dropped in behind the letter "F," before he slammed the drawer shut. The attack on Ted Donahue and Roxanne Foxx was now in the cold case file.

It was time to move on.

***

The moving van pulled away from the little stucco house on Susie Wilson Road, headed for the long trek to Oregon. April took a last look around the empty rooms, then pulled the front door closed and locked it. She handed the key to her dear friend, Connie, as they walked toward the car where Bill was waiting, the engine running. The woodie was packed full and Charley was jumping from the top of one suitcase to another, barking like an excited youngster. Bill twisted around and barked a little louder, so the dog dropped down into his bed, right behind the front seat. The man turned back around to listen, as Don dispensed a last bit of advice from outside the open driver's window.

"She's going to be very insecure for a while… maybe even for a lifetime, Bill. She knows you still think of that girl as the 'love of your life,' even with all the trouble that came with her." He leaned in closer. "You will have to bend over backwards, and you still may never fix it. Things will be different, but — hey — if you stick with some good Christian counseling, it will help a lot." At the approach of the two women, he looked up.

April stopped a few feet from the car door, to whisper an observation. "I never thought I would *ever* be glad to leave Vermont. Not ever. But I have to say, that is the way I truly feel right now." She looked at her friend. "The only thing I regret, is that we can't take you two with us."

There was a quick, hard embrace, and then April pulled the door open. As she slipped onto the seat, she had a quick reminder for both of them. "Let us know how it's going with the sale of the house."

"You bet," Connie reassured her.

Bill extended his hand to Don. "Thanks for everything."

The woodie back slowly out of the snowy driveway, then pulled around and headed toward Vermont Route 15 and pointed west.

Although there were numerous long-distance phone calls over the years, there was never another roast beef dinner together.

And Bill Flannigan pretty much forgot that the Collinses had misplaced his red croquet mallet.

CHAPTER THIRTY-FOUR

Letters

Principal Randy Marvin was grateful for the relative peacefulness which settled over the rest of the school year. Exams were passed, the senior prom was accomplished without incident, and June brought a fulfilling graduation for the class of 1953. He and his wife took a couple of days to enjoy a friend's cabin at Mallet's Bay, before he started a class at UVM to update his certification. He was snoozing on the beach when he got the news.

"Hey, Mr. Marvin!"

Randy opened his eyes and looked up into the face of Scottie Allen.

"I thought that was you," the youngster said, as he motioned back to the cabin which stood right beside the Marvin's borrowed facility. "I looked out the window, and you sure looked familiar."

"Well, how about that, Scottie. Do you folks have that place, or are you just guests, like we are?"

"Oh, it's ours... at least until I go to college. Mom's thinking about selling, anyway. It's a lot of trouble to keep it up. Plumbing's getting old, and stuff like that." He backed off, as if to leave. "Anyway, I just wanted to say 'Hi,' so I'll let you have your vacation. You get enough of us kids all year long."

"Appreciate it, young man."

Scottie hadn't gone three feet before he suddenly turned around. "Um, Mr. Marvin? Did my brother get in touch with you yet?" The principal looked surprised. The student approached once again. "He wanted to let you know that Roxie Foxx was being released at the end of this week." The man's mouth went into a supple pucker. "Yeah. They took her from Waterbury in February, straight over to that place in Vergennes for juvenile delinquents… uh, the Weeks School, right?" Mr. Marvin nodded. "Well, after four months they figure she's gotten straightened out, I guess. Anyway, I just thought I would let you know that Robbie wants to talk to you."

"I'll get in touch with him tomorrow night, Scottie. Thank you."

***

Part of the therapy Roxie went through in Vergennes included writing letters of apology to all those whom she had offended or harmed. This was accomplished over her last three weeks in custody. The first one went to her parents, it being delivered by her own hand during one of the weekly visits in the dayroom of the school. Her mother wept, of course, but when George read his letter, he kept shaking his head. "How did you remember all those rotten things you did to me? *I* can't even remember half of this stuff."

"I had a lot of time to think about those things. I am *so* sorry. I should never have treated you like that. You were just trying to be a good father. From now on, I promise to respect your authority. But right now, I just hope you will forgive me and give me another chance."

He looked at her, suspicious of her motives. However, she certainly was not twitching or rocking in place. In fact, all the drama seemed to have dissipated.

"Well, we can sure give it a try," he offered.

She looked up quickly, then back down. "I do want to ask you for one more thing."

The suspicion returned.

"I was wondering… if it would be okay if I… started to call you 'Dad.'"

"Oh… my… G—," Marilyn whispered.

The swarthy face softened. "Well, we can certainly give *that* a try, too," he murmured.

Penny received *her* letter the day before leaving for a summer job in New Hampshire. She shared it with Scottie, since it involved him, as well. The petite girlfriend slid across the sofa to draw near to him, there in the living room of the Allen home. He slipped a lanky arm around her and lowered his head to read over her shoulder, enjoying at the same time, the fragrance of her hair.

Gracie Allen spoke up from the easy chair at one end. "Should I leave?"

"No-no, Mrs. Allen. You really need to hear this." Slowly, she read it out loud.

Dear Penny,

I can hardly bear to write this letter, because I am so ashamed of how I hurt your knee that day. It was a horrible, horrible thing to do to somebody as sweet and loving as you are. I can't even think of you, without feeling like a monster. I don't know why you would ever forgive me, but I hope someday you will. I hope someday I can start going to a church youth group and learn to be more like Jesus. You are a good Christian girl, Penny, so don't ever change. If I ever had a sister, I would want her to be just like you. I mean that.

I hope you will forgive me for how I treated Scottie, too. I was horrible to that poor guy. He didn't deserve any of it. I would write to him, but he is YOUR boyfriend, and I don't want to give the wrong impression.

I will be coming back to EJHS next fall. I was hoping to try out for cheerleader squad again. Do you think they will let me? I hope so. It

"Oo-oh my," Gracie crooned. "Wasn't that a nice letter." She looked at her son. "So, what did she do to you, Scott?"

"Nothing, really," he lied. "Don't have any idea what she's talking about."

"Hmmm," she mused. "Maybe she was on pills or something."

The letter to Don and Connie lifted their hopes at first, because she indicated a desire to start attending a youth group. However, Don had one cautious comment.

"Either Stronghold has been rousted, or somebody's playing games."

"Yes, well, I am not passing any apologies on to the Flannigans, as she requested. Roxanne Foxx is forbidden to be in touch with those people under any circumstances. I wonder how that part of the letter got past the censor and into the mail."

"You'll notice she didn't use their actual name; just 'Please pass on my sincere apologies for all the bad things I did to any married couples.' You and I just assumed something, because we knew exactly whom she was talking about."

"So, she may be repentant, but she's still pretty slick."

"I married a smart woman," he said, as he gave her a peck on the cheek.

Then he filed the letter away.

Roxie's letter to Marsha was the shortest one.

Dear Marsha,

bother you, if you don't want me to. I will leave it up to you to make the first phone call.

Your friend,
Roxie

Marsha showed the letter to Shirley, who said, "We'll see."

***

Meanwhile, the wheels of justice were continuing to turn. Mindy Strong did a little writing of her own. A full confession to her illegal involvement with a child for ten years, and to the murder of Ted Donahue, whom, she claimed, she had paid back for accusing her little sweetheart of second degree assault. "That's how much I love her," she said. The law did go easier on her for cooperating, but she still went to prison for life. She figured it was better than a death sentence, since they could keep her behind walls, but — and this was her little triumph — they still couldn't keep her from being a witch. There were no geographical boundaries on those dark powers. She sent a short note to Roxie from the jail. It was passed to a trusted member of the witch's coven she belonged to, who addressed and mailed it to the girl's home address in Essex Junction.

Mindy Strong entered federal prison a week later, on the afternoon of June 11.

The very next day, Roxie was released from the Weeks School reformatory. She came home to a mini-celebration with her folks and the whole Bogue family. There were several cards to welcome her home, one of which had come in the mail, with a return address of Albany, New York. It disappeared before the time came to open those greetings.

Instead, much attention was focused on the handmade cards made by the twins, and special notes from both Shirley and Marsha Bogue, and a big, frilly one from her parents, Marilyn and stepdad George, who was enjoying being called "Dad" all afternoon.

It was a long, busy day, culminating with being tucked into bed, little-girl fashion, by a happy mother. But after Marilyn had turned out the light and closed the door, Roxie slipped back out of bed to pull out a flashlight from one of her dressing table drawers. As quietly as she could, she opened the Albany letter, which she had stashed in her dungaree pocket during the party. Back under the blanket, she unfolded the note and read it.

My dear little Butterfly,

Keep seeking the nectar. I am only a dream away.

Your loving Monarch

She turned off the flashlight and lay there a few minutes, enjoying the feeling. Then she started to tear up the small note, dropping the shreds into the envelope. It would all — including the shredded envelope — be flushed down the toilet in the morning.

But there was one more thing.

She slipped once again out of her bed, feeling for the dressing table. When she found the drawer, she turned the flashlight on and poked it deep into the recesses, searching for something special… something she had had to leave behind, with the rest of her jewelry, when she was taken into custody.

And there it was. Carefully, she removed a slender silver ring from the tangle of chains and bracelets, caressing the delicate circle of the ouroboros — a snake eating its own tail — admiring the artwork which her mentor had told her, represented eternal renewal. She had "won" it at the end of her first six months of dancing classes. At first, it was so big she could only wear it on her thumb. But gradually, over the years, it had moved to smaller fingers. Now it fit quite nicely on the smallest one. She had not been able to wear the ring since going to Waterbury. Marilyn had long since brought any personal items like that back home and placed them in the dressing table drawer. Gently, Roxie kissed the ring and slid it onto the little finger of her left hand. Then she crawled back under the light blanket, where she sighed in great relief.

She and Mindy were united, once again.

***

Scottie got his first postcard from Penny that same Friday. She had arrived at the campground where she would teach swimming and exercise classes to kids who were transported north every summer from the ghettos of New York City. She was excited, but she was missing him already. He made sure nobody was looking before he pressed the card to his lips and stuck it into the back pocket of his khaki shorts.

It was going to be another great day at the cabin. The weather was not hot and muggy, for once. He looked across the beach toward the glittering expanse of Lake Champlain, where he would soon be paddling canoes back and forth for the boat rental company which was located up close to the main beach of Mallet's Bay, just a quarter of a mile away. It was a dream job, offering both fun and good pay. At the end of the summer, he expected to have a deep tan, and his blondish hair would be bleached almost white, as usual. But the greatest thing right at the moment was that he was being allowed to live at the cabin, on the shores of this summer playground of the town of Colchester, just northwest of both Burlington and Essex Junction. He had a bike, but no car, and the distance for traveling by bus from Essex Junction to work was too involved. This was the most convenient and economical solution. Further, he was proud that his mother and older brother trusted him to take care of the place, like an adult.

Of course, there was a whole summer ahead.

The first teenagers to show up for a day at the beach were Diana and Jack. They played all day, then had a barbecue with Scottie after he got back from work, around seven that night. By nine, the couple left in the old farm truck, and Scottie fell into the bottom bunk bed and slept hard. That was during the middle of the first week.

He was joined by his mom on his first Monday off, and the two of them cooked and read and slept and enjoyed the warmish sunshine. She left the next morning, having several appointments for the day, and the young man was once again alone for the rest of the work week. But on Saturday, he came back to the cabin to find a half-dozen high school kids lounging on the little front porch of his abode. He looked around, and recognized only one person: Paula Donahue. She didn't look right.

"Hey-yyy, Scottie," she sang out. "I want you to meet some of my new friends." She came off the porch rail with a little wobble. "Hey, you guys! Introduce yourselves!"

He didn't hear one, single name. Instead, the hair on the back of his neck stood up. Instinctively, he waved and grinned as he moved back toward his bike. As soon as he was in the clear, he leaped onto the seat and peddled as fast as he could, back to the highway and the main beach. The phone booth near the bath house was empty, so he made the call. Thirty-five minutes later, Chief Robbie picked up his brother from the snack bar, and five minutes after that, the car slid to a stop at the cabin.

There was nobody there.

Robbie stayed the night, his police vehicle in the driveway. In the morning, some decisions were made. The very next day, Gracie arrived with a "NO TRESPASSING" sign, which she promptly nailed to the porch rail. If unwanted guests came calling, Scottie was within his rights to call the Colchester area law enforcement. Once that was all put in place, Gracie turned her concern toward Paula's welfare.

"Too much tragedy, all in just a few months. I wish she would join the youth group at church."

And that was how the First Congregational Church youth group ended up at the cabin in the middle of July. They arrived at noon on a Saturday, twelve loud young people descending onto the beach amidst the fling of beach bags and flapping towels. An extra barbecue was unloaded from Jack Wilson's truck, while a couple of kids started inflating beach balls, using Scottie's bicycle pump. Scottie, himself, had switched days off with a co-worker, in order to join the fun. He was surprised at the size of the crowd, but soon realized there were some new people in the group.

He figured Jack was there just because Diana invited him, but he wondered what Paula's status was. This girl, he knew, didn't even recognize the existence of God. But then, he knew also that his well-meaning mother was probably working on something behind the scenes, as usual.

Mark, the bright-eyed youth leader, helped Don Collins unload food and a box of picnic supplies from the Studebaker, while Connie and Gracie put the cold items in the old refrigerator.

As he spread his towel out on the beach, Scottie called out to his busy mother, "Mom! We have enough food to feed an army."

"Oh, not everybody is here, yet. We have another carload coming later this afternoon."

He was going to ask who they were, but somebody yelled for him to help set up the volleyball net. After that was done, it was discovered that somebody else forgot the ball, itself, but the enterprising crowd took to a game of "beach-ball volleyball." Same rules, more laughs.

Finally, Jack yelled, "I'm hot. Who's going in?" and started for the water. Suddenly, with great abandonment, most of the gang ran into the sloshing waves, screeching and yelping at the icy temperatures engulfing their overheated bodies. But several others stopped to remove eyeglasses and such, before diving in. Scottie had no glasses; however, he did drop his Timex inside one of his tennis shoes.

The last carload of young people arrived a few minutes later, pretty much unnoticed by the ones frolicking in the waves. The Collinses followed along as Mark went to greet the five special guests from Holy Family Roman Catholic Church. Father Tom emerged, followed by Marsha and the twins, all of whom they greeted warmly. This was, after all, an outreach for unity in the Family of God. Christian handshakes and hugs were being exchanged, when suddenly, Don and Connie got a real surprise. The last of the five newcomers out of the old green Ford was Roxie Foxx.

In the background, they heard Father explaining how his young folks had opted for a Catholic Youth Rally in Montreal, so he took the opportunity to enjoy the company of the Bogue children. But Roxie's former counselors were looking at a demure young lady with short, curly red hair. Her eyes quickly lowered after initial contact, the reddening of the cheeks an obvious indication of her deep embarrassment and shame.

"Oh, Lord," Connie whispered, as she stepped forward to embrace the girl. Roxie responded by melting into the woman's arms, her head buried deeply into the welcoming shoulder. A few seconds later, Don wrapped his arms around both of them.

It would be whatever it would be.

The fun just off-shore continued, as the new arrivals made themselves comfortable. It wasn't long before Marsha and one of the twins joined the water activities. Beach balls and body flips into the deeper waters had the happy group's attention.

Meantime, Roxie wandered around the beach, apparently unsure of what would happen when she was recognized. She placed a large straw hat over her head to keep the sun off her delicate skin, moving in and out of the shade whenever she could. But she did not join the swimmers. The chaperones tried to keep up light conversation between them and her, doing their best to ignore her obvious discomfort; after all, the girl knew she had a lot to make up for. She helped where she could, then wandered over to where the other twin, Paul, was apparently collecting pebbles on the beach. The slick black hair lay close across his young brow as he raised his head toward her footsteps. They exchanged a couple of words, then she squatted down to help him. The two of them became a team, moving from spot to spot amongst the beach bags and blankets, until the collection got too cumbersome. Then Roxie handed her hat to the boy, so he could have something in which he could carry it all. He gave her a grateful grin and ran to still another spot, this time kicking over a couple of shoes and getting sand on somebody's towel. The girl followed behind, straightening up the mess as she passed by.

Meanwhile, Paula Donahue was swimming only fifty yards away.

Actually, by the time of this picnic, the relationships between Roxie and her cheerleader associates had been pretty much mended. There had been several incidents of "testing" over the last few weeks, and she had passed every single one of them, convincing the girls that she was, indeed, repentant, and ready to "be one of the team."

Convincing all of them, that is, except Paula. The wounds were still too raw. It was the one letter of apology Roxie had not sent, for by doing so, she would have most certainly incriminated herself. Because of the situation, the two girls made it a point to keep a respectable distance between them. Neither one knew the other was at the beach party that day.

It was Scottie who spotted her first. He squinted, to make sure he was seeing right. Then he waded through the waist-high churning lake water, using his arms like paddles to push his body past all the activity, through to where Marsha was body-flipping Peter. "Hey, Marsha," he said in a low voice, "is that Roxie Foxx?"

Marsha ducked the big splash as Peter slapped into the cloudy depths, then followed Scottie's line of vision. "Yup. She's restricted from going over the border to Montreal with the rest of the group, so I stayed behind with her and we're the only two from the group who could make it today."

"She's going to church with you?" He was astounded.

"No, but she has been coming to our youth group once a week."

He thought about it for a second. "Well, I guess that's better than meeting with *our* youth group, since we've been trying to get *Paula* to join *us*." Then it hit him. "Uh-oh."

"What?"

"Paula is *here*."

"Oh my gosh. Nobody told me." She started for shore. "I'll let Roxie know. I'm sure she doesn't want any trouble."

A few minutes later, Roxie climbed into the green Ford, so that the priest could get her to the nearest bus stop. "This is very kind of you, Roxanne."

"It's just the right thing to do. Paula's life has been messed up too many times. I don't need to remind her of it."

When Father Tom returned to the party, most of the kids were chowing down. Don caught his eye. "Thanks for doing that," he whispered. "Was she okay with it?"

"More than just okay; it was *her* idea. I think maybe there have been some real changes in that one."

"That's great news, man." His voice reflected a glimmer of hope. "Now, we need to start working on Paula."

It was almost six o'clock when the little crowd climbed back into their vehicles. As the last one departed, Gracie heaved a sigh of relief. She watched her son amble down across the empty beach to pick up his tennis shoes and towel. It had been a great day.

"Hey, Mom!" Scottie came running toward her. "Have you seen my watch?"

CHAPTER THIRTY-FIVE

Bridges

Uncle had been holding his breath, so to speak, since hearing of Roxie's release. He greeted every bit of information about how much she had changed with a great deal of doubt, even though much of the news had come from his fishing partner, Father Tom Ladue. It was almost the end of July, as the two of them were driving back from their fishing hole, when the priest brought up the subject of the attack on her and Ted Donahue. In the course of the conversation, he revealed to Uncle that the beatings had actually originated from a demonic source, whereupon, the native's eyes grew wide.

"The hail you say!"

"Nope, I'm sure of it." He checked to make certain the fellow understood. "It was not another human being. Your plan to trap Roxie opened the floodgates on that one." His eyes went back to the road. "The demonic activity started to really manifest big time."

"You telling me I got a gawdim bogeyman on my butt?" The little man was sitting straight up.

"Well, no. She seems to be, uh, under control." The priest suddenly remembered there had been no exorcism. "At least, it looks that way."

Uncle was actually glaring at his friend. "What does that fricken' mean?" He saw the concern in Father Tom's frown.

"How the hail do I protect myself from a devil, will you tell me that?"

The freckled brow creased slightly. "Okay. Good question, and I have the answer: You belong to Jesus, and you have the Blood Covering. All you have to do, is command it to back off, in the Name of Jesus." A glance toward his passenger revealed more doubt. "That's it, Mr. Smart. It works. Trust me. You have power over those things, so if they come at you —"

"'Those things'? Did you say, '*things*'? What the fricken' hail do you mean, '*they*'? We talking a whole bunch of monsters, here?" There was a quiver in the voice. "Aw, hail, what've I gotten into? It's like Halloween, or something."

The priest hastened to calm the man. "No, it's not. Not by a long shot. *You* are the one in charge, not them. *You* have that special connection with Jesus, the Lord God Almighty. Those slimy losers can't even touch you, unless you run like a scared rabbit."

"Humph!" The Abnaki warrior was suddenly indignant. "I'm no gawdim rabbit, that's for sure." He followed it up with a sudden thought. "But I *do* know how to hide in plain sight. I can be right in front of them bah-serds and never let on that I'm, uh, about to wet my britches."

Father Tom smiled. "That's right. Although, I figure you don't have to even do that. All you need to do, is remember you have that special connection with God."

Uncle relaxed back in his seat. "Well, okay then. I got the connection. I tell them to get lost, in the fricken' Name — uh, the mighty Name of Jesus."

During supper that night, Raymond Rene' Smart expounded on this special connection between Christians and Jesus. At the end of it, the Thompsons quietly agreed, then Ceese changed the subject to what was growing in the garden. But as Winnie cleared the dishes a few minutes later, she suddenly remembered the conversation with her mother in that little boat. Yellow Flower had the concept, but it was a little too narrow. Winnie was not one of the bridges between people groups. It was Jesus who made all those wonderful connections, and they were all constructed out of the same material; unconditional love, and His blood. She stood there holding a stack of dirty plates, and marveled that she just learned all that from the mouth of a man who couldn't even talk without swearing.

***

Classes resumed at EJHS right after Labor Day weekend. Once more, it was time for basketball and cheerleader tryouts. And once again, the lists were posted. Roxie made only second substitute, and that only because of a reluctant bow to her apparently reformed ways. This didn't bother her so much, since the new rule was that the substitutes would attend every game, and do at least one cheer each during the course of the event. She could live with that.

In fact, she did more than just live with it; she pursued a closer friendship with Penny, who was reelected captain. There were friendly waves as they passed in the hallways, and a lot of joking around after practice. And there was the dancing, of course, with its many facets providing multiple venues for conversation. The sweet Penny never suspected the girl's ulterior motive. Even Diana was getting used to Roxie's more frequent presence.

One day after gym class, she and Roxie walked out of the locker room to spot Penny and Paula seated on the bottom row of the bleachers, in lively conversation. When Penny saw them coming, she jumped up and waved for them to join in on the fun.

"We have a new cheer!" she exclaimed.

"Really?" Roxie was delighted, for it meant more time invested with Penny, and another chance to show her own talent.

About ten minutes into the demonstration and tentative first tries, the cheer was interrupted by the arrival of Scottie Allen. He stood and watched, his square smile showing approval. As soon as the last move of the cheer had been performed, Roxie said, "Wow! That's great. I love it, Penny. But I need to scoot." She picked up her notebook and headed for the main building.

Diana's hands went to her hips, showing her frustration. "Ding blast! She just did it again!"

"What? You mean the 'walking off' thing?" Scottie asked.

"So, I'm not the only one who's noticed?"

"Actually, Scottie and I were talking about that, yesterday," Penny noted.

Diana wanted an answer. "Why do you think she does that?"

"That's easy," Paula asserted. "Guilt. Just plain guilt." She looked at her classmates as though they had no clue. "She did a whole bunch of..." That was all she allowed herself to say. She gave them all a dismissive wave, and went on her way.

Diana wasn't quite sure. "What guilt is she talking about? What the heck did she ever do to you, Scottie?"

He shrugged. "I don't know. I think she's referring to the attack."

"Of course she is, poor thing," Penny sympathized. "That was her brother, for Pete's sake." She led the other two toward the door.

Secretly, Scottie was pretty worried about Roxie's continual brush-offs. He was *sure* this girl never did something like that, without having an underlying plan. Not knowing why *he* was being included in that plan was the part that bothered him the most. His concern morphed slowly into real fear, as the weeks went by.

***

Late on the afternoon of October 9, Father Tom spotted Blow bounding joyfully across the traffic circle toward Robinson's Fuel on the corner of Pearl and Park Streets. There were two near-misses in a row, as the ebony terror continued around to race across Park Street, straight into the parking lot of the Lincoln Inn. When the well-meaning man caught up with the animal, the motivation for the high-spirited run became evident. The large garbage cans outside the inn's kitchen door stood overflowing on this Friday. Blow was just tipping one of them over, when a ruddy-faced cook came out, swinging a broom. The dog retreated almost into the priest's open arms.

"Hey, Blow! Whatcha doin,' boy?" He patted his knee.

The dog did the happy tongue-dangle and pounced at the ground around his prospective new playmate. Because Father Tom was blessed with pants that fit, he had no real use for the belt, so it came off, and after a half-dozen tries, became an effective, though rather short leash. He slowly brought the runaway into the Lincoln Street Greenhouse driveway and around to the back door of the house. There, he sat down on the back step, to catch his breath and give the dog a few more loving strokes before the poor, ugly thing was once again locked up.

Slowly, he became aware of voices coming from the open window near the door. They grew louder as if the speakers were coming in from another room.

"...so, all you have to do—"

"No! I'm not doing that, Roxie. I'm not." Her priest recognized Marsha Bogue's voice. He turned and looked at the screened lower half of the opened window, but he could not see the girls.

"No… Marsh… Marsh, I promise you, I will *never* ask you another favor, as long as I live. I just need this one thing." Blow's ears perked up and he focused on the window. "Just this one thing… so we can get a picture, and prove he was there and tried to—" The last few words were lost under the dog's low, soft growl.

"You know what, Roxie? My mother was right. You were big trouble. And it looks like you're *still* big trouble. I'm not doing any of this."

"Oh yeah? Well, how about if I tell her about the time you lied to her about going to the movies, and you were really riding the bus, helping me to seduce Sir William? How about if I tell her how you never told her how I met him that night I stayed over?"

There was silence.

The next threat was delivered in a deep, eerie voice. "Besides that, you owe me for squealing to the police about Ted and Mr. Smart. Did you think I would never find out about that? Did you?" There was a short hoot. "You made me look like a nut-case, you little snot. I went to reform school because of you."

The dog leapt to his feet, emitting another low growl.

"I'm gonna get busted," the priest whispered. Quickly, he rose to his feet. As he turned to go up the stairs, he could hear the bustling near the window screen. He tugged the rigid dog around and gently pulled him up the stairs. Before he could turn back around to knock on the door, it opened with a loud sucking noise.

"Hi, Father!" Marsha's voice was a little too chipper.

"Hey, Marsha." He pointed to Blow. "Guess who I found?"

She reached for the dog's collar. "Oh boy, I'm probably gonna hear about this." But the dog did not budge. Instead, he stared past her at Roxie, and growled again.

The beautiful redhead stopped in mid-greeting to Father Tom. "What's wrong with that stupid dog?"

Nobody seemed to know what to say, so Marsha knelt down and petted the tense animal. "Hey, Blow… it's okay. It's okay, boy." She signaled Roxie to move back, then gently tugged the animal into the kitchen. Then she motioned for Roxie to leave, with a firm tilt of her head.

Roxanne Foxx looked at her friend, long and hard. "See you right after the game tonight." She stepped through the doorway, then turned back for one last, sweet parting comment: "I know you won't let me down."

An hour later, Father Tom was in sweats and on his way to the Thompson farm. As his bicycle sped over the Old Colchester Road, he prayed for wisdom. He did not want to upset anybody, but that seemed an impossible goal. It was abundantly clear: Roxie Foxx was out to set somebody up. In the priest's mind, that was most likely his fishing pal, Mr. Smart, who had schemed with Teddy Donahue, to destroy her. Somehow, the little Abenaki warrior needed to be warned… and not by telephone… but in person, privately.

So great was his focus that he nearly ran over the little guy, who was toddling along on the side of the road. It was the rip-roaring rendition of the U. S. Army Hymn that caught his attention. Uncle was actually only on the first verse as the cyclist approached. It was something about caissons rolling along. He drew the bike to a slow wobble, following along behind the unaware singer, and listened as the chorus came forth in full volume. It was tempting to let the fellow finish, but there was urgent business ahead. The priest drew alongside the marching soldier, surprising him into shocked silence.

Father Tom slid off one side of the bike seat and balanced himself on the flat surface of the dry autumn road. "Mr. Smart, I need to let you know that something is up… I think, this very evening." He explained the situation quickly, ending with the precaution, "If I were you, I would get sober in a hurry, and stay that way for a good long time. You need to be on guard, sir. And it wouldn't hurt to pray the Rosary, that's how serious I believe this thing to be." He slid back onto the seat. "Mind you, this is just a gut feeling... I mean, like... like a Holy Ghost alert. Listen, I've had those before, and they have always proven to be accurate."

"Aw, gawd... it's another war."

"When it comes to 'good against evil,' we're always at war, Mr. Smart. This just happens to be the next battle."

As soon as it was dark, Uncle took his post at the upstairs kitchen window. Over the next ten hours, he duly noted all activities in the back yard. At four-thirty in the morning he went down to the barn. There, his carefully laid plans blew sky-high. A few minutes later, the little Abenaki warrior took his wallet and a couple of chocolate bars, and faded into the multicolored Vermont hills.

It was the night of the murder.

CHAPTER THIRTY-SIX

What?

"What do you mean, 'We all should have seen this one coming'?" Sheriff Duncan was irritated at the comment. "Can you ID this body, or not?"

"Yeah, I can. I recognize the hair, the hat, and the cheerleader outfit." Chief Allen straightened up. "That's Roxanne Foxx." He looked up at the loft and cursed softly.

"Ay-yuh, that's what I thought." The sheriff motioned to somebody. "I want an outline on this one." He walked out to the edge of the doorway, where he paused to look to the left, then to the right. "Somebody moved the door."

"Yeah, Mr. Thompson told me he did that. Spooked, I guess."

"Follow me, mister." Max Duncan moved slowly through the mud around the north end of the barn, stopping at the corner of the building.

"Norm! There's a camera here in the mud. Did you get a picture of it?" Norm replied that he had. "Okay, somebody mark that thing. It's evidence." He turned back toward Robbie and shoved his hands into his pants pockets. "So, what do you think happened here?"

"Maybe somebody lured her here. Or maybe *she* lured somebody here, and got caught in her own trap." The chief really didn't know how to answer the question. "I'm just guessing, but this was a girl who had a lot of people mad at her."

"And, she was a liar, in the first degree." Max waited for the next conclusion.

"Ay-yuh, that's probably true."

He looked Robbie in the eye. "Who's the first person comes to mind, that you figure would do this?"

"Somebody who really, really hated her, I guess."

"And who would that be?"

Robbie did not want to answer that. "Um, I just don't know. She had a lot of people mad at her."

"Like who?" The sheriff was persistent.

Robbie grasped at a straw in the wind. "Aw, jeez, Sheriff. Her own stepfather almost lost his job over her shenanigans. Who knows?"

Sheriff Duncan whipped out his notebook. "That right? And what is his name, again?"

For the next hour and a half, the two of them carefully circled the crime scene, making notes and then revising them.

Finally, the authorities arrived to remove the body. An ambulance had been standing by, the gurney out and ready, until the signal would be given to remove the corpse. Finally, the two uniformed men moved in to perform the task. They looked up for permission, then, given the nod, carefully removed the three-tined pitchfork. Somebody wrapped it securely, for it most certainly contained crucial evidence. The two medics waited for the next signal, then tenderly scooped their arms under the girl's body, to lift it gently onto the gurney. As they did that, the navy blue watch cap fell off the head, taking the golden-red curls with it.

Suddenly, there was someone else resting in the arms of the two ambulance drivers. As they laid the dead girl on the white sheet, Chief Allen leaned closer to view the frozen face. He gasped as he beheld the familiar greasy blonde hair, now plastered across the forehead and around the edges of the pale cheeks.

It was Marsha Bogue.

***

The task of notifying Shirley Bogue was one the sheriff, as tough as he was, did not care to do alone. First, he notified Father Tom. But then he turned to Robbie. "You know the Bogues?"

"Yes, sir, I do."

"You should probably go with me." It was the turning point in the relationship between the two law officers.

The autumn morning was in full light as the two official vehicles pulled in next to Shirley's old car. The twins spotted them from the kitchen window and pulled the front door open before the two men were even up the porch steps.

"Mama!" Paul shouted over his shoulder. "Better get up!" He pulled his brother to the side, to let the two officers in.

"'Morning, boys," Robbie said softly. "Where's your mother?"

"She worked until midnight," Peter said, shyly.

Shirley's bedroom door opened, just the left of where they were all standing. She was tying the belt on her flannel bathrobe as she stepped forward. When she looked up, her sleepy eyes widened. "O-oh my gosh! What happened?"

"We need to speak to you privately, Shirley," Robbie said. "Hey, guys... we need you to go upstairs for a few minutes, okay?" The boys looked at their mother, who gave the nod. As soon as she shut the stairway door behind them, the disheveled head turned and she was furious.

"What has he done *now*?" She smoothed her hair with both hands. "Have a seat." As the two men sat down uneasily on the sofa, she took the chair across the room near the back window. "In jail again? What?"

Robbie realized she was talking about the twins' father. "Uh, it's not him this time… it's Marsha."

"What? No. She's a good kid." She started toward the girl's room. "Marsha! You need to get out here, kiddo!"

Robbie stopped her before she got past the coffee table. "She's not there, Shirley," he said, as he placed his hands gently on her shoulders.

The front door swung open. Father Tom and Anna, the church secretary, came in. They came to a sudden halt at the look on Robbie's face. Then Father Tom took over.

She was inconsolable.

There was no way the sheriff could do anything else there, but before they left, Robbie thought to check on the two children. He opened the stairway door and slowly made his way to the top of the stairs. There, his heart nearly broke.

The twins were huddled against the bricks of the chimney through which the oil stove was vented, holding fast onto each other, their faces hidden. They had been listening through the ornate heat vent in the floor, just above the stove.

"Father Tom!" His voice cracked. "You need to come up here."

***

When Sheriff Duncan and Chief Allen knocked on the door, Marilyn answered. "What's wrong?"

"Sorry, ma'am, but we need to talk to Roxanne."

"What for, Sheriff?"

"Is she here?"

"Y-yes... down in the basement, doing some laundry."

"We'll need to talk to her, Mrs. Foxx. Appreciate if you would have her come upstairs for a few minutes."

Marilyn stood still and stared at the men.

"Um, we need your permission to enter the premises, Marilyn." It was going to be "good cop–bad cop," and Robbie was the former. He gave her an "It's okay" wink, and then she motioned for them to come in.

"Sit down," she whispered. Then she went back to the kitchen and called her daughter. The two men sniffed the air and made eye contact.

"Is that skunk?"

"Definitely skunk," Robbie whispered.

Roxie seemed prepared to have this interview. She glanced at the two men before she sat down heavily beside her mother on the sofa. "I suppose you want to know where I was last night."

"We could start there." The sheriff caught the gist of the "victim" approach. If she wanted to play that game, he knew how to play it very well.

"I was trying to get a picture of somebody cheating on his girlfriend." She reached over and took her mother's hand. "I'm sorry, Mom, but it was too awful. I just couldn't tell you somebody killed Marsha."

Marilyn's mouth dropped open, then shut, then opened again, but no words came. The question was in her eyes.

"We dressed her up to look like me, in my cheerleading outfit and some of my hair that I had stored in the jar, and she was going to meet him in the hayloft, and I was going to take a picture and we would run like heck... only, it didn't work out that way."

"We're talking about the Thompsons' hayloft in their barn, right?" The sheriff was taking notes, while at the same time, trying to help Marilyn get the setting. "Alright, so tell us how it *did* work out."

"We sneaked over the railroad track and hid behind the big maple tree at the end of the driveway. When we saw him go into the barn, we waited a minute, then Marsha went ahead of me. She went to the big door, and I stayed back far enough so I couldn't be seen from the hayloft." She hugged herself, rubbing her upper arms with her hands. "So then, she got to the doorway, and she did my little laugh, like I taught her. And then I heard him say 'Ha-a-ey!' all sexy-like. So she kind of put her head down, like... like she was scared." Roxie turned to her mother. "Oh, Mom... I just know she was scared." The voice cracked, but neither mother nor daughter moved.

Robbie started his "good cop" thing. "Aw jeez, Roxie... this has to be hard for you. But listen, kiddo, just try to relax and help us out, here." He gave her a friendly nod. "Just tell it like it happened, as best you can."

Her head dropped suddenly, to hide a little smirk. But then she got control and lifted her sufferer's countenance to continue. "I was counting on his attention being on Marsha as she started to climb the ladder. I was so scared, too, Mom. But I got in behind the car, and took my position. When I got brave enough, I peeked over the hood, and I could see him standing up at the top of the ladder, watching her climb. She was almost at the top, so I held the camera up to my eye, so I could get the shot. She was... she was..." The girl stopped and took a moment. When she continued, her voice was a solemn monotone: "Her head was just barely above the top of the ladder, when he leaned back, like he was going to hit a home run, and... then he... he swung so *hard*." Her whole body shivered.

Marilyn covered her face, but Roxie continued: "She fell backwards. I heard how hard she hit against the car, and then... she slipped down onto the floor."

"Aw, kiddo," Chief Allen sympathized, "you must have been terrified. What did you do?"

"I froze. I just dropped down. Then I could hear him coming down the ladder, which was a little noisy, so... I rolled under the car."

"Good move," the chief commented. "So, what happened next?"

The girl leaned forward, as though to concentrate on something. Her fingertips came together, and began to tap, just a little. Robbie noted the sudden look of concern on the mother's face, but he allowed Roxie to continue.

"I could see his feet. He walked over and kind of kicked her foot. Then he bent down and checked her wrist. I guess she must have been dead, 'cause he stood back up and just stood there for a couple of seconds. Then he went over to the big door and stopped there. Then he took off down the driveway. I could hear his footsteps. He was running."

"How long did you wait before you came out from under the car?" Robbie asked.

"As soon as I was sure he was gone. Then I sneaked around the front of the car, to check on my friend. I... I checked for a heartbeat, on her throat, like I've seen them do in the movies. But she was definitely dead." The voice started to go weak. "I started to cry, and I got scared that he might come back and hear me, so I ran out the back door and over the tracks. Then I came home."

"What time did your daughter come home last night?" the sheriff was now questioning Marilyn.

"I was working until midnight. Both Shirley and I had to work last night." Suddenly, she remembered Shirley. Tears welled up. "That poor woman." She wiped her eyes before she finished her reply. "Anyway, it was so late, and I wanted to avoid a drenching between the car and the door. I never checked on her. I just went to bed." She looked to Roxie for the answer, but the sheriff was still wanting answers from the mother.

"What about your husband? Does he know what time she got home?"

"He's in New York City, picking up a 'new' used bus for Burlington Transit. He'll be back tonight."

It was back to Roxie, who gave a ready answer. "I was home by eleven, I think, because it was starting to rain pretty good by then. It was a mess, because I scared a skunk when I put my bike in the back yard. Got sprayed. Had to take my clothes off outside, then come in to take a shower. Then I sprayed some of my mom's perfume around, before I got into bed."

Robbie leaned forward. "Roxie, why didn't you call me? Or the sheriff? Or even an ambulance?"

"I just panicked. Besides, *you* sure wouldn't have believed me."

"*I* wouldn't have believed you? Why not?"

"'Cause it was your little brother that we were trying to trap."

The two law officers exchanged a quick look, then both sat back in their chairs. It was quiet while Max Duncan made another note. Finally, Robbie spoke up: "Scottie has been 'catting around' behind Penny's back?"

"Well, he's certainly been trying. He's been chasing me for months."

The chief studied the living room carpet, then raised his focus back to the girl. "That right? Well, if that young man has been doing anything unseemly, I would certainly like to know the details."

A scornful hoot preceded her words. "Believe me, you don't want to know."

"Be that as it may," the sheriff interrupted, "you should have called me. You could have used the telephone right there at the Thompsons' house."

"I wouldn't go near that man."

"Who? Cecil Thompson?"

"Nope. That drunk, Mr. Smart. He's crazy as a loon."

The sheriff's hands dropped to his lap. "So, you just panicked and came home, and left your friend lying there, dead. Is that correct?"

"That... just... sounds so... awful..." The girl's head bowed slowly.

Sheriff Duncan stood up abruptly, followed closely by Chief Allen. Slipping his notebook into his jacket pocket, he left instructions for her to be available for a formal statement. "And don't try to run this time. If you do, I'll see that you get charged as an accomplice to murder." It was a bluff, but he was sure he made his point.

Robbie pulled the door open, letting Max exit first, then turned back to Roxie. "By the way, Scottie was sick all night. He has the flu."

"Oh, sure he does..." she sneered.

He pulled the door closed behind him, and followed the sheriff back to his vehicle. Max was already at the wheel, but with the window down. The chief leaned against the man's car. "That was very interesting. My little brother is scared stiff of that girl. Besides, he really does have the flu. My mom was up with him half the night." He shook his head. "Hard to tell how much of that story is actually true."

"I can tell you at least one part of it, that is not true," Max Duncan said. "She wasn't really going to take pictures."

"How do we know that?"

"Remember the camera we tagged for evidence? Had her fingerprints on it, but there was no film in it." He grinned. "I doubt she would have overlooked that."

"I see." Rob suddenly had a thought. "And did you notice what else she forgot?"

"Oo-oh, yeah," the sheriff said, "she never even *mentioned* the pitchfork."

CHAPTER THIRTY-SEVEN

Rainbows

"Hey, Mom," Robbie called downstairs just before Sunday morning breakfast. "I don't suppose I can talk you into skipping church this morning?"

"What's up?" she answered from the kitchen.

"Look out the window!" he said as he came bouncing down the stairs. "It's fall out there. The whole world is a *Vermont Foliage* calendar. We should take a drive."

"Oh, I don't know…"

"Yeah, we should. How long has it been since we've done that?" He poured a cup of coffee. "Tell you what… why don't we take a drive up through Colchester? Make one last visit to the cabin. We could even barbecue. I need to put some things away for the winter, anyway."

She looked thoughtful. "I was going to do that this week."

"Look, I can help you. Today. But not next week."

It was still fairly warm when they unlocked the cabin door at noon. The inside of the place still smelled of wood smoke from the small potbellied stove. Rob bent over and opened the stove's door. In a few minutes, the inside of the cabin had lost its chill, and the two of them were busy wiping down and stacking and storing. The box they had brought with them was filled with items to be taken back to the village, and he loaded it into the trunk of Grace's car. The pace of work was steady, and the conversation limited, and they decided not to dirty the barbecue, but it was time together and that was enough.

The fire in the stove was nearly out by the time they were finished. So, they decided to sit out on the small porch for a while, to let the coals die down. Rob unfolded two of the chairs from where they had been stacked on the bottom bunk and they sat down to enjoy the view of the lake. The quiet of the beach was broken only by the gentle lapping of the waves upon the pebbly shore.

"We sure enjoyed this summer, didn't we?"

"We sure did, son. Too bad we can't go back to those peaceful months."

"Well, that's life, right, Mom?" He shifted his weight on the chair. "I wish we could go back to when we still had Dad with us."

From there, the conversation turned to the good times, when they were a whole family. It was actually more uplifting than sad, and went on for a good half-hour. But then it was time to check the fire and head on home.

Rob took the two folded chairs back into the cabin, where he paused in front of the lower bunk once more.

"Say, Mom, would do me a favor?"

"Sure," she said, as she came back in. "What do you need?"

"I think it would be better to roll up that mattress, and store the chairs on the slats. These metal chairs get wet and rusty, and that's a new mattress."

He set the chairs aside, and the two of them commenced to roll the plastic five-inch-thick mattress, starting at the bottom edge, until it could be secured into a fat roll with the ties at the end. Just as Rob reached for the last tie, something fell out from under the slippery roll, hitting the floor with a faint clink.

"What was that?"

"Yeah, I heard that, too. Move your foot, son."

"Soon as I tie this thing... Okay. Which way?"

"Never mind," she said, as she reached down. "Oh my gosh! Will you look at this?!"

"What?"

She held out her hand. In the center lay Scottie's lost watch.

"Well, I'll be darned," Robbie exclaimed. "That'll make Scottie's day."

***

The news of Marsha's murder spread quickly at EJHS on Monday. It was at a special assembly at two-thirty in the afternoon that Mr. Marvin addressed the whole school. On the stage with him were members of the local clergy, including Father Tom, and the school counselor, Mrs. Collins. Mr. Marvin's word to the students was short and to the point.

"We have lost one of our dear classmates from the sophomore class, Marsha Bogue. It is a heartbreaking situation. I'm sure we will agree, and it will take a long time to get over it, if ever. Meanwhile, I am asking your cooperation in several areas, so please let me have your complete attention.

"First, we do not have all the facts surrounding this sad event. We must be careful not to speculate or make judgments concerning the circumstances or the *people* involved in these circumstances. We have an excellent law enforcement system in place, and those folks need to do their jobs with the least possible amount of hindrance. Please do not spread rumors. Please don't hurt anybody else. There's been enough damage, already.'

"Second, I believe we have a fine bunch of youngsters here at EJHS. We have All-State caliber students in this school, and every one of you has an extraordinary shot at outstanding success. That's who we are, people. Are you listening? Each one of you is a gifted person, a possibility, a promise, and a great source of hope for the future of this community, this state, this country, and the world. Never forget that. We may have sad days like this one, but we *will* find a reason to move forward, and that's the way Marsha would want it to be."

The principal went on to express condolences to the victim's family and friends, encouraging everyone to remember and cherish Marsha's talents and accomplishments, and the privilege of having her special smile in their lives. He concluded the short tribute with a word of advice: "Finally, I encourage each of you to seek out and spend some time with your parents, priest, or pastor, and of course, we have Mrs. Collins, who is our school counselor. It is important that you have someone who is older and wiser right now. Otherwise, the conversation sinks into despair, and that's not where we want to go with this. Again, it is a very hard day for all of us, but we can honor Marsha by coming through it, each of us, wiser and stronger."

Each of the clergy prayed a short prayer, and then Mrs. Desmond hit the introductory chords to **Be Still My Soul**. It was the perfect piece to end the day. Its mournful melody expressed the grief of the crowd, but the carefully crafted words actually encouraged them. For just a little while, a beautiful spiritual rainbow arched gracefully over that small-town high school assembly.

But rainbows are fragile, often appearing only after a storm. So far, this community had weathered the deaths of two students. Sadly, there were more clouds on the horizon.

***

The murder of the two teenagers, combined with the disappearance of her beloved Uncle, had a deep effect on Winnie. She called in sick on Monday morning, because she had slept only a few hours over the last two nights. She spent most of the day in bed, praying and crying and falling into short, vivid dreams. At about three in the afternoon, she decided she needed to do some kind of strenuous activity to keep her mind occupied, and make her body more able to rest at bedtime. She arose and dressed, and for two hours, she deep-cleaned the kitchen. Not one inch of it escaped a scrubbing. At last, she was mopping up the floor, every bone in her body so weary, she could hardly move.

Cecil came in from the barnyard, took one look at her, and gently led her to her gold recliner. "Now listen," he said gently, "I know this is not what you normally do when you get worried, but this is not a normal situation." He went into the kitchen and made a quick half-sandwich of peanut butter and apple butter, which he put on a small plate, and brought it to her. In his other hand, he held a little fruit juice glass, filled halfway with his favorite whiskey. He held it in front of her face as he spoke. "I know. This is not your style. But do me a favor and sip on this slowly, as you eat your sandwich." He placed the drink down beside the radio next to her chair. "Just take it like you would take a medicine. It will help you sleep." Then he turned on the radio and sat down next to her, watching to make sure she got it all down and noting with satisfaction, the gradual softening of her shoulders. Over the low music of the radio, he chatted about the color of the maple tree this year, and the golden ones over in the Wilsons' front yard, and of how relieved he was that the Guernsey, Ruby, was finally back producing her full ration of milk... until Winnie's eyelids began to lower. He reached over and turned the radio down to a whisper, then got up and put on his milking jacket. At six o'clock, Ceese was still a little reluctant to leave her alone in the house, but, as he had said so many times before, "Those cows aren't going to milk themselves."

The radio continued to play. This time, it was Vera Lynn, singing her 1942 hit, White Cliffs of Dover. This time, the bluebirds were flying near those cliffs, celebrating the end of the ravages of war. For a moment, the promise of a free world seemed entirely possible, and Winnie's eyes slowly closed. The little lady slipped into a fretful sleep.

She never even heard the back door open.

***

Marilyn had once again taken time off work, due to problems with her daughter's health, so there had been a couple of days to watch and assess the girl's behavior. By Monday evening, the woman had reached some alarming conclusions. The most disturbing thing was Roxie's lack of grief over the murder of her very best friend. Although she asked not to go back to school just yet, she seemed pretty much her regular self, spending a lot of time in front of the television or alone in her room, doing her nails, laying out different outfits of clothing for the upcoming winter... just performing little tasks which most teenage girls did every day. There were no sudden outbursts of tears, no nightmares, no sad recollections of the blonde friend. Occasionally, there were the moments of tapping fingers, or doing the little rocking dance as she stood in front of a window, looking out at nothing. She had seen Roxanne do these things many times before. But then, there was that new little habit of twisting the ring on her little finger. That was odd.

Marilyn was also uneasy about her daughter's version of what happened last Friday, the night Marsha was killed. Yes, she had been tired when she got home, and yes, she should have checked to see if Roxanne was alright, but she had not. That decision haunted her, because she did *not* remember the skunk smell. Surely, it would have been throughout the house. Surely, she would have noticed it, and checked with

524

her daughter about it. But the only skunk smell she could remember was that which she had awakened to the next morning. What did that mean? She knew, but fear pushed the answer to the back of her mind.

And there was George's reaction to the news on Saturday night. He simply shook his head and walked away. Further, he stubbornly refused to get involved with any of it. Even Roxie had been surprised, but in a few minutes, she just hooted and went on her way. Marilyn had witnessed this behavior before. It had been replayed many times, before her second husband had finally left.

And so, as she lay wide awake in her bed, the doting mother became the doubting mother, and she made the decision to ask Don Collins to get those demons out of her girl… and she wanted it done soon.

She would make the call the first thing in the morning.

***

The dream is vivid, like the others. This time she is dreaming that Ceese is hugging her as they walk through the garden out back. It is a bright, sunny day, and there are string beans to be picked, and they are laughing at how hard it is for them to bend down. Suddenly, Ceese reaches behind and pulls forth a small stepstool, like the one she had as a child up there in Swanton, where she stood in front of the sink and brushed her teeth, like a good girl. But now, Ceese helps her to sit down on the stepstool, and they pluck the long, green, stringy vegetables off the wobbly plants. It is then that she realizes her husband's basket contains fine, healthy beans, but her own battered container is filling up with a shriveled, stringy, harvest.

In the midst of her frustration, she is distracted by a darkness upon the dirt path between the green beans. It is the shadow of her father, Chief Raven's Wing. Magically, his stern face appears, as he turns to his companion, her cousin from the university. "Tall Tree, please speak to your cousin, who is engaging in such foolishness."

"No," she objects. "I am only picking string beans, my father."

"What string beans?" he asks. "I see no string beans."

She tries to rise from the little stepstool of her youth. "I am only picking the string beans, my father," she insists. But then there is a touch upon her face, and...

She was suddenly awake, and the two men in front of her were very real.

"The chief's daughter drinks firewater now?" It was Tall Tree speaking.

"No... no... not usually." She blinked her eyes to focus on the two men.

"What does that mea—?" Tall Tree stopped as the Abenaki chief raised his hand.

"We come to give you news of Shining Waters," he spoke in the native tone.

She sat up eagerly, then remembered to lower her head in respect. It was then she realized the room was dim because the lights were not on. Instinctively, she knew it was nearing dusk outside the big window.

"Thank you, my father. I have been very worried."

"You will worry no more, Firstborn Daughter. He has made it to the safe place."

She looked at Tall Tree, wanting confirmation that the Canadian reservation was the same safe place she knew as a teenager. He nodded affirmatively. She took a joyful breath. "He's safe." But then she had another question, so she lowered her head to ask rightly. "What has he done?"

"He has done nothing," the chief answered.

"Then, why does he run?"

"He runs because he is Abenaki," came the younger one's reply.

"But Abenaki warriors do not run, Tall Tree. They disappear into the forest."

"Exactly right," the young activist said firmly. "They disappear to throw the enemy off the trail. Remember that."

She covered her face, not knowing whether to laugh or cry. It took her a little bit before she asked the next question. Then, without uncovering her face, she spoke it carefully: "Will he ever come back, Father?"

There was no answer.

Slowly, she uncovered her eyes. The two men were gone, as quietly as they had come. She turned to look through the large window. Somewhere out there in the darkening autumn night, two warriors were moving toward the woodlands.

She turned back around and leaned into the comfort of the gold recliner. Above her, the bluebirds arched in non-flight, as Winnie-the-Pooh drew a grateful breath and smiled.

Rehema Foster's prophecy had come true, or so it seemed.

CHAPTER THIRTY-EIGHT

Investigations

Marilyn made the call from The Harvest during her break. She wanted to speak with Don Collins, without Roxanne being present. The phone rang until the live operator notified her that there was "…no answer. Please try again, later." She put down the phone, frustrated, and headed back to work.

"Got any more doughnuts?"

It was Don Collins. Marilyn grabbed him by the arm and pulled him back into the breakroom. It took her only five minutes to fill him in. "I think it's the demons, and I think she knows it, and doesn't care. And I also think something is going on with George — he might be leaving me." By this time, she was weeping. At the end of the conversation, they agreed to confront Roxie at her home, the very next Saturday morning.

Meanwhile, the girl had returned to school, cocky and defiant in the faces of those who dared to cast furtive looks her way. She hooted and cavorted at cheerleading practice, as though nothing had ever happened. When Paula walked out, the beautiful redhead emitted an especially disdainful hoot-laugh.

"Roxie." Mrs. Collins was having none of that.

It was almost other-worldly, but the whole student body walked through the rest of the week under the watchful eyes of the teaching staff, trying to avoid "a situation." At three o'clock Friday afternoon, there was almost an audible sigh, as the school emptied out for the weekend.

At nine o'clock Saturday morning, the Collinses arrived to find Roxie still in her pajamas, watching *The Mickey Mouse Club* from her seat on the couch. She jumped up and ran for the bedroom, but Marilyn got there first, and held her robe out toward her. "Just put it on," the mother said firmly.

"No!"

"Look, the sooner you talk to them, the sooner they will leave."

The girl processed that thought. Then she snatched the robe from her mother and slipped quickly into it. "This had better be short and sweet," she muttered, as she headed back out to the living room.

Marilyn turned off the Disney program and took a seat on the sofa beside the Collinses. Roxie glared at them for taking her own special place, then plopped into George's recliner, pulling the side handle to tilt it back so far that she was looking at the ceiling.

"Roxanne, don't be rude," Marilyn said.

"It's rude to show up at somebody's house, uninvited."

"I invited them."

"It's rude to invite company and not tell me."

Don used his military officer's voice to interrupt this nonsense. "Hey, young lady, you need to get with the program. Sit up and pay attention."

She didn't move.

Suddenly, the robust man bounded across the room, bent down, and yanked the recliner's handle, letting the back of the chair slam to an upright position. Roxie's head shot forward, almost touching her knees. She stayed there a second, then raised a furious face, which was quickly turning purple. Her hands shot up like claws, as she let forth a drooling snarl.

Don never budged. If he was fearful, he did not let this thing know it. Instead, he immediately put both hands on his hips. "Are you kidding me?" he said sarcastically. "*I'm* the one under the Blood Covering, not you." He bent closer to the clicking teeth. "Shut up and back off. I command you in the Mighty Name of Jesus."

The hands turned toward the girl's face, ready to claw it. "Stop right there, Devil! You will *not* touch her face. I have the authority, and you know it. You *must* stop!"

The battle continued for several minutes, but in the end, Don had the information he needed.

The demons claimed they were part of a "marriage ceremony" which united Mindy and Roxie, and if *they* were removed, the girl would be killed in the process. It was some kind of witch's covenant, sealed by a satanic symbol, they said, and the curse could not be removed, ever, because of the seal. They had a right to be there.

None of the three adults really knew much about witchcraft, but they did know Who had the real supernatural power.

"In the Name of Jesus," Don said, quite calmly, "I rebuke your lying tongues. I command a hedge of protection around this—" He paused at Connie's touch on his arm.

"Wait just a second," she whispered, as she positioned herself at Roxie's left side. In one swift move, she reached for the girl's hand and pulled the ring off, ducking her head to avoid the fierce swipe of the clawed right hand. Roxie's whole body turned toward Connie, spewing a foul-smelling breath. *"Give tha-a-at back! Give it ba-aa-aack!"*

"I felt it in my spirit!" she yelled over the noise. She clenched the ring tightly inside her fist. "*This* is the seal for that satanic marriage covenant!" She stepped back. "It's been removed, so now the demons can be removed. Go for it, Don—!"

She was stopped by the sudden pain. "Ow!" Her hand flew open from the pain. "Ow-ow-ow!" She turned her palm toward the floor, trying to shake the biting thing off. Don grabbed her wrist and tried to pull the tiny, uncoiled snake from the center of her hand, but it hung on, its rigid metal body dangling like a grotesque bobble.

"Oh, Lord, it's eating into my hand. Ow-ow-ww! Don...!"

He dragged her toward the kitchen. "Pliers!" he yelled to Marilyn. In a flash, the woman shoved them into Don's hand. "Hold on, babe!" One good yank removed the thing.

Immediately, the pain ceased. Connie looked for the damage in her palm.

There was none.

"Look!" Marilyn was pointing at the thing Don was holding in the pliers. It had curled back into a silver ring, in the shape of a snake that was eating its own tail. "It was an illusion...!"

"It's witchcraft," Connie muttered.

Immediately, Don ran for the bathroom and flung the thing into the toilet. As the two women watched, he flushed, then flushed the refilled tank, again. Then once more.

Suddenly, there was a movement behind them, out in the hallway.

"Mom? What's going on out here?"

"The ring is gone," Marilyn said firmly. "There is no more marriage to Mindy."

"WHAT?" The girl looked at her bare finger. A look of pure fury signaled the blow which was meant for her mother, so Don managed to block Roxie's left arm before she could complete it. "I hate you! I hate your *guts.*" She pulled loose from Don's grip.

"Take authority, Marilyn!" he yelled, as he grabbed for the arm again.

"What...?"

"In the Name of Jesus...!" Connie prompted her. She grabbed Roxie's other arm. "Tell them to stop, in the Name of Jesus!"

"Stop!" Marilyn shrieked. "In the N-Name of Jesus."

Roxie's face was turning color as she threw both Don and Connie to the hallway floor. The demons could feel the mother's fear, and they moved on it.

From where they lay on the carpet, Don and Connie turned and shouted the same command, almost simultaneously. "I command you to stop in the Name of Jesus!"

The girl's body stood still, but there were low growls coming from deep in her throat.

Marilyn could not believe what had just happened. Her own daughter had attacked her. But no, she suddenly realized, no, not really; it was those things inside... inside her beautiful girl.

Suddenly, she was mad. She was *really* mad.

Slowly, she approached Roxie's stiffened form. Her head bobbed up and down like a mama eagle protecting her nest, and she meant business. She stopped just inches from the girl's face.

"You listen to me, you filthy scum. You can't touch me. No-no-no, you can't. I actually have the Blood all over me. Take a good look... the Blood of Jesus Christ... all over me. Yeah, that's right... all over me. You can't touch me, because that Pure Blood makes *me* the boss, *not you.*" She inhaled through the nostrils. "*I belong to God.* You got that? Huh? You got that?" She snorted in another breath. "*Now*, in the *Mighty Name of Jesus*, I command you to not hurt my daughter, and not hurt my husband, and not hurt me. You lie down and be quiet, until it's time for you to leave. You got that? Huh?" This time, the breath was inhaled through her teeth… "So… *DO* it… *NOW!*"

It was crude, but right on the mark. Marilyn Foxx finally *got it.*

After she got her girl safely into bed, however, she also got the fact that Roxie probably could not keep out the demons… not yet. This whole incident would have to be chalked up as another aborted attempt at an exorcism.

***

The coroner's report came back to Sheriff Duncan the very next week. He was quick to share it with Chief Allen, because he still had some questions for that young man. The two met Cecil Thompson at the barn on Tuesday morning.

"Mainly what it says," Max said, as he led the way into the crime scene, "is that the girl died of a blow to the head, which resulted in a broken neck, which might have happened when she hit the car on the way down to the floor. It says that the neck could have been broken when the blow was struck, but more likely it happened when she hit the side of the car, considering the angle and all." He turned to address both Robbie and Mr. Thompson. "Interestingly enough, the attack with the pitchfork happened after death had occurred." He looked at the stain on the floor. "Can't quite figure that one out. What do you guys think?"

"Sounds like the latecomer wanted to be sure she was dead, saw the thing hanging over there, and used it." The chief's training enabled the prompt answer; Cecil, on the other hand, did not feel qualified to even offer a suggestion.

"According to your statements, you and your wife never heard anything going on out here that night, am I correct?" Cecil nodded. "Is there a chance that someone else could have stumbled on the scene, recognized the girl as a troublemaker, and made sure the job was done right?"

"Oh gee-awd, I can't imagine such a thing."

"Reason I ask, the coroner estimates the time of death around eleven-thirty that night. On the other hand, the amount of blood and how long it had been drained from the body, etcetera, etcetera, indicate that the actual stabbing probably took place sometime around four in the morning."

"Oh, Lord…" The man was genuinely incredulous.

"Well," the sheriff reassured him, "it might take a while, but we'll get to the bottom of it." He glanced around. "The other thing, sir, is that the murder weapon is described in the report as being a circular object, three-and-a-half to four inches across… extremely solid, possibly one of these new hard plastics, or a hardwood of some sort. It was swung hard against the right temple of the victim, actually cracking the skull above the ear… which brings up the next thing in the report: the killer was left-handed." He paused to check on Mr. Thompson. "You okay there, sir?" Cecil took a pack of Camels out of his pocket, then realized he was in a hay barn, and put them away. "Well, let me get to the last thing, then. We need to do a search of the crime scene to try and locate that murder weapon. The way *you* might help us is by pointing us at something that sounds like that description."

"Oh, I thought of it right away," Mr. Thompson said, as he hurried over to the workbench. He reached across a bunch of tools and lifted out an object. As he held it toward them, the two officers exchanged a triumphant look. It was a solid wood sledge hammer, obviously handmade, and very old. The head was fashioned from a tree limb which was reinforced with iron bands near both ends, and the long wooden handle, made from some sort of hardwood, was wedged into a hole in the hammer's head. Someone had driven a nail into the hole, obviously to tighten the fit.

"Put it down, Mr. Thompson, and don't touch it anywhere else." He watched the man gently place it on the front edge of the shelf. "Very good." He went to the doorway and yelled to the deputy in his vehicle. "Smith! Get me an evidence packet, medium size." He turned back around. "Don't touch it," he cautioned again, because Robbie was peering more closely at it.

"I don't know," the chief murmured. "Don't see any blood stains on it."

"We're not looking for stains, mister. We're looking for hair, and skin, and maybe even some fingerprints."

"Gee-awd, that was my father's, too." Cecil looked at Max. "Am I even going to get this stuff back?"

"Are you sure you *want* them back? I mean, they are murder weapons, you know?"

"Not to me."

"Well, as soon as the investigation is over, I will ask that they be returned to you. Would that be alright, sir?"

"Appreciate it."

The sledge hammer was carefully wrapped and placed in the trunk of the car. Just to be sure, however, Sheriff Duncan ordered a complete search of the area. At the end of an hour, the three lawmen were confident that there were no other items which fit the description. They thanked Mr. Thompson and left.

An hour later, Max Duncan called Robbie Allen's office.

"I believe it's time to get a formal statement from Miss Foxx. Since you were there for the informal one, I thought we should continue to work on this angle of the investigation together. We will be bringing her in tomorrow morning, so you may want to work that into your schedule. You can help me pinpoint any discrepancies. If all goes well, we may even book her for murder."

On Wednesday morning, Roxie was picked up by the Chittenden County sheriff and a social worker, just as she was leaving the house to go to school. Her folks were already at their workplaces in Burlington, so the appropriate phone calls were made, to inform them. George refused to attend, but Marilyn took off her apron and left The Harvest, even though she knew it meant that she was fired.

At the end of the morning, Max Duncan and Robbie Allen were sitting on a bench in City Hall Park, where they could eat a take-out sandwich from The Harvest, and insure the privacy of their conversation. People moved up and down the walkways, all intent on other goals, but the two men carefully guarded their talk.

"Did you notice her mother's face while Roxie was talking about getting home at about eleven o'clock?"

"Yeah, good ol' mom knew she was lying," Robbie concluded.

"That means she will have to be questioned, if there's a trial. Think she'll lie for her daughter?"

Robbie lifted an "I don't know" eyebrow. He glanced around. "I'm actually wondering what time Roxie got back home. I mean, it really smelled like skunk in that place, and it was about noon when we were there, right?"

"Ay-yuh, somewhere around there. I've got it in my notes, anyway."

"I'm guessing she was out a lot later than she's saying." He caught the slight nod from the corner of his eye. "I mean... a *lot* later."

The sheriff was unwrapping his salami sandwich. "Because...?"

"It didn't even start raining until half an hour after midnight."

"No kidding? How do you know that?"

"I had just gotten off swing shift, myself. I checked out, and Ed checked in, at just a couple of minutes after the hour. It started to rain just as I was pulling into my driveway." He pulled his sandwich out of the brown paper bag. "I live only a mile or so from the Thompson farm." He started to unfold the waxed paper from his egg salad on rye. "But here's the thing… it was just the first of several downpours. They kept waking me up, all night." He inspected the first half of the sandwich, deciding where to take the first bite. "Now, let's think about this. If the kid had gone home and gotten sprayed in the back yard at about eleven, she would have stunk up the whole house, and her mother would have noticed it. That didn't happen." He held up the corner where he would take the bite. "On the other hand, if she stayed out all night, in the rain, she would have had to been sprayed by a skunk sometime early in the morning."

"Why do you say that?"

"Because skunks don't go out and play in the rain, sir. They do not like a lot of heavy downpours." He took a bite and waited for the next question.

"So, how do you know that?"

"Statistics show that when there is a lot of rain, the skunk population declines. That's because when skunks get soaked, they get pneumonia." He took a sip of his coffee. "Isn't that interesting?"

"So, when Roxie Foxx got sprayed by a skunk, it had to be *after* the rain tapered off."

"Ay-yuh."

"And what time was that, Chief?"

"According to Ed, who got off at six that morning, it finally stopped raining just one hour before he went home. That would be at around five, I'm thinking."

"How do you know he was so aware of all that?"

"He didn't have a raincoat, and he knew he was walking home to his apartment up the street." He grinned. "You get these uniforms soaked, you have to send them to the cleaners."

"Yeah, that's true. You can't get a decent press on them until you do." Max took another bite, then chewed through to the next question. "So what do you suppose she was doing out there, all night?"

"Well, covering her tracks, I guess. It takes a lot of scheming to get your story straight. Probably spent a lot of time in the neighborhood, just making sure she got it all right. Probably walked the whole thing out, planted the camera, cleaned off the murder weapon and put it back on the workbench… whatever." Robbie took a sip from his coffee. "I really don't know. Maybe she just didn't want to walk home in all that rain. Maybe found shelter and waited until it stopped."

The sheriff went on, to another subject. "I also found it interesting that she seemed to want to incriminate your little brother. What can you tell me about that?"

"If it involved normal kids, I would qualify it as just 'high school crap.'" He smoothed out the waxed paper on his lap. "But this girl… she's just not a normal kid, I swear." He glanced around again. "It's like she can't let go. She just has to get even, or something."

"What do you think she was talking about at this interview this morning, when she said we should have found evidence that Scottie was there?"

"Wasn't that interesting, Sheriff? Wasn't that interesting that she was so sure there was evidence that Scottie was there, and she was apparently busy *doing something* until the wee hours of the morning?" He took another bite, but this was a small one. "Almost like she knows something we don't know. That's curious."

The sheriff took a final bite from his first half of the sandwich. "Think she may have planted something?"

"Can't prove it."

Across the park, the Vermont Transit buses hissed and groaned through their usual manipulations. People moved back and forth through the autumn color of the park. Little children frolicked at the edge of the gyrating water fountain, under the watch of their young mothers. It was a beautiful, peaceful scene.

Sheriff Max Duncan washed down that last bite with a little coffee. "If you went anywhere *near* that hayloft before I got there, I don't want to know anything about it. Got that?"

"No problem, sir."

CHAPTER THIRTY-NINE

Sacrifice

Roxanne Foxx could not be charged with the murder of Marsha Bogue, because the antique sledge hammer turned out to be nothing more than just that. There were no traces of evidence to link it with the killing. Other than the fact that Roxie had certainly been present at the murder scene, and probably was lying about what time she got home, there was nothing conclusive. She was labeled as "a person of interest" and released. Her mother enrolled her at Edmunds High School right after Thanksgiving.

On that very same day, there was a fire on Case Road.

Shirley had not been able to bring herself to completely let go of her girl. She kept the bedroom just the way Marsha had left it. Further, every night she turned on the little battered lamp, which had served as the girl's night light. It was a ritual which gave much comfort, but proved to be almost fatal, for on that particular night, the frayed cord sparked a fire which raged throughout the old structures, leveling both the house and the shed. Shirley and the boys made it out by the skin of their teeth. The Wilsons took them in for a couple of nights, before her estranged husband showed up, hat-in-hand, and begged her to come back home. It was time for a new beginning.

A few days later, Rob Allen and his younger brother, Scottie, stood at the edge of the charred ruins, watching Sheriff Duncan conduct his own investigation.

"Had to be here," he said, pointing to the spot where the melted lamp lay.

The other two walked over and took a look.

"How do you know?" Robbie was intrigued.

"You can tell by the progress of the fire." The lawman went on to explain a few details, as Scottie continued around toward the back. Neither one of the officers was aware of the youngster's whereabouts, until they heard the sound of cracking wood, followed by a yell. They turned to look across the burned ground to where the shed had been. Scottie's head and shoulders were the only parts still above ground. He had gotten too close to the outhouse pit.

The two men burst out in robust laughter. As the young man lifted his arms to try and push himself out, more charred wood broke off. Again, more laughter.

"Um," Scottie grinned and flapped his elbows like wings. His dignity was sacrificed. "Soon as you're done having fun about this…"

Walking carefully, they got close enough to each grab one arm, and, on the count of three, hauled the lanky kid up out of the smelly hole. As his feet cleared the edge of the opening, something dropped back into the pit. The chief got a good look at it.

"Hold on, guys," he said, as he dropped carefully down onto his belly. "Scottie, hold onto my feet," he commanded, as he finished a slow crawl to the drop-off. The sheriff grabbed one foot, and Scottie the other. There was a long, long stretch, and then Robbie arched his back and pushed himself back with one hand.

In the other hand, he held a soiled red croquet mallet.

The two law officers exclaimed it together: "Bingo!"

"What's that doing down there?" Scottie couldn't believe his eyes.

"A certain young lady probably hid it there," Robbie said.

"Now we know what she was doing half the night, out in the rain," Max said.

"Ay-yuh."

"You guys talking about Roxie?"

"That's right, son," the sheriff replied. "You're probably looking at the murder weapon." As Max headed for the car to get an evidence packet, Robbie smiled at his brother.

"Good fumble, kid. This will probably put her in jail."

He was right. Roxanne Foxx was tried and convicted of the murder of her very best friend. There was some dialogue about whether she had come back to deliver the bloody pitchfork finale for the murder, but it was something the jury seemed to think was a "given." Sheriff Max Duncan did not concur with that part of the verdict; he was sure there was another party involved, and he was determined to find that person, no matter how long it took.

In the end, because she claimed throughout the trial that it was the work of demons, and then had exacerbated that point by exhibiting disturbing animal-like behavior during her sentencing, Roxanne Foxx was taken away to Waterbury State Hospital.

Nobody there even wanted to try to get rid of demons. The Foxxes and the Collinses were never allowed to try, either. Instead, they were viewed as religious fanatics. Consequently, the girl would languish there for the rest of her life, suffering periodic episodes of strange, almost erotic spasms over her whole body, which left her close to death each time. No medication or therapy was sufficient to stop these damaging spells. She finally succumbed to an early demise at the age of thirty-eight, a mindless soul in a wasted body. That coroner's report recorded the cause of death as heart failure, brought on by a particularly violent episode. There were no other contributing factors, it stated, although it did make note of the presence of an odd tattoo-like imprint, looking much like a ring, on the little finger of her left hand…

***

Life had pretty much gotten back to normal at the Thompson farm. Cecil had his two prized antiques back, Winnie was sleeping better, and life was looking up. In fact, the spring of 1954 brought a new guy into their household. A happy, bouncing fellow named Blow. He accompanied Cecil into the barn for milking chores. He went out into the garden to supervise early plowing. Then he trotted down the pathways between planting rows, stopping to nuzzle Winnie's face as she tried to push the dark soil over the seeds. He sniffed the compost pile, then peed on it, to notify the night creatures of his presence. He went out into the pasture to visit the cows, running in circles around them, until Ruby gave him a sharp kick. He romped and played his day away, and then sat whacking his tail against the kitchen floor as his two humans ate their supper, knowing his was to come immediately afterward. He got dog food and leftovers, and some fresh water.

But at night, he wanted to go out, and he wanted to stay out… in the barn. Winnie had long since decided it was useless to have his dog bed there next to the phone stand between the kitchen and dining room, so it was decided to haul the whole thing out to where Blow liked to settle down every night: on the floor between the whitewashed wall which divided the barn's two sections, and the stanchions of the three cows. There was just room enough for a man to walk through, and the bed fit there perfectly.

"It's like he's guarding the girls," Cecil observed.

In the meantime, Winnie was keeping Uncle's apartment swept and dusted. She made weekly trips upstairs every Friday, when Ceese was milking. Sometimes she would spot a sign... a dent in the bed, a crumpled terrycloth on the bathroom towel bar, a little piece of candy wrapper in the wastepaper basket... and she would smile. He had been home. He was letting her know he was doing fine, just not putting her in a place where she would have to lie if anyone asked whether she had seen him.

Meanwhile, the Wilsons noticed the occasional visits of a Chittenden County sheriff's vehicle, slowly passing around the curve between the two houses, sometimes late at night. Laura remarked about this to Winnie, who brushed it off as coincidence. But she never said a word about the little hints of Uncle's presence, because it had always been this way. These two Abenakis had a long history of taking care of each other. She took comfort in knowing that he *would* be back, eventually, and things would be the same again. Meanwhile, she would keep things ready. And she was so grateful to God for Cecil, who loved her, and provided for her and her dear Uncle. "He's been a great husband for me, Lord. Thank you so much."

Neither Cecil nor Winnie were ready for the news that came in mid-July. Chief Raven's Wing and Tall Tree were waiting in front of the long row of windows in the milking parlor when Cecil stepped inside the door, early on a Sunday morning. He knew immediately that it was not good news.

"You will comfort your wife today, sir," the chief said, soberly.

"Oh no..."

"Shining Waters, her uncle, has left us."

"Oh no..." He looked at the younger man for an explanation.

"We have received word from the safe place. It was a black bear and her cub. He wandered between them. He did not realize — he meant no harm, but the sow attacked him. He did not survive."

"Aw, gee-awd…"

The next month was the most difficult time of their marriage. Nothing could lessen the grief of her loss: not hugging, not soft words of comfort, not visits from Father Tom, not even whiskey with a half-sandwich. Winnie's mourning took over her life. In just a few days, she was having nightmares again.

"I hate that black monster… that stupid, stupid, ugly thing that killed Uncle. I should have been there to warn him. I should have protected him from it," she murmured over and over, even though it made no sense.

All that week, she could not make it to work. Cecil asked for a leave of absence, due to a death in the family.

But, at the beginning of the second week, she was falling apart. He was constantly waking up to find her wandering around the house at night. It was to the point where he was not getting enough rest, himself. Something had to be done. He would have to hospitalize her, just for a little while.

On the same evening of that sad, but firm decision, he tucked her back into bed, then turned over, sighed, and dropped off into a much-needed sleep.

***

He awakened suddenly, to a deep foreboding. A quick check revealed that Winnie was not in the bed. He arose and went out into the dining room, where he immediately noticed a light coming in through the large window. He moved quickly to locate its source.

The undulating light was glinting gently over the old Dodge, and Blow was barking, barking, barking. There was no time to pull on barn boots.

When he got to the front barn door, he spotted the empty space for his winnowing fork. Then he heard Blow's soft whine from the milking parlor.

Cecil pounded across the floor in his slippers, screaming as his went, "No-o-o, Winnie, no!"

She was standing near the dog's empty bed, half-awake and confused, with the pitchfork in her hand. Blow was hiding over behind the cows. She looked at Cecil, and started to cry. "That thing… that ugly black bear…"

***

It turned out that the ladies of the Maple Leaf Sewing Circle came to the rescue, so Winnie never did have to be hospitalized. One of them showed up each day, faithfully, for the next month, to help her get to her "new normal." Mostly, it was Laura Wilson, from across the road, and Gracie Allen, with Anna Morgan from Holy Family, coming in for a close third. The others had daily jobs which prohibited such frequent visits, but Connie and Lily tried. Shirley Bogue, however, kept it to cheerful get well cards, all the way from the little family's rented home down there on Flynn Avenue, near a local woodworking factory. She was not up to visiting the place where her Marsha had died, no matter what was happening with Winnie.

But it was during one of Gracie Allen's visits, that things started to turn around for the little Abenaki woman. She was standing on the back porch, getting ready to leave after the usual time of prayer and encouragement.

"I can't thank all of my friends enough, Gracie, including you. It's like a connection that has kept me encouraged and grounded."

The friend paused. "And isn't that what we're all supposed to be doing, Winnie? Aren't we supposed to be supporting each other, as we go through the testings of this whacky world?"

"Um..." she was not sure.

The would-be comedienne caught that. "Hey, we can handle this stuff, right?"

"Um..." came the doubtful reply.

The lady laughed out loud. "Listen, missy, if you believe that, I have a bridge in Brooklyn I'd like to sell you...!"

It was the bridge reference that drew her into the revelation. Suddenly, it was quite clear: Yellow Flower had certainly not gotten it all straight, but she had the concept about the bridges between people. Winnie now saw the bigger picture of what had been happening recently in her own life. There had been loving help from both Roman Catholic and Pentecostals, from that lovely black couple who tried to remove the threat of Roxie Foxx, in the efforts of Raven's Wing and Tall Tree to encourage their Abenaki family, and in the godly presence of the Maple Leaf Sewing Circle ladies. "My goodness," she whispered, "even those law officers were doing the self-sacrificing thing, whether they knew it or not!" She smiled, reminding herself that the sheriff's vehicles were no longer doing the oh-so-slow drive-bys. Turning back to the happy mental picture, she was sure there were many others who had helped, but it was too overwhelming to fathom. Instead, she closed her eyes and let the love flow down into her innermost soul. The grieving was not over, but the healing had begun.

It was during a visit from Connie Collins that another little piece of the puzzle in the story was discovered. She was retrieving a photograph from the top of the piano in the parlor — Winnie was putting together an album for Uncle's memorial dinner after the Mass — and she was suddenly stopped short by the chain pattern on the old chaise lounge's brocade covering. She drew closer for a better look. The angle of the early Saturday morning sunlight spotlighted its theme in shocking detail. Each loop in the chain was a snake, eating its own tail.

Mrs. Case had been into much more than just playing with the Ouija board.

"No wonder Uncle had such devastating times in there," Winnie moaned. "And all he wanted was to be near Yellow Flower."

"I'm guessing he opened the door to the demonic depression — temporary though those episodes may have been — with the alcohol," Connie said softly.

That evening, Cecil dragged the chaise out to the back of the garden, and burned it.

By the end of September, the Mass for Uncle had been held, and Winnie had progressed through the initial healing. As the next couple of weeks went by, the lady was precariously back to her old schedule... even invited to come back to work at Sears. That, in itself, encouraged her greatly.

***

She was sitting out on the porch with Cecil and Father Tom that Friday, just a year after the murder. The priest had joined the Thompsons for a bit of supper after the milking was done. Winnie was rocking the porch swing gently, while the two men sat at the far end of it, each finishing a cup of coffee. Outside this screened sanctuary, fall colors were glowing in the sunset, as the evening crickets' erratic syncopation trilled forth from dry hideaways. Inside, Blow lay in an ebony heap upon the porch floor, half-asleep.

"It was a terrible thing," she said, reflecting on the killing. "And here we are, exactly one year later, and now Uncle is gone, too." The two men waited for her to finish the thought. "I still wish none of it had ever happened."

Father Tom crossed his legs, attempting to change the direction of the conversation. "I had some wonderful talks out here with him." He laughed softly. "He was an enigma… tough and tender at the same time… a victim, and yet a rescuer. Really, a warrior who loved his family and would do anything for them, sort of like…" He fixed his eyes on the gray floor, failing to end the sentence.

"What I can't get over," Cecil mused, "is how he took the blame for the pitchfork thing."

"Oh yeah!" The priest came back to the subject. "Everybody thought it was him, because he ran."

"He threw them off," the petite woman said. "He protected me."

"He took the blame, Winnie." Her priest took the last little sip from the cup. "Sort of like…" He stopped short, again. "You know, I think your uncle's actions were very meaningful, Winnie," the freckled-face clergyman finally said.

She stopped the swing to hear this. "In what way?"

"It's sort of like Jesus." He spoke cautiously. "Mind you, he was not Jesus. But, like I just said, he was tough, yet tender; a victim, yet a rescuer; loved his family more than his own life." He waited to see if either of them were following his train of thought. "And he knew, when the chips were down, exactly what he was called to do. *He sacrificed himself to save someone he loved.* That's a noble, even godly thing, for a mere human to do. Of course, your uncle was not Jesus! I mean, he will not be resurrected after three days, or anything like that." He continued toward his point: "So… so, he wasn't exactly like Jesus, but when it comes to this 'unconditional love' thing… do you see the similarities?"

"Well, maybe." She was sorting things out as she spoke. "I mean, I was Uncle's closest family. I get that about him, that he would have my back, no matter what." There was more sorting out. "But with Jesus, it's different, you know? I mean, where's the similarity?"

In the pregnant silence, the answer seemed to come from nowhere.

"Wait. Are you saying that Jesus was, or is…?" She was a little surprised to hear her own next words, considering all those years of contemplation up there in Canada: "Oh… oh, really?" There was a brief moment of revelation, before she spoke it out: "Um… I guess I always got that about Uncle, but just never *really, really* understood that about Jesus."

"Again… 'unconditional love.' Uncle didn't want anything from you, except that you loved him, just as he was." Father Tom was almost whispering.

"So, let me get this straight: Jesus has been seeing me as *His* closest family all along, covering me, all this time?" She clucked her tongue softly. "I thought I had to measure up to somebody like Sainte Jeanne d'Arc, before I was really worthy of that kind of love."

"A lot of folks think that," the priest said, as he rose to leave. "But, just like Uncle, all Jesus actually wants from you, Winnie, is you… loving Him back."

***

Before the two of them went in to bed, Winnie asked for a little favor from her husband. "Could you go upstairs with me, just for old times' sake, to put a final closure on Uncle's departure, please, Ceese?"

The two of them climbed the back stairs, her behind him, and crossed over into the small kitchen. There, they both stopped in surprise.

"I thought you and the ladies had removed this stuff," Cecil said, as he focused on Uncle's half-full cup of coffee on the table. Over in the sink, the empty coffee pot was turned upside-down, the dark grounds still glistening in the strainer.

Her face paled.

Cecil waited.

After a minute, she squeezed his big farmer's hand, as a faint smile passed over her lips. Her countenance regained its color.

"We *did*. We cleaned that very cup and that very pot, and put them away last year," she said softly. "And you know what? Those things haven't been out of the cupboard ever since then, Ceese."

"Are you sure?"

"Absolutely. I check the place every Friday night."

Firstborn Daughter reached out to pull her husband slowly over to the kitchen window. "Oh, my goodness... oh, my goodness!" she murmured as she leaned in close to the window's glass, scanning the dusky-edged woodlands of upper Case Road.

"What?"

"He's alive!"

"Really, Win? You think so?" He could not hide the doubt. "How can that be?"

"I don't know... but maybe we need to talk to Tall Tree and my father. Maybe they know something we don't know... about that bear, or whatever." Her eyes glinted with certainty. "All I know is *I* didn't put this stuff up here. He did this, in just the last few hours. Look at the coffee grounds... they're still wet!" She turned and saw the confirmation in her husband's eyes.

"I can't explain this, me, but he's the only one who knew how he left this stuff lying around... just exactly the same items, in the very same places." Her head nodded firmly. "He's been here, Ceese, and he'll be coming back again."

"You sure about this?"

"Positive. He's coming back again."
"When do you think he'll be back?"
"Only God knows..."

It was sort of like Jesus, after all.

THE END

From L. E. Fleury's *Junctions Murder Mystery Series*:

Book One: LOST

Book Two: HAUNTED

Book Three: PORTALS

Book Four: HEROES

Book Five: DAMAGED

Stay tuned for more to come!

9 7 9 8 9 8 9 0 2 3 6 1 5